VELVET
THE MAN WHO STOLE
THE WORLD

IMAGE COMICS, INC.
Robert Kirkman – Chief Operating Officer
Erik Larsen – Chief Financial Officer
Todd McFarlane – President
Marc Silvestri – Chief Executive Officer
Jim Valentino – Vice-President

Eric Stephenson – Publisher
Corey Murphy – Director of Sales
Jeff Boison – Director of Publishing Planning & Book Trade Sales
Jeremy Sullivan – Director of Digital Sales
Kat Salazar – Director of PR & Marketing
Branwyn Bigglestone – Controller
Sarah Mello – Accounts Manager
Drew Gill – Art Director
Jonathan Chan – Production Manager
Meredith Wallace – Print Manager
Briah Skelly – Publicist
Sasha Head – Sales & Marketing Production Designer
Randy Okamura – Digital Production Designer
David Brothers – Branding Manager
Olivia Ngai – Content Manager
Addison Duke – Production Artist
Vincent Kukua – Production Artist
Tricia Ramos – Production Artist
Jeff Stang – Direct Market Sales Representative
Emilio Bautista – Digital Sales Associate
Leanna Caunter – Accounting Assistant
Chloe Ramos-Peterson – Library Market Sales Representative
IMAGECOMICS.COM

ED BRUBAKER
WRITER

STEVE EPTING
ARTIST

ELIZABETH BREITWEISER
COLORS

CHRIS ELIOPOULOS
LETTERS

ERIC STEPHENSON
EDITS

SEBASTIAN GIRNER
EDITORIAL COORDINATOR

DREW GILL
PRODUCTION

SPECIAL THANKS TO SIDNEY STONE

SPECIAL THANKS TO SIDNEY STONE

A NOTE ON FOREIGN LANGUAGES:
Dialogue in an italic font should be read as a foreign language.

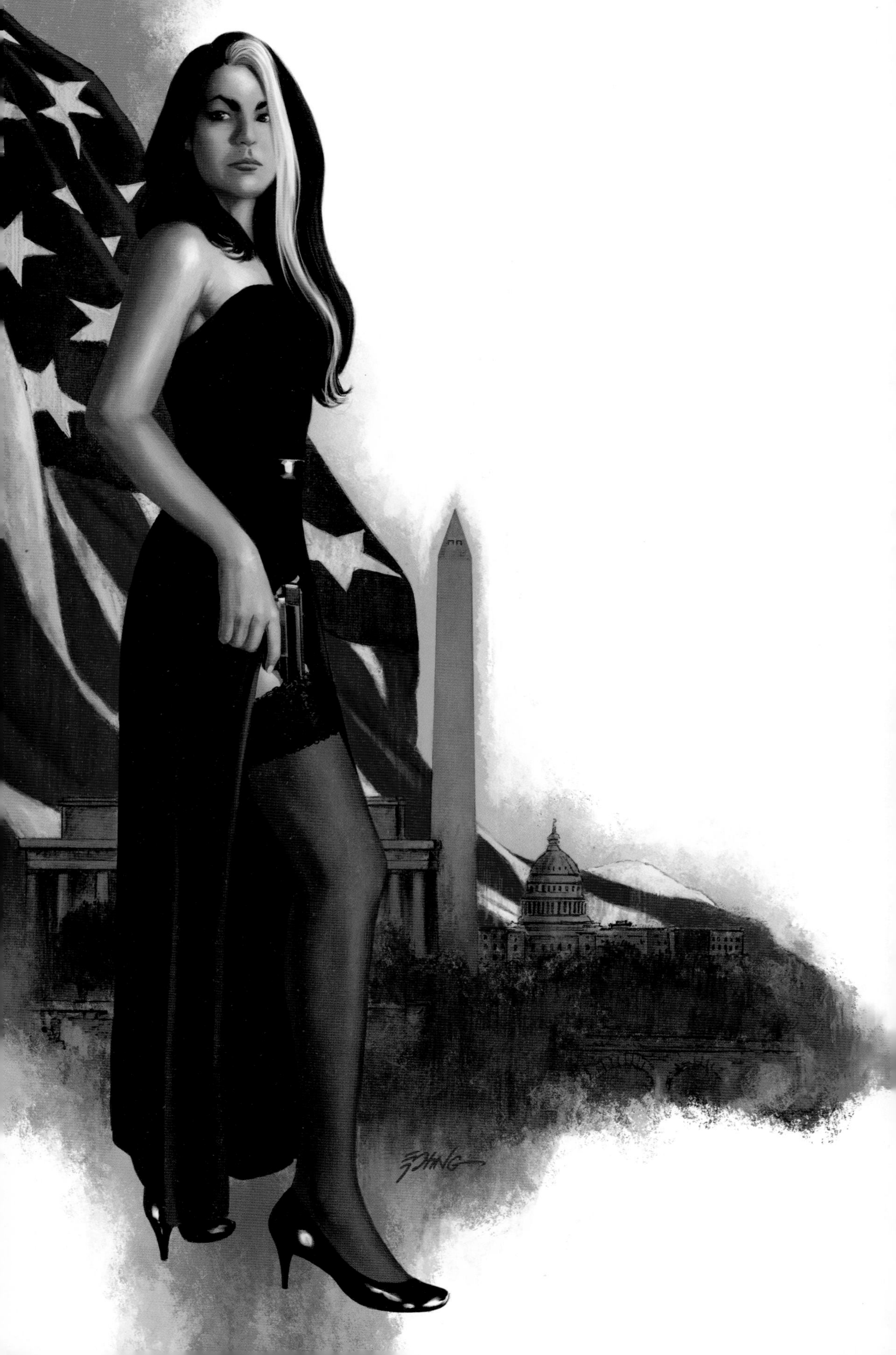

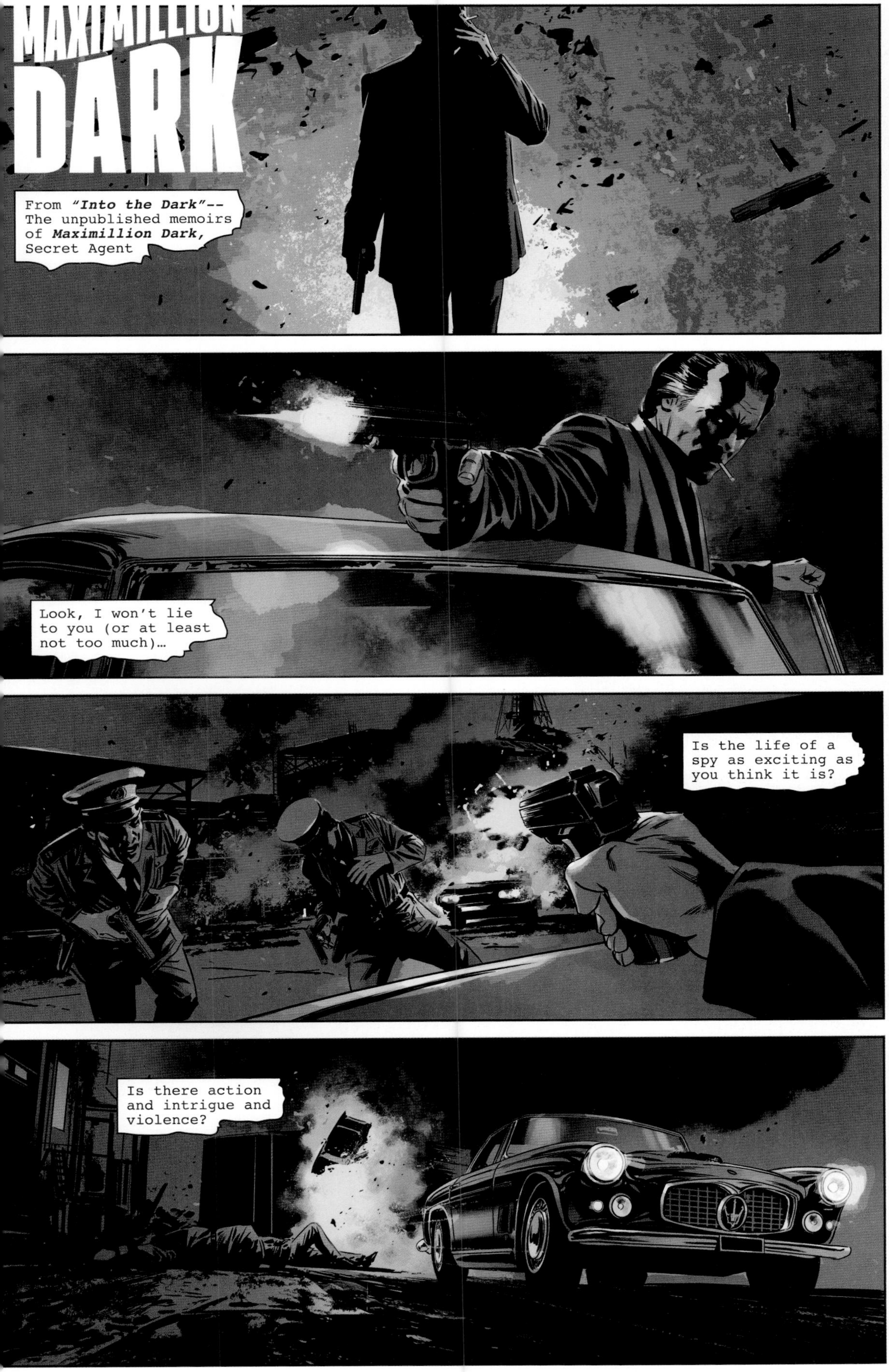
MAXIMILLION DARK
From "Into the Dark"-- The unpublished memoirs of Maximillion Dark, Secret Agent
Look, I won't lie to you (or at least not too much)...
Is the life of a spy as exciting as you think it is?
Is there action and intrigue and violence?

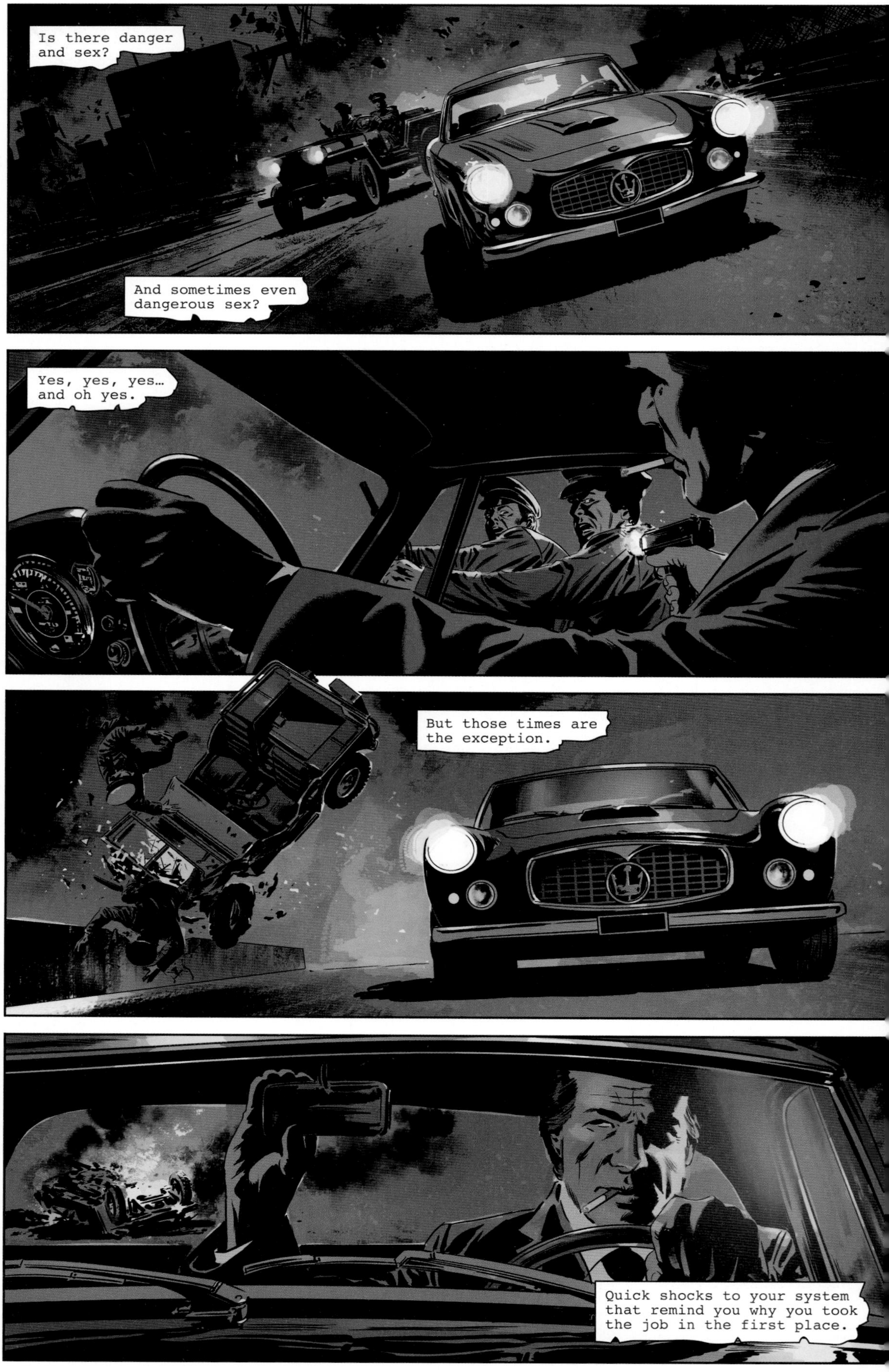
Is there danger and sex?
And sometimes even dangerous sex?
Yes, yes, yes… and oh yes.
But those times are the exception.
Quick shocks to your system that remind you why you took the job in the first place.

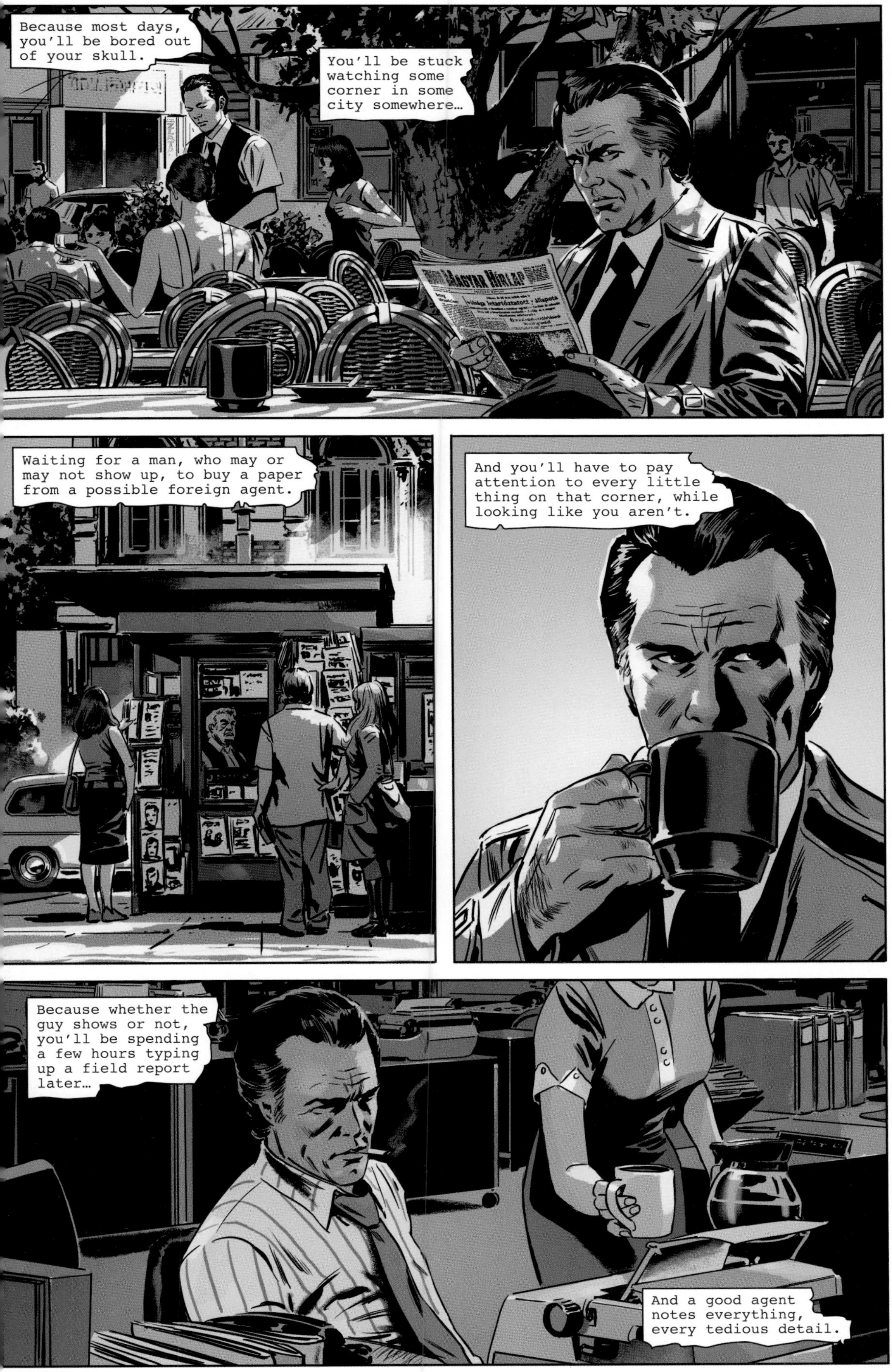
Because most days, you'll be bored out of your skull.
You'll be stuck watching some corner in some city somewhere…
MAGYAR HÍRLAP
Waiting for a man, who may or may not show up, to buy a paper from a possible foreign agent.
And you'll have to pay attention to every little thing on that corner, while looking like you aren't.
Because whether the guy shows or not, you'll be spending a few hours typing up a field report later…
And a good agent notes everything, every tedious detail.

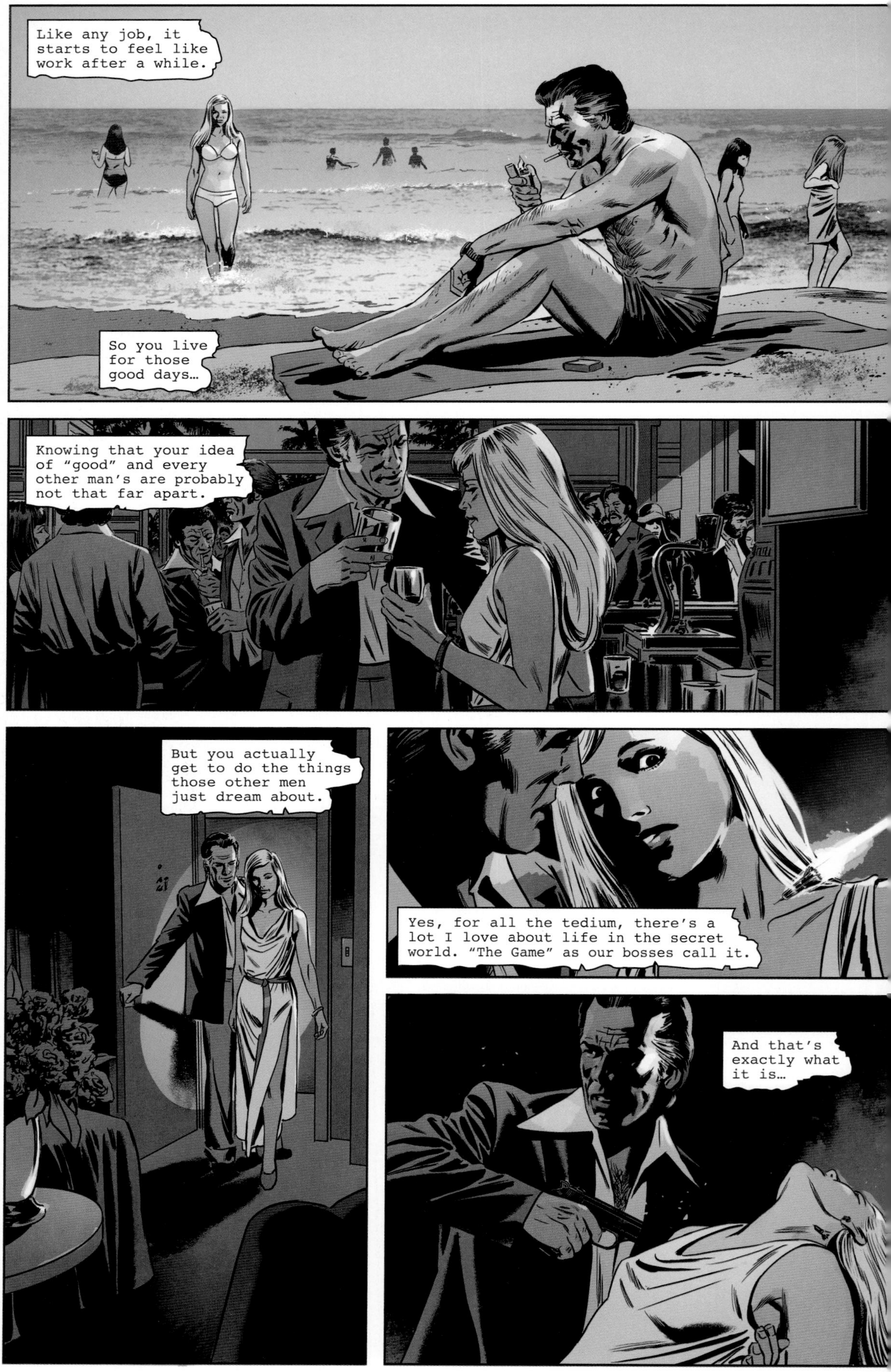
Like any job, it starts to feel like work after a while.
So you live for those good days…
Knowing that your idea of "good" and every other man's are probably not that far apart.
But you actually get to do the things those other men just dream about.
Yes, for all the tedium, there's a lot I love about life in the secret world. "The Game" as our bosses call it.
And that's exactly what it is…

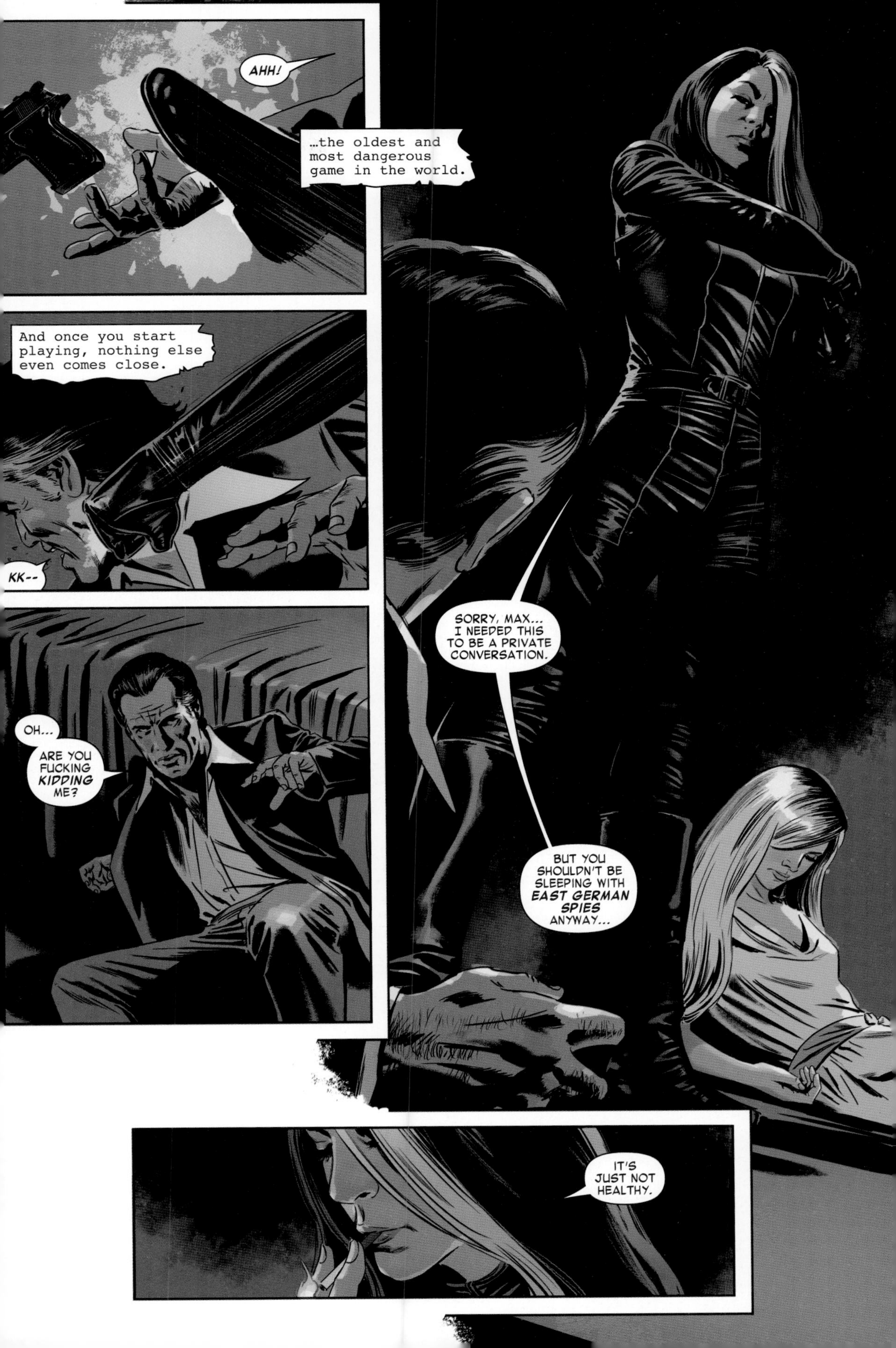
AHH!
...the oldest and most dangerous game in the world.
And once you start playing, nothing else even comes close.
KK--
OH...
ARE YOU FUCKING KIDDING ME?
SORRY, MAX... I NEEDED THIS TO BE A PRIVATE CONVERSATION.
BUT YOU SHOULDN'T BE SLEEPING WITH EAST GERMAN SPIES ANYWAY...
IT'S JUST NOT HEALTHY.

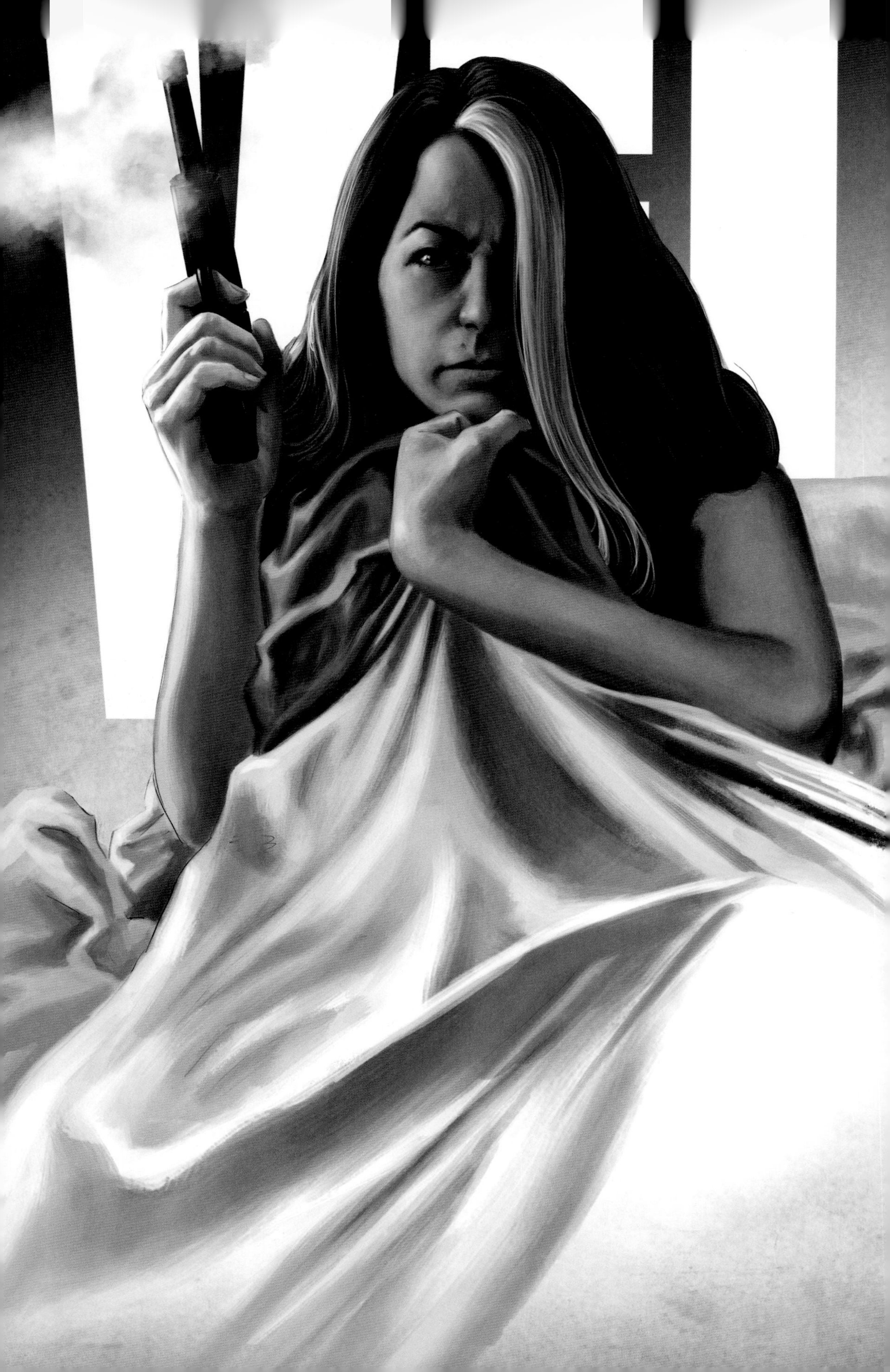

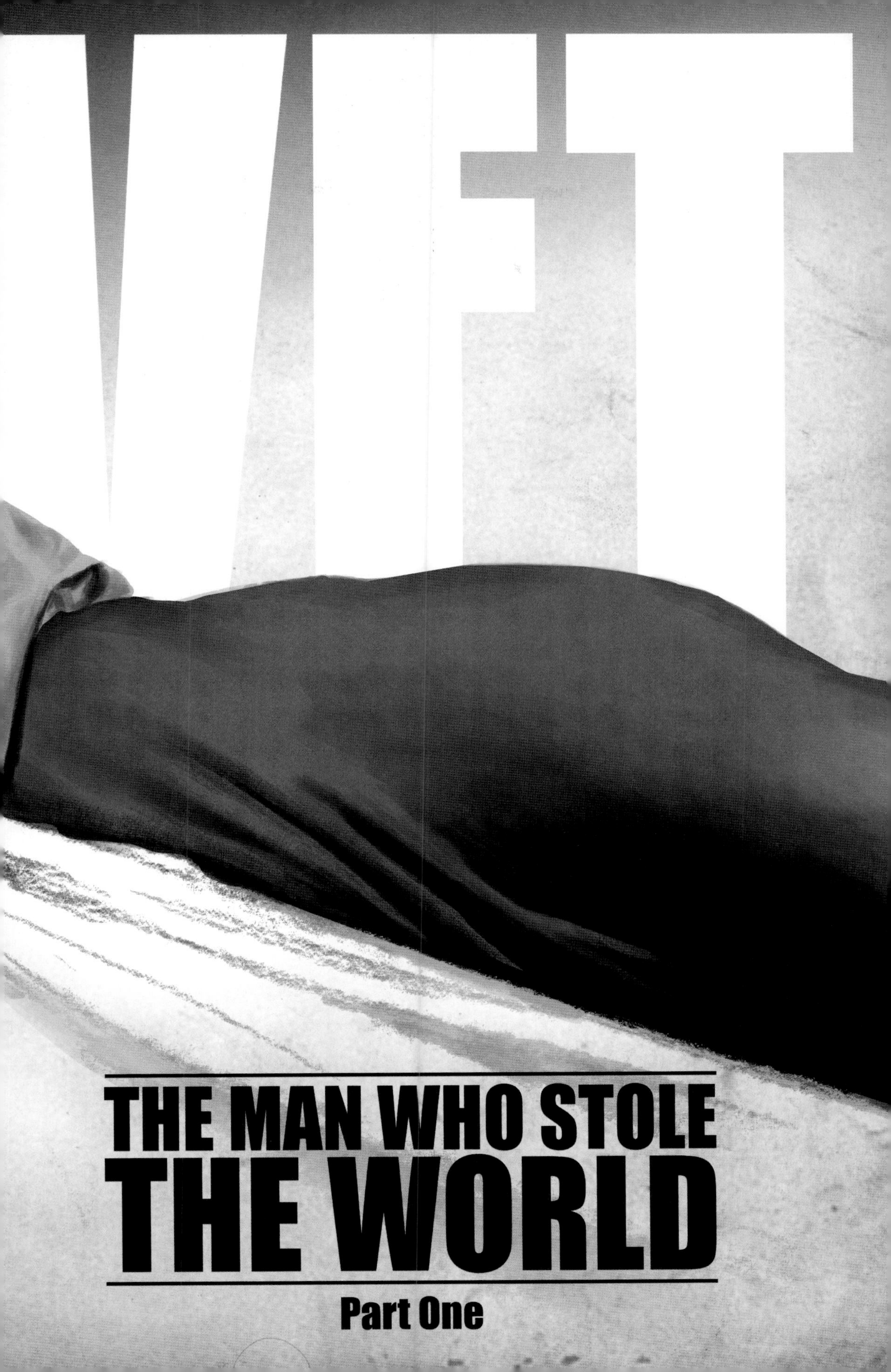

THE MAN WHO STOLE THE WORLD

Part One

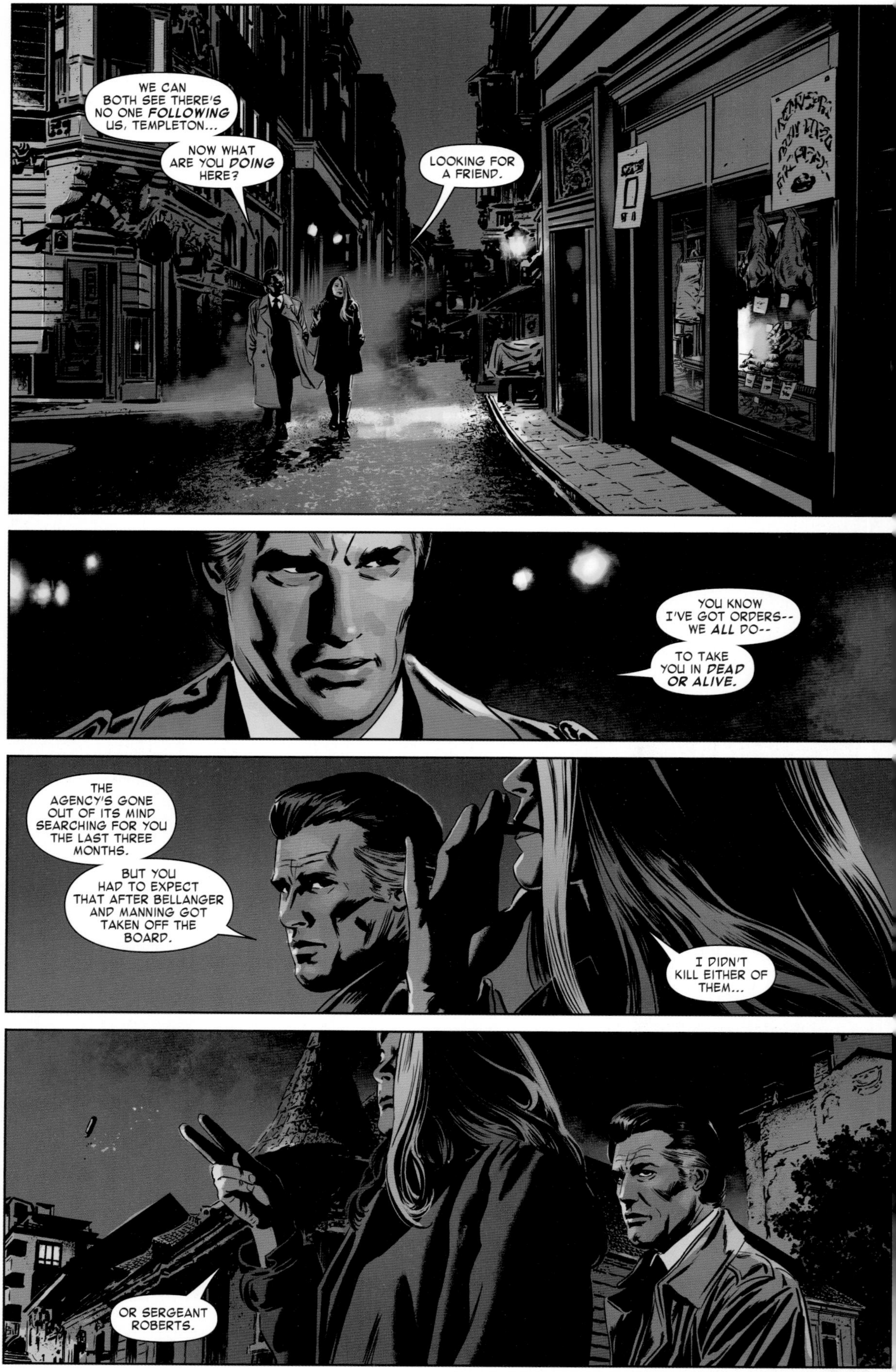
WE CAN BOTH SEE THERE'S NO ONE FOLLOWING US, TEMPLETON...
NOW WHAT ARE YOU DOING HERE?
LOOKING FOR A FRIEND.
YOU KNOW I'VE GOT ORDERS-- WE ALL DO--
TO TAKE YOU IN DEAD OR ALIVE.
THE AGENCY'S GONE OUT OF ITS MIND SEARCHING FOR YOU THE LAST THREE MONTHS.
BUT YOU HAD TO EXPECT THAT AFTER BELLANGER AND MANNING GOT TAKEN OFF THE BOARD.
I DIDN'T KILL EITHER OF THEM...
OR SERGEANT ROBERTS.

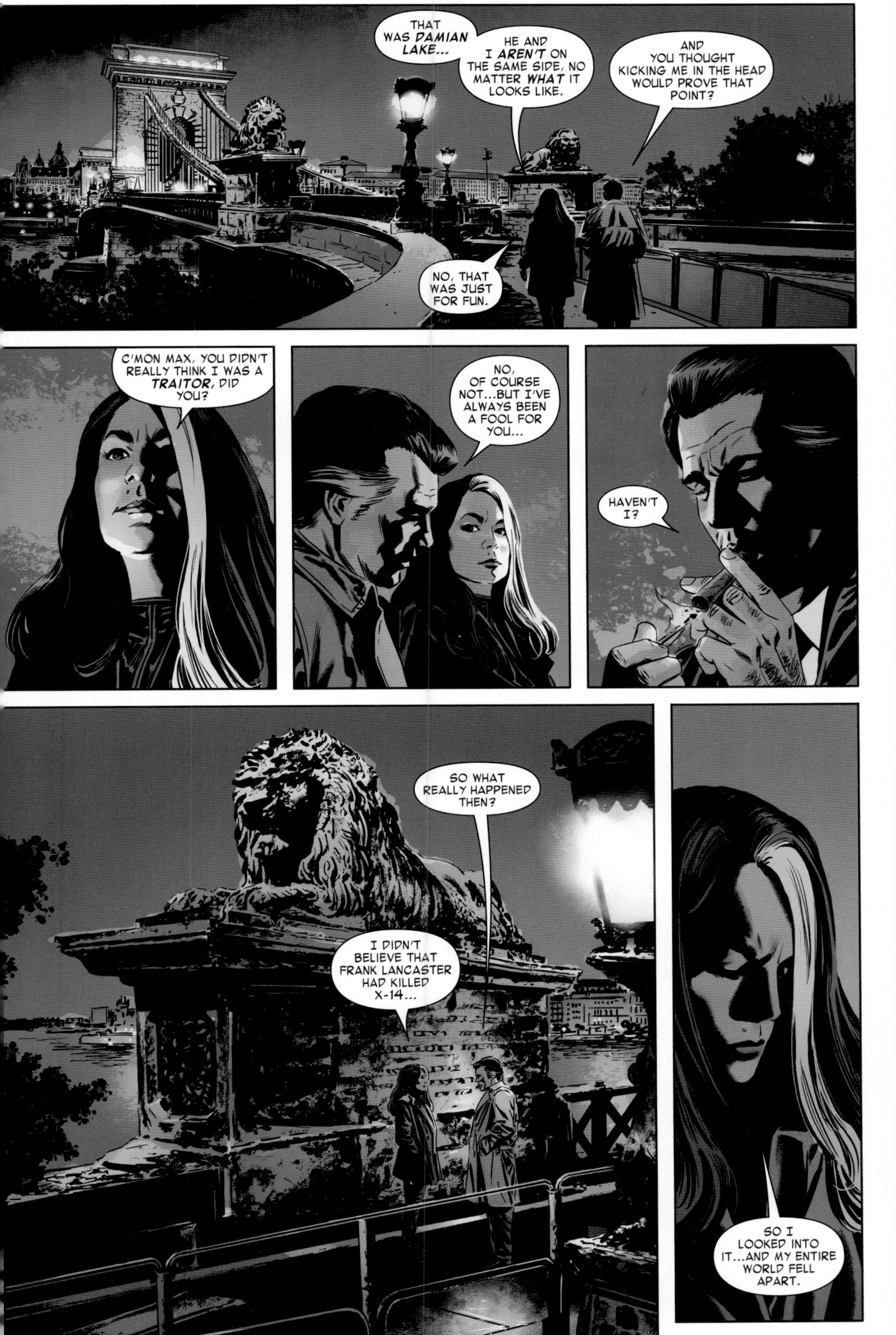

THAT WAS DAMIAN LAKE...
HE AND I AREN'T ON THE SAME SIDE, NO MATTER WHAT IT LOOKS LIKE.
AND YOU THOUGHT KICKING ME IN THE HEAD WOULD PROVE THAT POINT?
NO, THAT WAS JUST FOR FUN.
C'MON MAX, YOU DIDN'T REALLY THINK I WAS A TRAITOR, DID YOU?
NO, OF COURSE NOT...BUT I'VE ALWAYS BEEN A FOOL FOR YOU...
HAVEN'T I?
SO WHAT REALLY HAPPENED THEN?
I DIDN'T BELIEVE THAT FRANK LANCASTER HAD KILLED X-14...
SO I LOOKED INTO IT...AND MY ENTIRE WORLD FELL APART.

YOU WERE X-14'S *AMERICAN FRIEND*...

I THOUGHT YOU MIGHT HELP ME GET HIM SOME JUSTICE.

THIS... THIS IS *STILL* ABOUT JEFF'S MURDER?

IT'S *BIGGER* THAN THAT...BUT YES...

THAT'S WHY I PICKED YOU, NOT JUST BECAUSE OF OUR HISTORY.

JUSTICE...?

CHRIST, I REALLY AM A FOOL...

WHAT DO YOU WANT ME TO DO?

NOT MUCH...

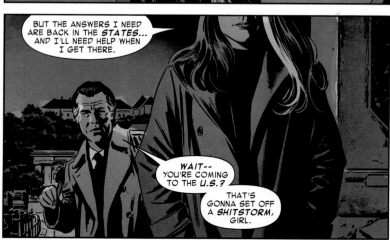

BUT THE ANSWERS I NEED ARE BACK IN THE *STATES*... AND I'LL NEED HELP WHEN I GET THERE.

WAIT-- YOU'RE COMING TO THE *U.S.?*

THAT'S GONNA SET OFF A *SHITSTORM,* GIRL.

I HOPE SO...THE LAST FEW MONTHS HAVE BEEN *BORING* AS HELL.

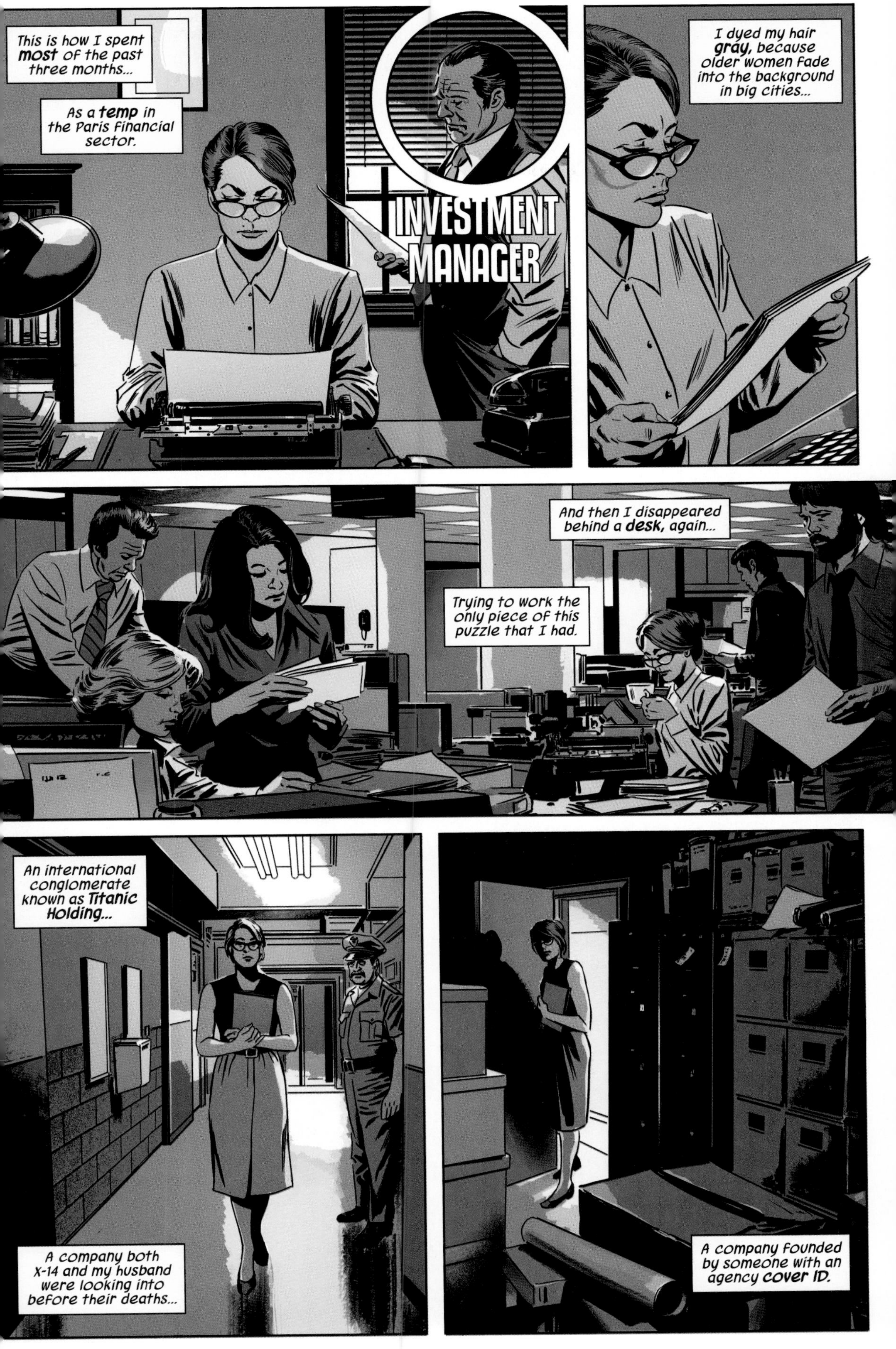

This is how I spent most of the past three months...
As a temp in the Paris financial sector.
INVESTMENT MANAGER
I dyed my hair gray, because older women fade into the background in big cities...
And then I disappeared behind a desk, again...
Trying to work the only piece of this puzzle that I had.
An international conglomerate known as Titanic Holding...
A company both X-14 and my husband were looking into before their deaths...
A company founded by someone with an agency cover ID.

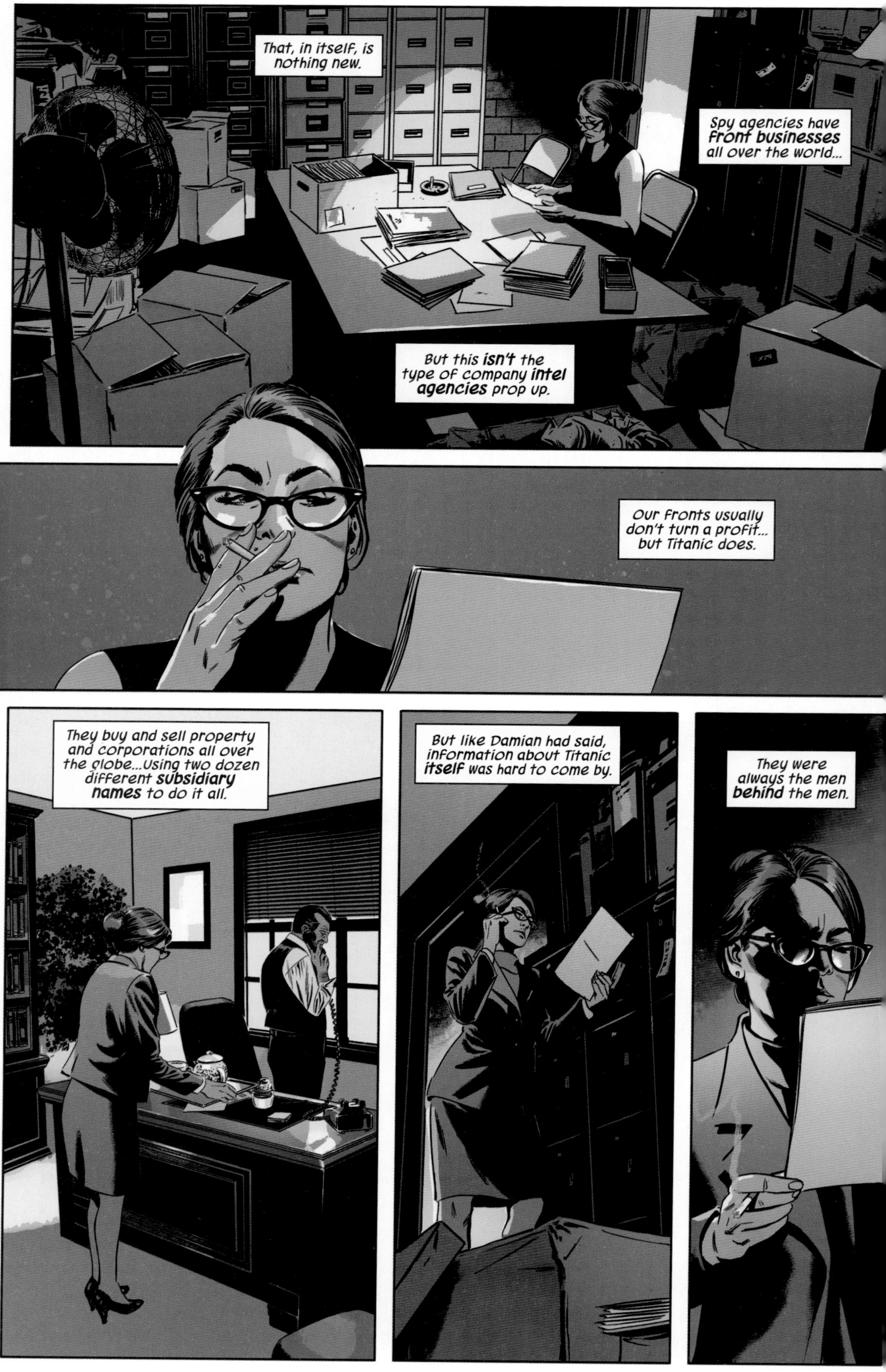
That, in itself, is nothing new.
Spy agencies have front businesses all over the world...
But this isn't the type of company intel agencies prop up.
Our fronts usually don't turn a profit... but Titanic does.
They buy and sell property and corporations all over the globe...Using two dozen different subsidiary names to do it all.
But like Damian had said, information about Titanic itself was hard to come by.
They were always the men behind the men.

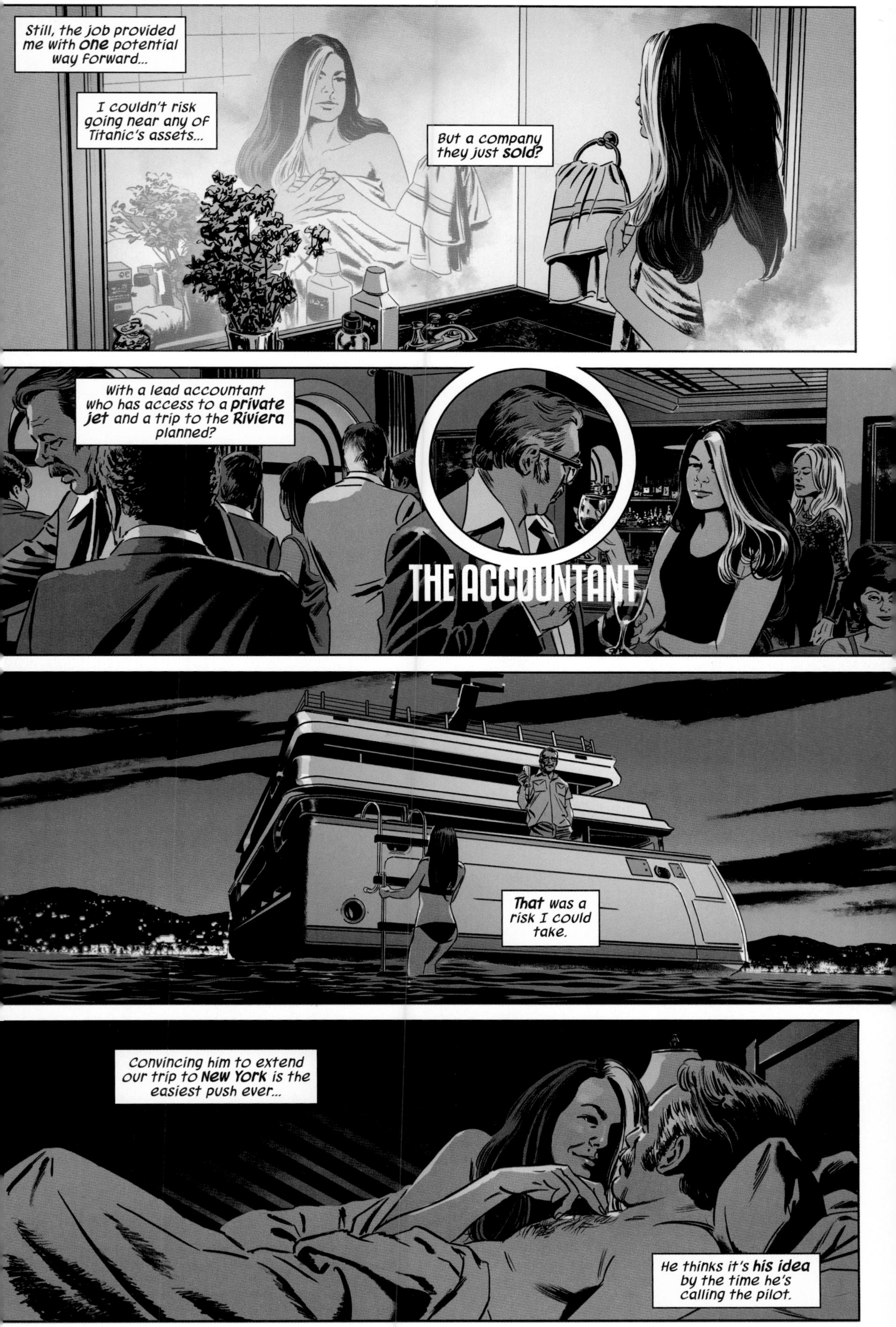
Still, the job provided me with one potential way forward...
I couldn't risk going near any of Titanic's assets...
But a company they just sold?
With a lead accountant who has access to a private jet and a trip to the Riviera planned?
THE ACCOUNTANT
That was a risk I could take.
Convincing him to extend our trip to New York is the easiest push ever...
He thinks it's his idea by the time he's calling the pilot.

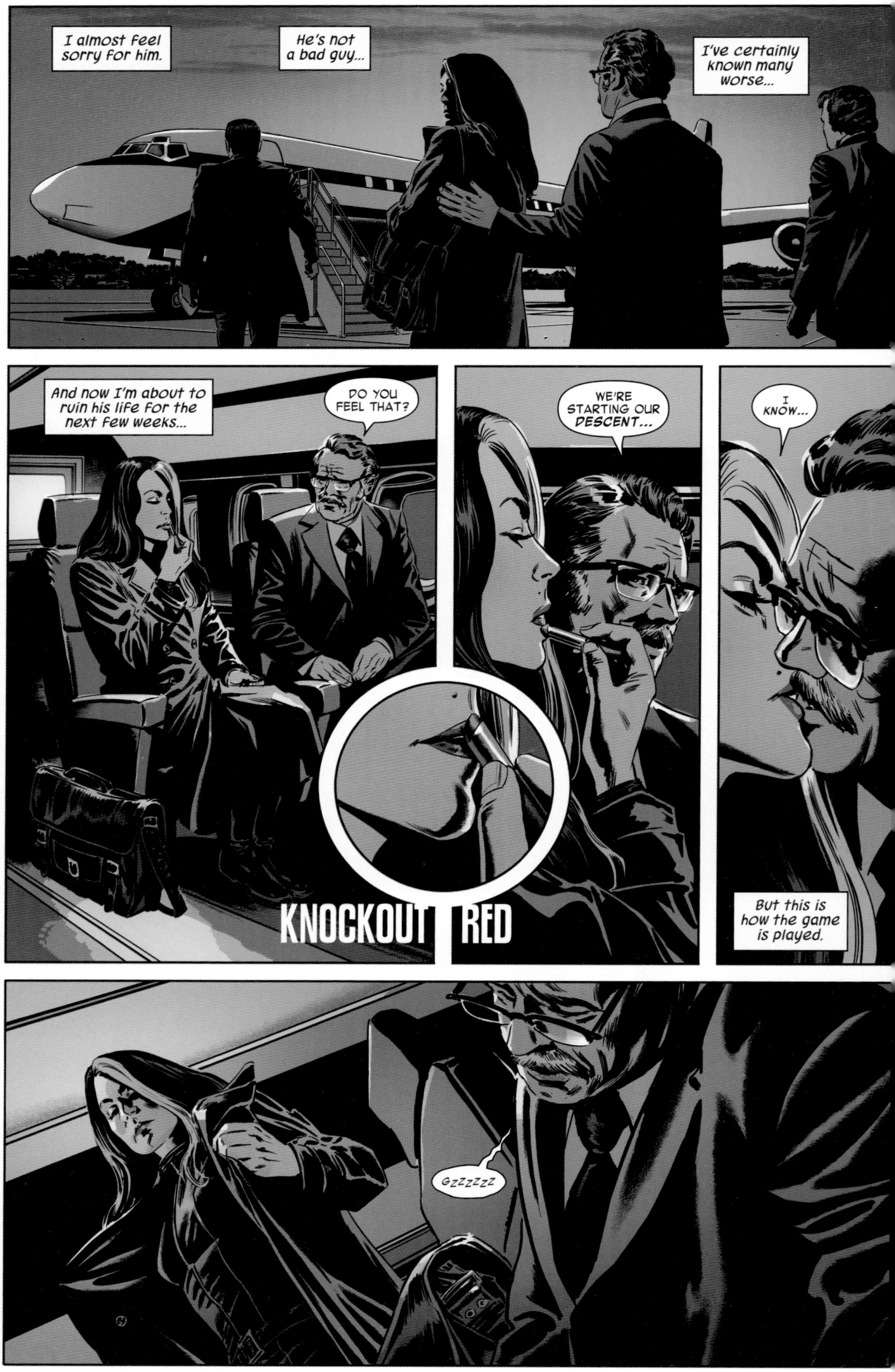
I almost feel sorry for him.
He's not a bad guy...
I've certainly known many worse...
And now I'm about to ruin his life for the next few weeks...
DO YOU FEEL THAT?
WE'RE STARTING OUR DESCENT...
I KNOW...
KNOCKOUT RED
But this is how the game is played.
GZZZZZZ

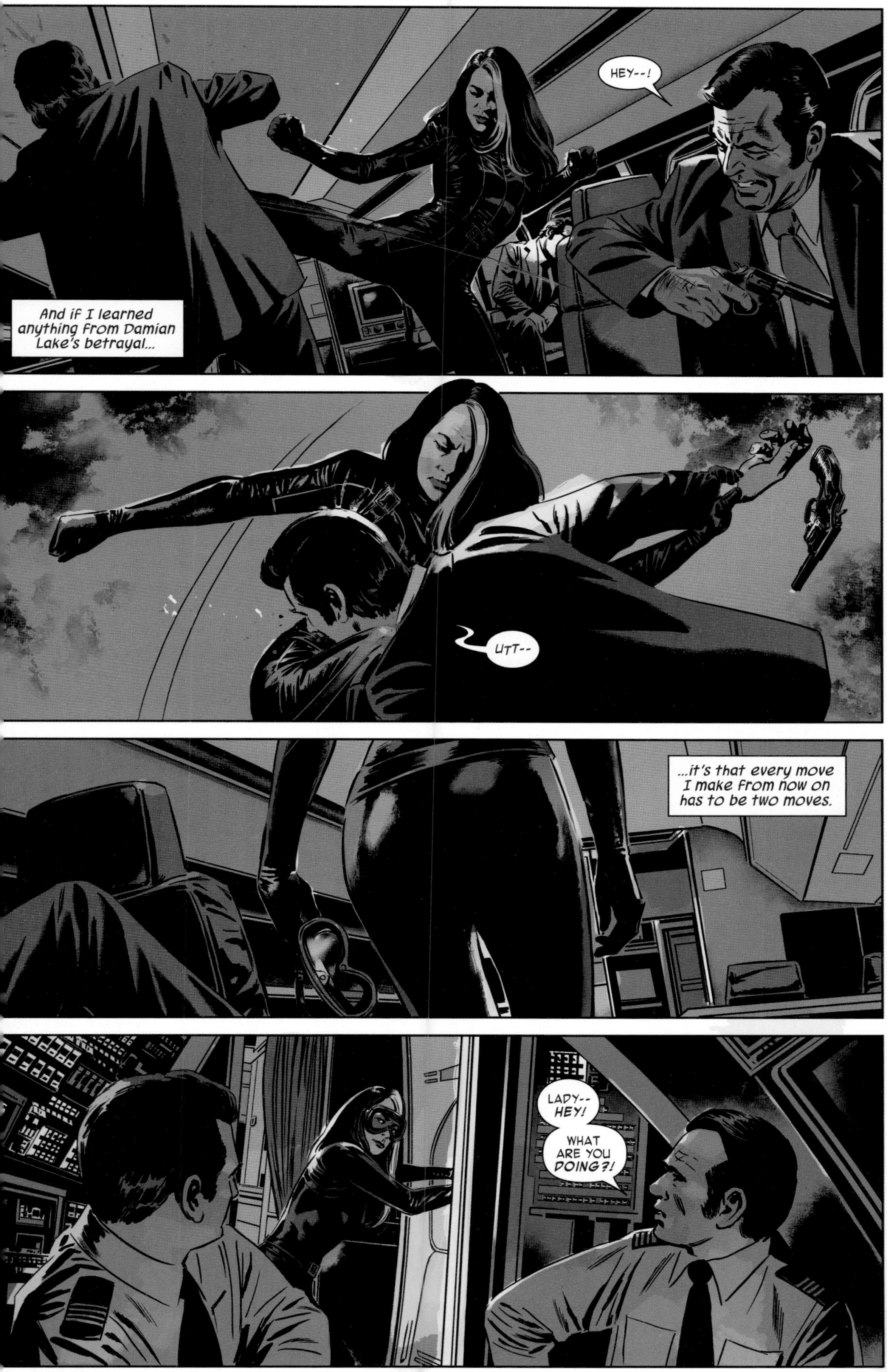
HEY--!
And if I learned anything from Damian Lake's betrayal...
UTT--
...it's that every move I make from now on has to be two moves.
LADY-- HEY!
WHAT ARE YOU DOING?!

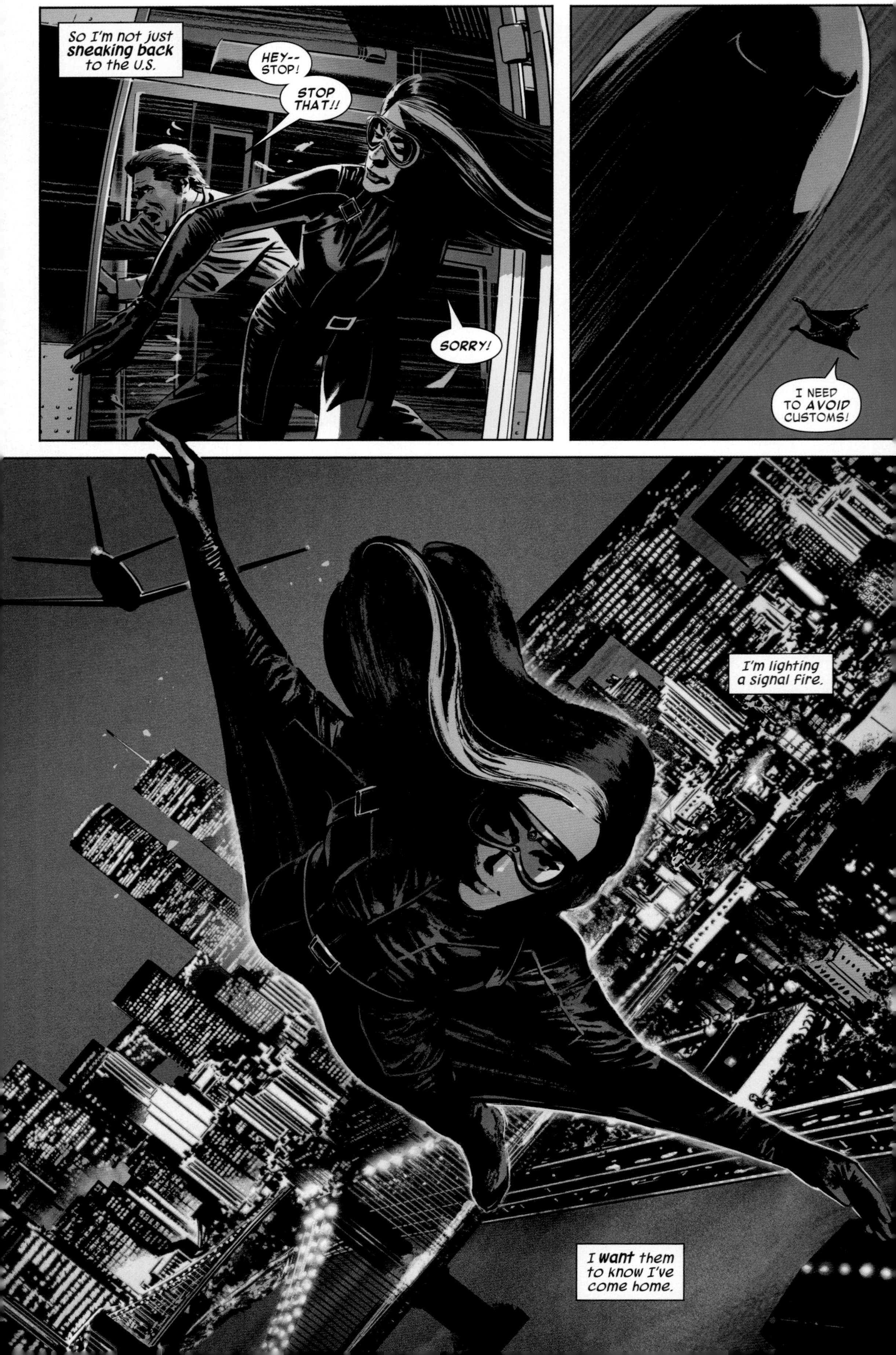
So I'm not just sneaking back to the U.S.
HEY-- STOP!
STOP THAT!!
SORRY!
I NEED TO AVOID CUSTOMS!
I'm lighting a signal fire.
I want them to know I've come home.

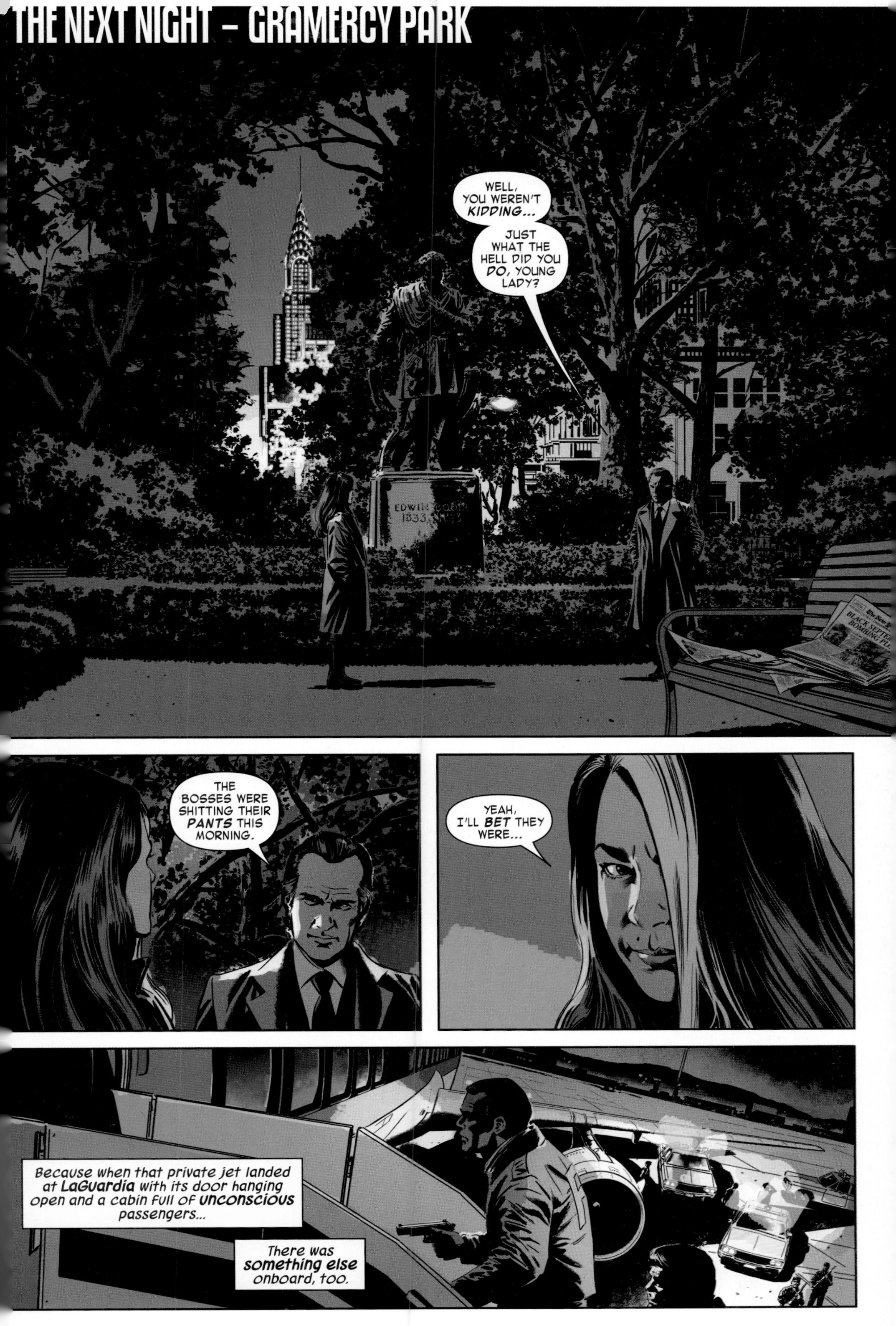
THE NEXT NIGHT – GRAMERCY PARK
WELL, YOU WEREN'T KIDDING...
JUST WHAT THE HELL DID YOU DO, YOUNG LADY?
THE BOSSES WERE SHITTING THEIR PANTS THIS MORNING.
YEAH, I'LL BET THEY WERE...
Because when that private jet landed at LaGuardia with its door hanging open and a cabin full of unconscious passengers...
There was something else onboard, too.

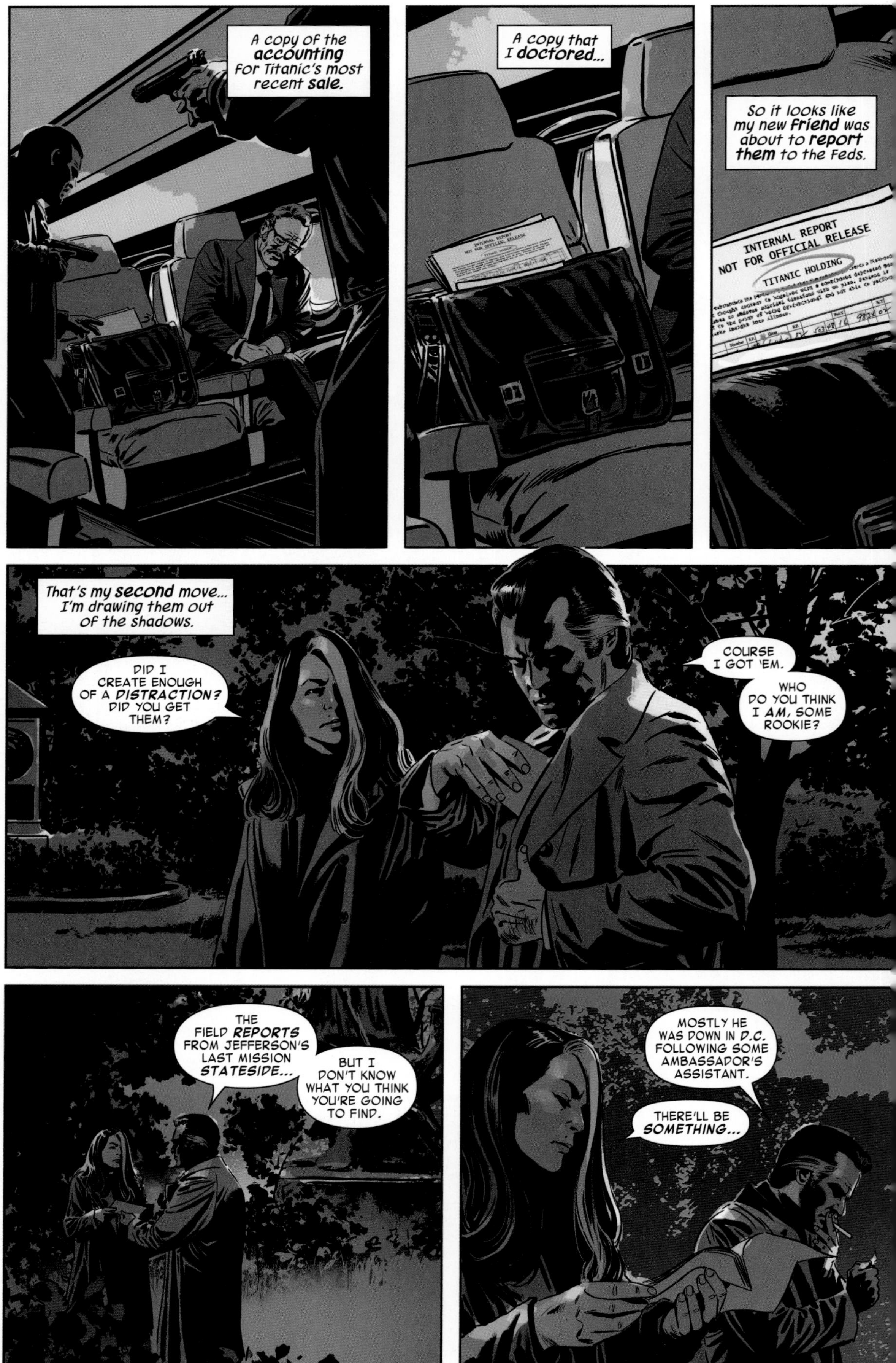

A copy of the **accounting** for Titanic's most recent **sale.**
A copy that I **doctored...**
So it looks like my new **friend** was about to **report them** to the Feds.
INTERNAL REPORT
NOT FOR OFFICIAL RELEASE
TITANIC HOLDING
That's my **second** move... I'm drawing them out of the shadows.
DID I CREATE ENOUGH OF A *DISTRACTION?* DID YOU GET THEM?
COURSE I GOT 'EM.
WHO DO YOU THINK I *AM,* SOME ROOKIE?
THE FIELD ***REPORTS*** FROM JEFFERSON'S LAST MISSION ***STATESIDE...***
BUT I DON'T KNOW WHAT YOU THINK YOU'RE GOING TO FIND.
MOSTLY HE WAS DOWN IN *D.C.* FOLLOWING SOME AMBASSADOR'S ASSISTANT.
THERE'LL BE ***SOMETHING...***

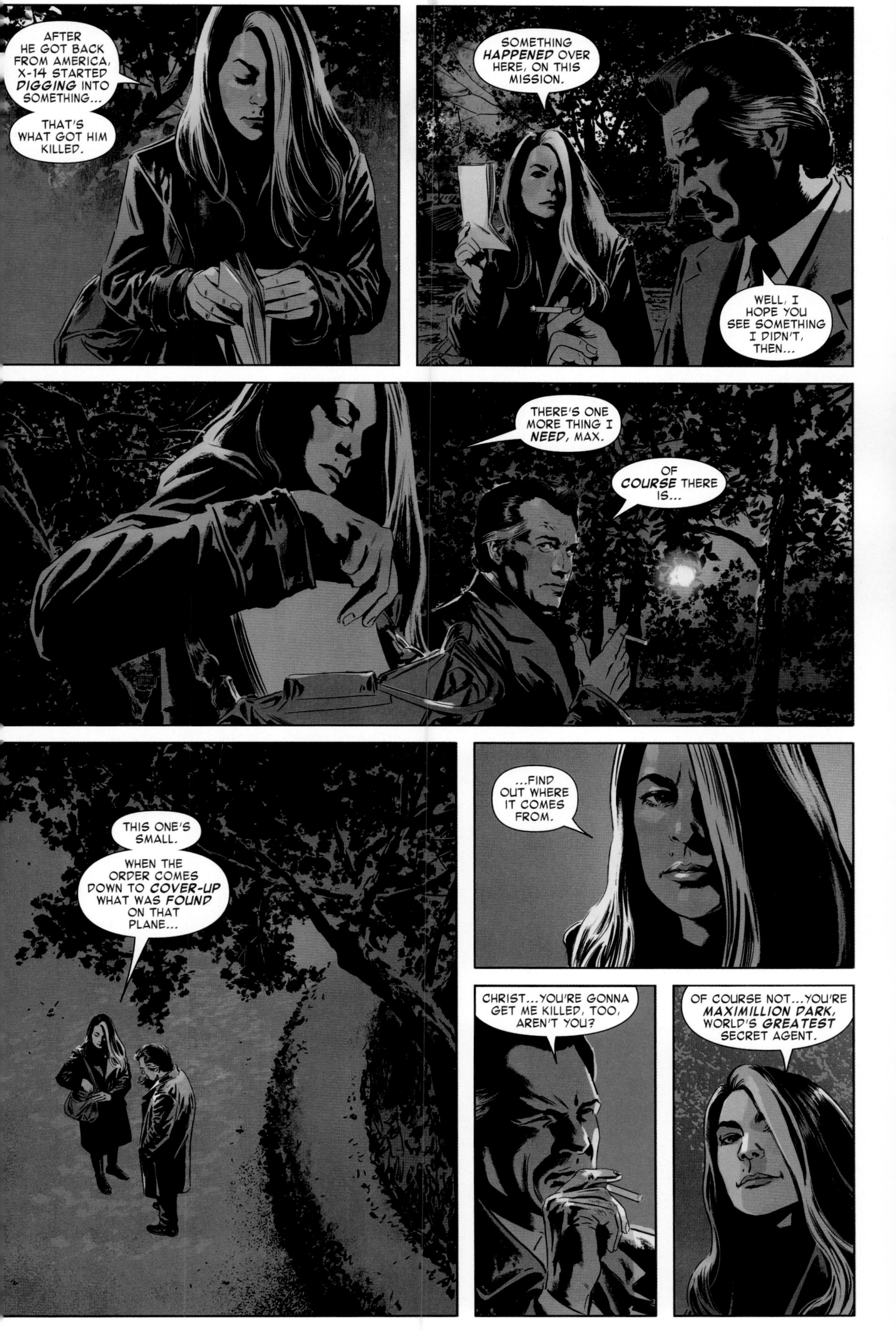

AFTER HE GOT BACK FROM AMERICA, X-14 STARTED DIGGING INTO SOMETHING...
THAT'S WHAT GOT HIM KILLED.
SOMETHING HAPPENED OVER HERE, ON THIS MISSION.
WELL, I HOPE YOU SEE SOMETHING I DIDN'T, THEN...
THERE'S ONE MORE THING I NEED, MAX.
OF COURSE THERE IS...
THIS ONE'S SMALL.
WHEN THE ORDER COMES DOWN TO COVER-UP WHAT WAS FOUND ON THAT PLANE...
...FIND OUT WHERE IT COMES FROM.
CHRIST...YOU'RE GONNA GET ME KILLED, TOO, AREN'T YOU?
OF COURSE NOT...YOU'RE MAXIMILLION DARK, WORLD'S GREATEST SECRET AGENT.

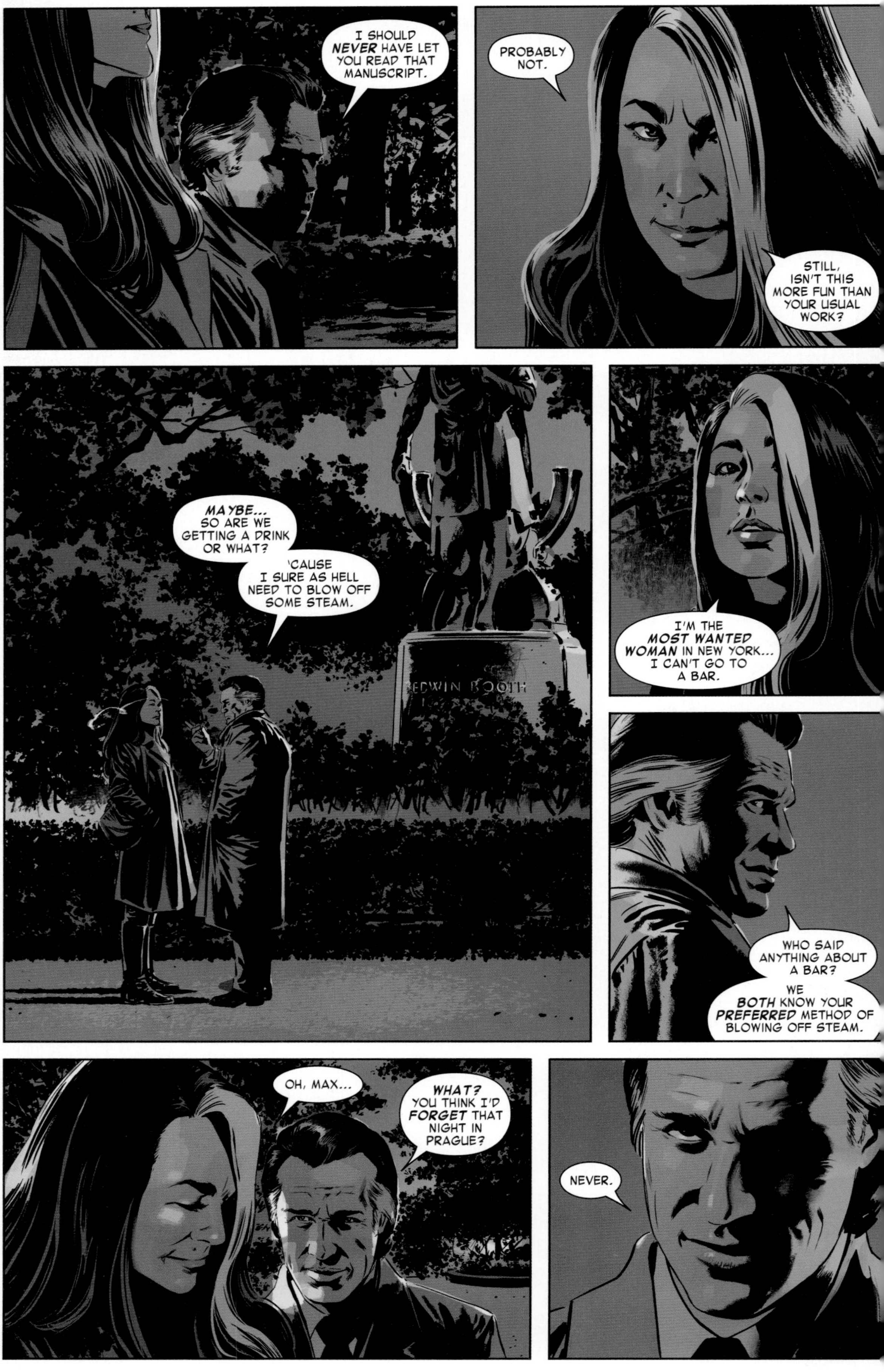
I SHOULD NEVER HAVE LET YOU READ THAT MANUSCRIPT.
PROBABLY NOT.
STILL, ISN'T THIS MORE FUN THAN YOUR USUAL WORK?
MAYBE... SO ARE WE GETTING A DRINK OR WHAT?
'CAUSE I SURE AS HELL NEED TO BLOW OFF SOME STEAM.
EDWIN BOOTH
I'M THE MOST WANTED WOMAN IN NEW YORK... I CAN'T GO TO A BAR.
WHO SAID ANYTHING ABOUT A BAR?
WE BOTH KNOW YOUR PREFERRED METHOD OF BLOWING OFF STEAM.
OH, MAX...
WHAT? YOU THINK I'D FORGET THAT NIGHT IN PRAGUE?
NEVER.

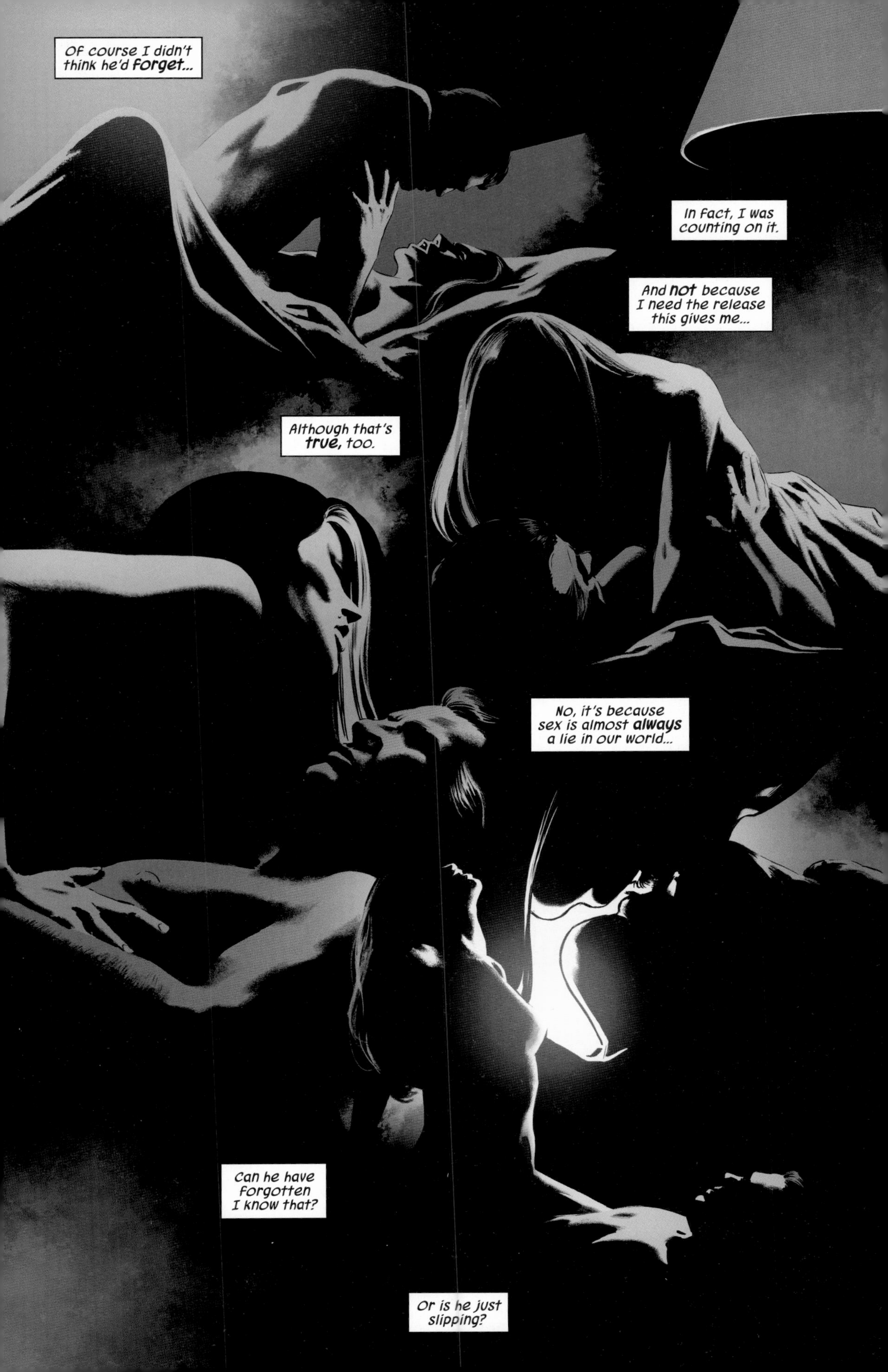
Of course I didn't think he'd forget...
In fact, I was counting on it.
And not because I need the release this gives me...
Although that's true, too.
No, it's because sex is almost always a lie in our world...
Can he have forgotten I know that?
Or is he just slipping?

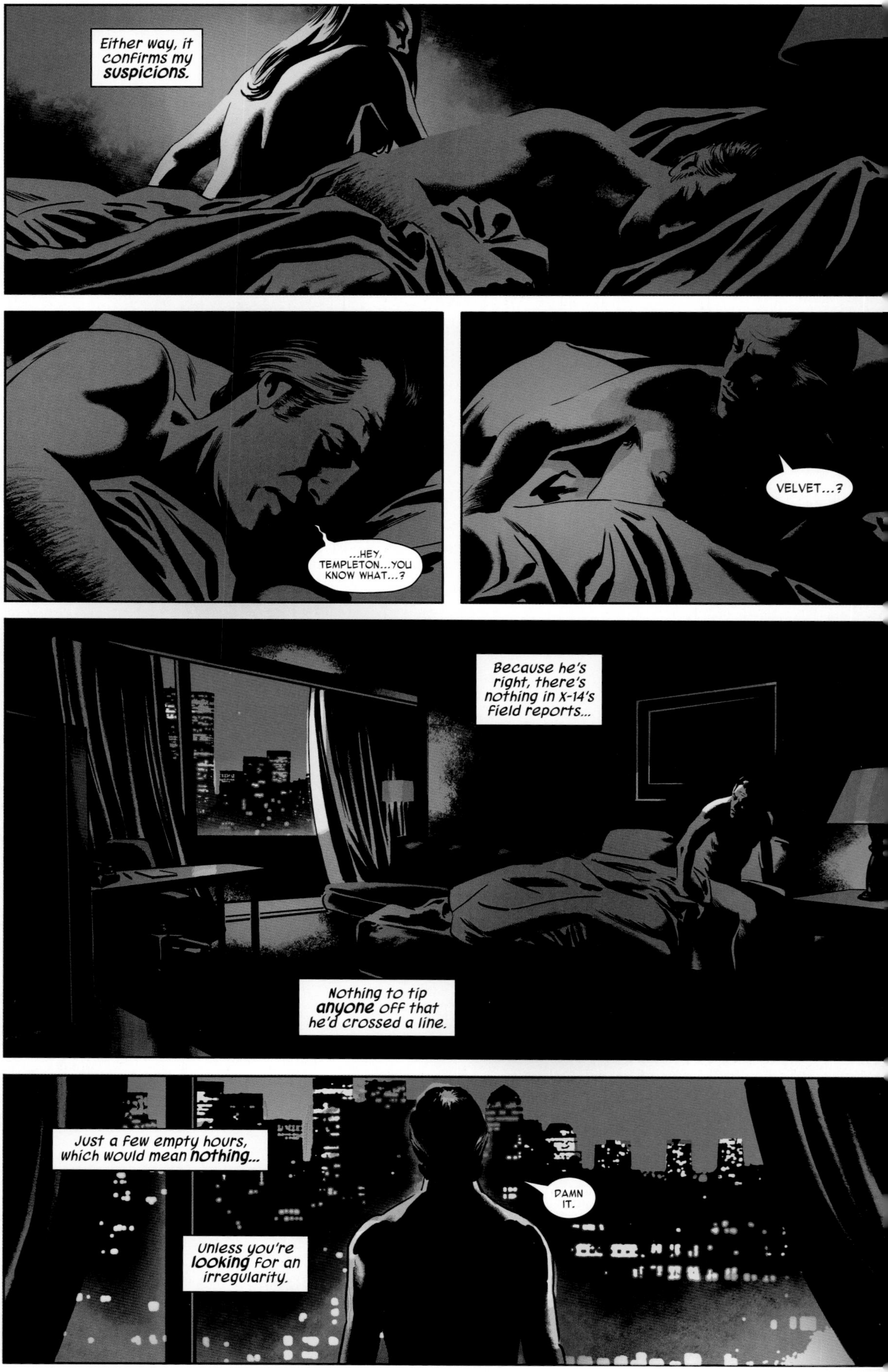
Either way, it confirms my suspicions.
...HEY, TEMPLETON...YOU KNOW WHAT...?
VELVET...?
Because he's right, there's nothing in X-14's field reports...
Nothing to tip anyone off that he'd crossed a line.
Just a few empty hours, which would mean nothing...
DAMN IT.
Unless you're looking for an irregularity.

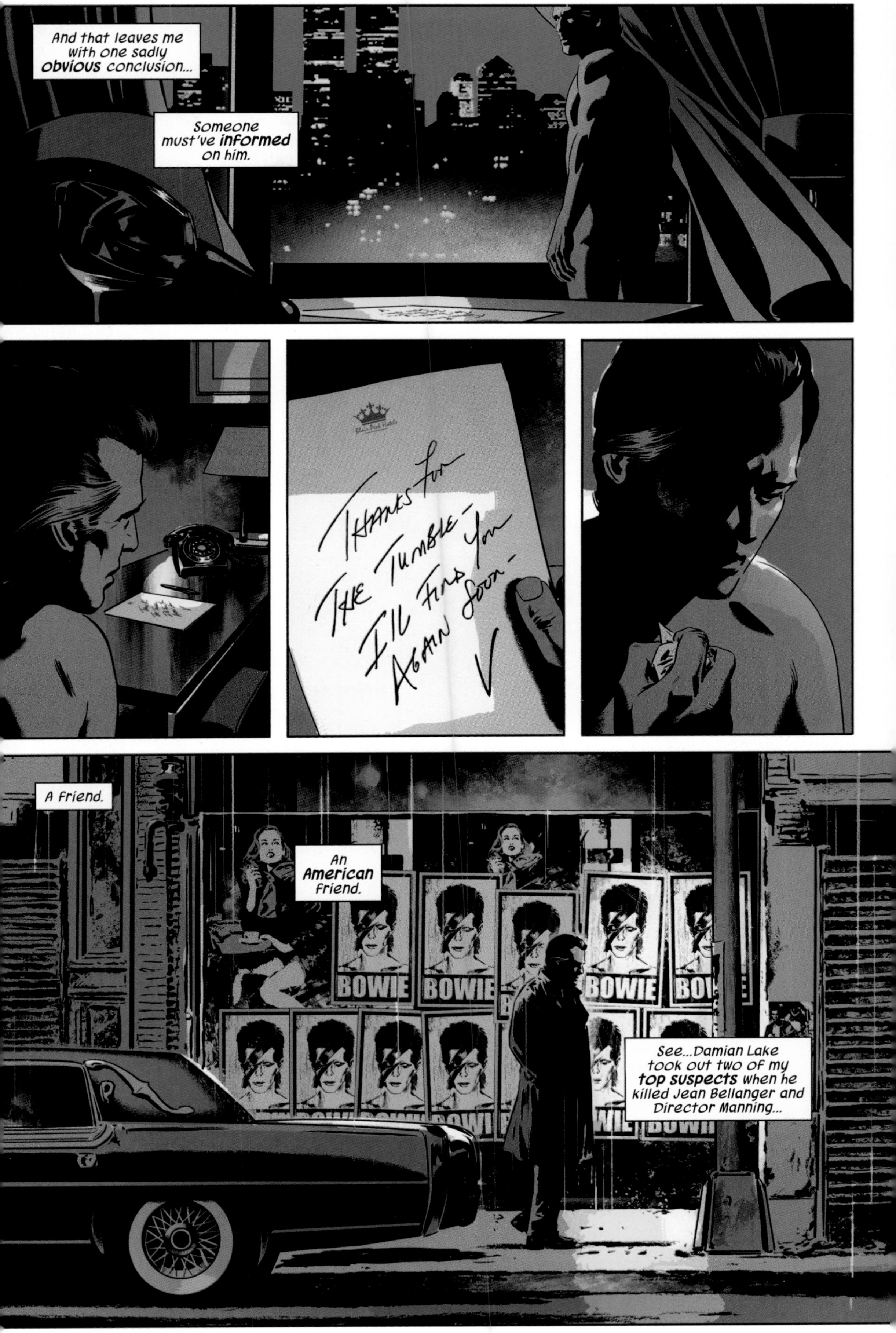
And that leaves me with one sadly obvious conclusion...
Someone must've informed on him.
Thanks for the tumble - I'll find you again soon - V
A Friend.
An American friend.
BOWIE
See...Damian Lake took out two of my top suspects when he killed Jean Bellanger and Director Manning...

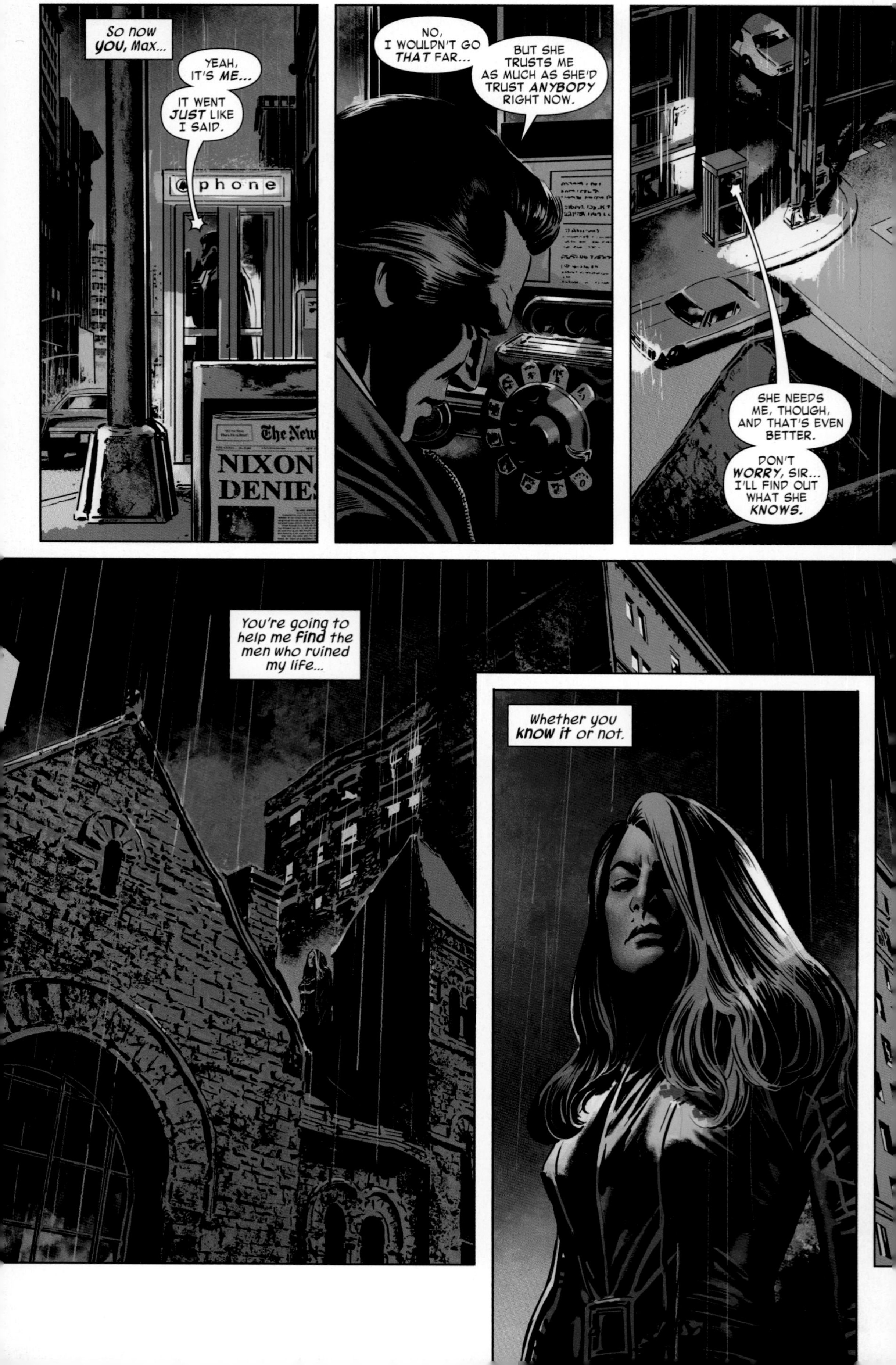

So now YOU, Max...
YEAH, IT'S ME...
IT WENT JUST LIKE I SAID.
phone
The New
NIXON DENIES
NO, I WOULDN'T GO THAT FAR...
BUT SHE TRUSTS ME AS MUCH AS SHE'D TRUST ANYBODY RIGHT NOW.
SHE NEEDS ME, THOUGH, AND THAT'S EVEN BETTER.
DON'T WORRY, SIR... I'LL FIND OUT WHAT SHE KNOWS.
You're going to help me find the men who ruined my life...
Whether you know it or not.

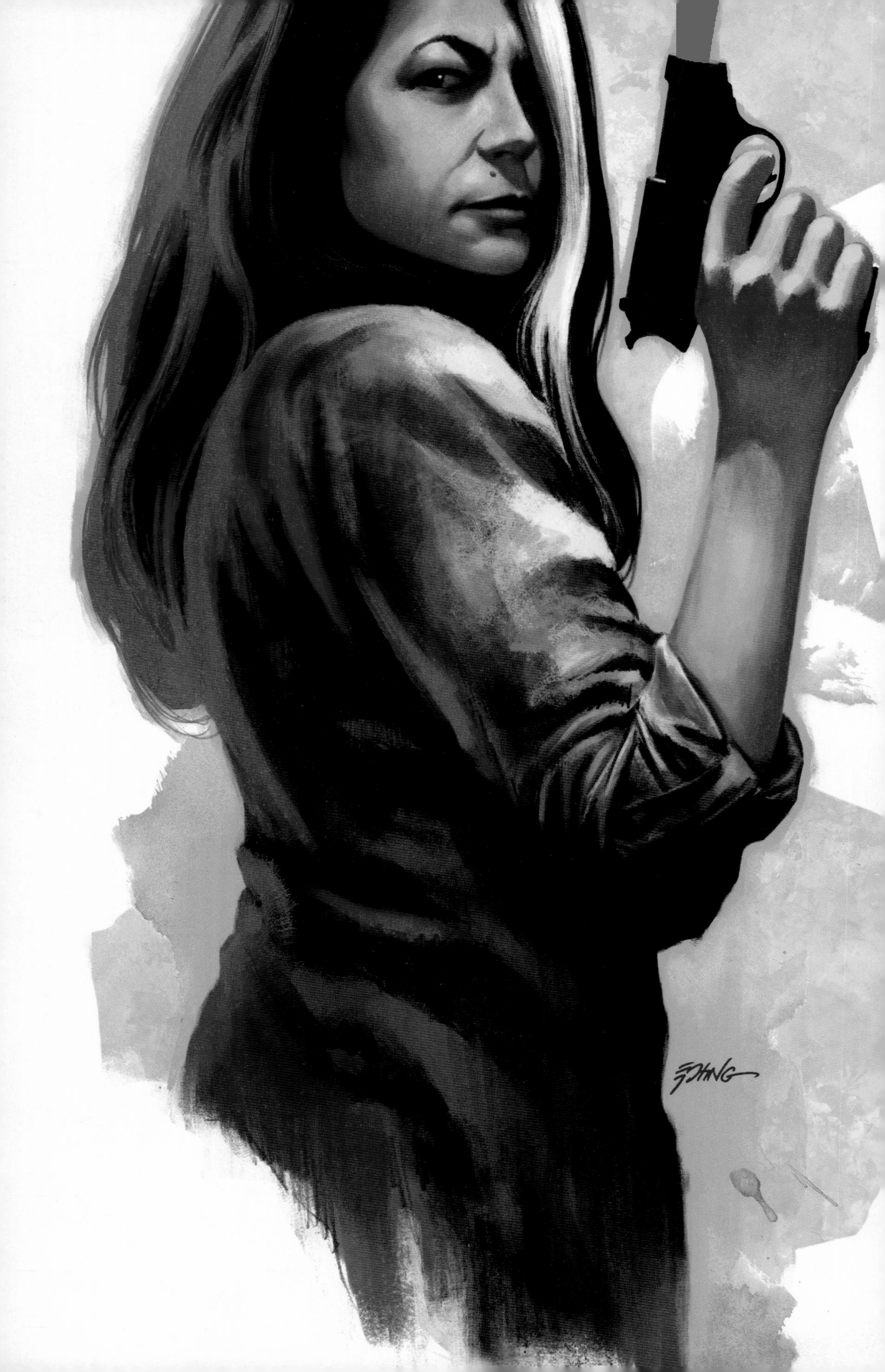

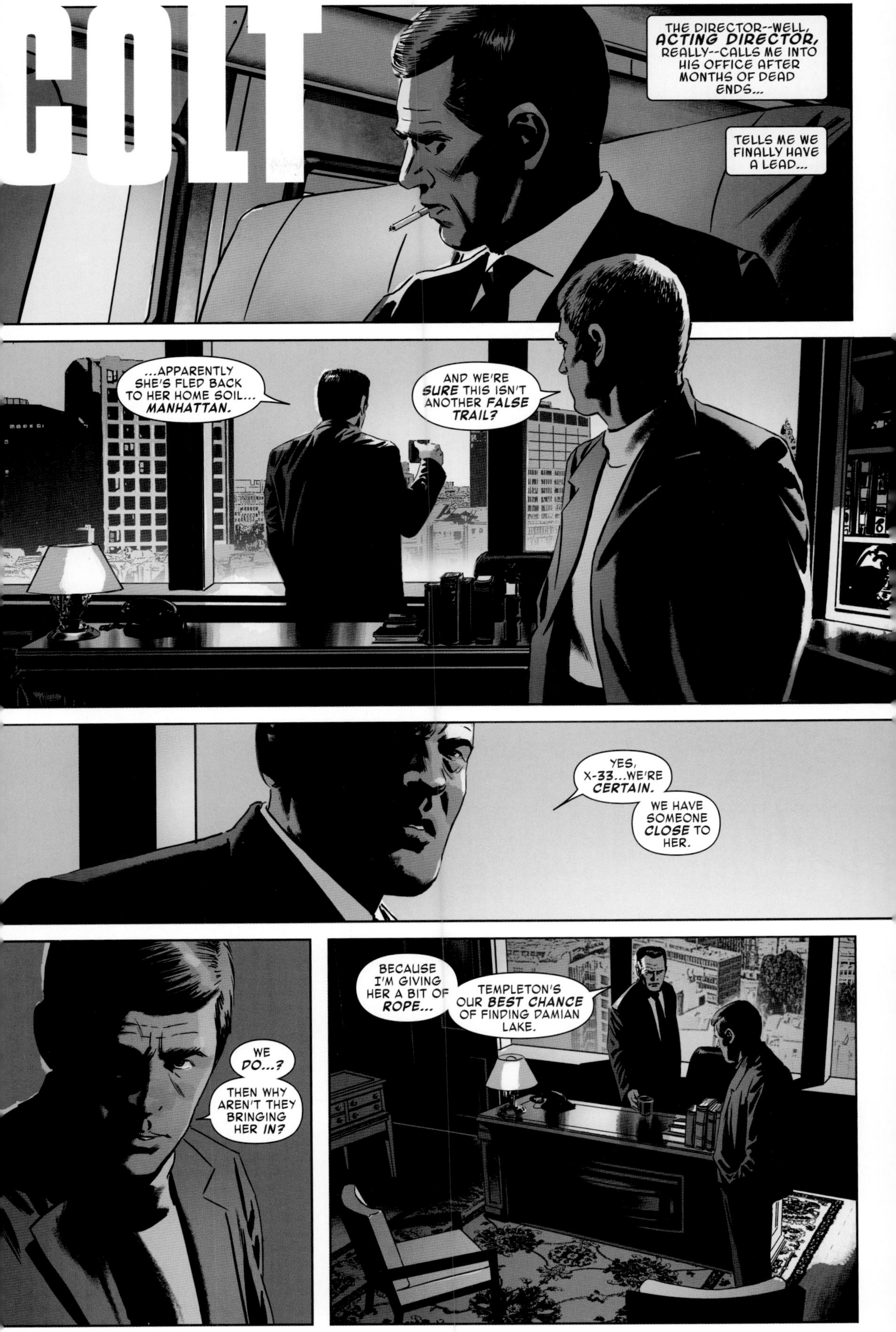
COLT
THE DIRECTOR--WELL, ACTING DIRECTOR, REALLY--CALLS ME INTO HIS OFFICE AFTER MONTHS OF DEAD ENDS...
TELLS ME WE FINALLY HAVE A LEAD...
...APPARENTLY SHE'S FLED BACK TO HER HOME SOIL... MANHATTAN.
AND WE'RE SURE THIS ISN'T ANOTHER FALSE TRAIL?
YES, X-33...WE'RE CERTAIN.
WE HAVE SOMEONE CLOSE TO HER.
WE DO...?
THEN WHY AREN'T THEY BRINGING HER IN?
BECAUSE I'M GIVING HER A BIT OF ROPE...
TEMPLETON'S OUR BEST CHANCE OF FINDING DAMIAN LAKE.

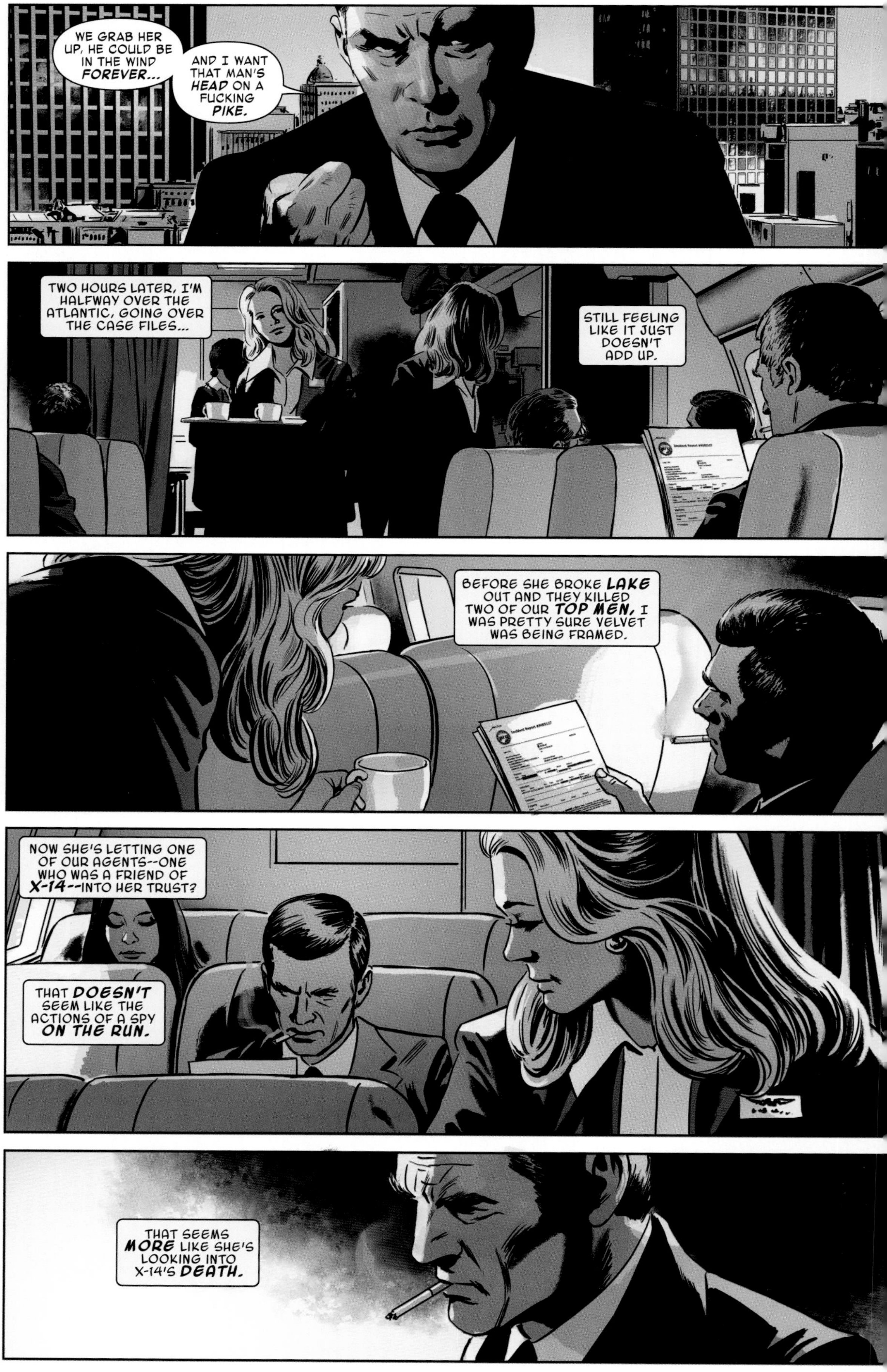
WE GRAB HER UP, HE COULD BE IN THE WIND FOREVER...
AND I WANT THAT MAN'S HEAD ON A FUCKING PIKE.
TWO HOURS LATER, I'M HALFWAY OVER THE ATLANTIC, GOING OVER THE CASE FILES...
STILL FEELING LIKE IT JUST DOESN'T ADD UP.
BEFORE SHE BROKE LAKE OUT AND THEY KILLED TWO OF OUR TOP MEN, I WAS PRETTY SURE VELVET WAS BEING FRAMED.
NOW SHE'S LETTING ONE OF OUR AGENTS--ONE WHO WAS A FRIEND OF X-14--INTO HER TRUST?
THAT DOESN'T SEEM LIKE THE ACTIONS OF A SPY ON THE RUN.
THAT SEEMS MORE LIKE SHE'S LOOKING INTO X-14'S DEATH.

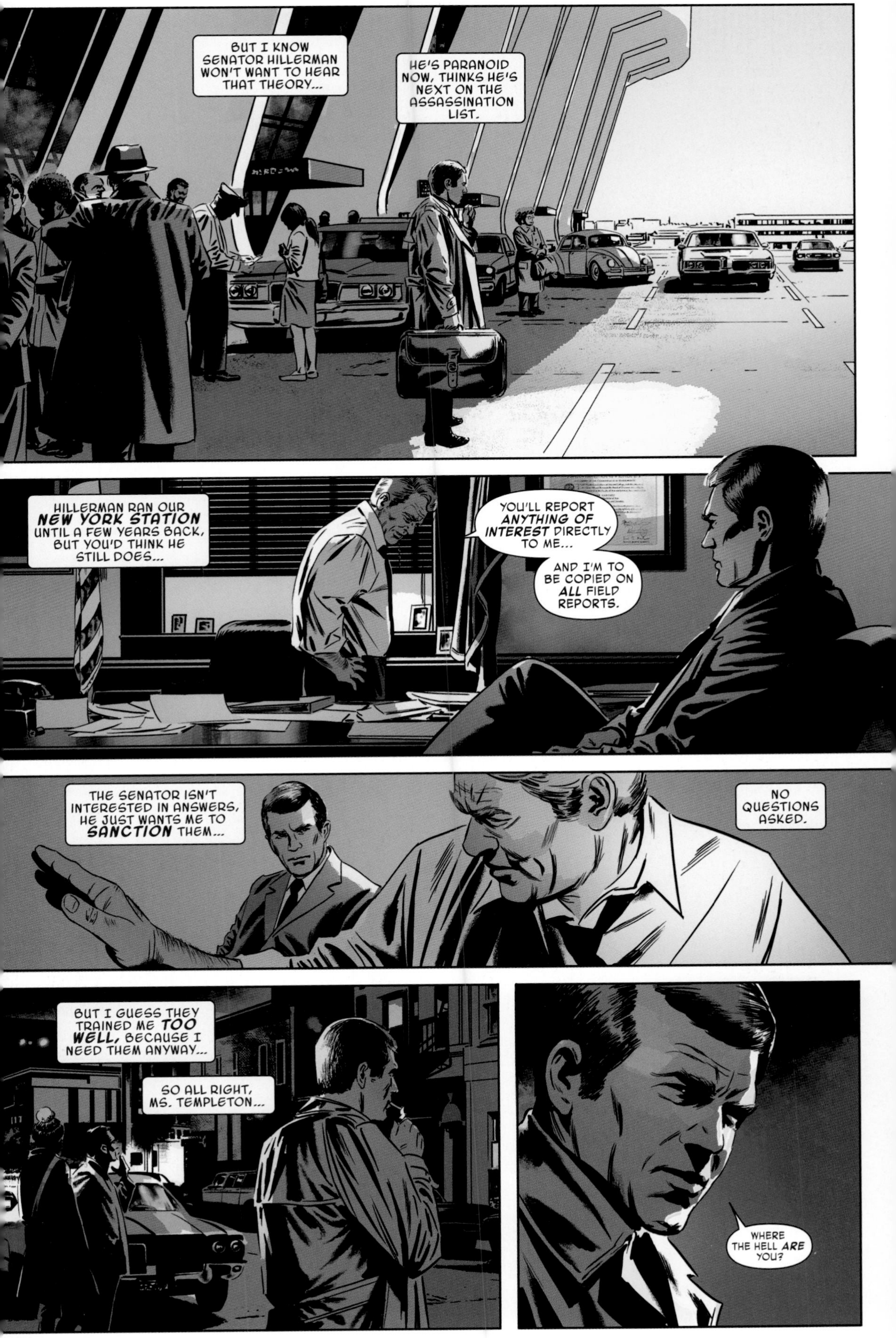
BUT I KNOW SENATOR HILLERMAN WON'T WANT TO HEAR THAT THEORY...
HE'S PARANOID NOW, THINKS HE'S NEXT ON THE ASSASSINATION LIST.
HILLERMAN RAN OUR NEW YORK STATION UNTIL A FEW YEARS BACK, BUT YOU'D THINK HE STILL DOES...
YOU'LL REPORT ANYTHING OF INTEREST DIRECTLY TO ME...
AND I'M TO BE COPIED ON ALL FIELD REPORTS.
THE SENATOR ISN'T INTERESTED IN ANSWERS, HE JUST WANTS ME TO SANCTION THEM...
NO QUESTIONS ASKED.
BUT I GUESS THEY TRAINED ME TOO WELL, BECAUSE I NEED THEM ANYWAY...
SO ALL RIGHT, MS. TEMPLETON...
WHERE THE HELL ARE YOU?

PART TWO

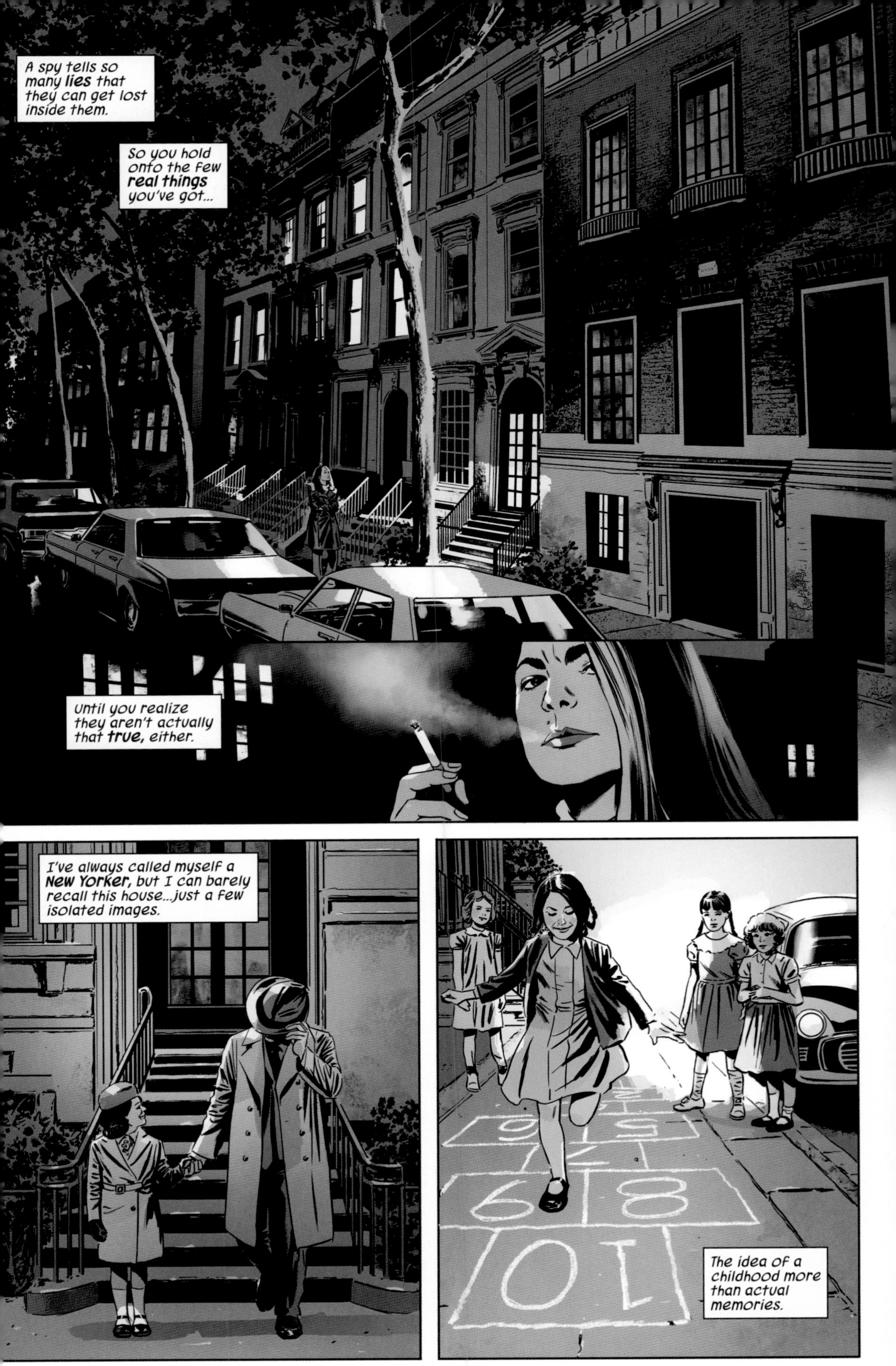
A spy tells so many **lies** that they can get lost inside them.
So you hold onto the few **real things** you've got...
Until you realize they aren't actually that **true,** either.
I've always called myself a **New Yorker,** but I can barely recall this house...just a few isolated images.
The idea of a childhood more than actual memories.

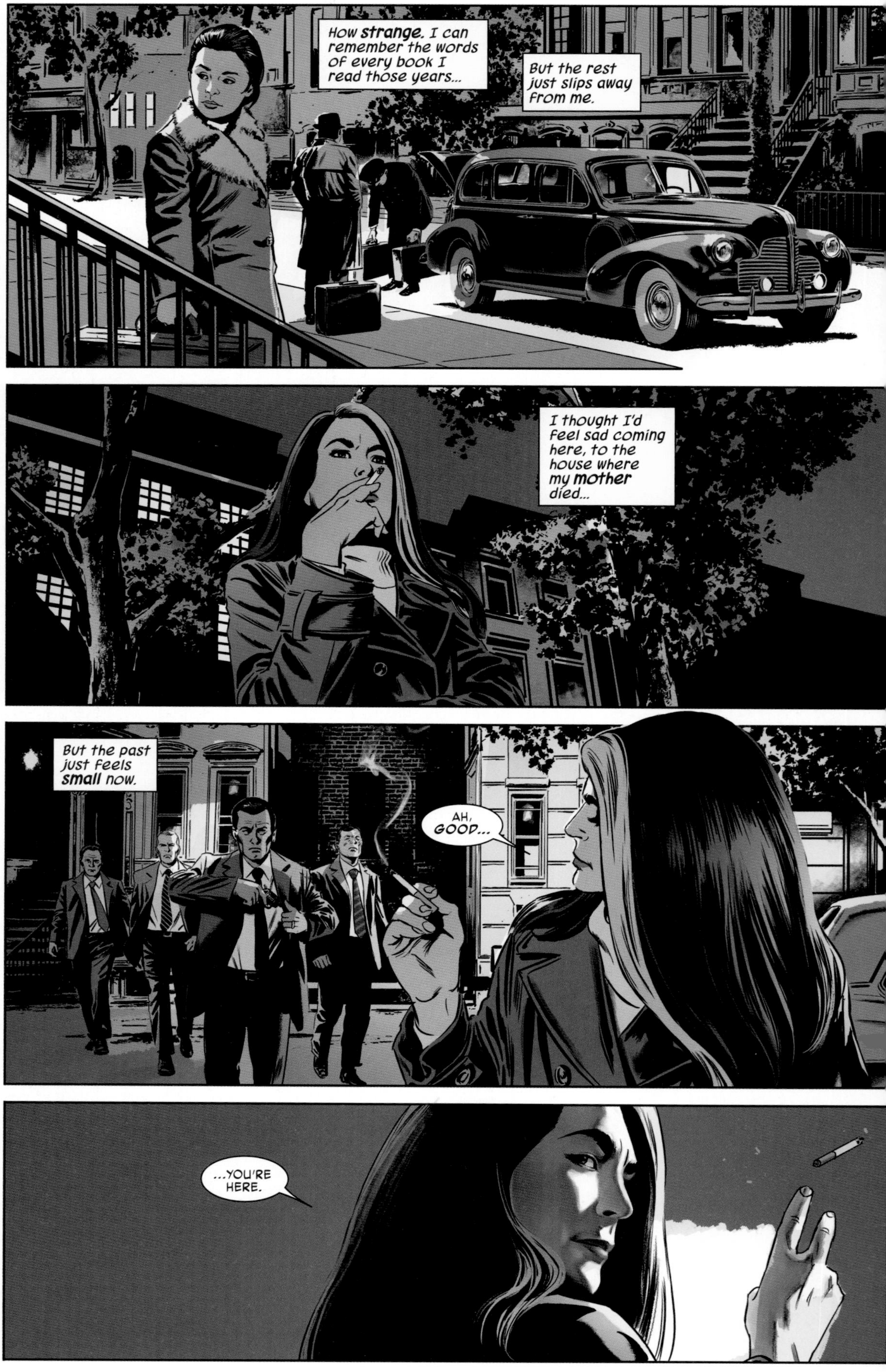
How strange. I can remember the words of every book I read those years...
But the rest just slips away from me.
I thought I'd feel sad coming here, to the house where my mother died...
But the past just feels small now.
AH, GOOD...
...YOU'RE HERE.

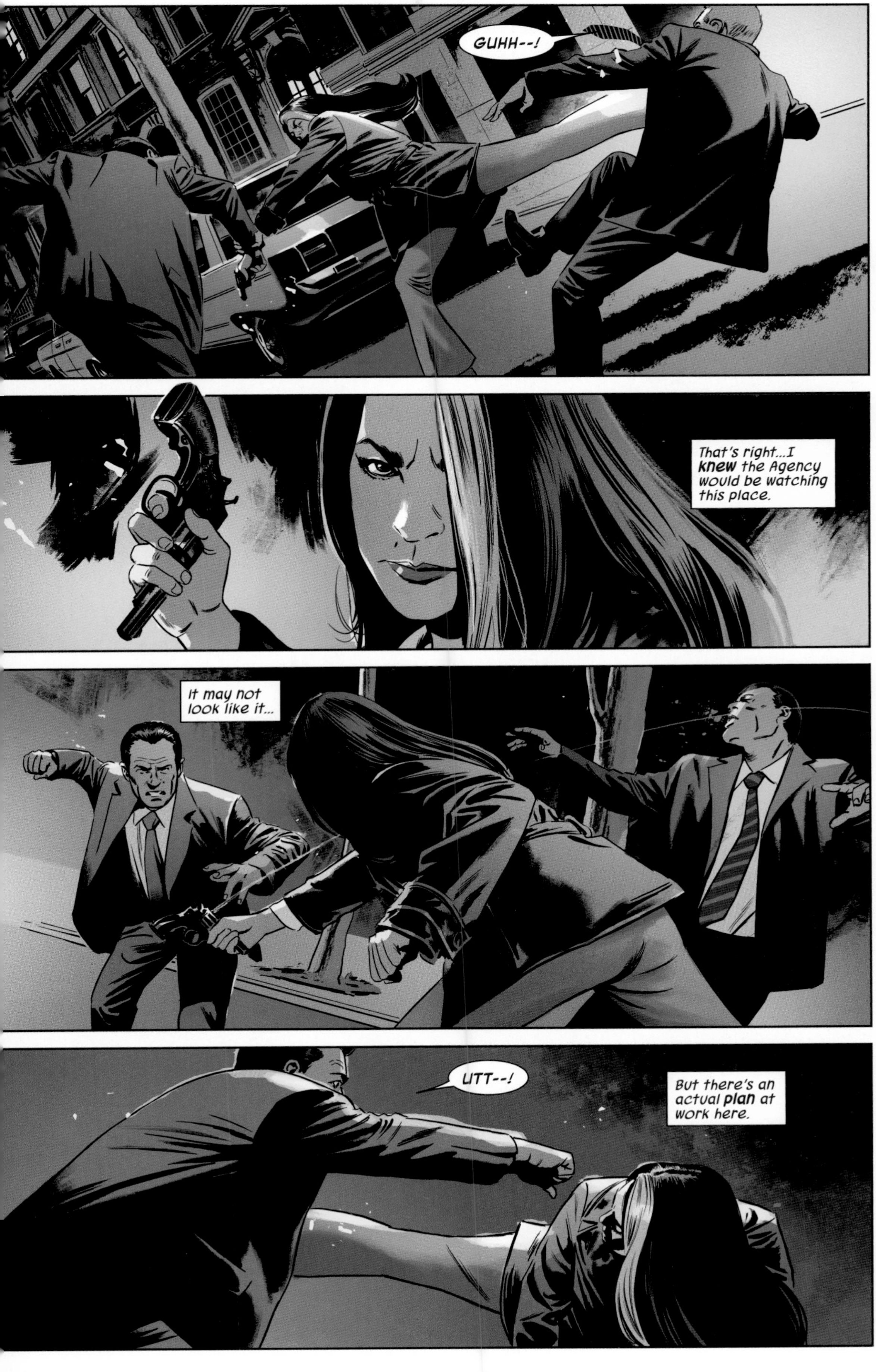
GUHH--!
That's right...I **KNEW** the Agency would be watching this place.
It may not look like it...
UTT--!
But there's an actual **plan** at work here.

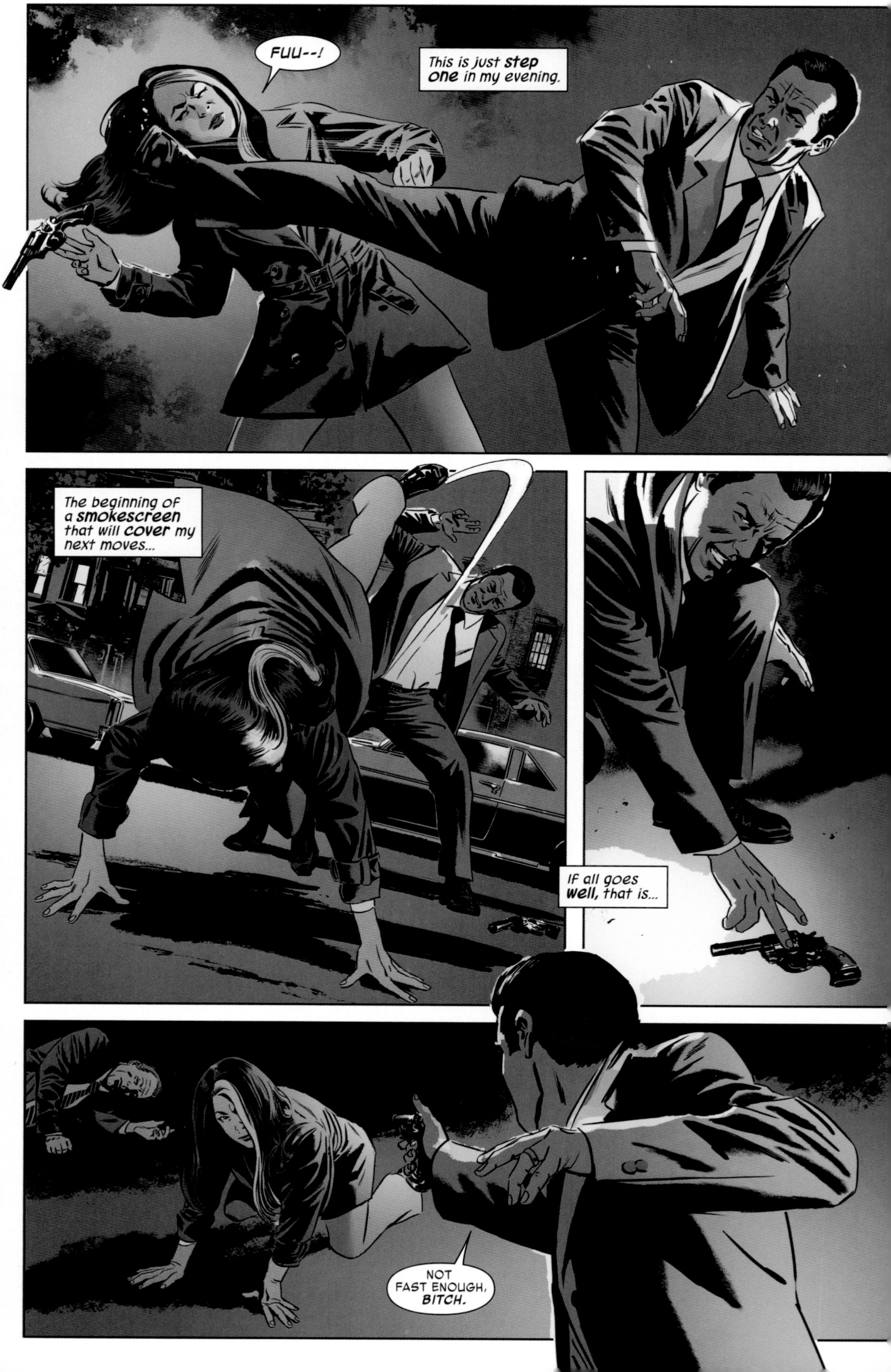
FUU--!
This is just step one in my evening.
The beginning of a smokescreen that will cover my next moves...
If all goes well, that is...
NOT FAST ENOUGH, BITCH.

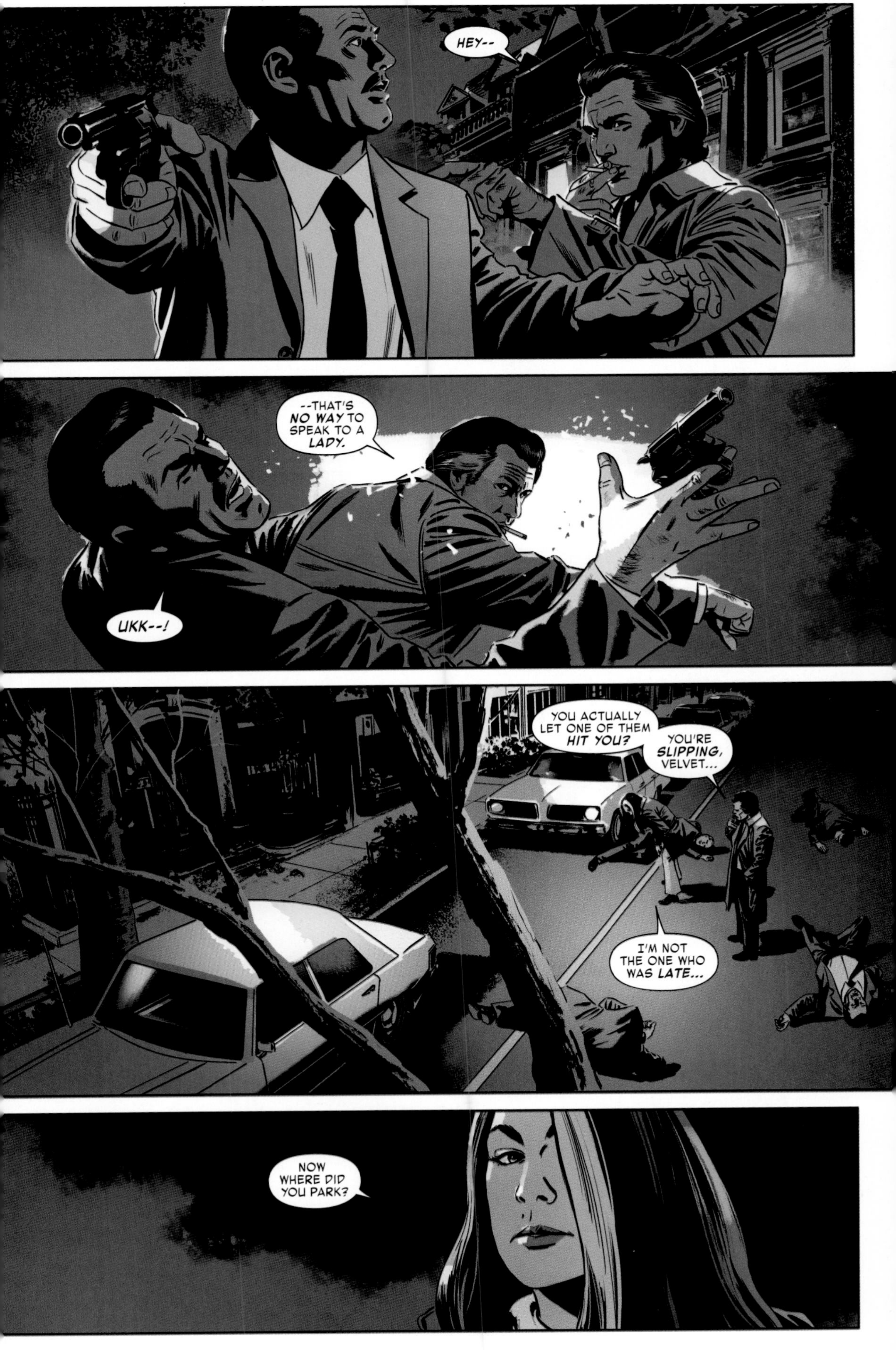
HEY--
--THAT'S NO WAY TO SPEAK TO A LADY.
UKK--!
YOU ACTUALLY LET ONE OF THEM HIT YOU?
YOU'RE SLIPPING, VELVET...
I'M NOT THE ONE WHO WAS LATE...
NOW WHERE DID YOU PARK?

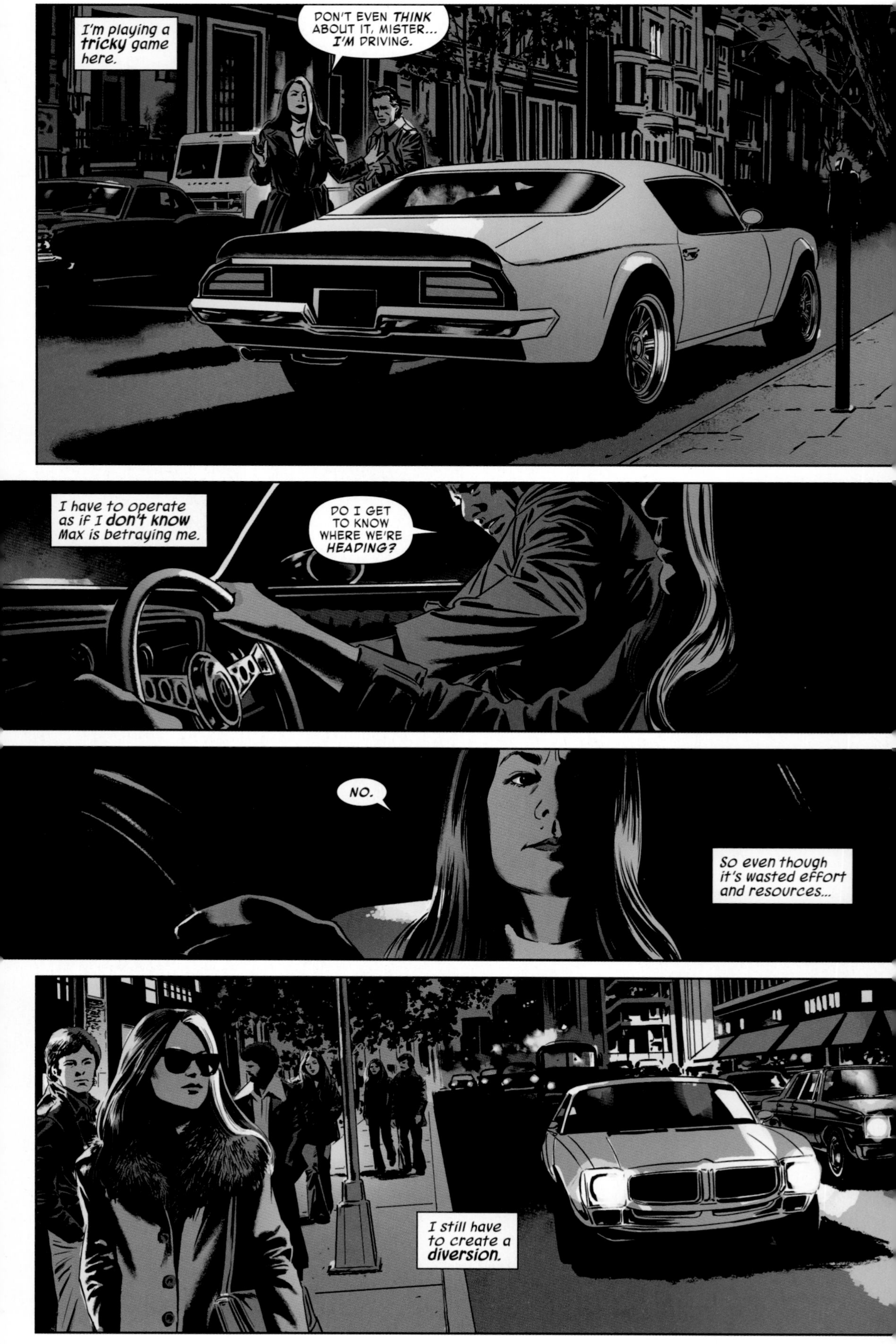
I'm playing a tricky game here.
DON'T EVEN THINK ABOUT IT, MISTER... I'M DRIVING.
I have to operate as if I don't know Max is betraying me.
DO I GET TO KNOW WHERE WE'RE HEADING?
NO.
So even though it's wasted effort and resources...
I still have to create a diversion.

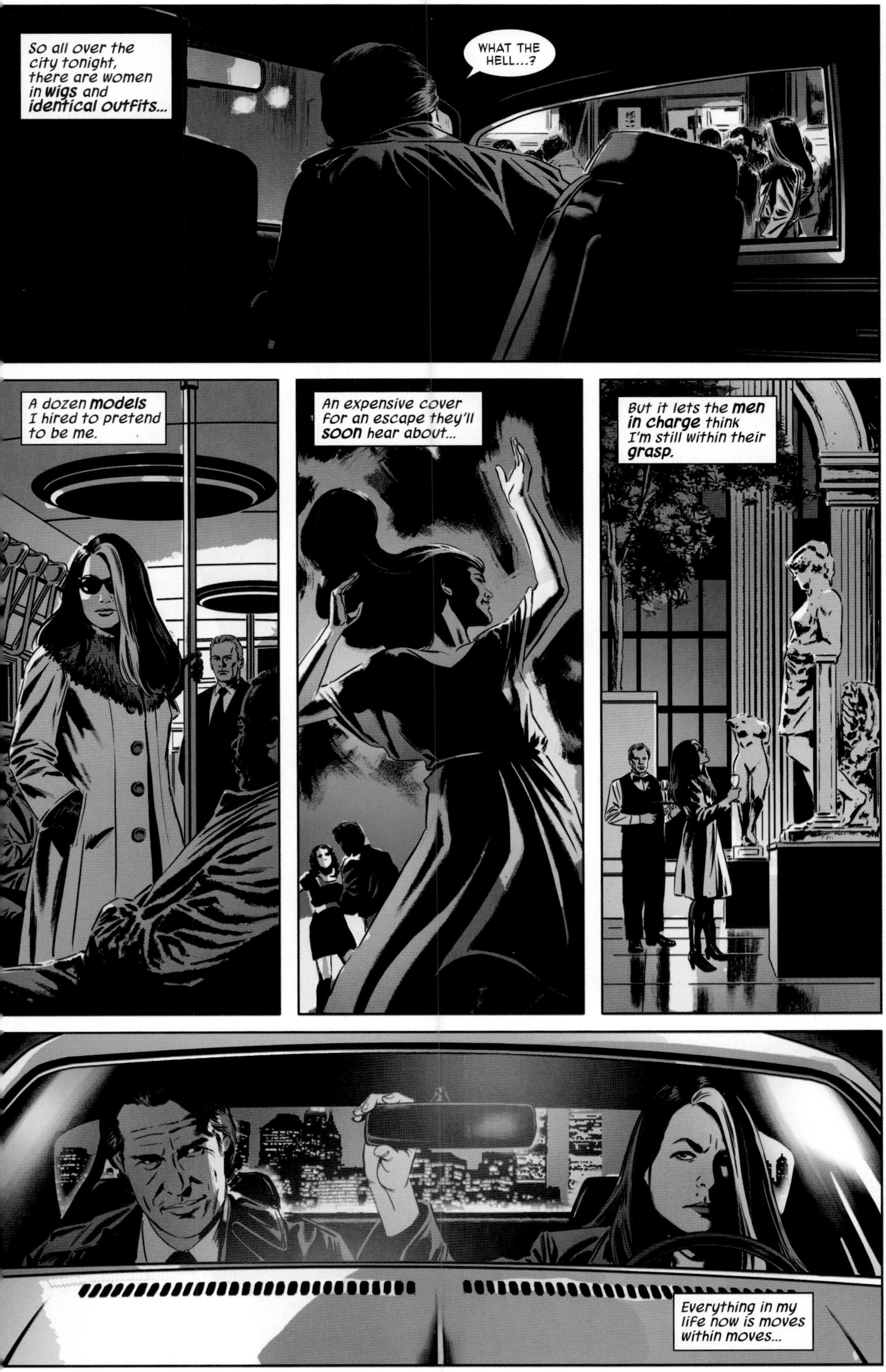
So all over the city tonight, there are women in wigs and identical outfits...
WHAT THE HELL...?
A dozen models I hired to pretend to be me.
An expensive cover for an escape they'll soon hear about...
But it lets the men in charge think I'm still within their grasp.
Everything in my life now is moves within moves...

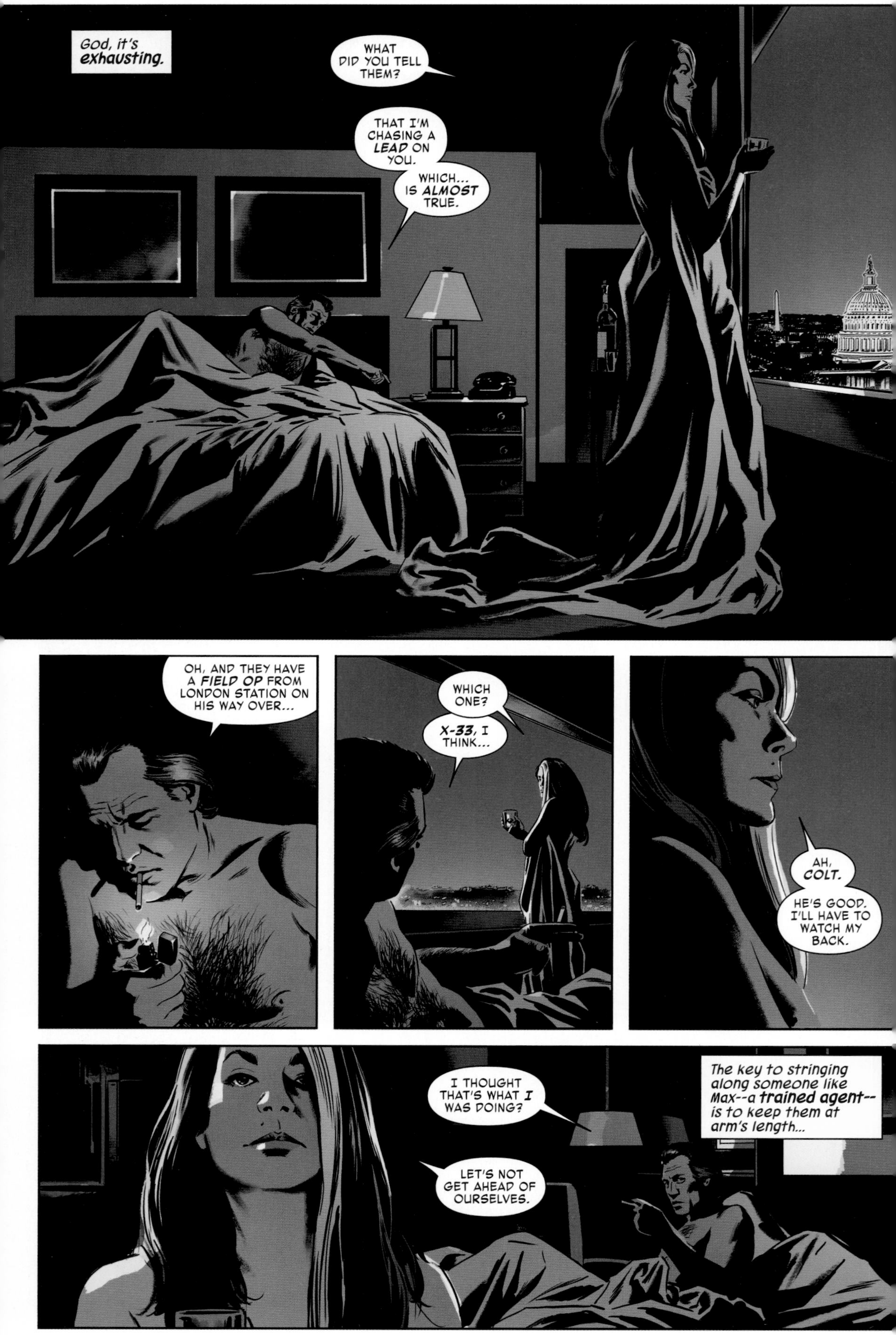
God, it's exhausting.
WHAT DID YOU TELL THEM?
THAT I'M CHASING A LEAD ON YOU.
WHICH... IS ALMOST TRUE.
OH, AND THEY HAVE A FIELD OP FROM LONDON STATION ON HIS WAY OVER...
WHICH ONE?
X-33, I THINK...
AH, COLT.
HE'S GOOD. I'LL HAVE TO WATCH MY BACK.
I THOUGHT THAT'S WHAT I WAS DOING?
LET'S NOT GET AHEAD OF OURSELVES.
The key to stringing along someone like Max--a trained agent--is to keep them at arm's length...

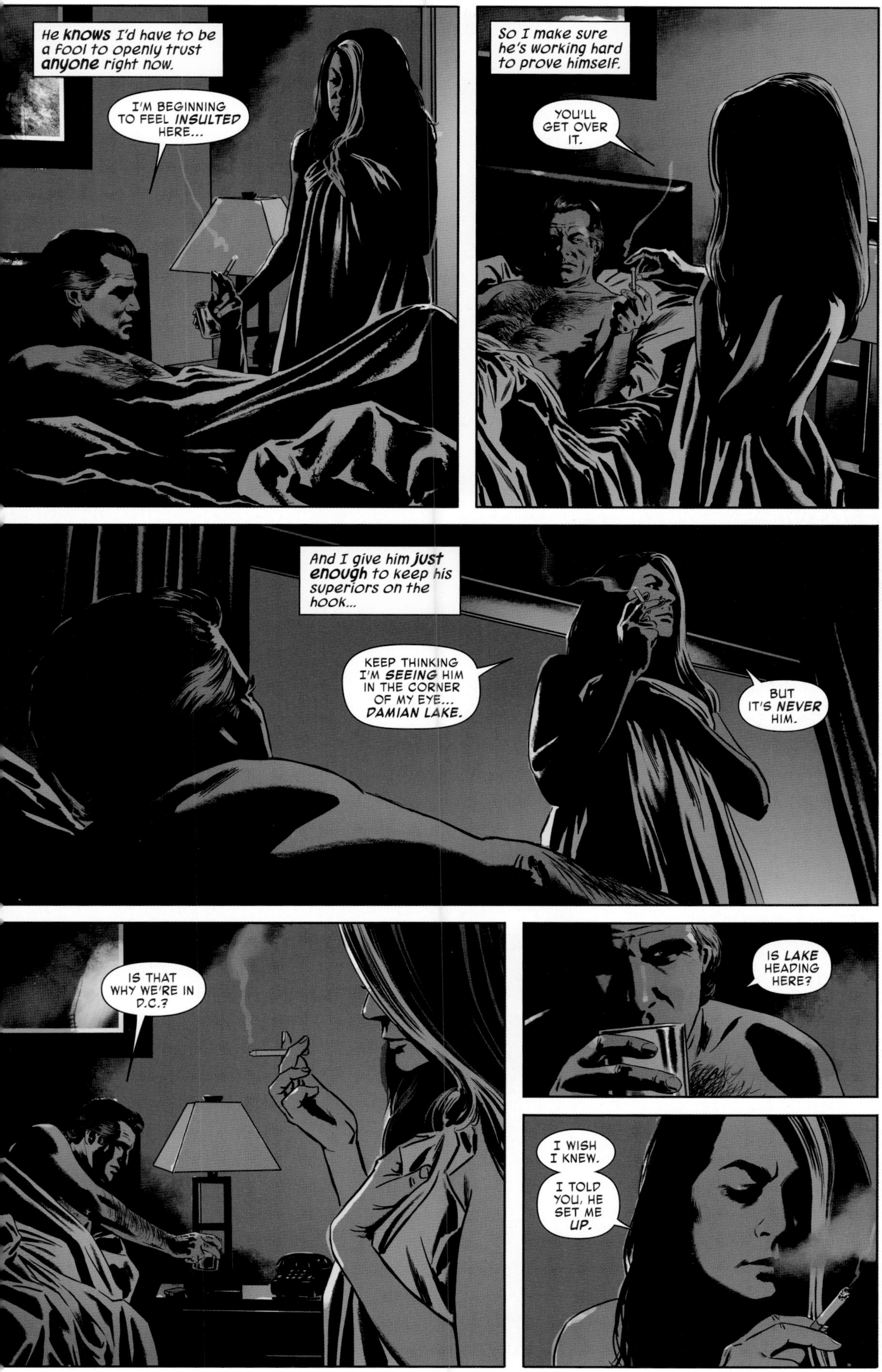

He KNOWS I'd have to be a fool to openly trust anyone right now.
I'M BEGINNING TO FEEL INSULTED HERE...
So I make sure he's working hard to prove himself.
YOU'LL GET OVER IT.
And I give him just enough to keep his superiors on the hook...
KEEP THINKING I'M SEEING HIM IN THE CORNER OF MY EYE... DAMIAN LAKE.
BUT IT'S NEVER HIM.
IS THAT WHY WE'RE IN D.C.?
IS LAKE HEADING HERE?
I WISH I KNEW.
I TOLD YOU, HE SET ME UP.

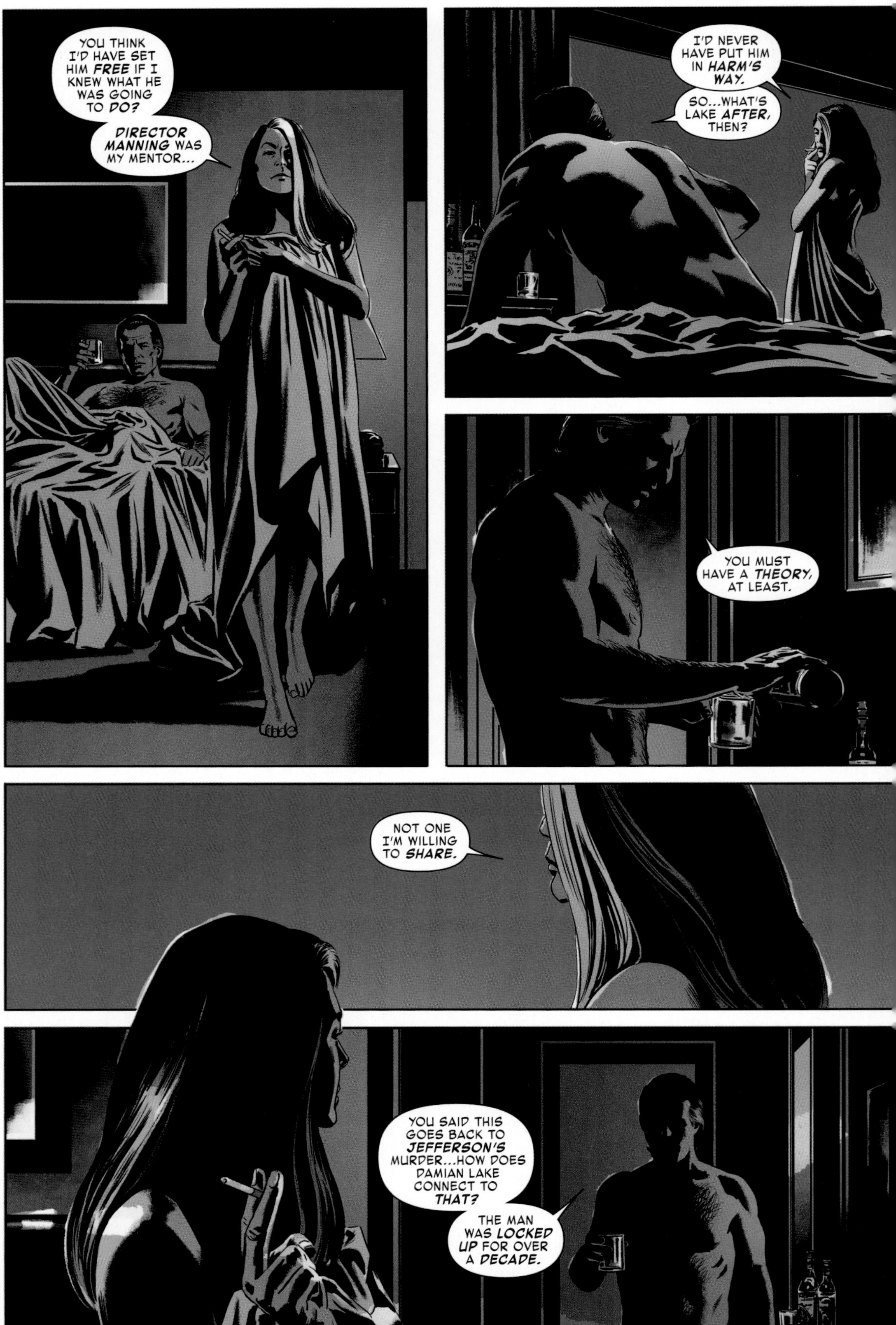
YOU THINK I'D HAVE SET HIM FREE IF I KNEW WHAT HE WAS GOING TO DO?
DIRECTOR MANNING WAS MY MENTOR...
I'D NEVER HAVE PUT HIM IN HARM'S WAY.
SO...WHAT'S LAKE AFTER, THEN?
YOU MUST HAVE A THEORY, AT LEAST.
NOT ONE I'M WILLING TO SHARE.
YOU SAID THIS GOES BACK TO JEFFERSON'S MURDER...HOW DOES DAMIAN LAKE CONNECT TO THAT?
THE MAN WAS LOCKED UP FOR OVER A DECADE.

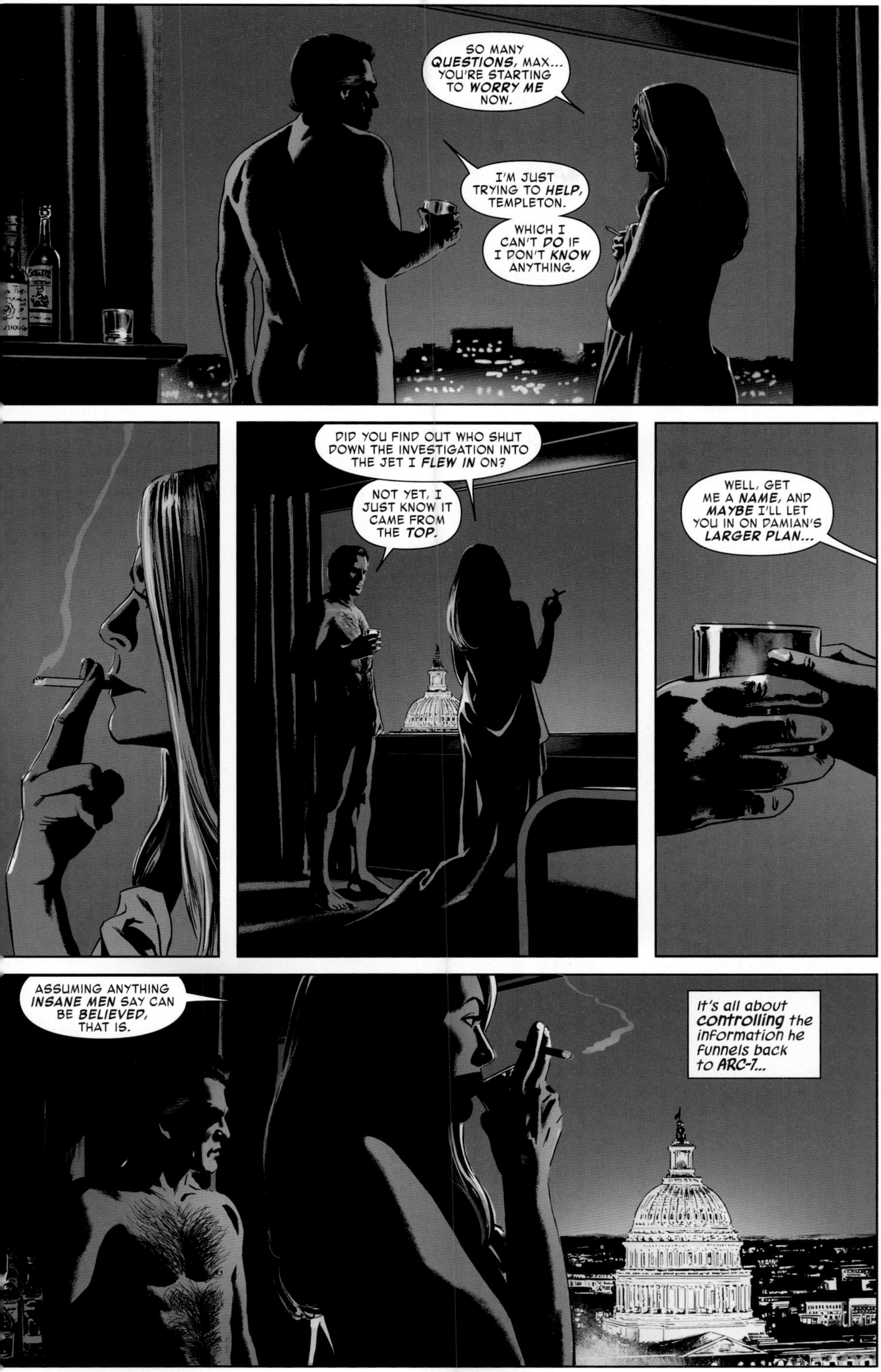
SO MANY QUESTIONS, MAX... YOU'RE STARTING TO WORRY ME NOW.
I'M JUST TRYING TO HELP, TEMPLETON.
WHICH I CAN'T DO IF I DON'T KNOW ANYTHING.
DID YOU FIND OUT WHO SHUT DOWN THE INVESTIGATION INTO THE JET I FLEW IN ON?
NOT YET, I JUST KNOW IT CAME FROM THE TOP.
WELL, GET ME A NAME, AND MAYBE I'LL LET YOU IN ON DAMIAN'S LARGER PLAN...
ASSUMING ANYTHING INSANE MEN SAY CAN BE BELIEVED, THAT IS.
It's all about controlling the information he funnels back to ARC-7...

If I can use Max to keep them looking the **wrong way**...

I **may** be able to get the **answers** I'm after.

And while he's phoning in his latest report--heavy on Damian Lake **paranoia**, I'm sure--that's **exactly** what I do.

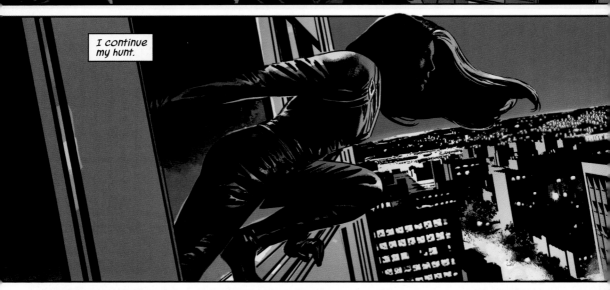

I continue my hunt.

In the most-boring way possible...

A middle-of-the-night **break-in** at the phone company.

Last time he was in **D.C.**, X-14 was shadowing a Diplomat's **Assistant**--Rachel Tanner.

The **Diplomat** was transferred overseas and the Assistant's address has another girl living there now...

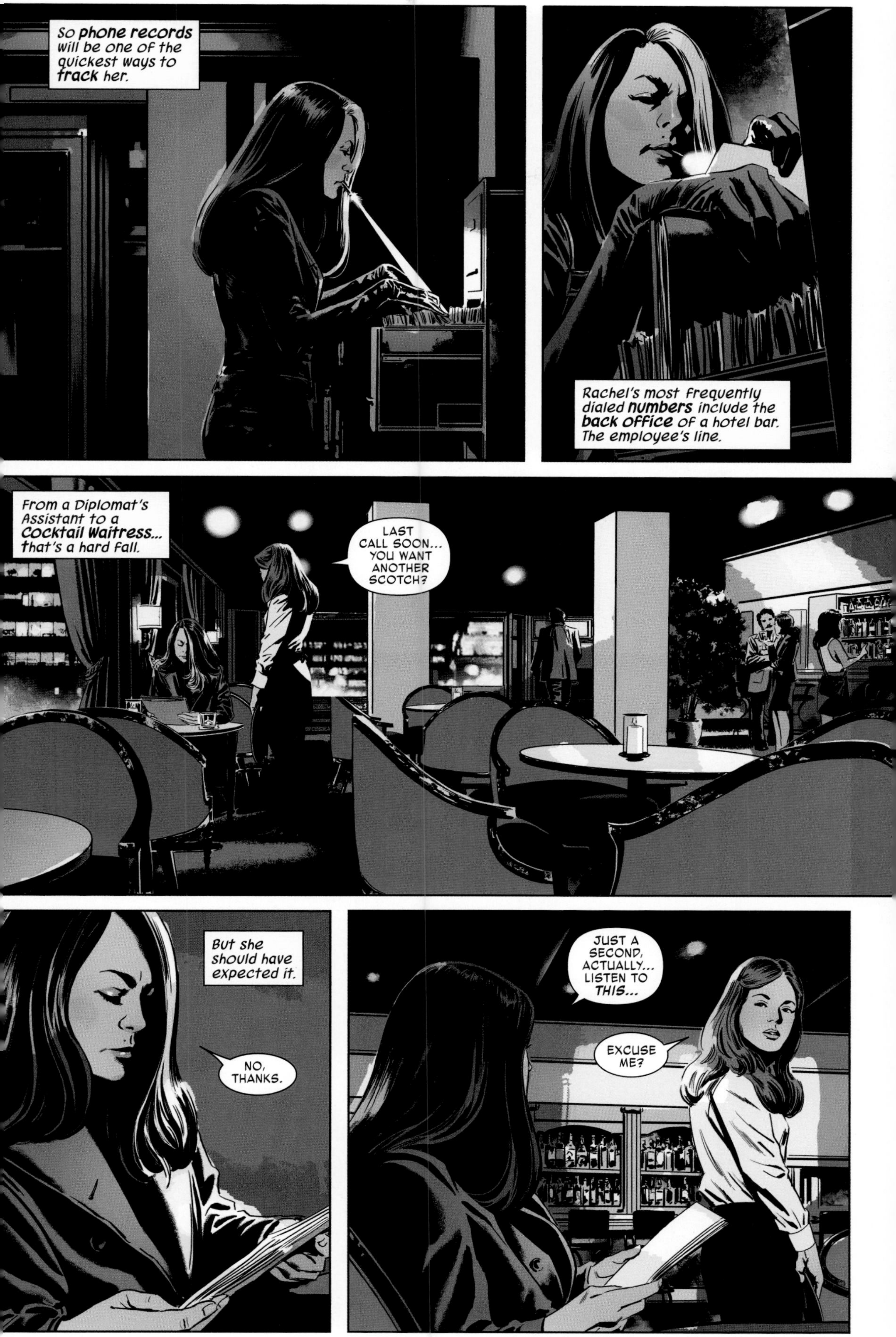
So phone records will be one of the quickest ways to track her.
Rachel's most frequently dialed numbers include the back office of a hotel bar. The employee's line.
From a Diplomat's Assistant to a Cocktail Waitress... that's a hard fall.
LAST CALL SOON... YOU WANT ANOTHER SCOTCH?
But she should have expected it.
NO, THANKS.
JUST A SECOND, ACTUALLY... LISTEN TO THIS...
EXCUSE ME?

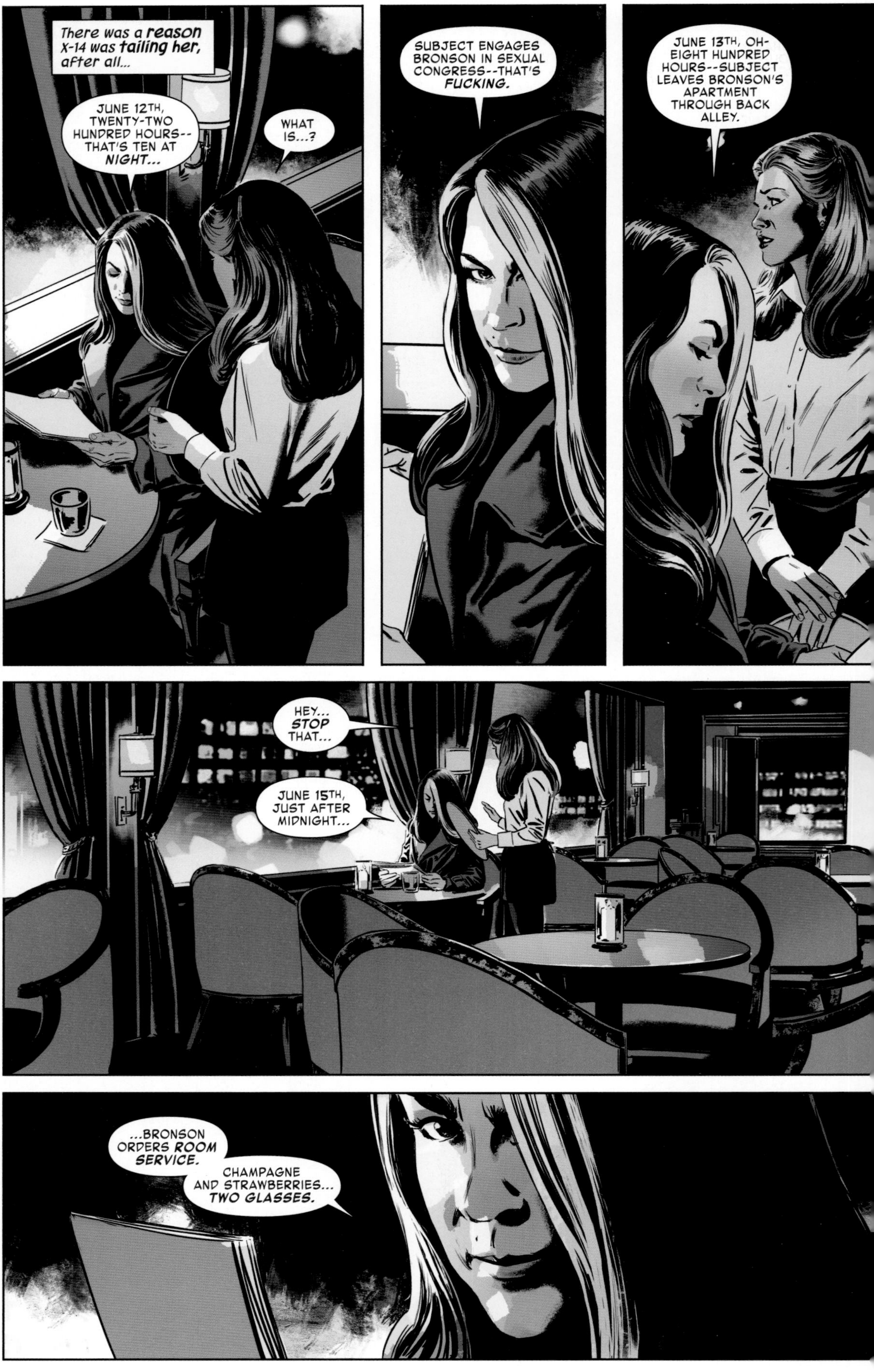
There was a reason X-14 was tailing her, after all...
JUNE 12TH, TWENTY-TWO HUNDRED HOURS--THAT'S TEN AT NIGHT...
WHAT IS...?
SUBJECT ENGAGES BRONSON IN SEXUAL CONGRESS--THAT'S FUCKING.
JUNE 13TH, OH-EIGHT HUNDRED HOURS--SUBJECT LEAVES BRONSON'S APARTMENT THROUGH BACK ALLEY.
HEY... STOP THAT...
JUNE 15TH, JUST AFTER MIDNIGHT...
...BRONSON ORDERS ROOM SERVICE.
CHAMPAGNE AND STRAWBERRIES... TWO GLASSES.

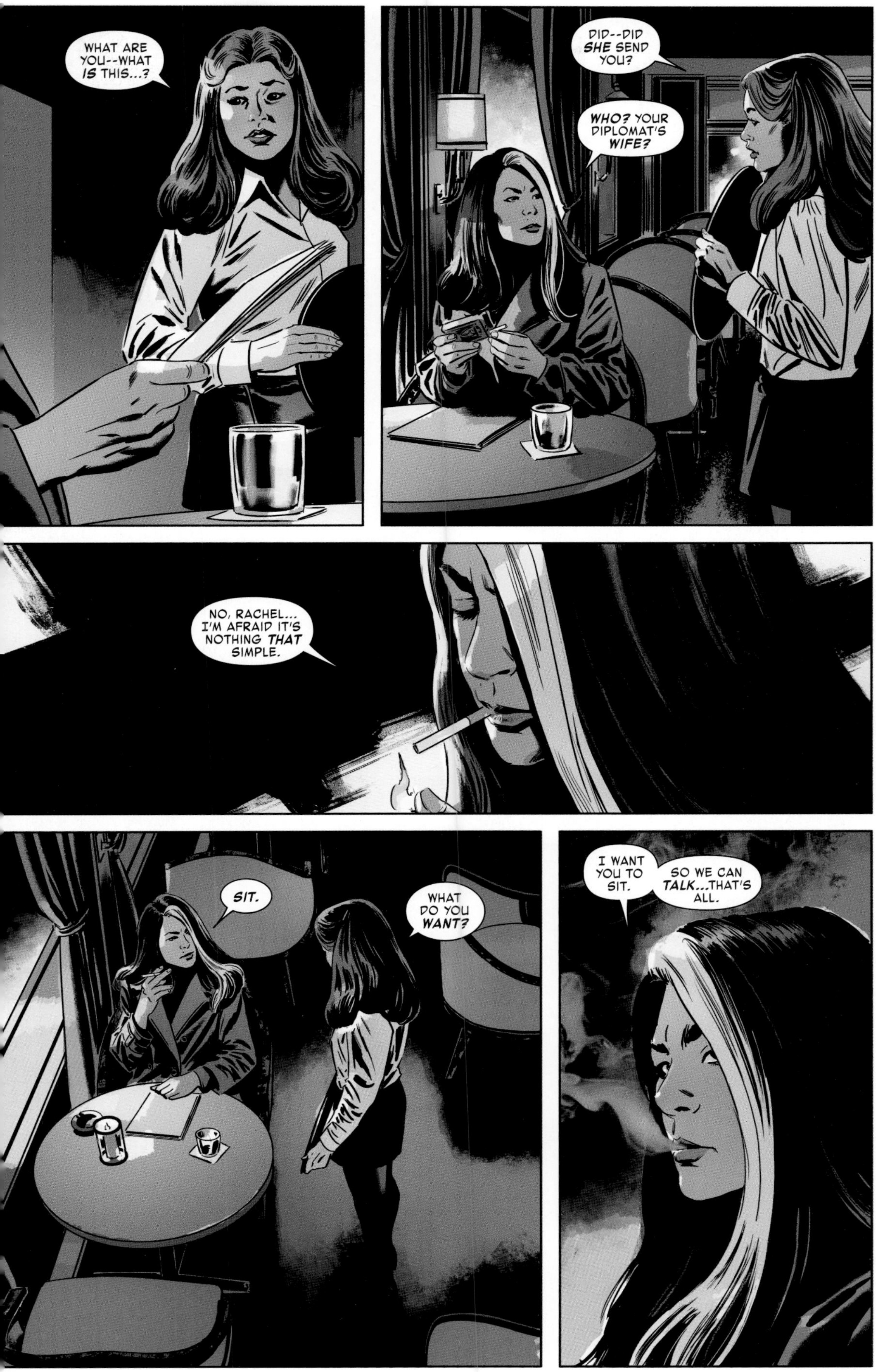
WHAT ARE YOU--WHAT *IS* THIS...?
DID--DID *SHE* SEND YOU?
WHO? YOUR DIPLOMAT'S *WIFE?*
NO, RACHEL... I'M AFRAID IT'S NOTHING *THAT* SIMPLE.
SIT.
WHAT DO YOU *WANT?*
I WANT YOU TO SIT.
SO WE CAN *TALK*...THAT'S ALL.

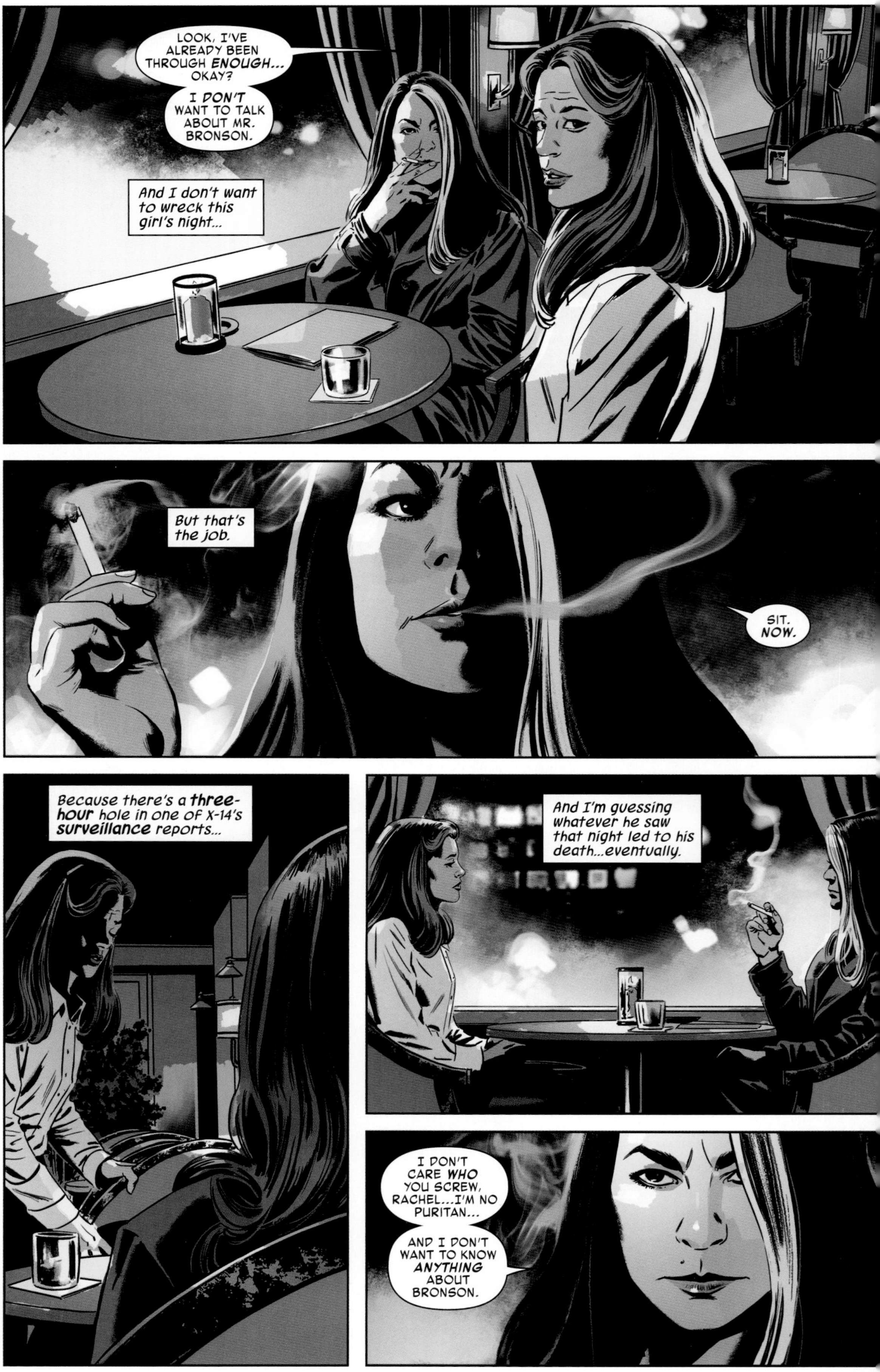
LOOK, I'VE ALREADY BEEN THROUGH ENOUGH... OKAY?
I DON'T WANT TO TALK ABOUT MR. BRONSON.
And I don't want to wreck this girl's night...
But that's the job.
SIT. NOW.
Because there's a three-hour hole in one of X-14's surveillance reports...
And I'm guessing whatever he saw that night led to his death...eventually.
I DON'T CARE WHO YOU SCREW, RACHEL...I'M NO PURITAN...
AND I DON'T WANT TO KNOW ANYTHING ABOUT BRONSON.

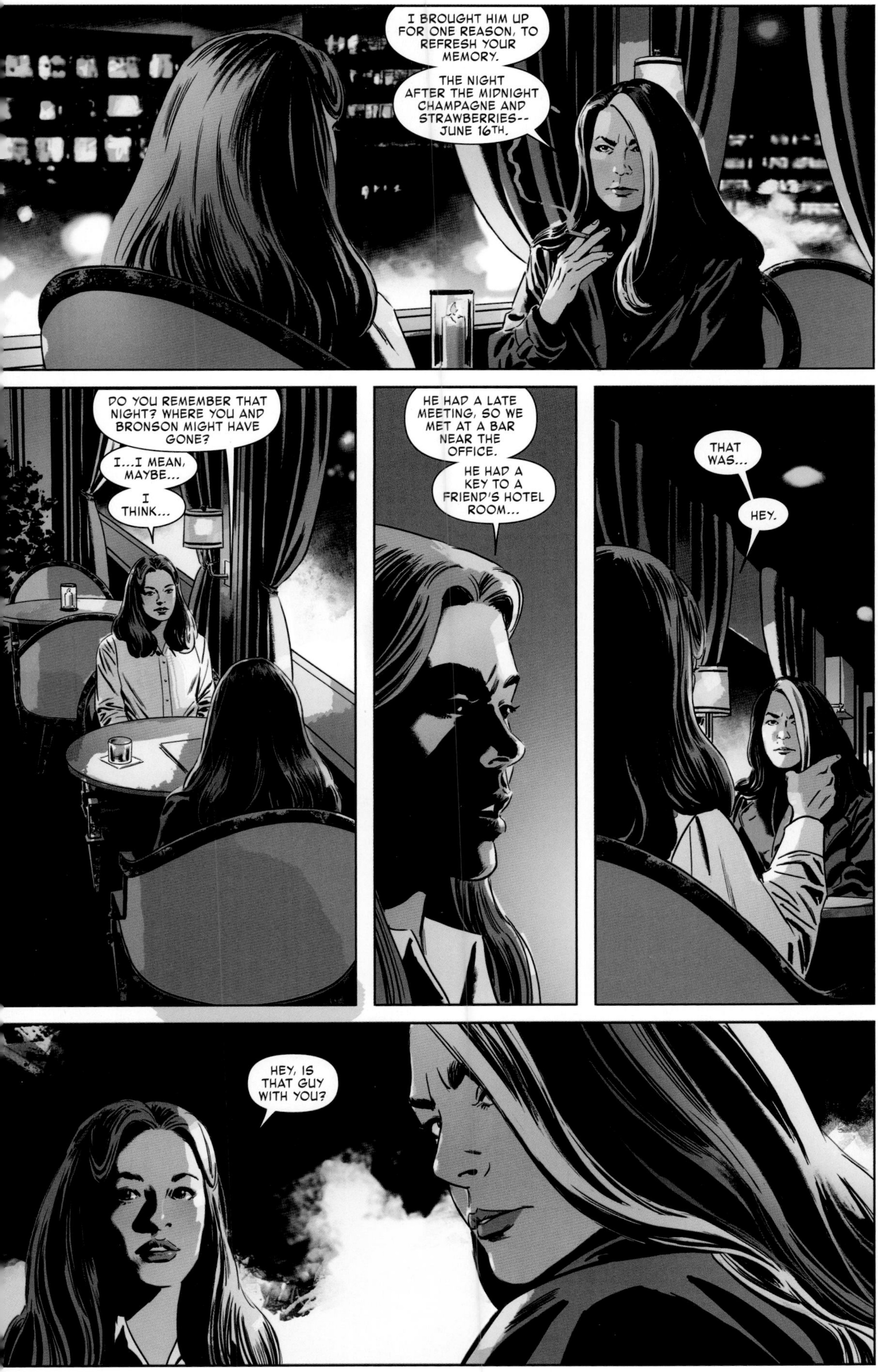
I BROUGHT HIM UP FOR ONE REASON, TO REFRESH YOUR MEMORY.
THE NIGHT AFTER THE MIDNIGHT CHAMPAGNE AND STRAWBERRIES-- JUNE 16TH.
DO YOU REMEMBER THAT NIGHT? WHERE YOU AND BRONSON MIGHT HAVE GONE?
I...I MEAN, MAYBE...
I THINK...
HE HAD A LATE MEETING, SO WE MET AT A BAR NEAR THE OFFICE.
HE HAD A KEY TO A FRIEND'S HOTEL ROOM...
THAT WAS...
HEY.
HEY, IS THAT GUY WITH YOU?

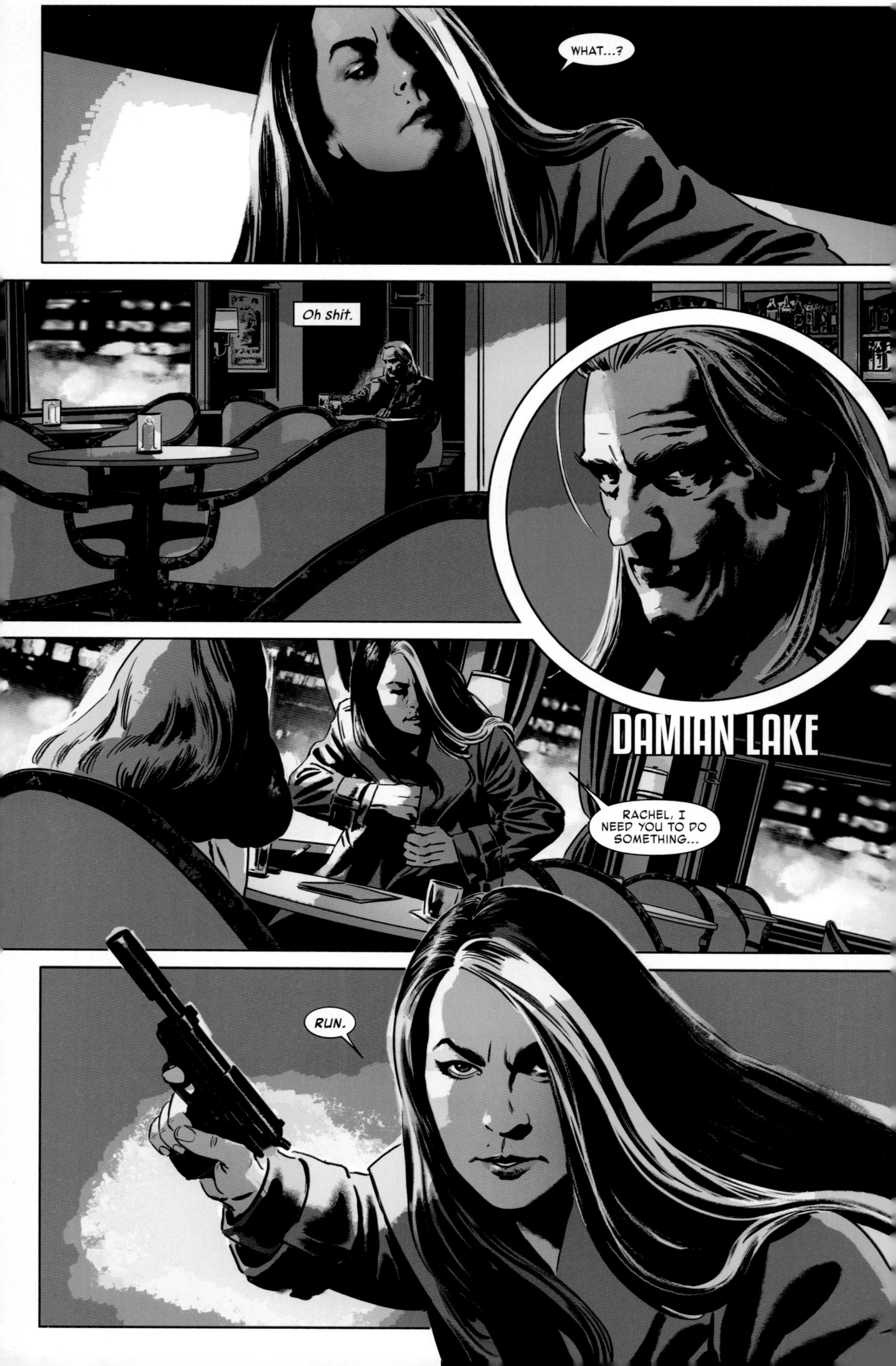
WHAT...?
Oh shit.
DAMIAN LAKE
RACHEL, I NEED YOU TO DO SOMETHING...
RUN.

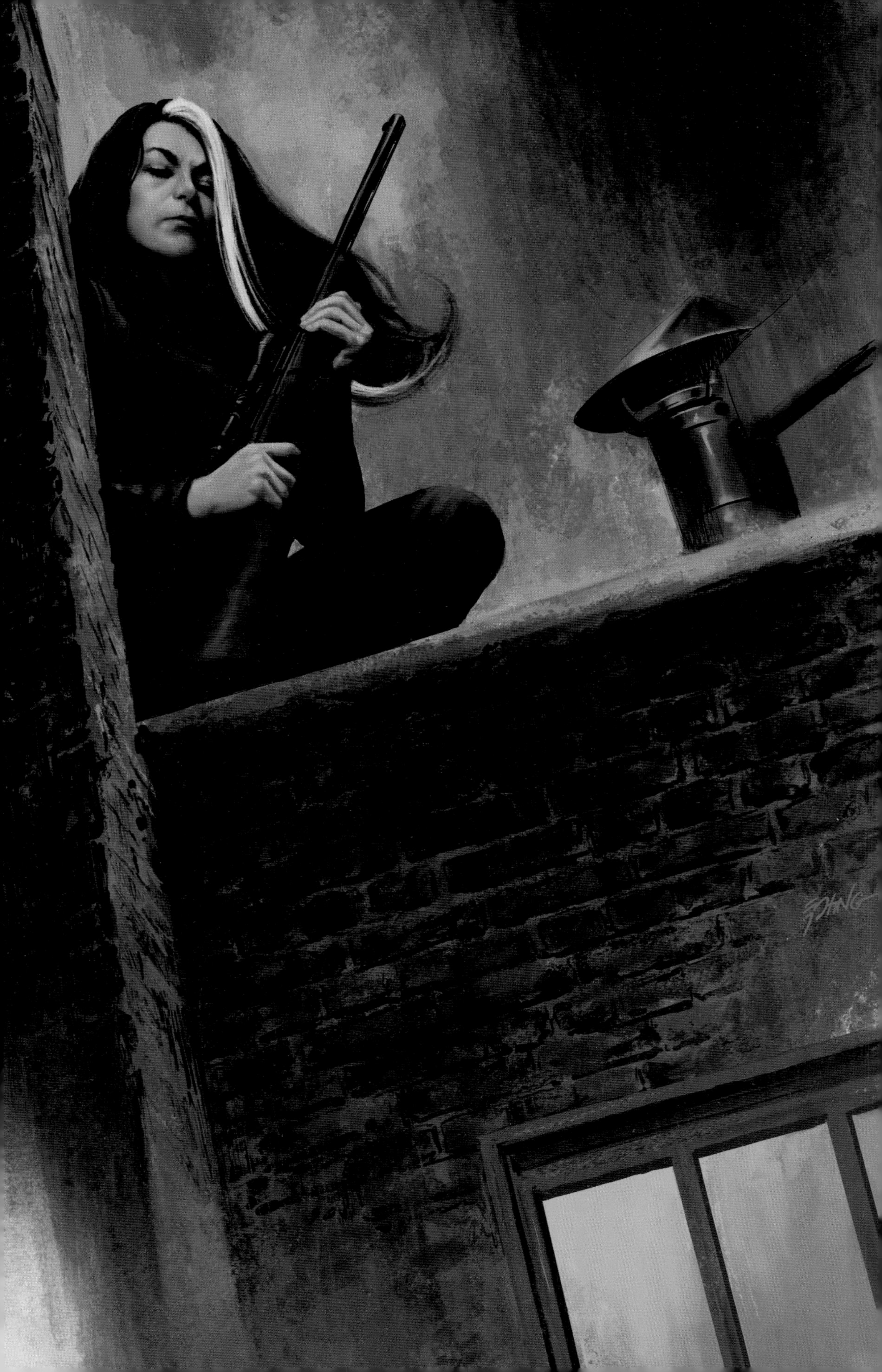

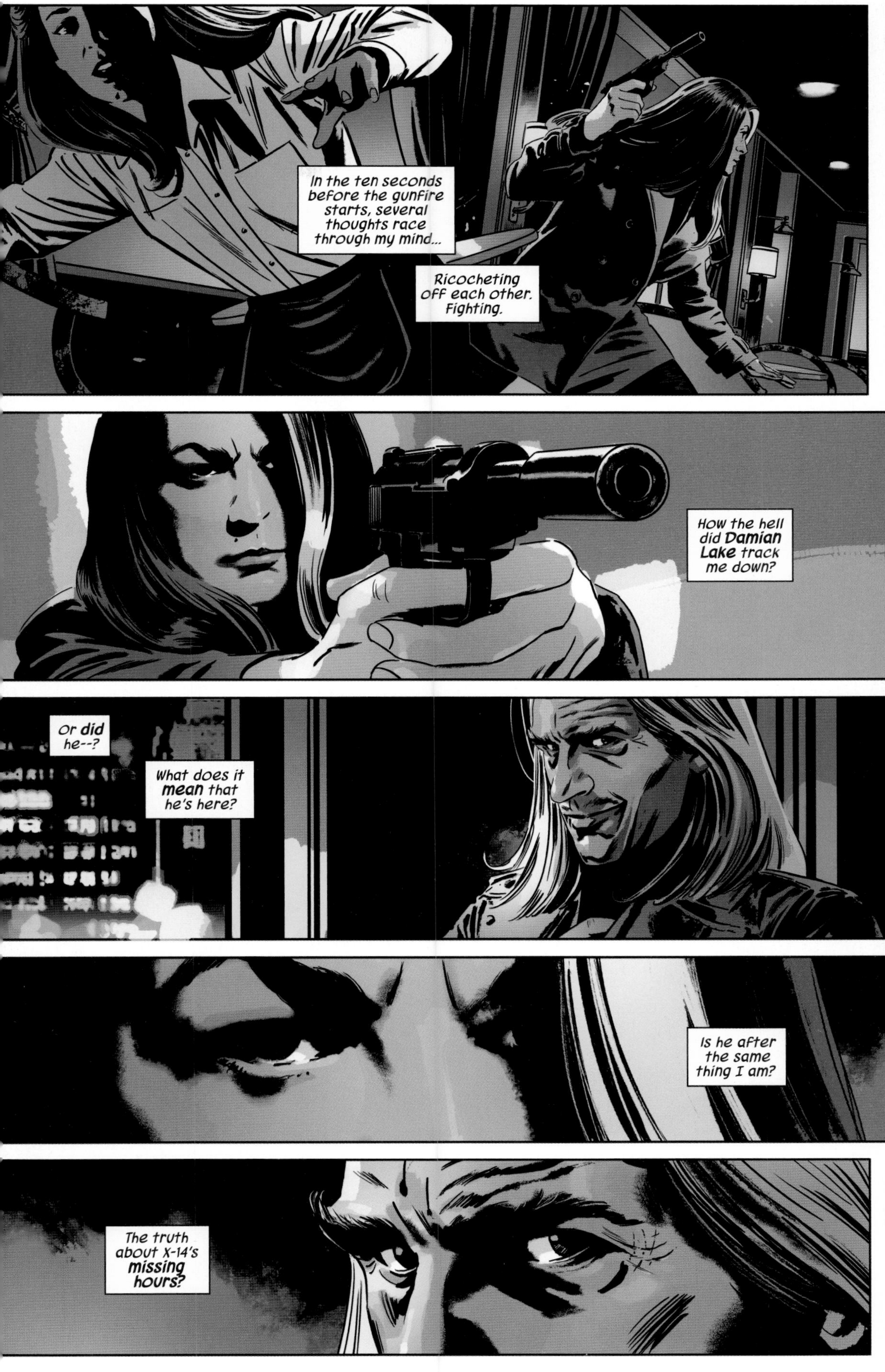
In the ten seconds before the gunfire starts, several thoughts race through my mind...
Ricocheting off each other. Fighting.
How the hell did Damian Lake track me down?
Or did he--?
What does it mean that he's here?
Is he after the same thing I am?
The truth about X-14's missing hours?

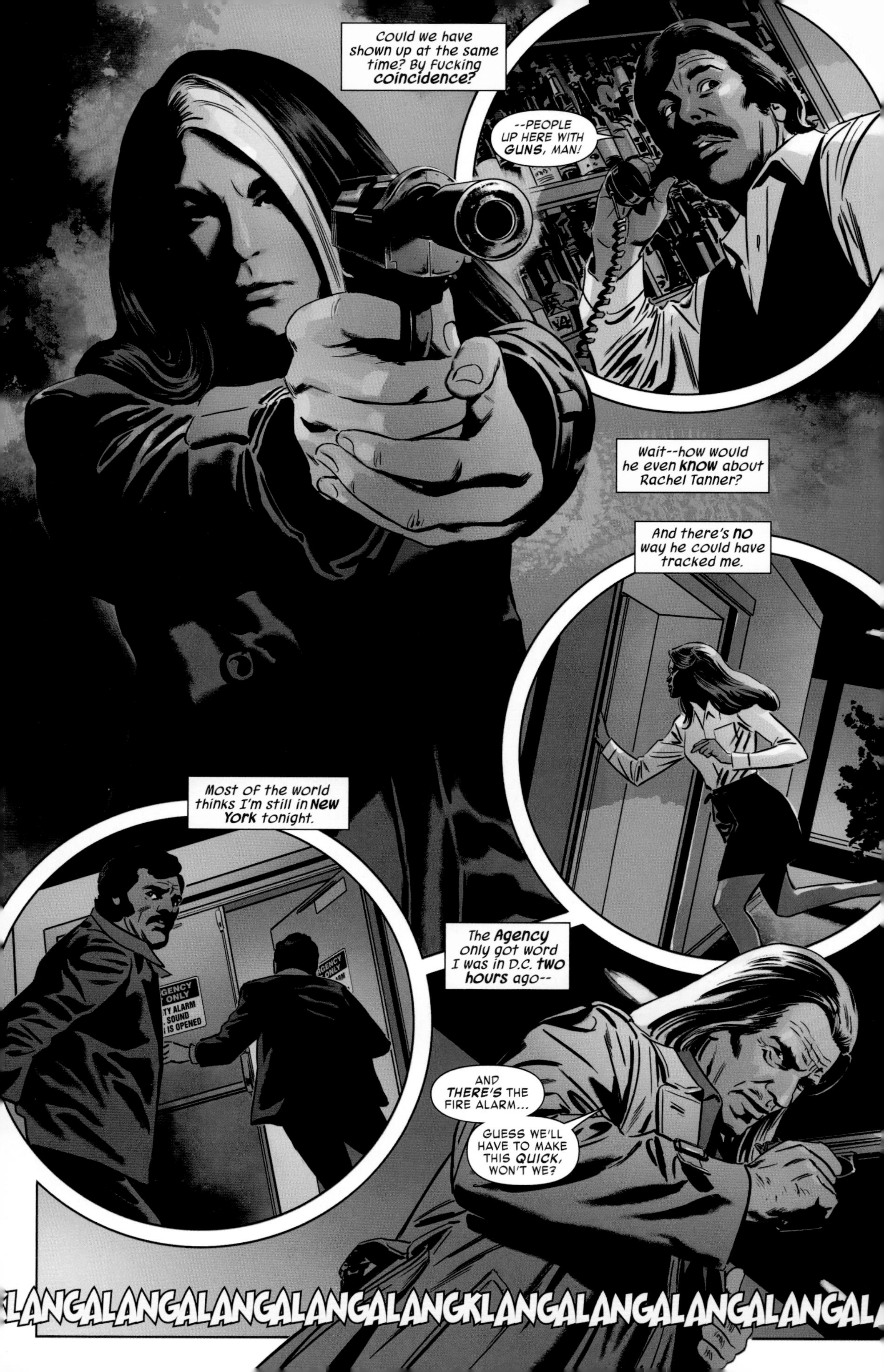

Could we have shown up at the same time? By Fucking coincidence?
--PEOPLE UP HERE WITH GUNS, MAN!
Wait--how would he even KNOW about Rachel Tanner?
And there's NO way he could have tracked me.
Most of the world thinks I'm still in New York tonight.
The Agency only got word I was in D.C. two hours ago--
AND THERE'S THE FIRE ALARM...
GUESS WE'LL HAVE TO MAKE THIS QUICK, WON'T WE?
LANGALANGALANGALANGKLANGALANGALANGALANGAL

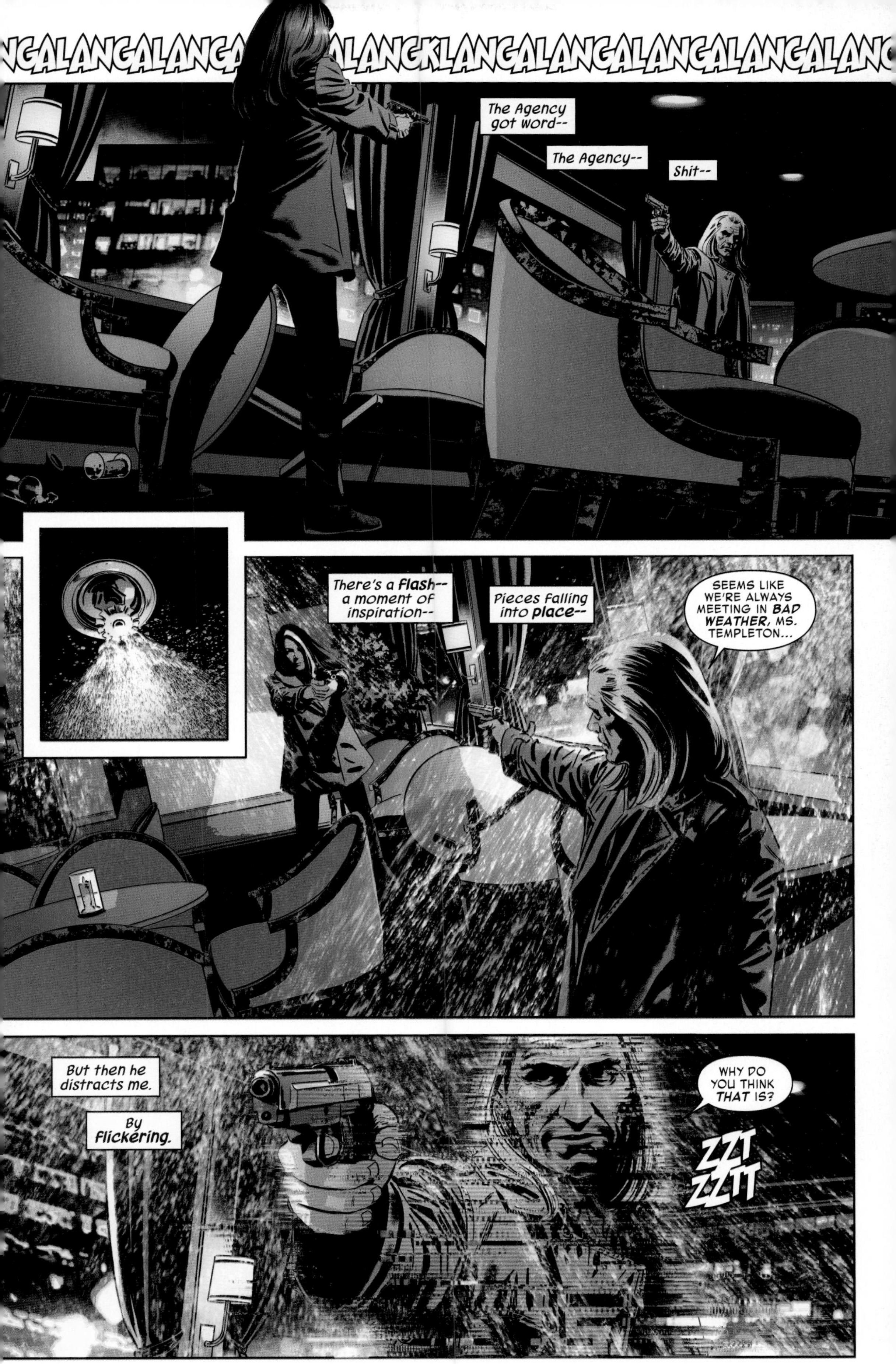

KLANGALANGALANGALANGKLANGALANGALANGALANGALANG
The Agency got word--
The Agency--
Shit--
There's a **flash**-- a moment of inspiration--
Pieces falling into **place**--
SEEMS LIKE WE'RE ALWAYS MEETING IN **BAD WEATHER**, MS. TEMPLETON...
But then he distracts me.
By Flickering.
WHY DO YOU THINK **THAT** IS?
ZZT ZZTT

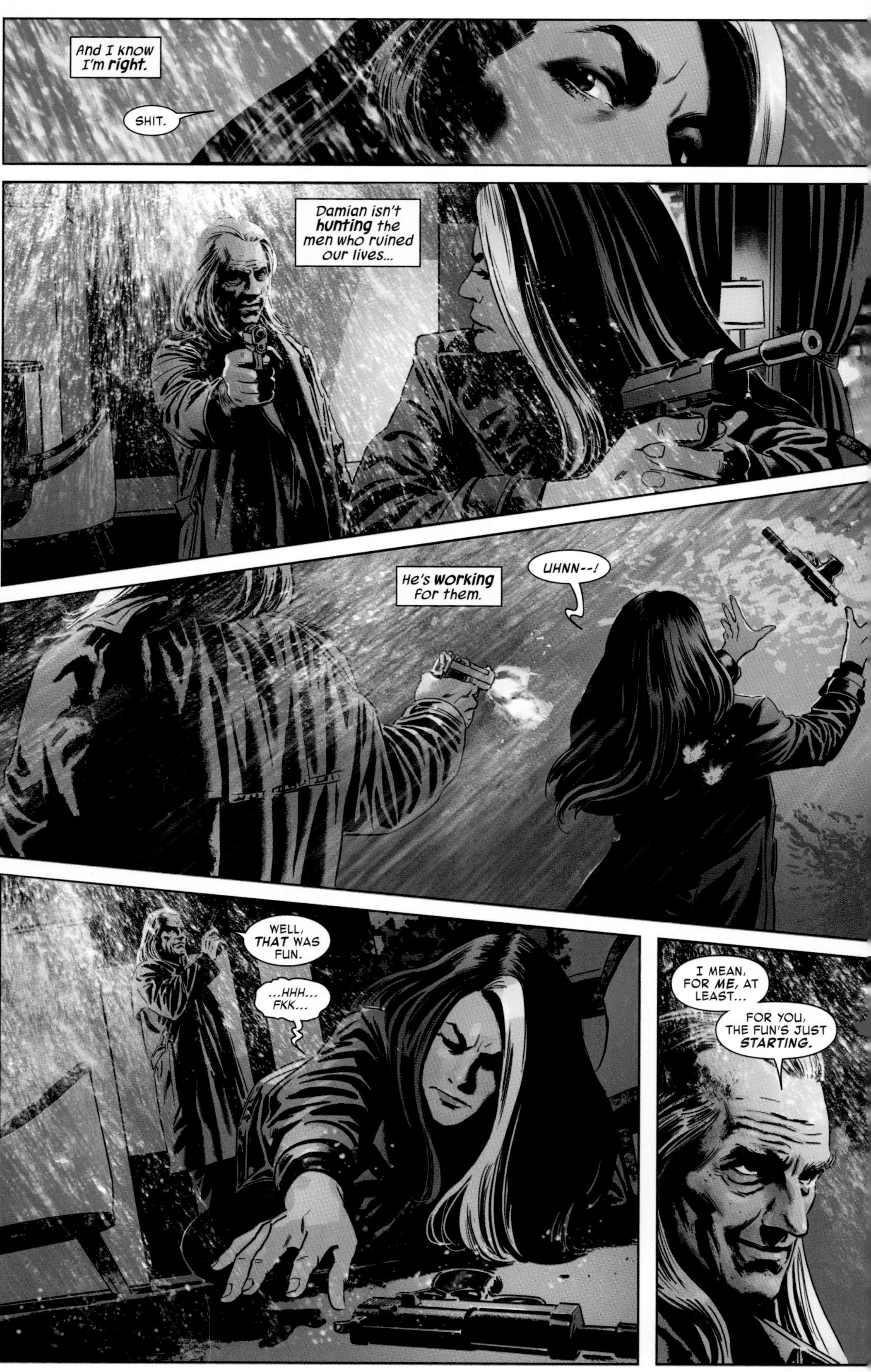
And I know I'm **right.**
SHIT.
Damian isn't **hunting** the men who ruined our lives...
He's **working** for them.
UHNN--!
WELL, *THAT* WAS FUN.
...HHH... FKK...
I MEAN, FOR *ME*, AT LEAST...
FOR YOU, THE FUN'S JUST *STARTING.*

PART THREE

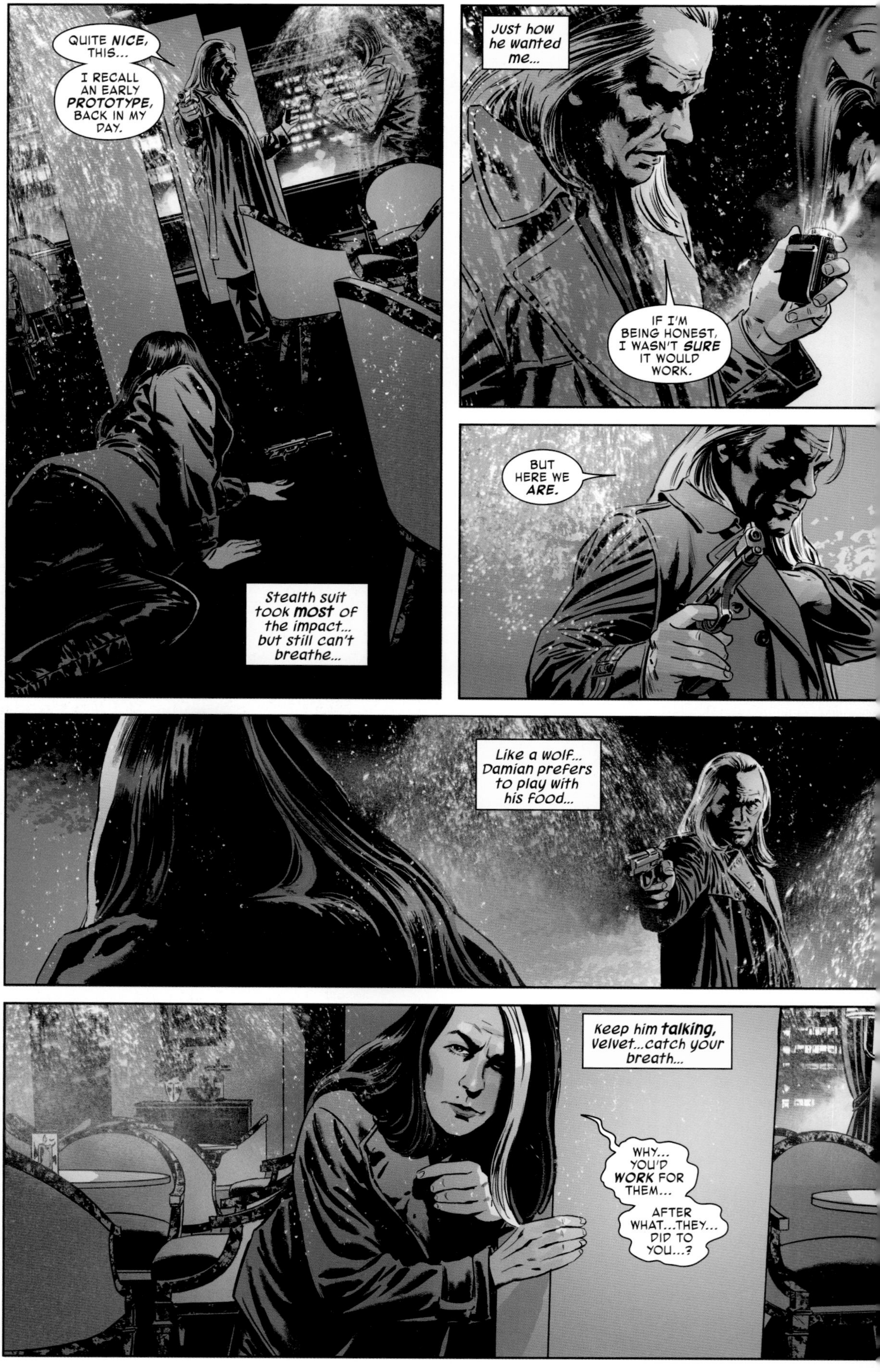
QUITE NICE, THIS...
I RECALL AN EARLY PROTOTYPE, BACK IN MY DAY.
Stealth suit took most of the impact... but still can't breathe...
Just how he wanted me...
IF I'M BEING HONEST, I WASN'T SURE IT WOULD WORK.
BUT HERE WE ARE.
Like a wolf... Damian prefers to play with his food...
Keep him talking, Velvet...catch your breath...
WHY... YOU'D WORK FOR THEM...
AFTER WHAT...THEY... DID TO YOU...?

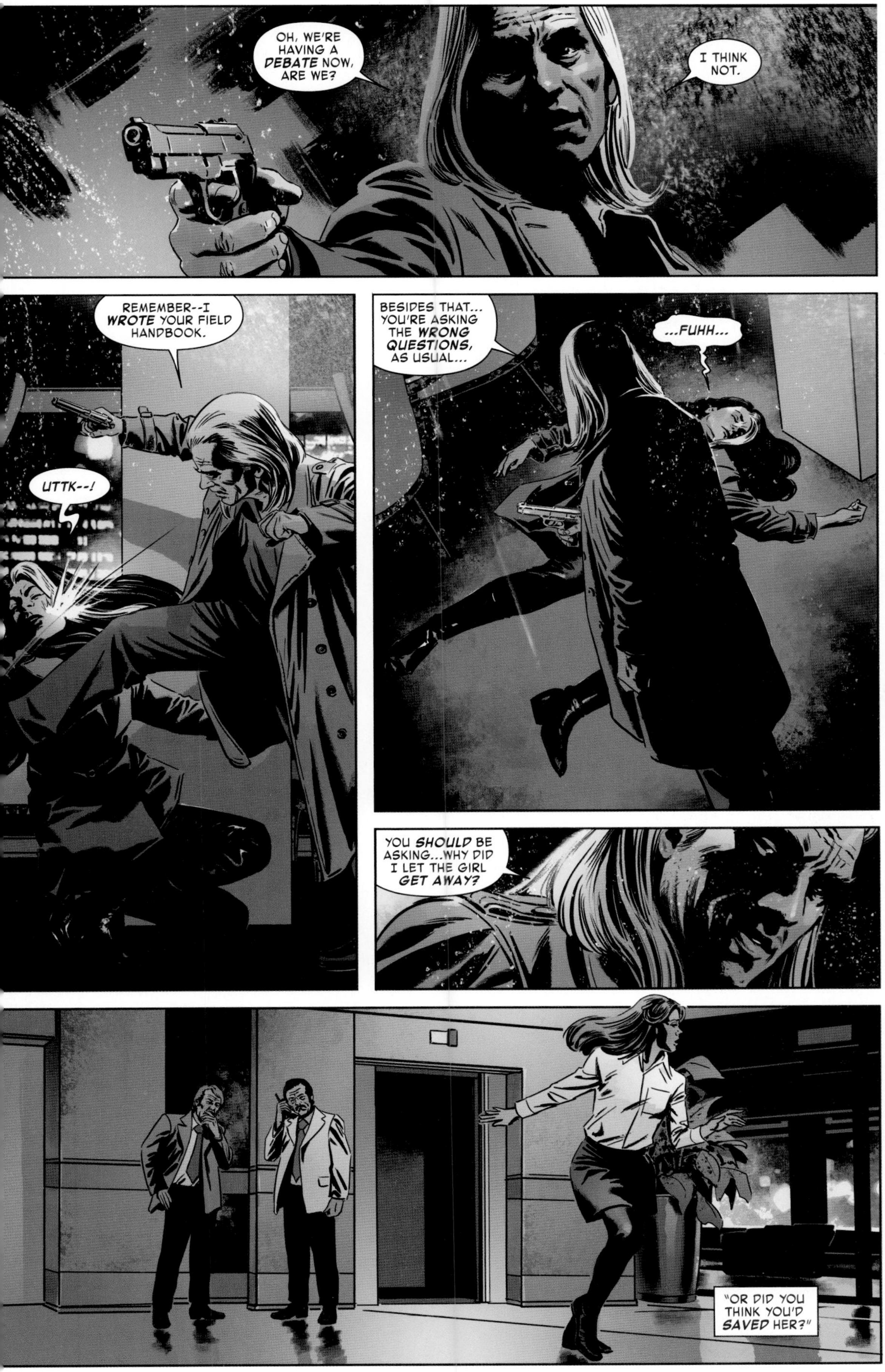
OH, WE'RE HAVING A DEBATE NOW, ARE WE?
I THINK NOT.
REMEMBER--I WROTE YOUR FIELD HANDBOOK.
UTTK--!
BESIDES THAT... YOU'RE ASKING THE WRONG QUESTIONS, AS USUAL...
...FUHH...
YOU SHOULD BE ASKING...WHY DID I LET THE GIRL GET AWAY?
"OR DID YOU THINK YOU'D SAVED HER?"

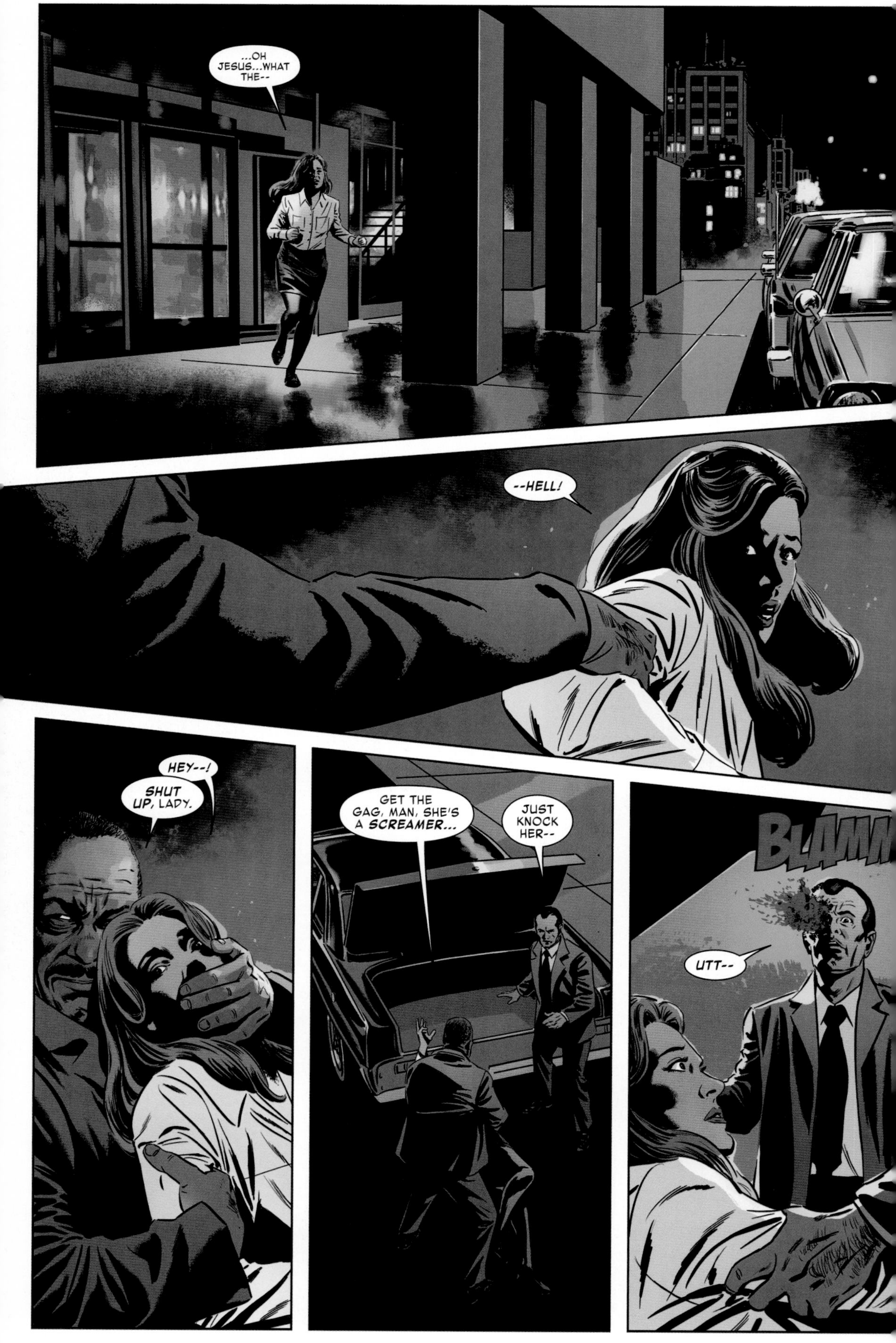
...OH JESUS...WHAT THE--
--HELL!
HEY--!
SHUT UP, LADY.
GET THE GAG, MAN, SHE'S A SCREAMER...
JUST KNOCK HER--
BLAMM
UTT--

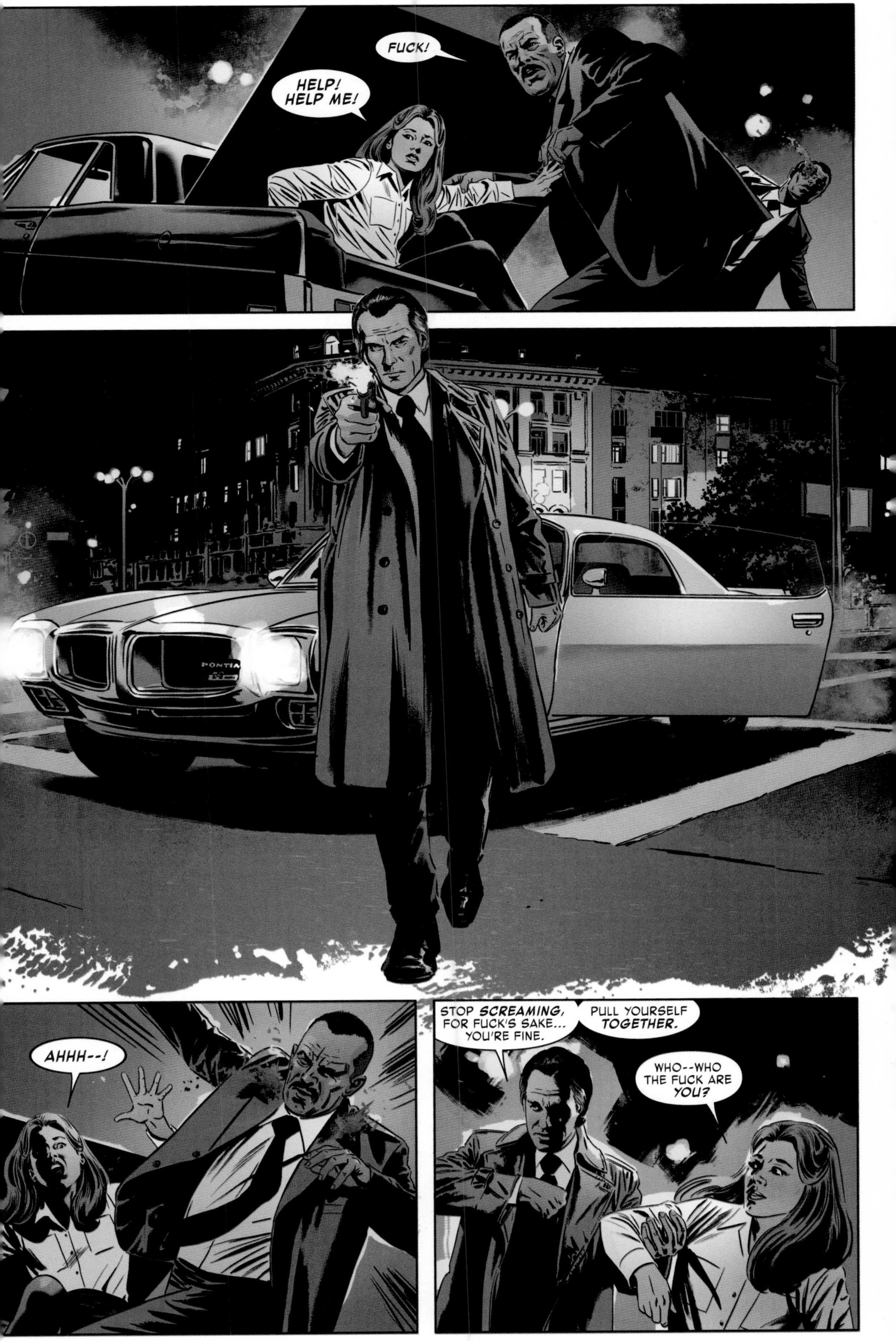
FUCK!
HELP! HELP ME!
PONTIAC
AHHH--!
STOP SCREAMING, FOR FUCK'S SAKE... YOU'RE FINE.
PULL YOURSELF TOGETHER.
WHO--WHO THE FUCK ARE YOU?

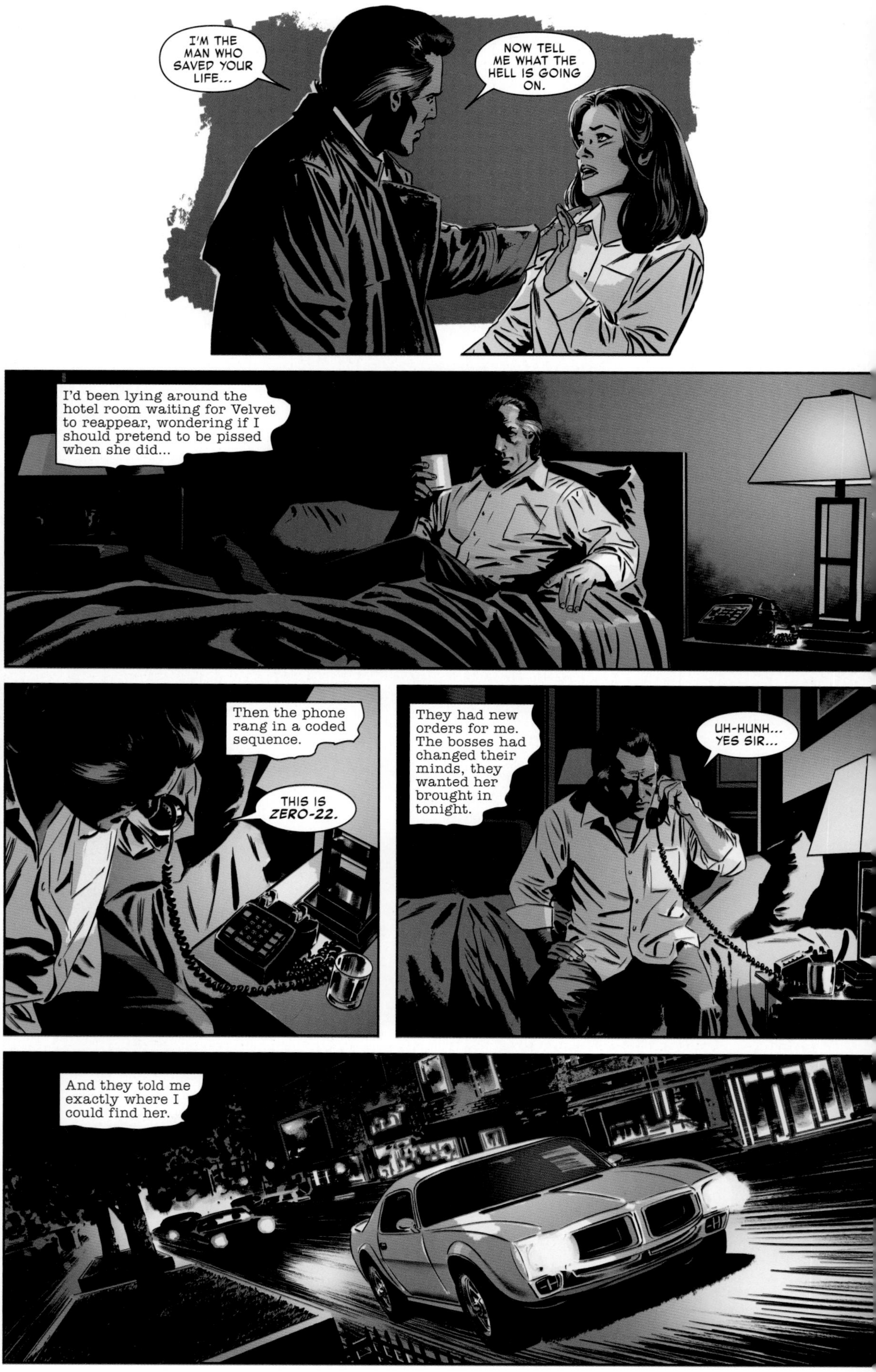
I'M THE MAN WHO SAVED YOUR LIFE...
NOW TELL ME WHAT THE HELL IS GOING ON.
I'd been lying around the hotel room waiting for Velvet to reappear, wondering if I should pretend to be pissed when she did...
Then the phone rang in a coded sequence.
THIS IS ZERO-22.
They had new orders for me. The bosses had changed their minds, they wanted her brought in tonight.
UH-HUNH... YES SIR...
And they told me exactly where I could find her.

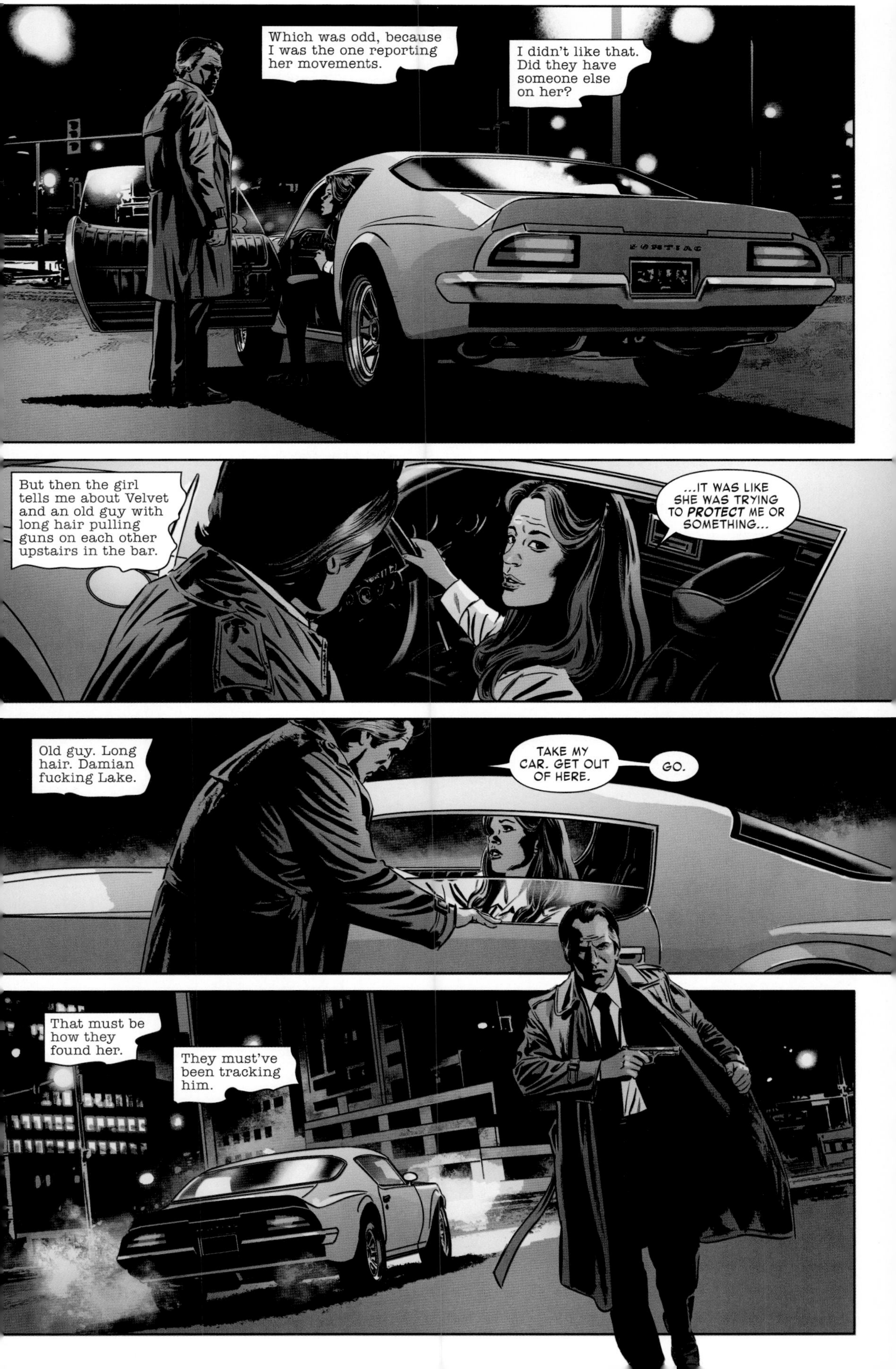
Which was odd, because I was the one reporting her movements.
I didn't like that. Did they have someone else on her?
But then the girl tells me about Velvet and an old guy with long hair pulling guns on each other upstairs in the bar.
...IT WAS LIKE SHE WAS TRYING TO PROTECT ME OR SOMETHING...
Old guy. Long hair. Damian fucking Lake.
TAKE MY CAR. GET OUT OF HERE.
GO.
That must be how they found her.
They must've been tracking him.

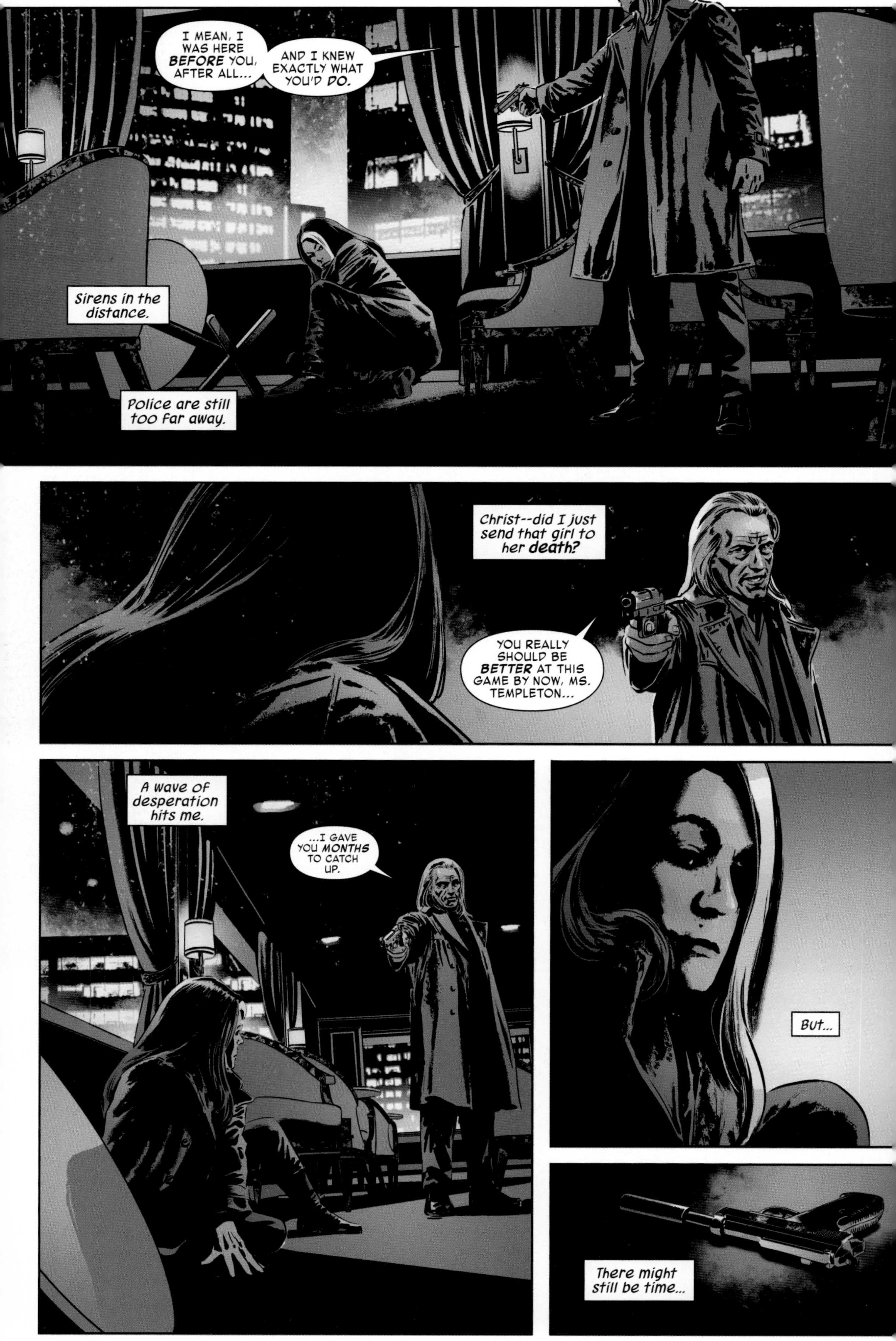
I MEAN, I WAS HERE BEFORE YOU, AFTER ALL...
AND I KNEW EXACTLY WHAT YOU'D DO.
Sirens in the distance.
Police are still too far away.
Christ--did I just send that girl to her death?
YOU REALLY SHOULD BE BETTER AT THIS GAME BY NOW, MS. TEMPLETON...
A wave of desperation hits me.
...I GAVE YOU MONTHS TO CATCH UP.
But...
There might still be time...

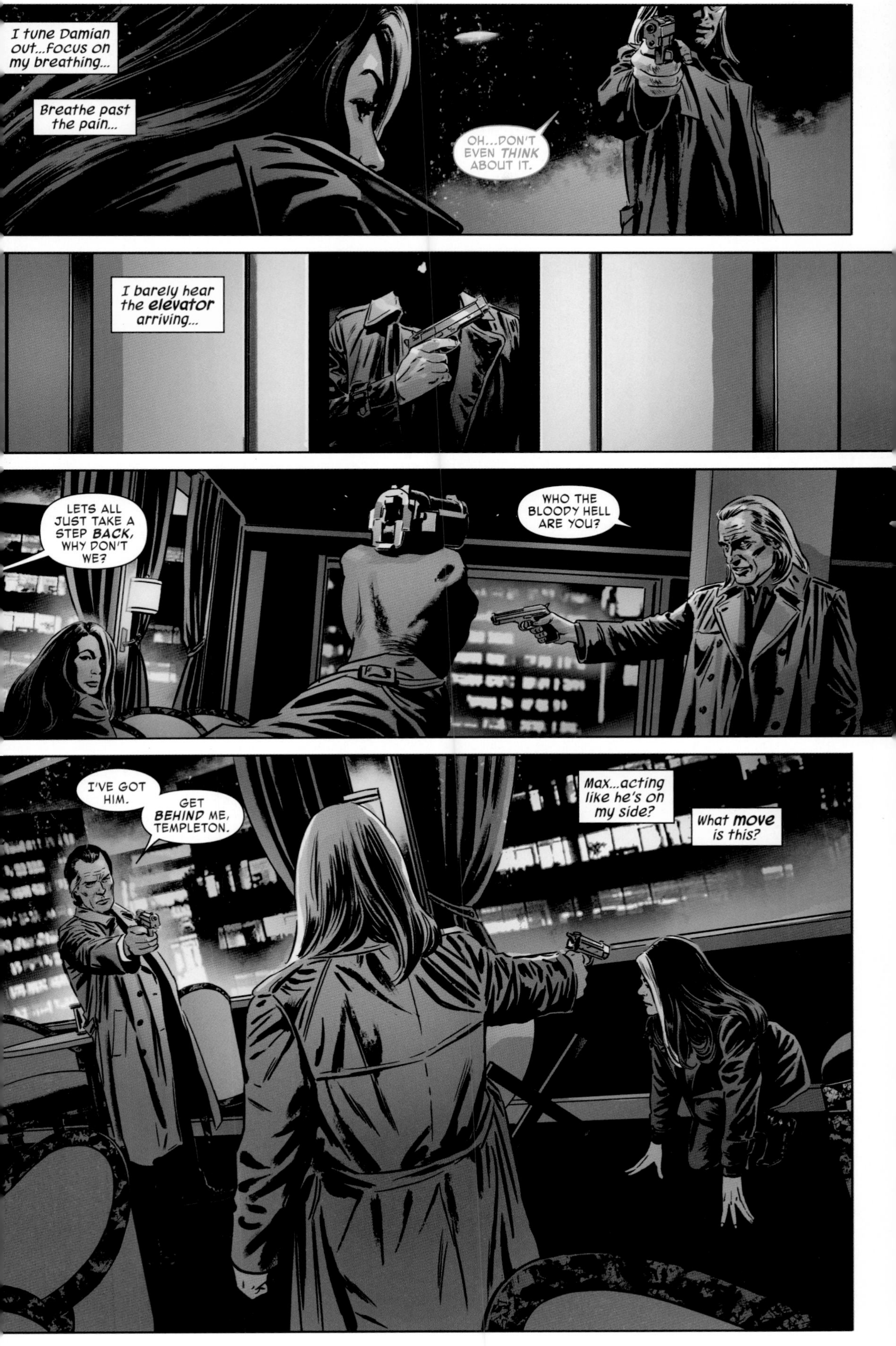
I tune Damian out...focus on my breathing...
Breathe past the pain...
OH...DON'T EVEN THINK ABOUT IT.
I barely hear the elevator arriving...
LETS ALL JUST TAKE A STEP BACK, WHY DON'T WE?
WHO THE BLOODY HELL ARE YOU?
I'VE GOT HIM.
GET BEHIND ME, TEMPLETON.
Max...acting like he's on my side?
What move is this?

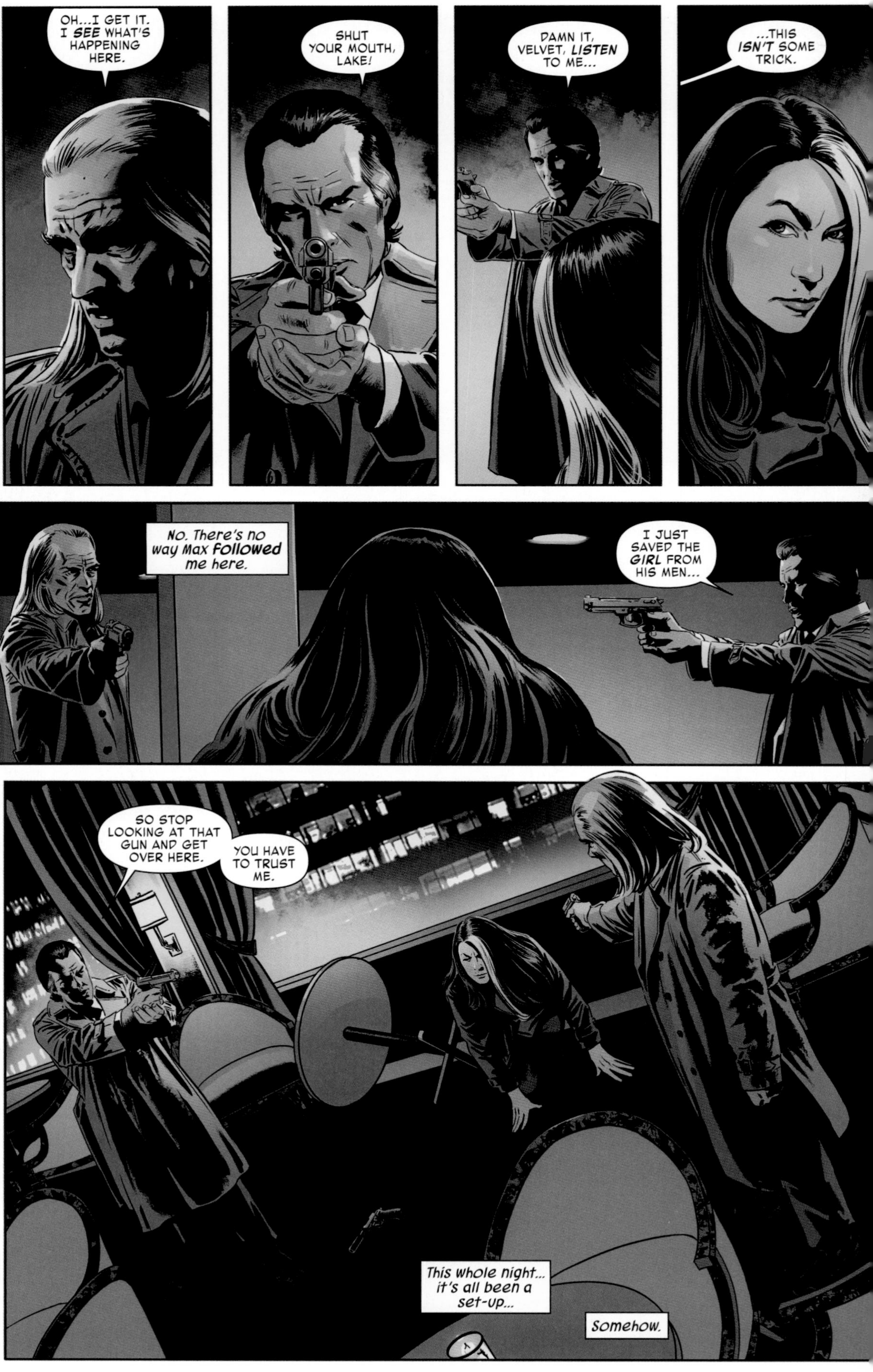
OH...I GET IT. I SEE WHAT'S HAPPENING HERE.
SHUT YOUR MOUTH, LAKE!
DAMN IT, VELVET, LISTEN TO ME...
...THIS ISN'T SOME TRICK.
No. There's no way Max followed me here.
I JUST SAVED THE GIRL FROM HIS MEN...
SO STOP LOOKING AT THAT GUN AND GET OVER HERE.
YOU HAVE TO TRUST ME.
This whole night... it's all been a set-up...
Somehow.

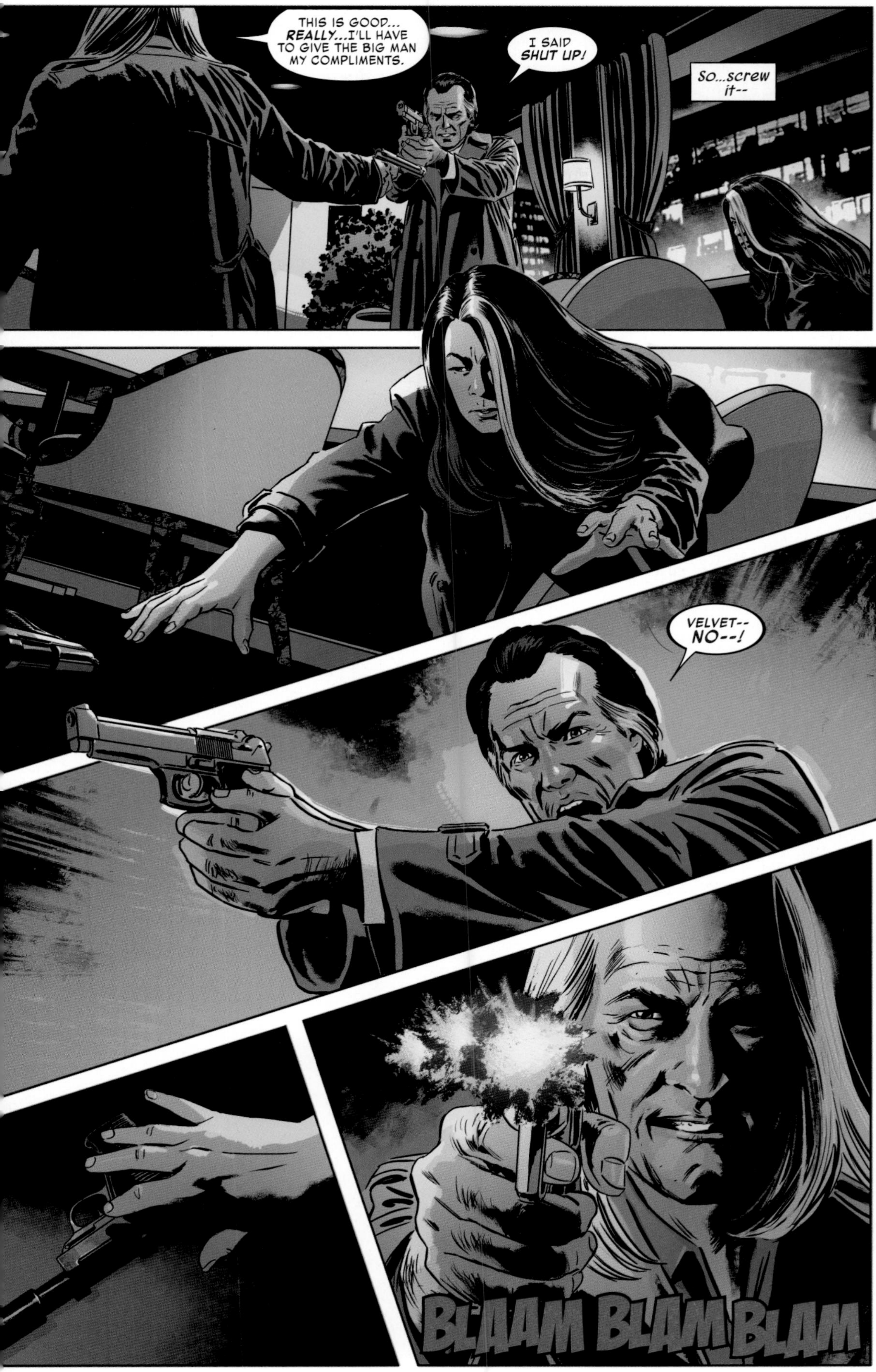
THIS IS GOOD... REALLY...I'LL HAVE TO GIVE THE BIG MAN MY COMPLIMENTS.
I SAID SHUT UP!
So...screw it--
VELVET-- NO--!
BLAAM BLAM BLAM

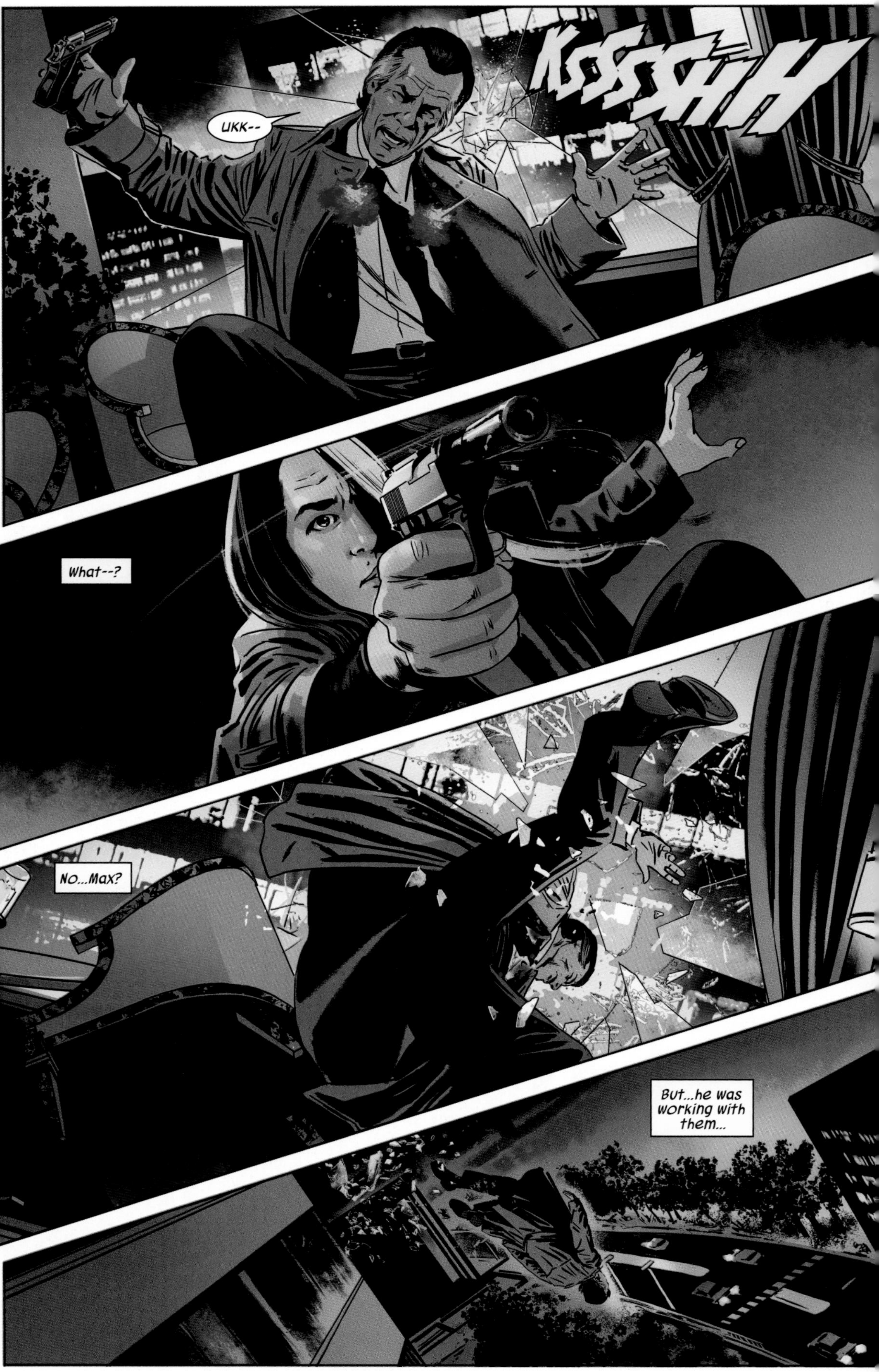
KSSSHH
UKK--
What--?
No...Max?
But...he was working with them...

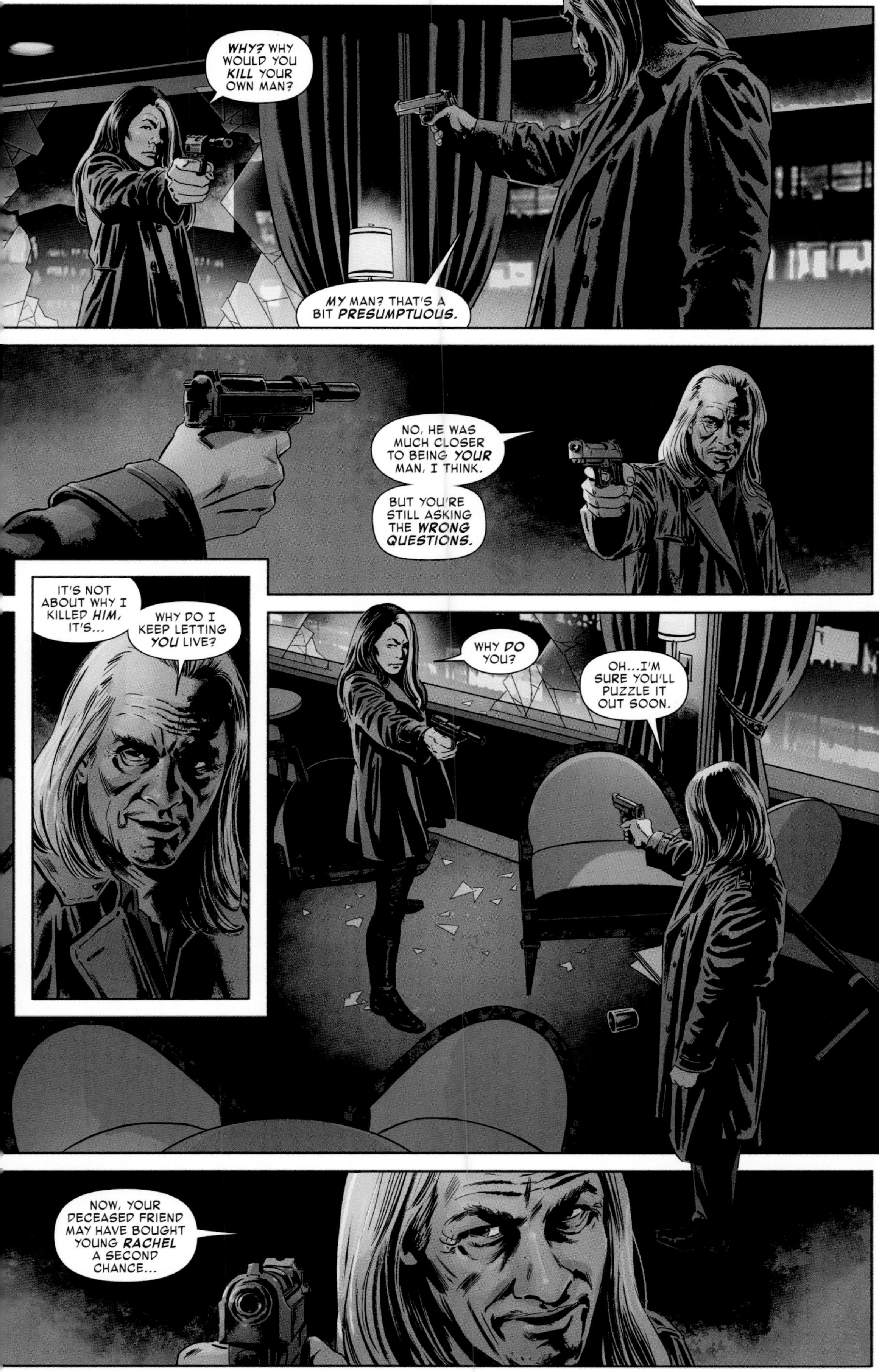
WHY? WHY WOULD YOU KILL YOUR OWN MAN?
MY MAN? THAT'S A BIT PRESUMPTUOUS.
NO, HE WAS MUCH CLOSER TO BEING YOUR MAN, I THINK.
BUT YOU'RE STILL ASKING THE WRONG QUESTIONS.
IT'S NOT ABOUT WHY I KILLED HIM, IT'S...
WHY DO I KEEP LETTING YOU LIVE?
WHY DO YOU?
OH...I'M SURE YOU'LL PUZZLE IT OUT SOON.
NOW, YOUR DECEASED FRIEND MAY HAVE BOUGHT YOUNG RACHEL A SECOND CHANCE...

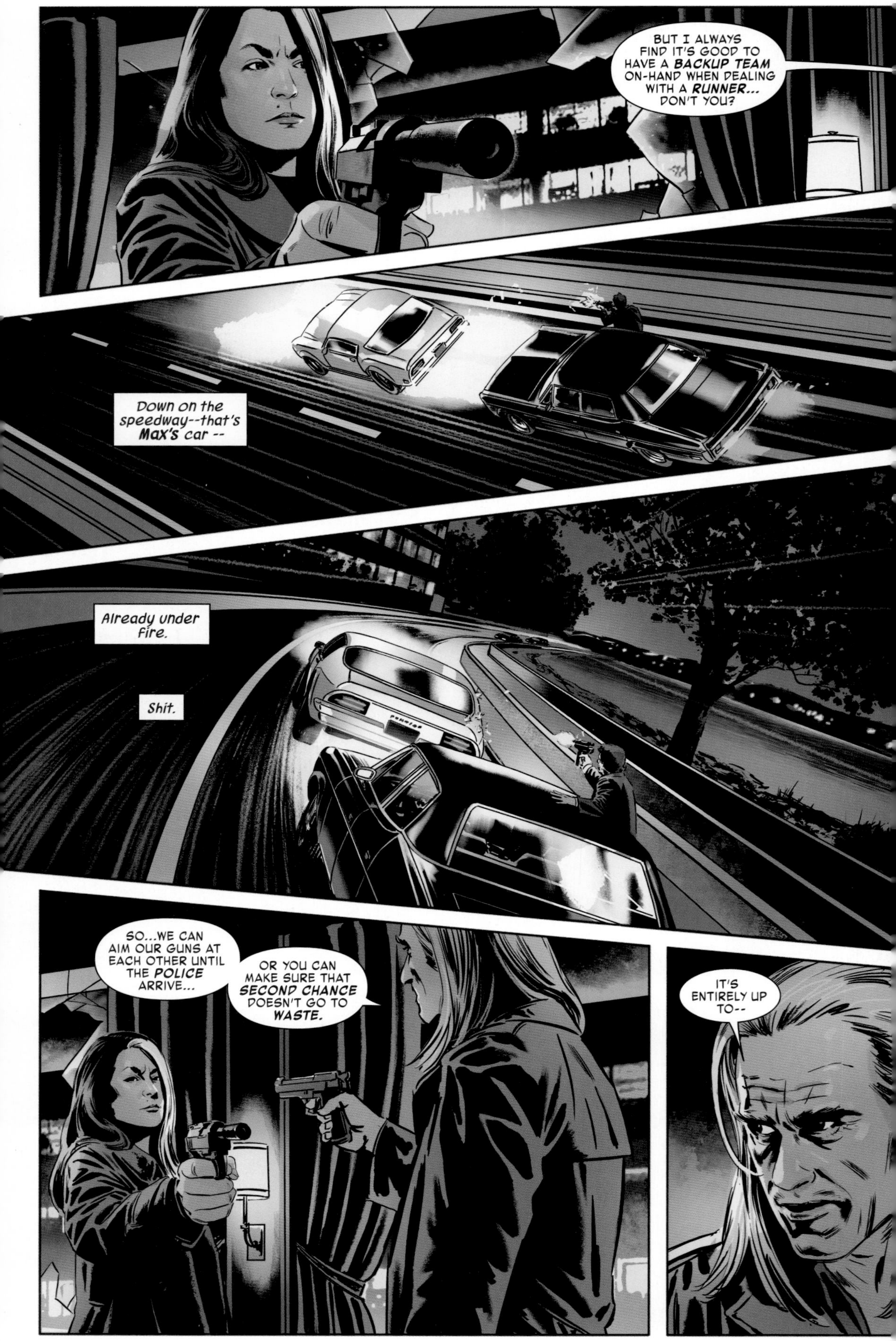
BUT I ALWAYS FIND IT'S GOOD TO HAVE A BACKUP TEAM ON-HAND WHEN DEALING WITH A RUNNER... DON'T YOU?
Down on the speedway--that's Max's car --
Already under fire.
Shit.
SO...WE CAN AIM OUR GUNS AT EACH OTHER UNTIL THE POLICE ARRIVE...
OR YOU CAN MAKE SURE THAT SECOND CHANCE DOESN'T GO TO WASTE.
IT'S ENTIRELY UP TO--

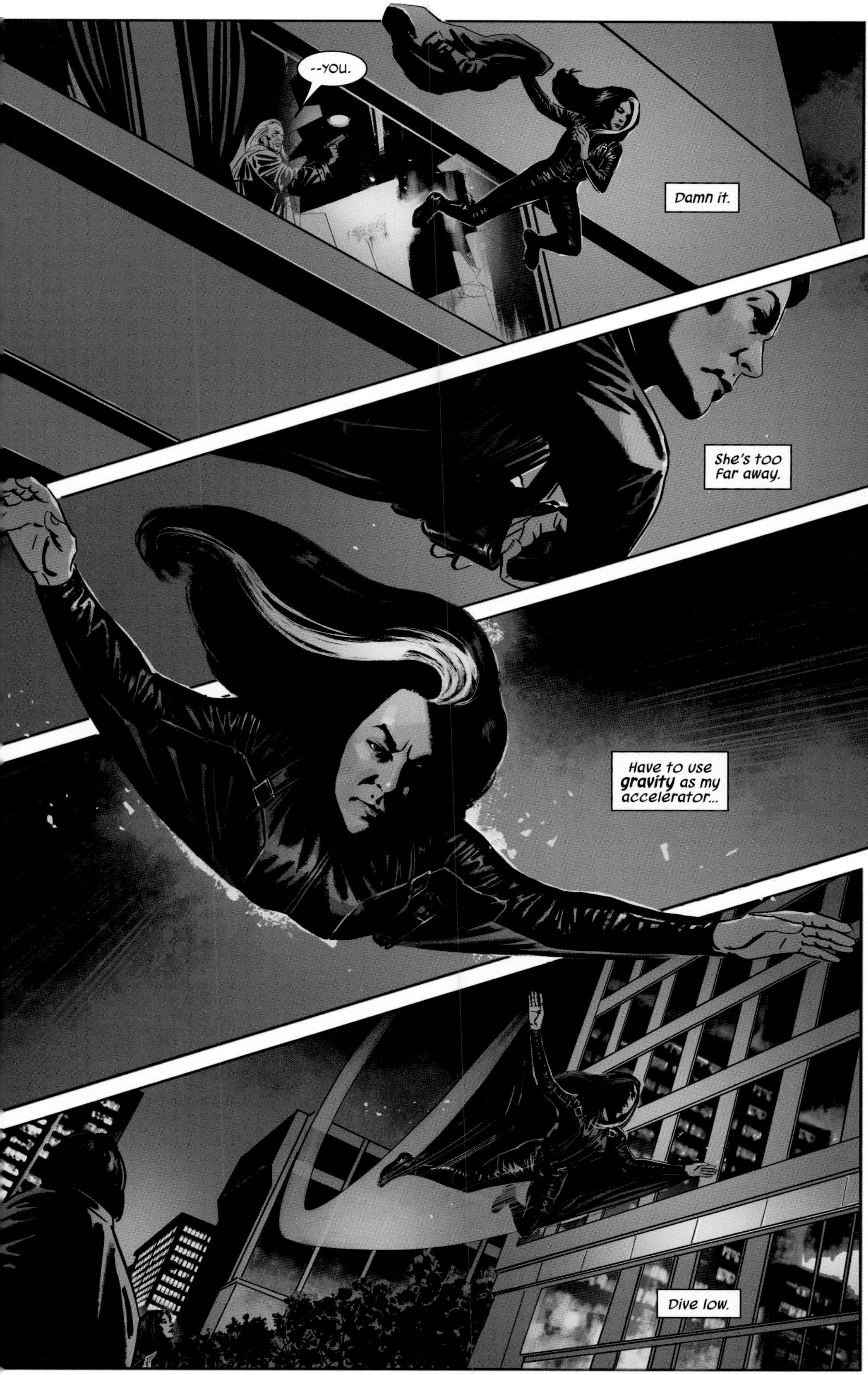
--YOU.
Damn it.
She's too far away.
Have to use **gravity** as my accelerator...
Dive low.

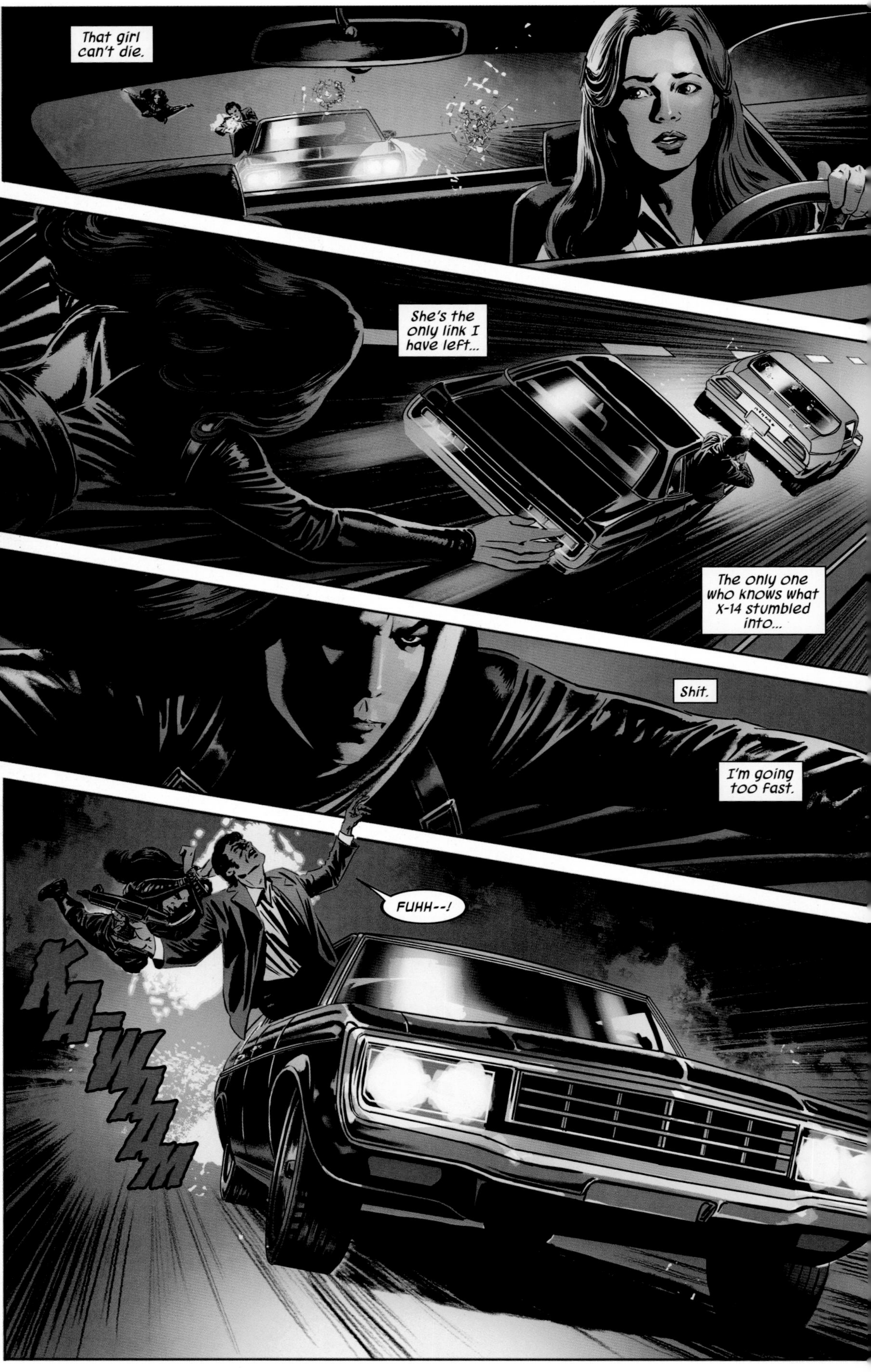
That girl can't die.
She's the only link I have left...
The only one who knows what X-14 stumbled into...
Shit.
I'm going too fast.
FUHH--!
KA-WHAM

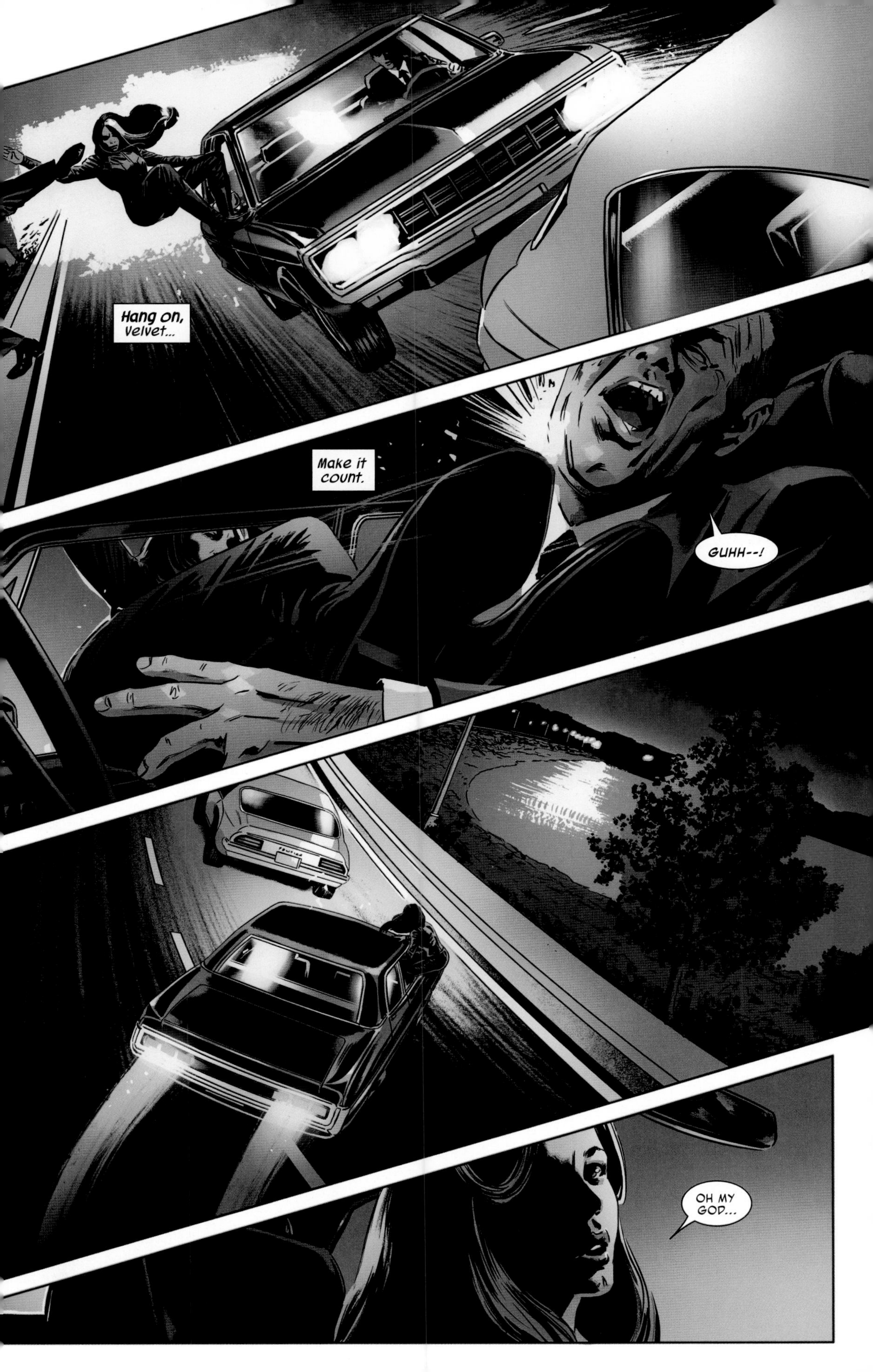
Hang on, velvet...
Make it count.
GUHH--!
OH MY GOD...

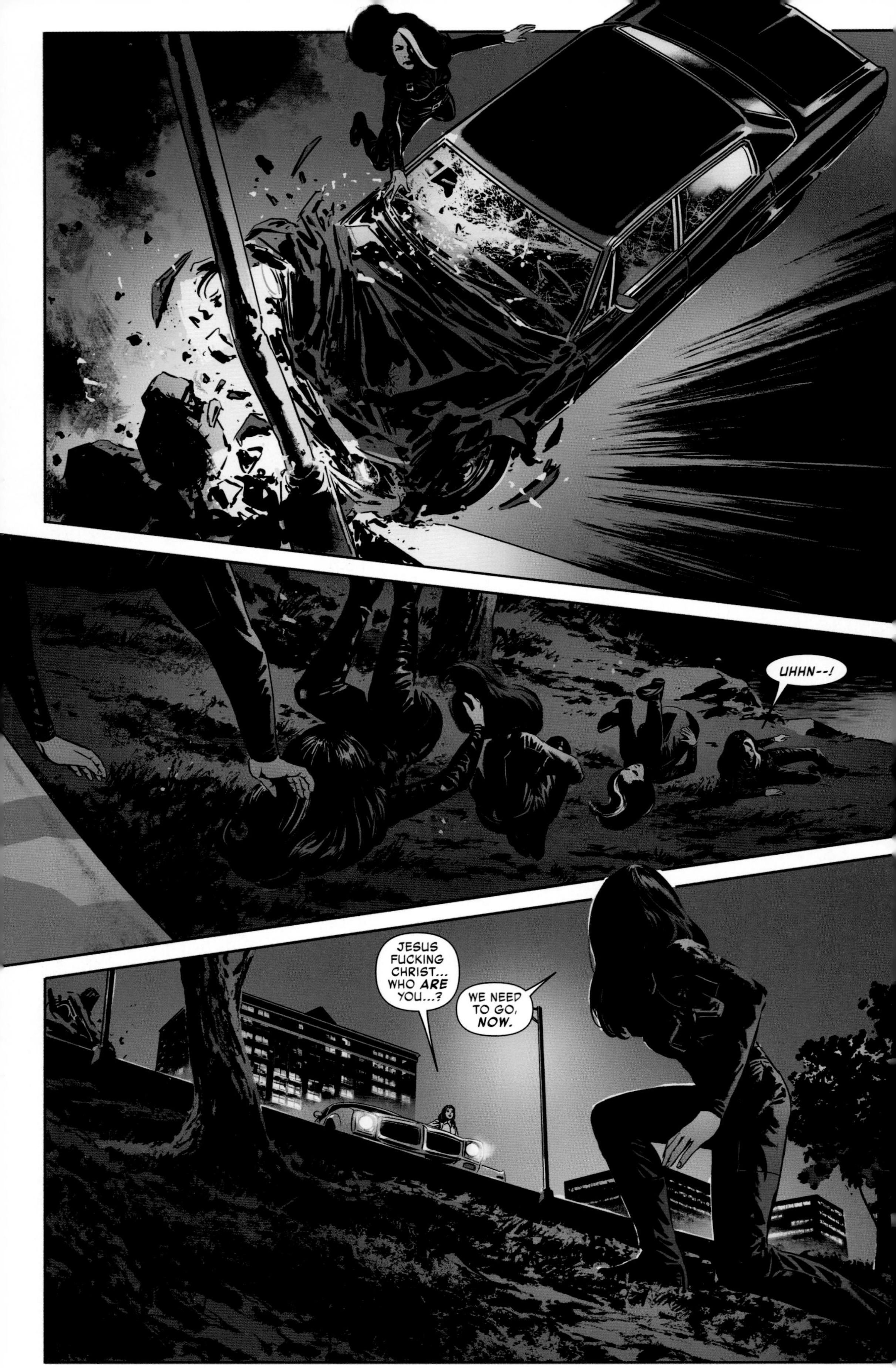
UHHN--!
JESUS FUCKING CHRIST... WHO ARE YOU...?
WE NEED TO GO, NOW.

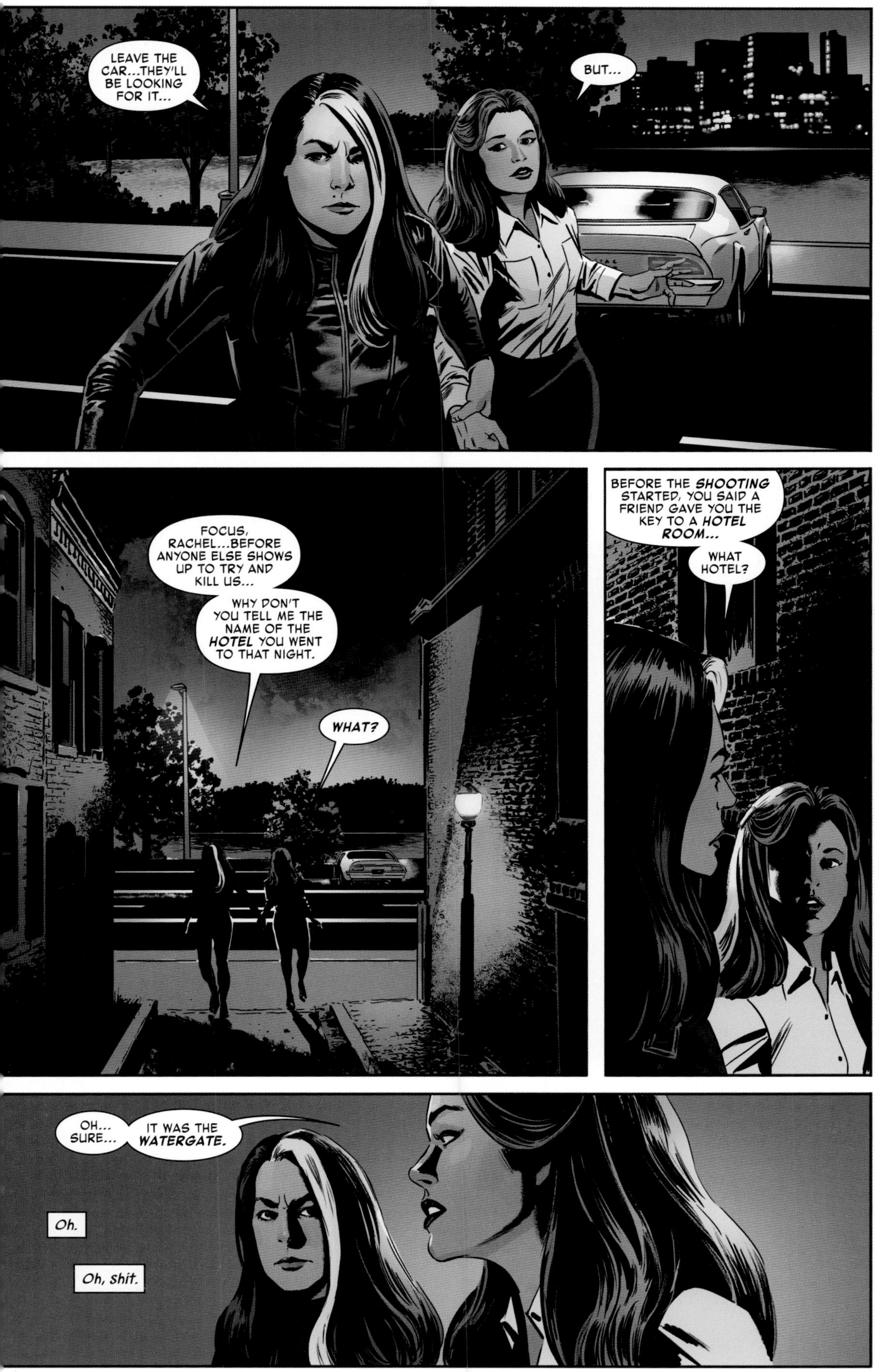
LEAVE THE CAR...THEY'LL BE LOOKING FOR IT...
BUT...
FOCUS, RACHEL...BEFORE ANYONE ELSE SHOWS UP TO TRY AND KILL US...
WHY DON'T YOU TELL ME THE NAME OF THE HOTEL YOU WENT TO THAT NIGHT.
WHAT?
BEFORE THE SHOOTING STARTED, YOU SAID A FRIEND GAVE YOU THE KEY TO A HOTEL ROOM...
WHAT HOTEL?
OH... SURE...
IT WAS THE WATERGATE.
Oh.
Oh, shit.

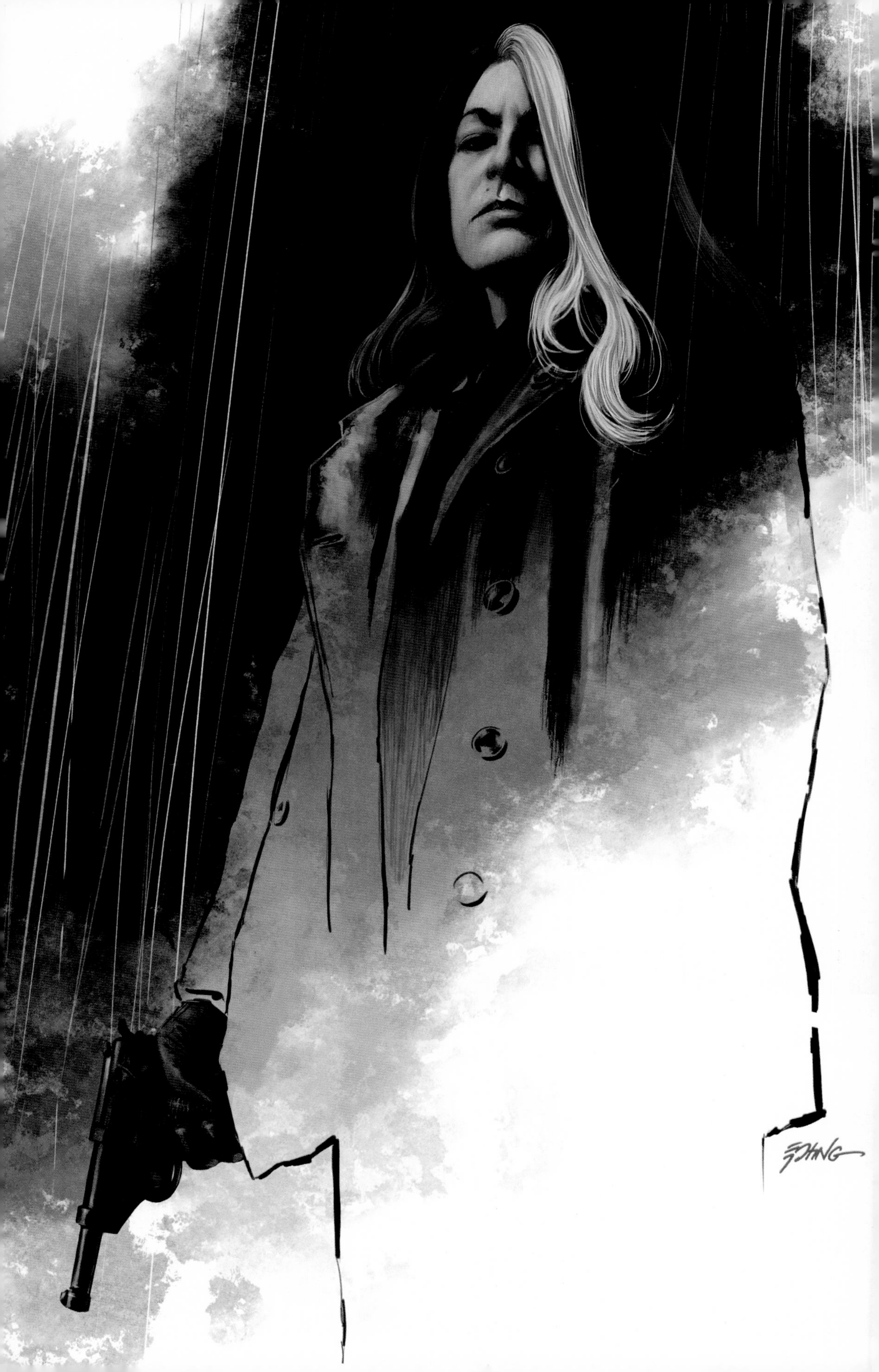

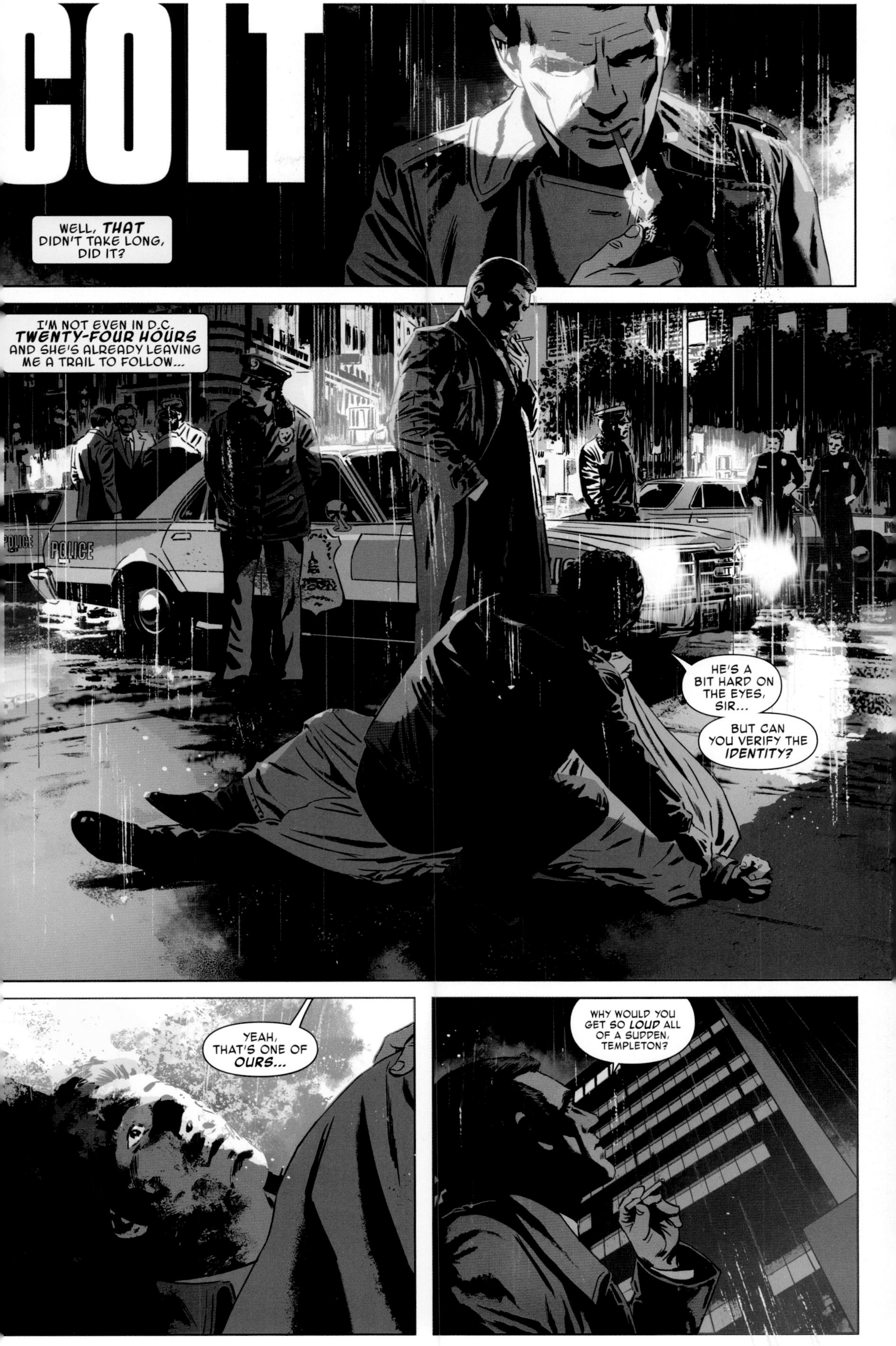
COLT
WELL, THAT DIDN'T TAKE LONG, DID IT?
I'M NOT EVEN IN D.C. TWENTY-FOUR HOURS AND SHE'S ALREADY LEAVING ME A TRAIL TO FOLLOW...
POLICE
POLICE
HE'S A BIT HARD ON THE EYES, SIR...
BUT CAN YOU VERIFY THE IDENTITY?
YEAH, THAT'S ONE OF OURS...
WHY WOULD YOU GET SO LOUD ALL OF A SUDDEN, TEMPLETON?

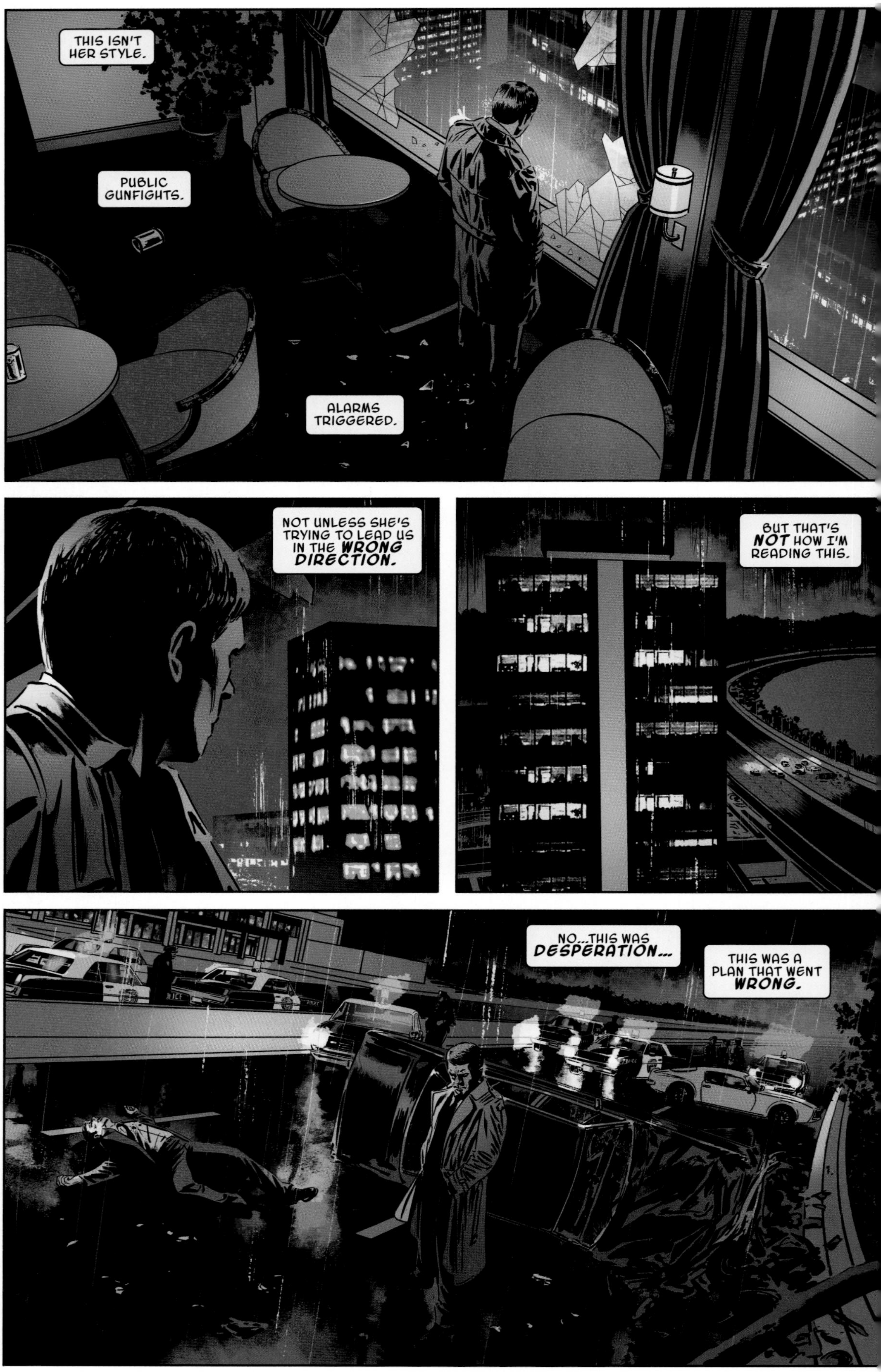
THIS ISN'T HER STYLE.
PUBLIC GUNFIGHTS.
ALARMS TRIGGERED.
NOT UNLESS SHE'S TRYING TO LEAD US IN THE WRONG DIRECTION.
BUT THAT'S NOT HOW I'M READING THIS.
NO...THIS WAS DESPERATION...
THIS WAS A PLAN THAT WENT WRONG.

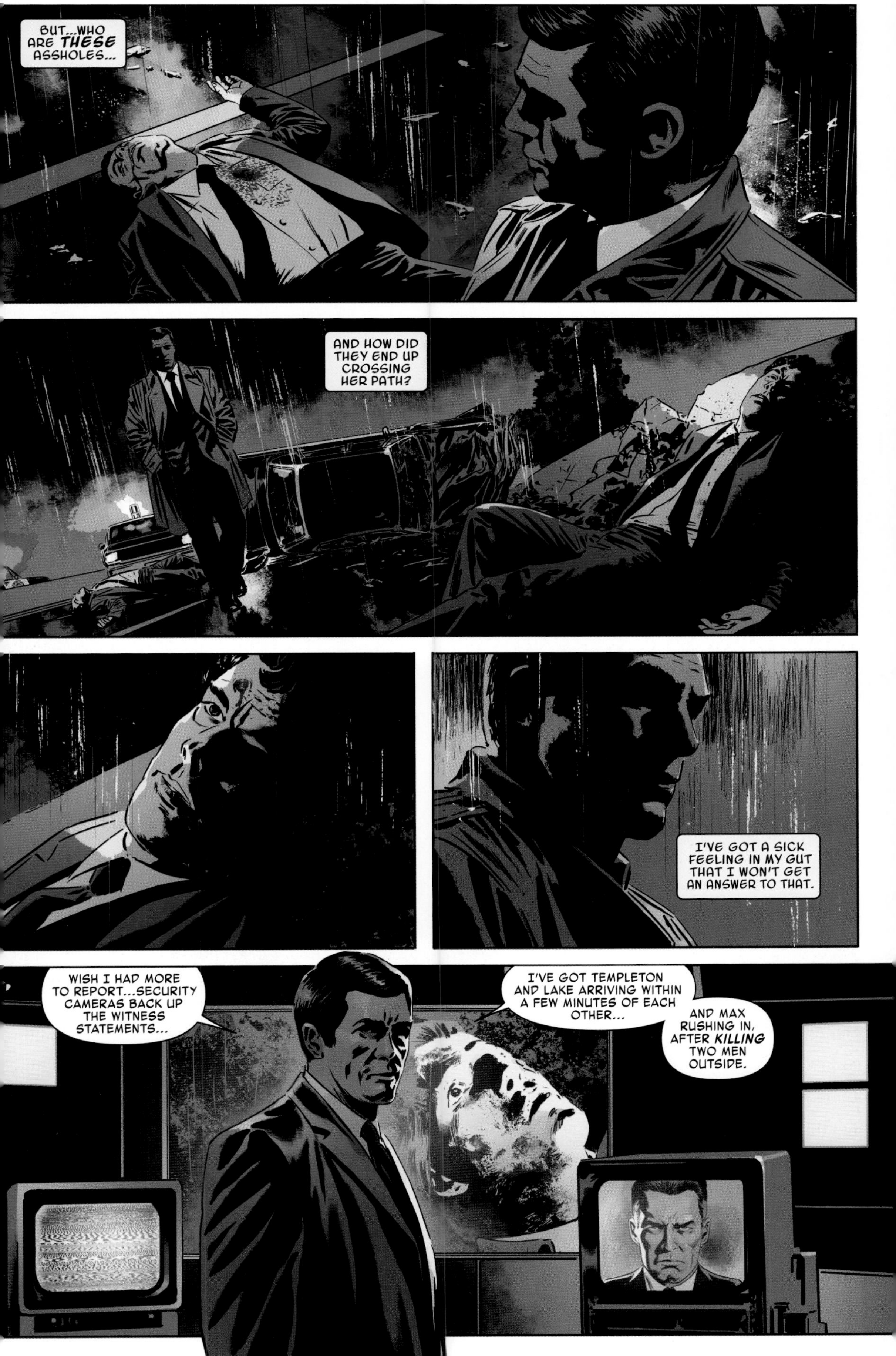

BUT...WHO ARE *THESE* ASSHOLES...
AND HOW DID THEY END UP CROSSING HER PATH?
I'VE GOT A SICK FEELING IN MY GUT THAT I WON'T GET AN ANSWER TO THAT.
WISH I HAD MORE TO REPORT...SECURITY CAMERAS BACK UP THE WITNESS STATEMENTS...
I'VE GOT TEMPLETON AND LAKE ARRIVING WITHIN A FEW MINUTES OF EACH OTHER...
AND MAX RUSHING IN, AFTER *KILLING* TWO MEN OUTSIDE.

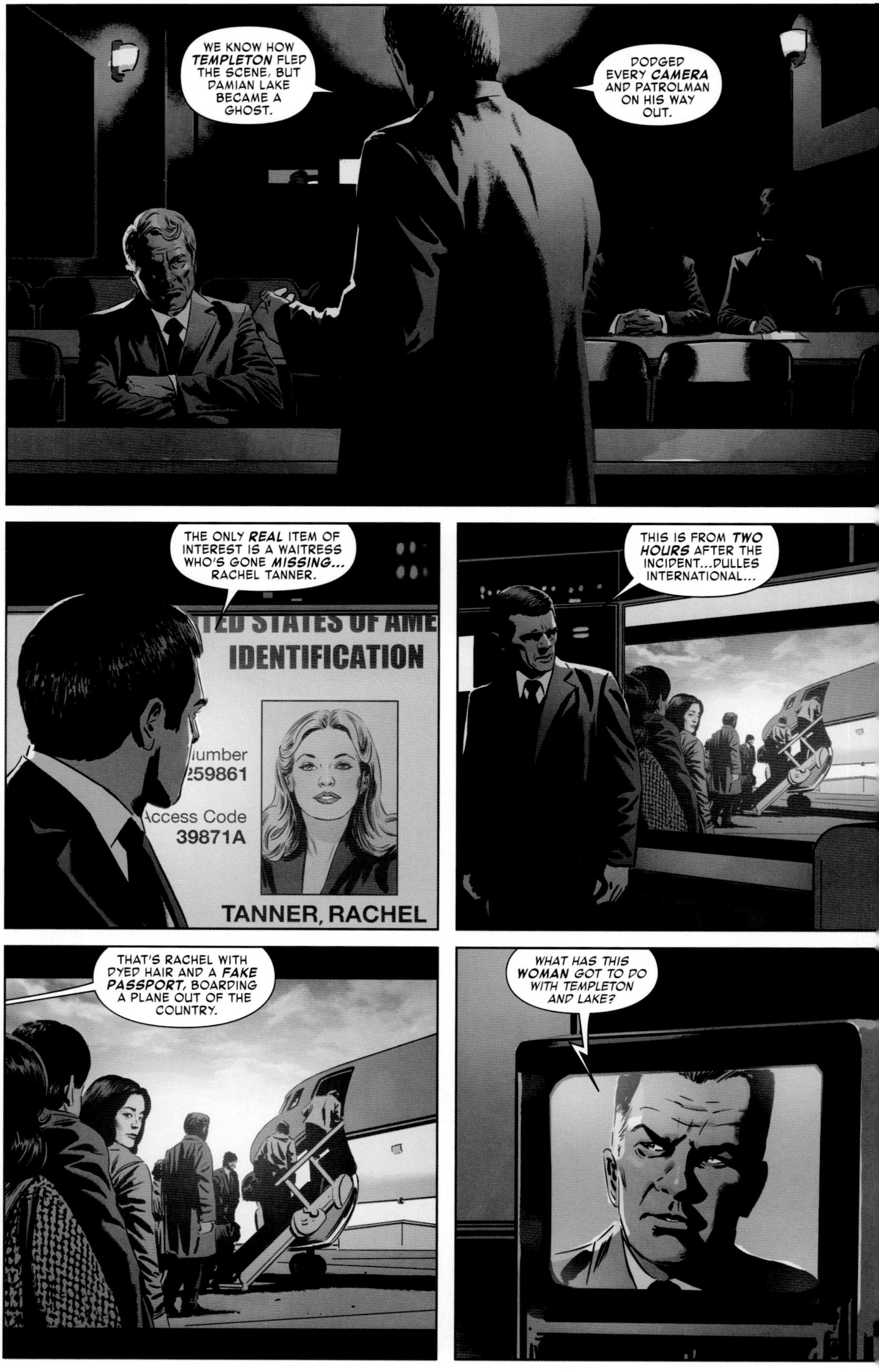
WE KNOW HOW TEMPLETON FLED THE SCENE, BUT DAMIAN LAKE BECAME A GHOST.
DODGED EVERY CAMERA AND PATROLMAN ON HIS WAY OUT.
THE ONLY REAL ITEM OF INTEREST IS A WAITRESS WHO'S GONE MISSING... RACHEL TANNER.
TED STATES OF AME
IDENTIFICATION
umber
259861
ccess Code
39871A
TANNER, RACHEL
THIS IS FROM TWO HOURS AFTER THE INCIDENT...DULLES INTERNATIONAL...
THAT'S RACHEL WITH DYED HAIR AND A FAKE PASSPORT, BOARDING A PLANE OUT OF THE COUNTRY.
WHAT HAS THIS WOMAN GOT TO DO WITH TEMPLETON AND LAKE?

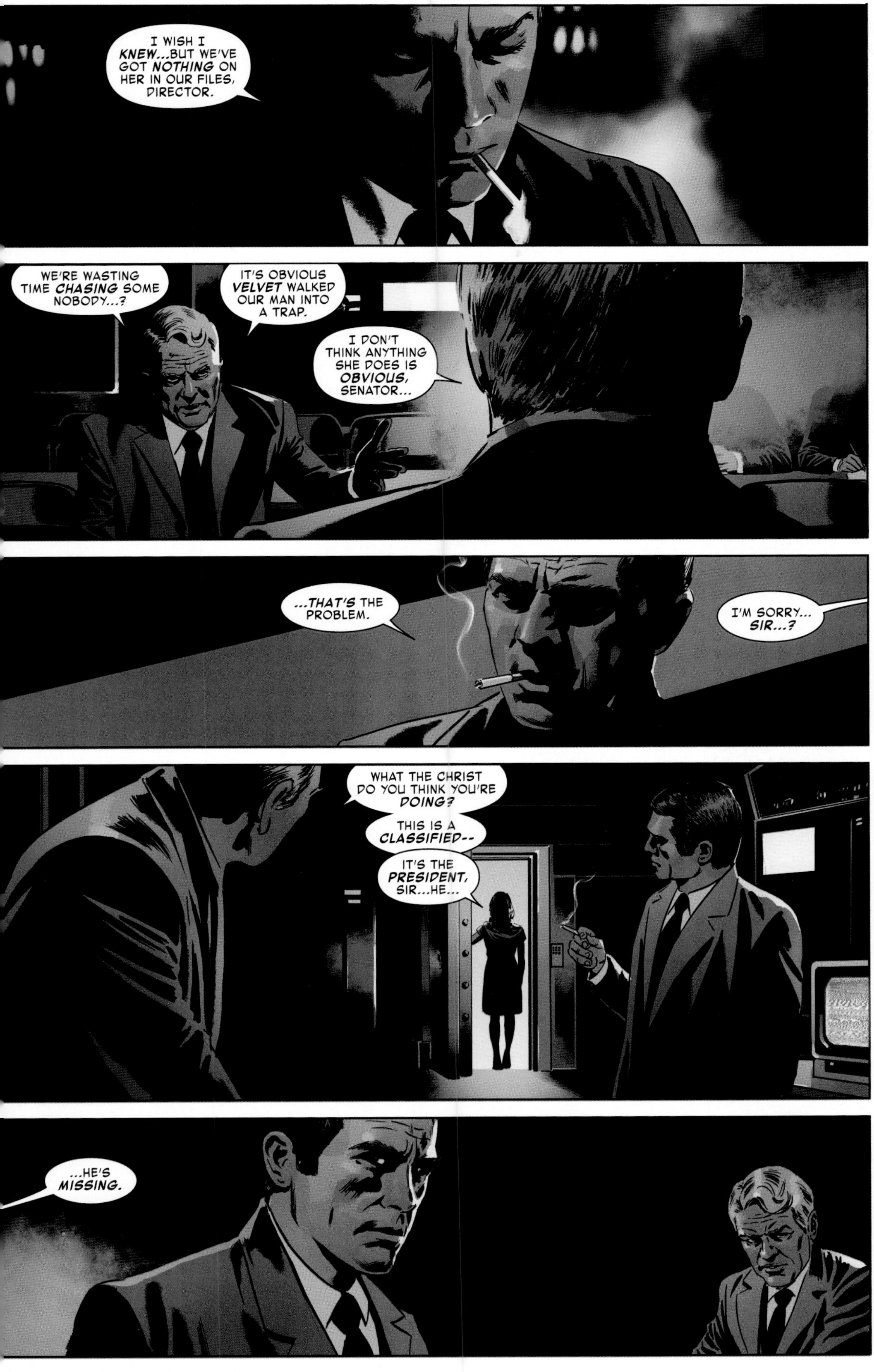
I WISH I KNEW...BUT WE'VE GOT NOTHING ON HER IN OUR FILES, DIRECTOR.
WE'RE WASTING TIME CHASING SOME NOBODY...?
IT'S OBVIOUS VELVET WALKED OUR MAN INTO A TRAP.
I DON'T THINK ANYTHING SHE DOES IS OBVIOUS, SENATOR...
...THAT'S THE PROBLEM.
I'M SORRY... SIR...?
WHAT THE CHRIST DO YOU THINK YOU'RE DOING?
THIS IS A CLASSIFIED--
IT'S THE PRESIDENT, SIR...HE...
...HE'S MISSING.

PART FOUR

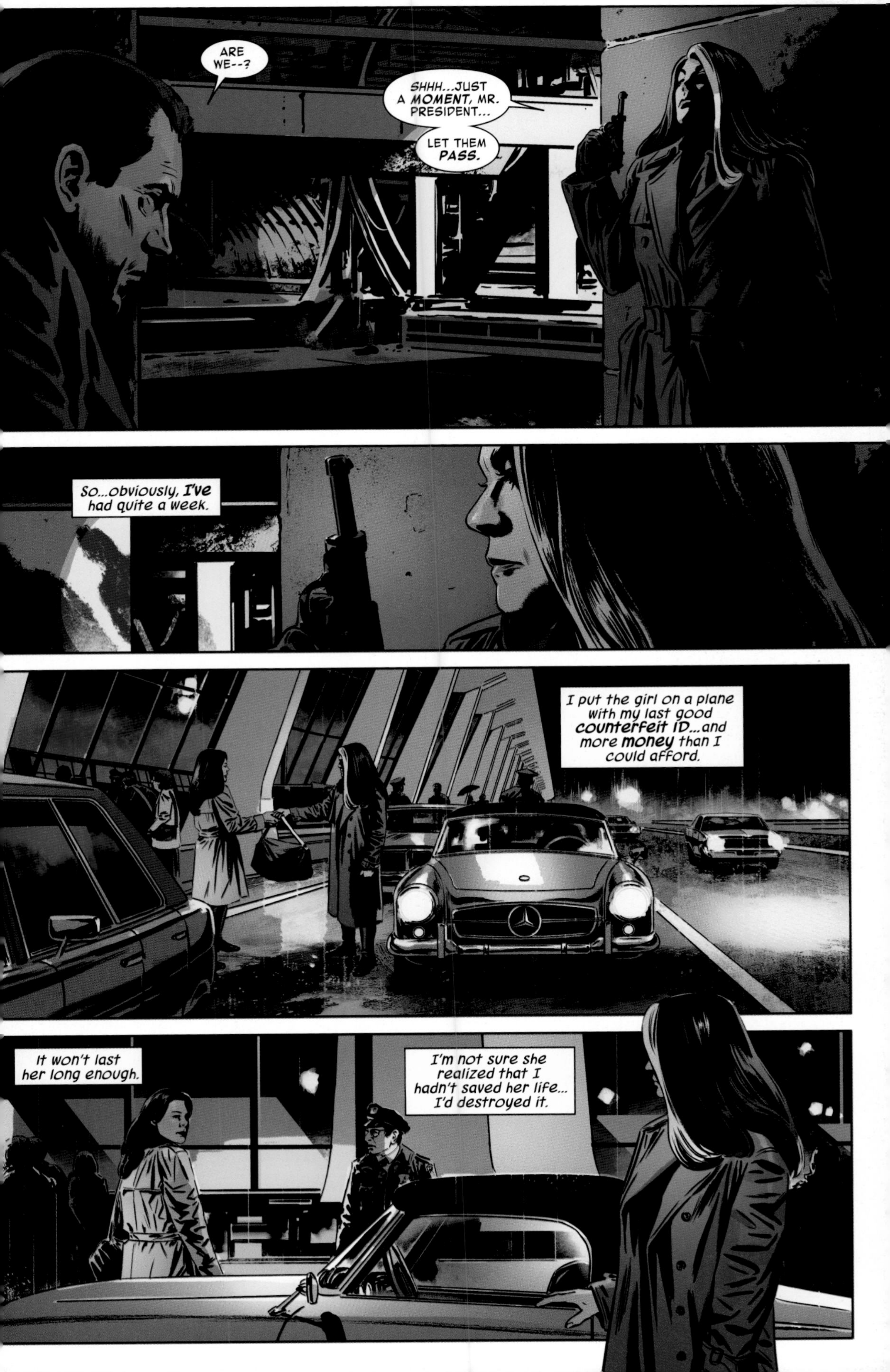
ARE WE--?
SHHH...JUST A MOMENT, MR. PRESIDENT...
LET THEM PASS.
So...obviously, I've had quite a week.
I put the girl on a plane with my last good counterfeit ID...and more money than I could afford.
It won't last her long enough.
I'm not sure she realized that I hadn't saved her life... I'd destroyed it.

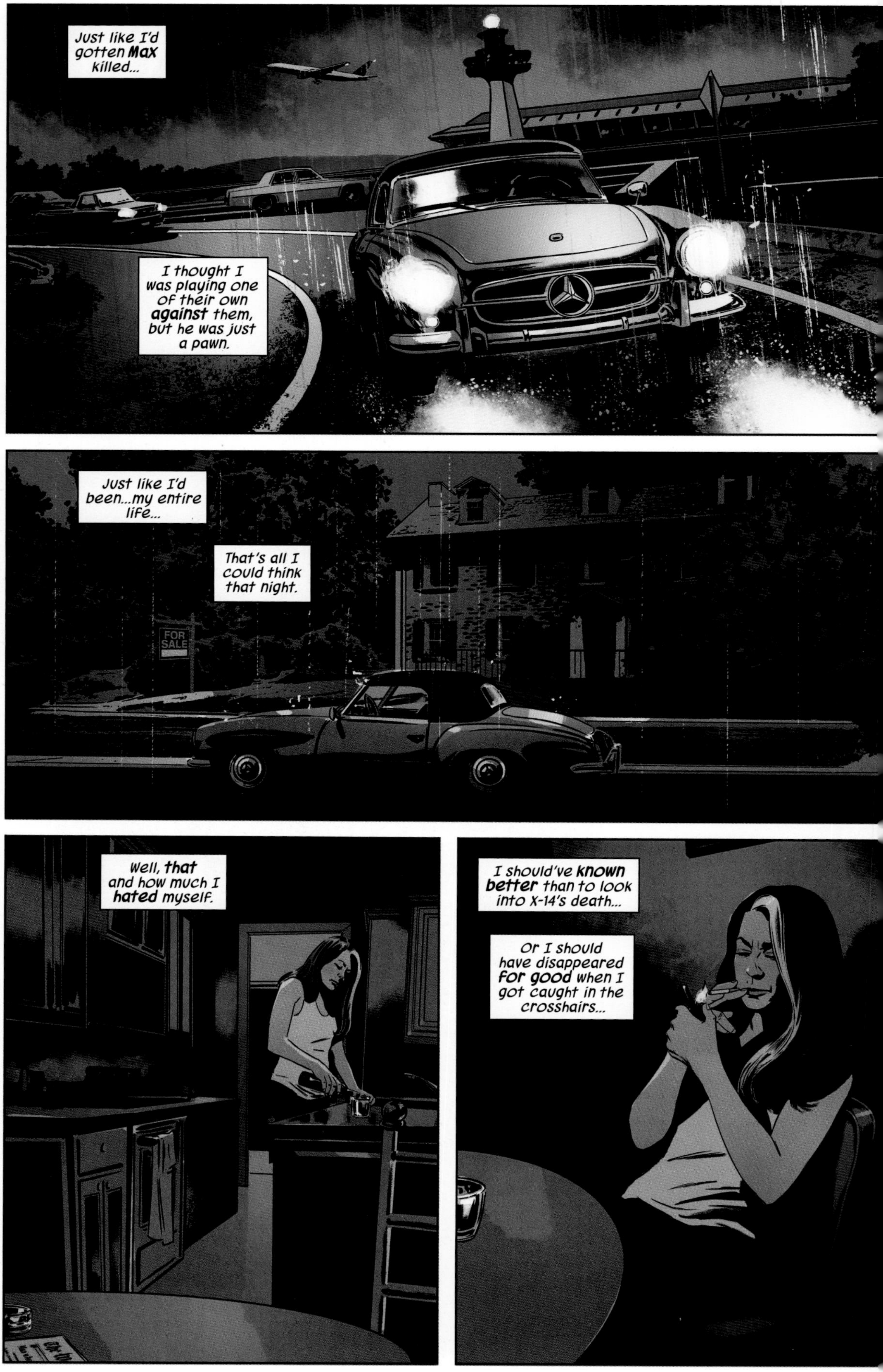
Just like I'd gotten Max killed...
I thought I was playing one of their own against them, but he was just a pawn.
Just like I'd been...my entire life...
That's all I could think that night.
FOR SALE
Well, that and how much I hated myself.
I should've known better than to look into X-14's death...
Or I should have disappeared for good when I got caught in the crosshairs...

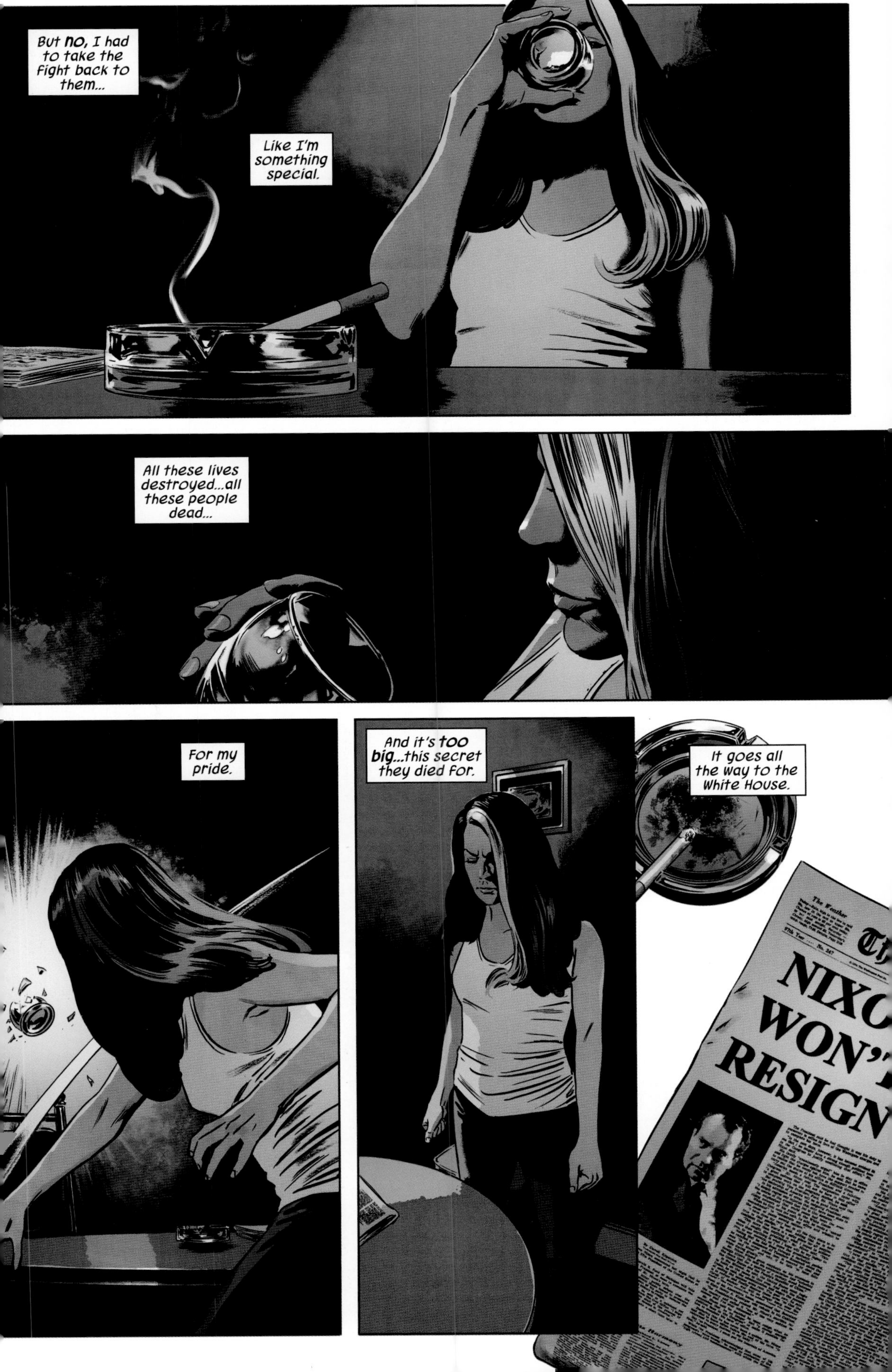

But **no**, I had to take the fight back to them...
Like I'm something special.
All these lives destroyed...all these people dead...
For my pride.
And it's **too big**...this secret they died for.
It goes all the way to the White House.
NIXO
WON'
RESIGN

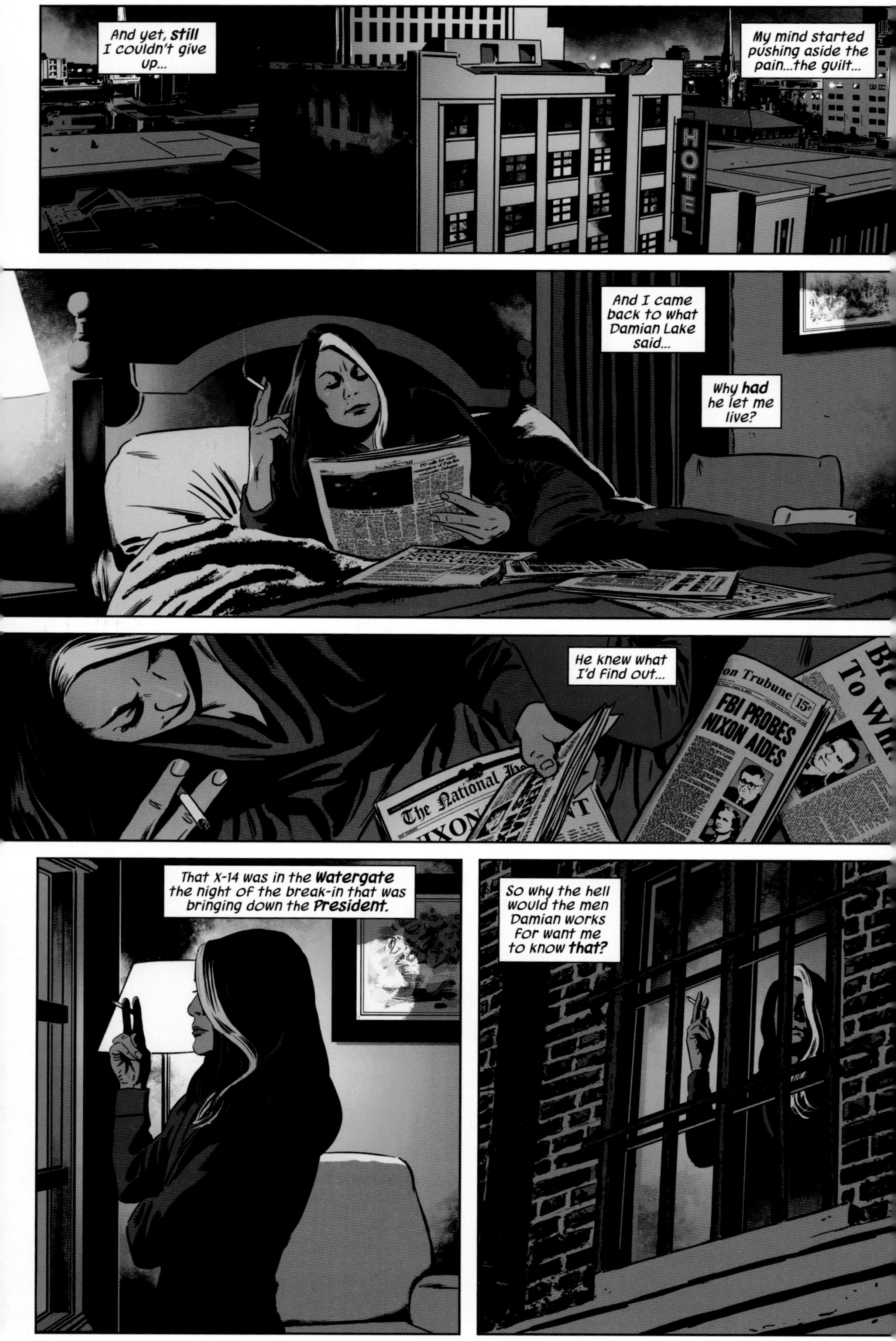
And yet, still I couldn't give up...
My mind started pushing aside the pain...the guilt...
HOTEL
And I came back to what Damian Lake said...
Why had he let me live?
He knew what I'd find out...
FBI PROBES NIXON AIDES
15¢
That X-14 was in the Watergate the night of the break-in that was bringing down the President.
So why the hell would the men Damian works for want me to know that?

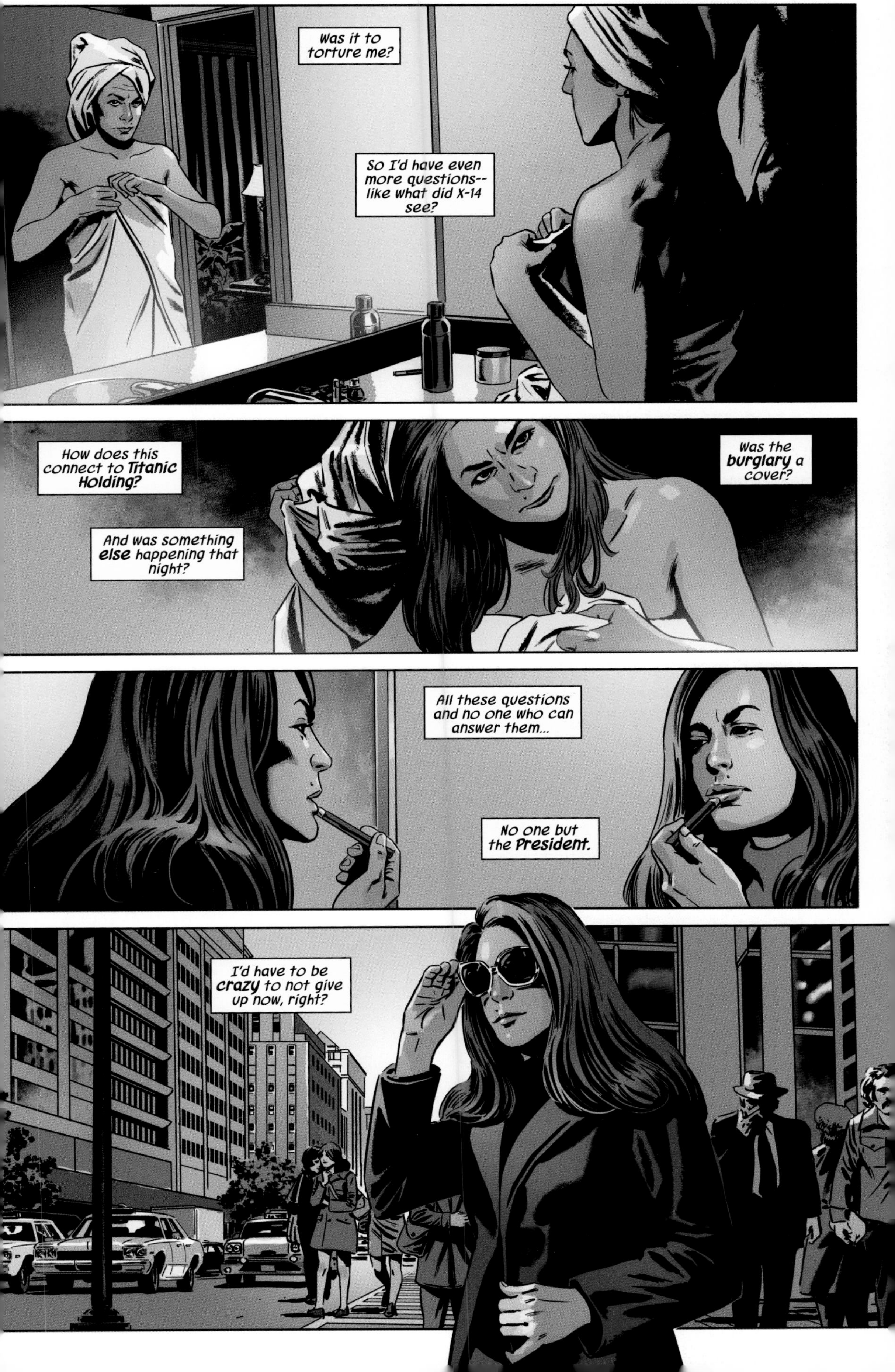

Was it to torture me?
So I'd have even more questions-- like what did X-14 see?
How does this connect to **Titanic Holding?**
Was the **burglary** a cover?
And was something **else** happening that night?
All these questions and no one who can answer them...
No one but the **President.**
I'd have to be **crazy** to not give up now, right?

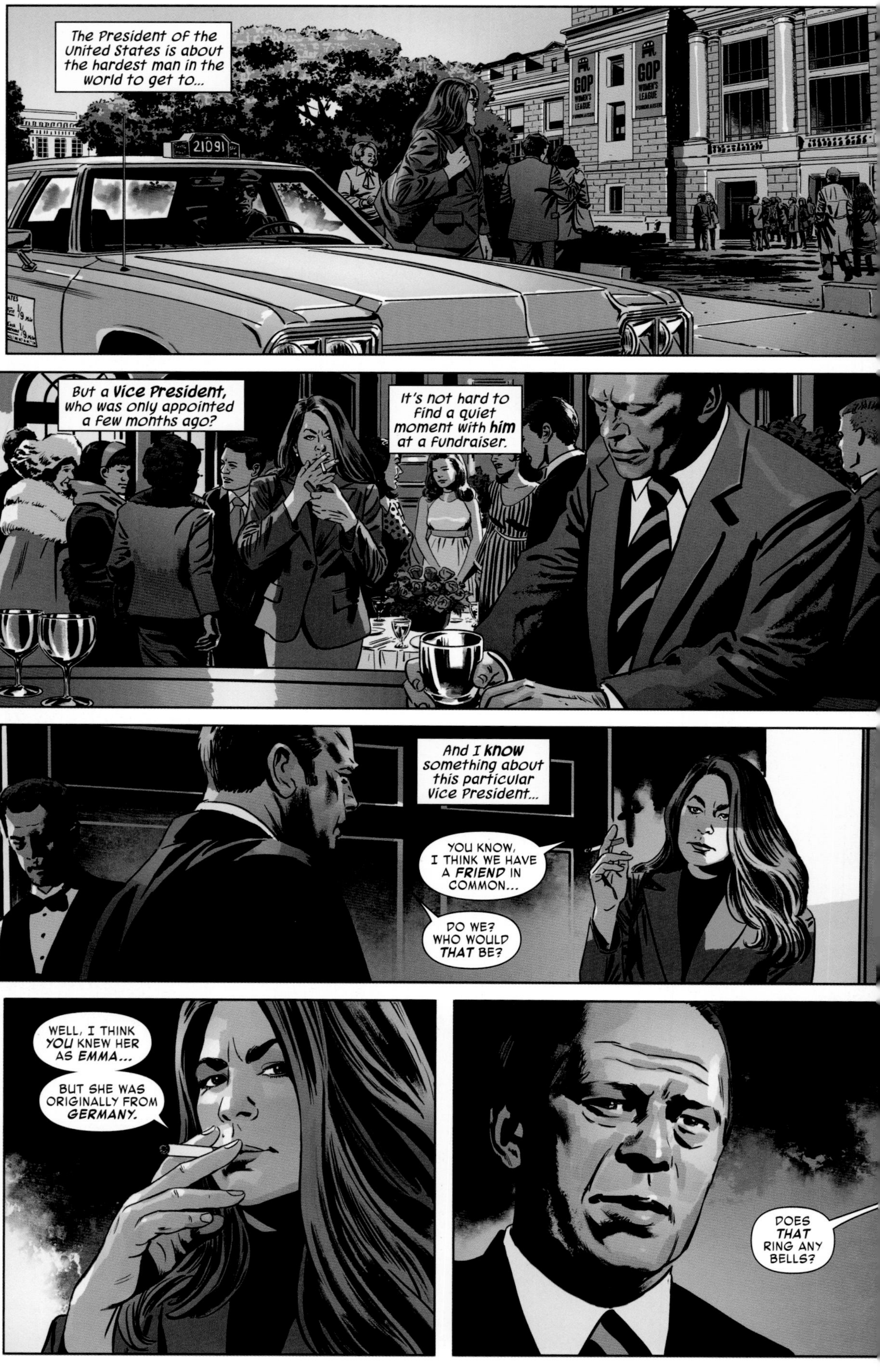
The President of the United States is about the hardest man in the world to get to...
21091
GOP WOMEN'S LEAGUE FUNDRAISER
GOP WOMEN'S LEAGUE FUNDRAISER
But a Vice President, who was only appointed a few months ago?
It's not hard to find a quiet moment with him at a fundraiser.
And I know something about this particular Vice President...
YOU KNOW, I THINK WE HAVE A FRIEND IN COMMON...
DO WE? WHO WOULD THAT BE?
WELL, I THINK YOU KNEW HER AS EMMA...
BUT SHE WAS ORIGINALLY FROM GERMANY.
DOES THAT RING ANY BELLS?

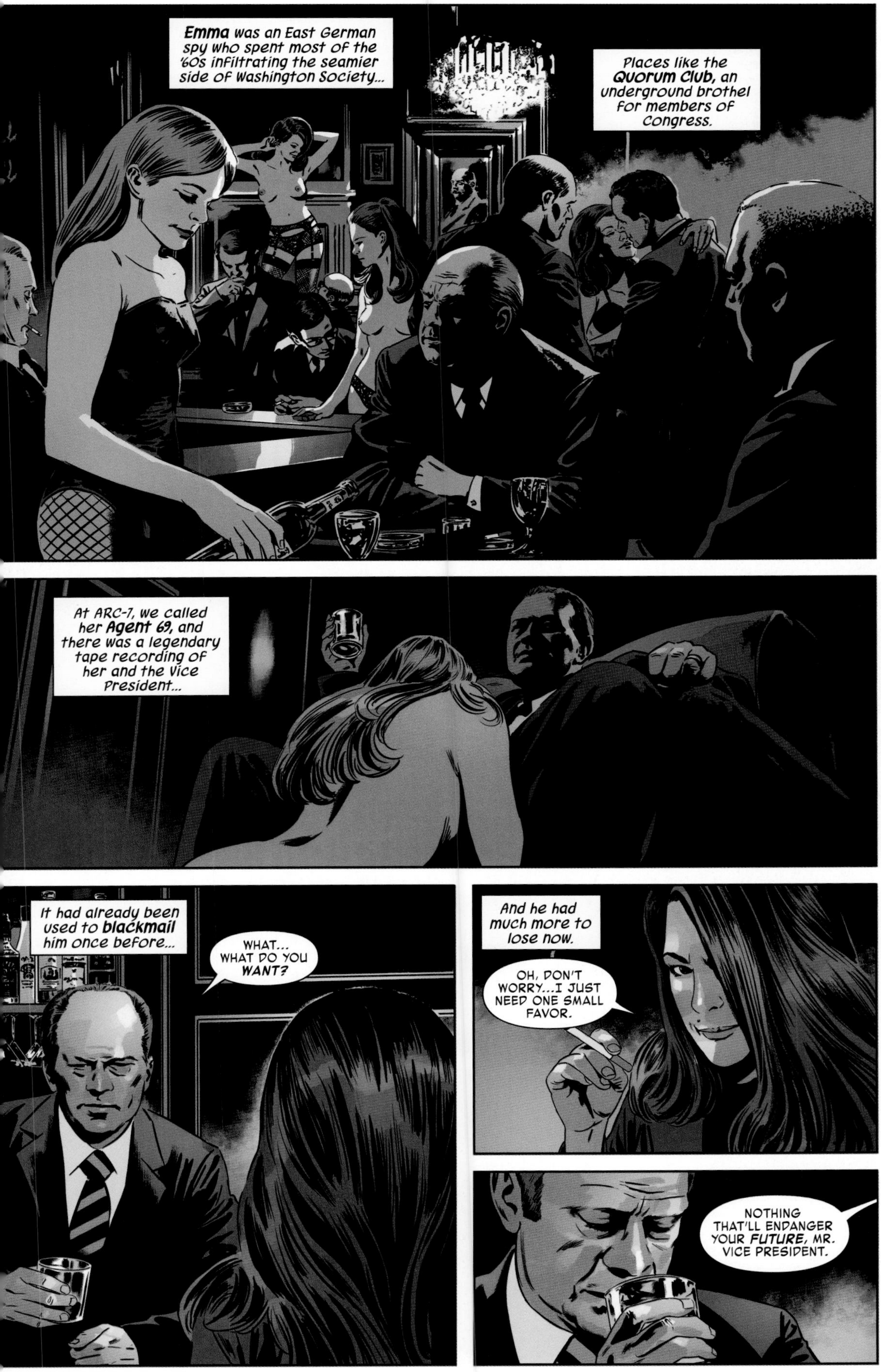
Emma was an East German spy who spent most of the '60s infiltrating the seamier side of Washington Society...
Places like the Quorum Club, an underground brothel for members of Congress.
At ARC-7, we called her Agent 69, and there was a legendary tape recording of her and the Vice President...
It had already been used to blackmail him once before...
WHAT... WHAT DO YOU WANT?
And he had much more to lose now.
OH, DON'T WORRY...I JUST NEED ONE SMALL FAVOR.
NOTHING THAT'LL ENDANGER YOUR FUTURE, MR. VICE PRESIDENT.

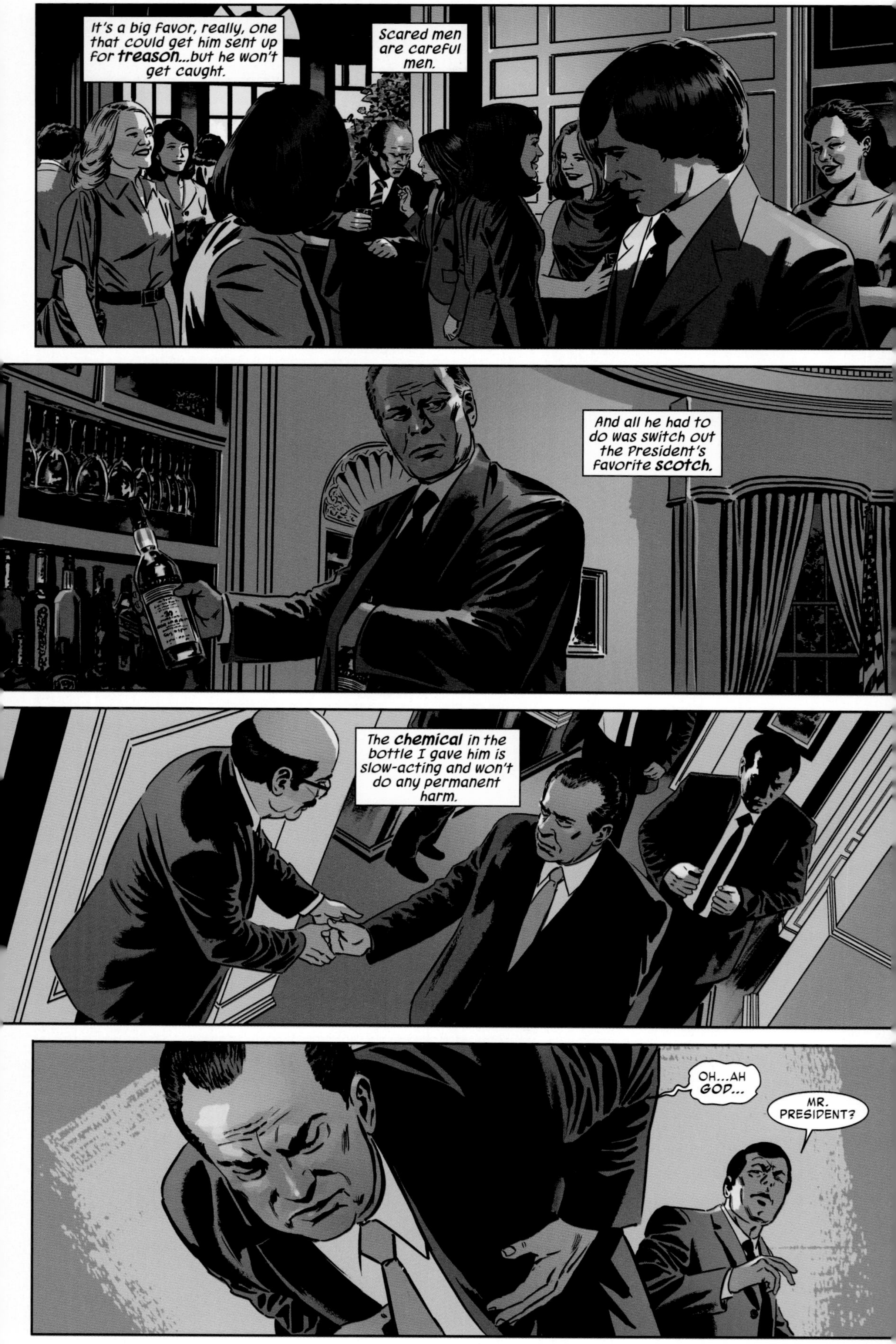
It's a big favor, really, one that could get him sent up for treason...but he won't get caught.
Scared men are careful men.
And all he had to do was switch out the President's favorite scotch.
The chemical in the bottle I gave him is slow-acting and won't do any permanent harm.
OH...AH GOD...
MR. PRESIDENT?

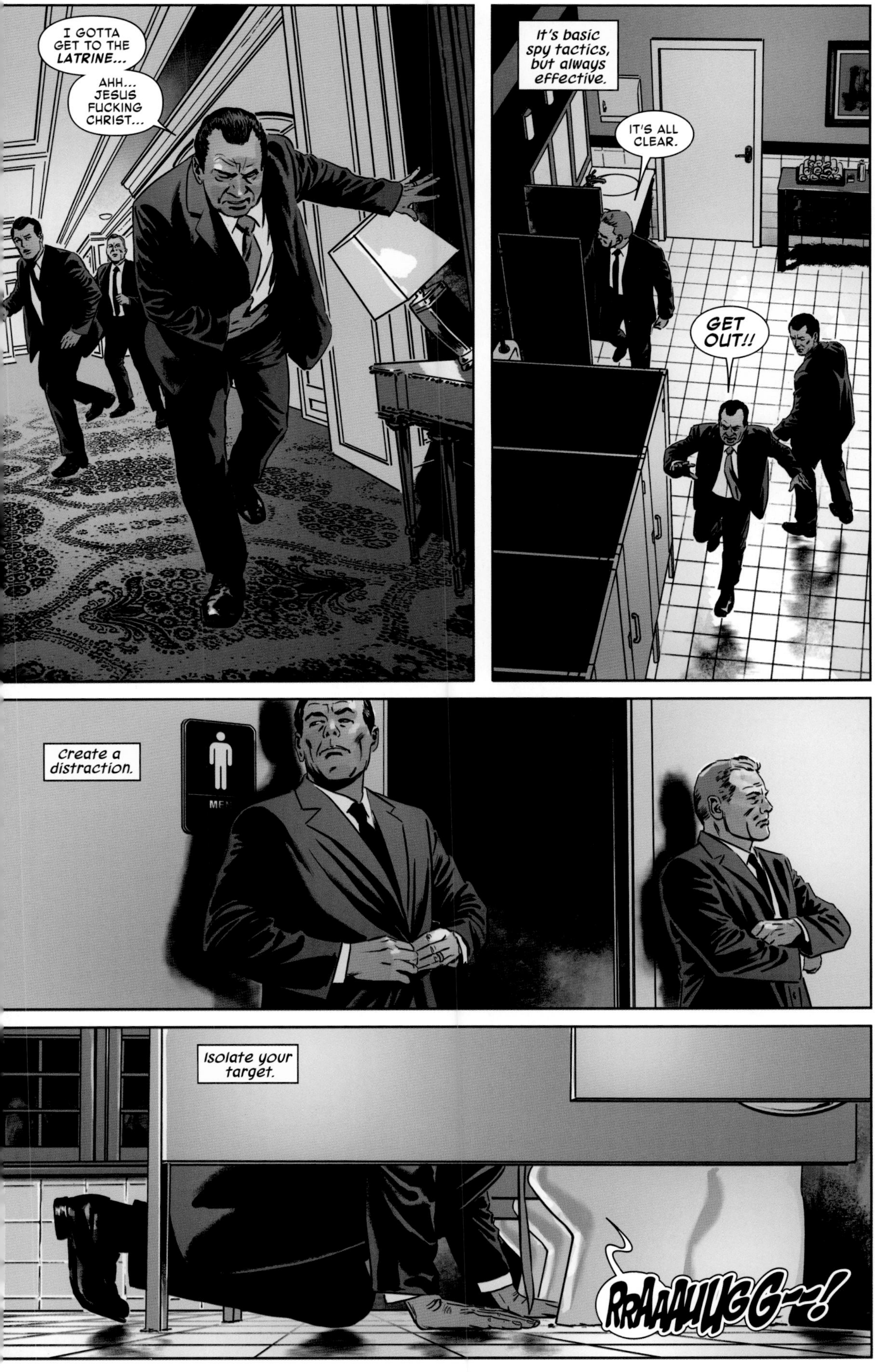
I GOTTA GET TO THE LATRINE...
AHH... JESUS FUCKING CHRIST...
It's basic spy tactics, but always effective.
IT'S ALL CLEAR.
GET OUT!!
Create a distraction.
MEN
Isolate your target.
RRAAAUUGG~~!

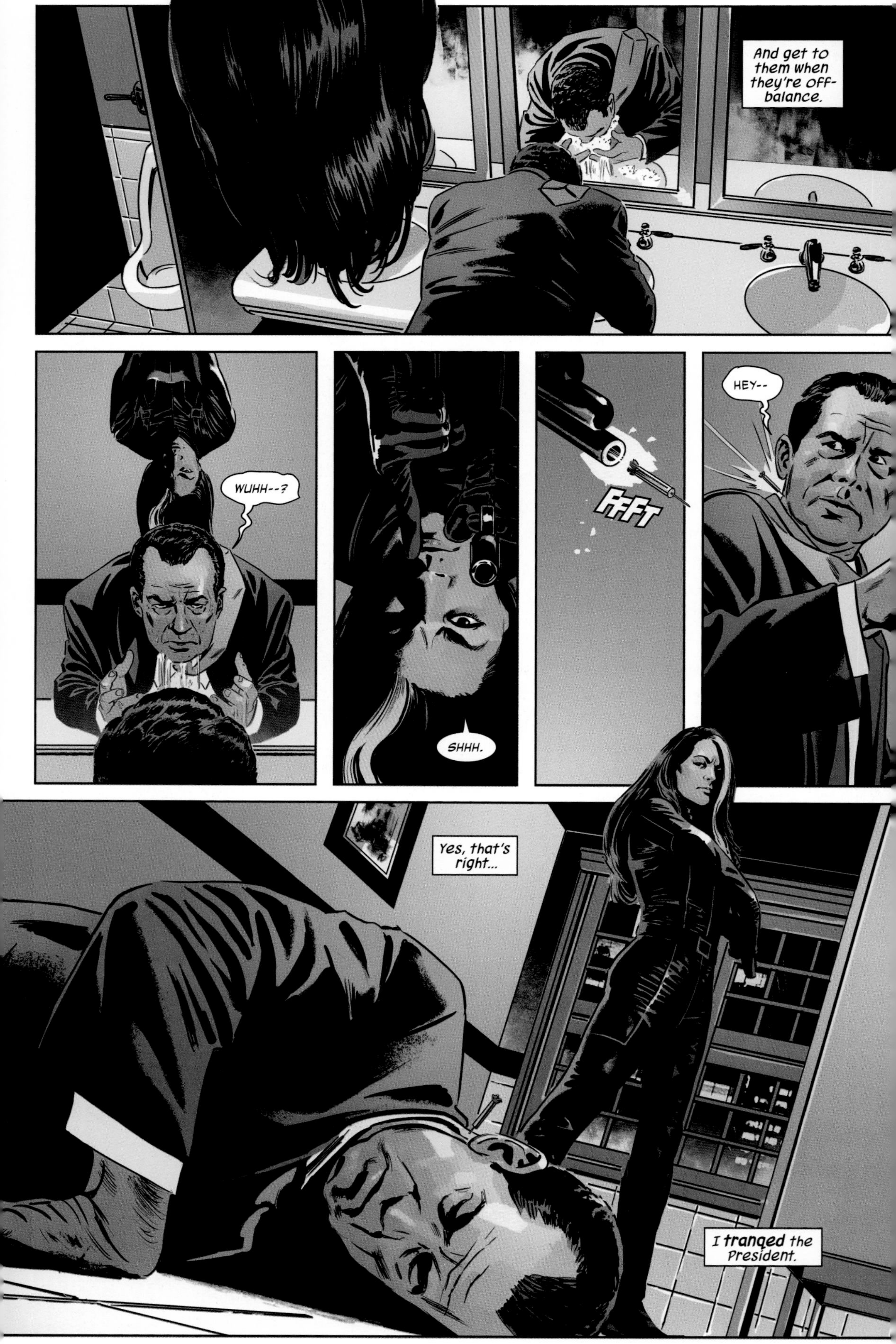
And get to them when they're off-balance.
WUHH--?
SHHH.
FFFT
HEY--
Yes, that's right...
I tranqed the President.

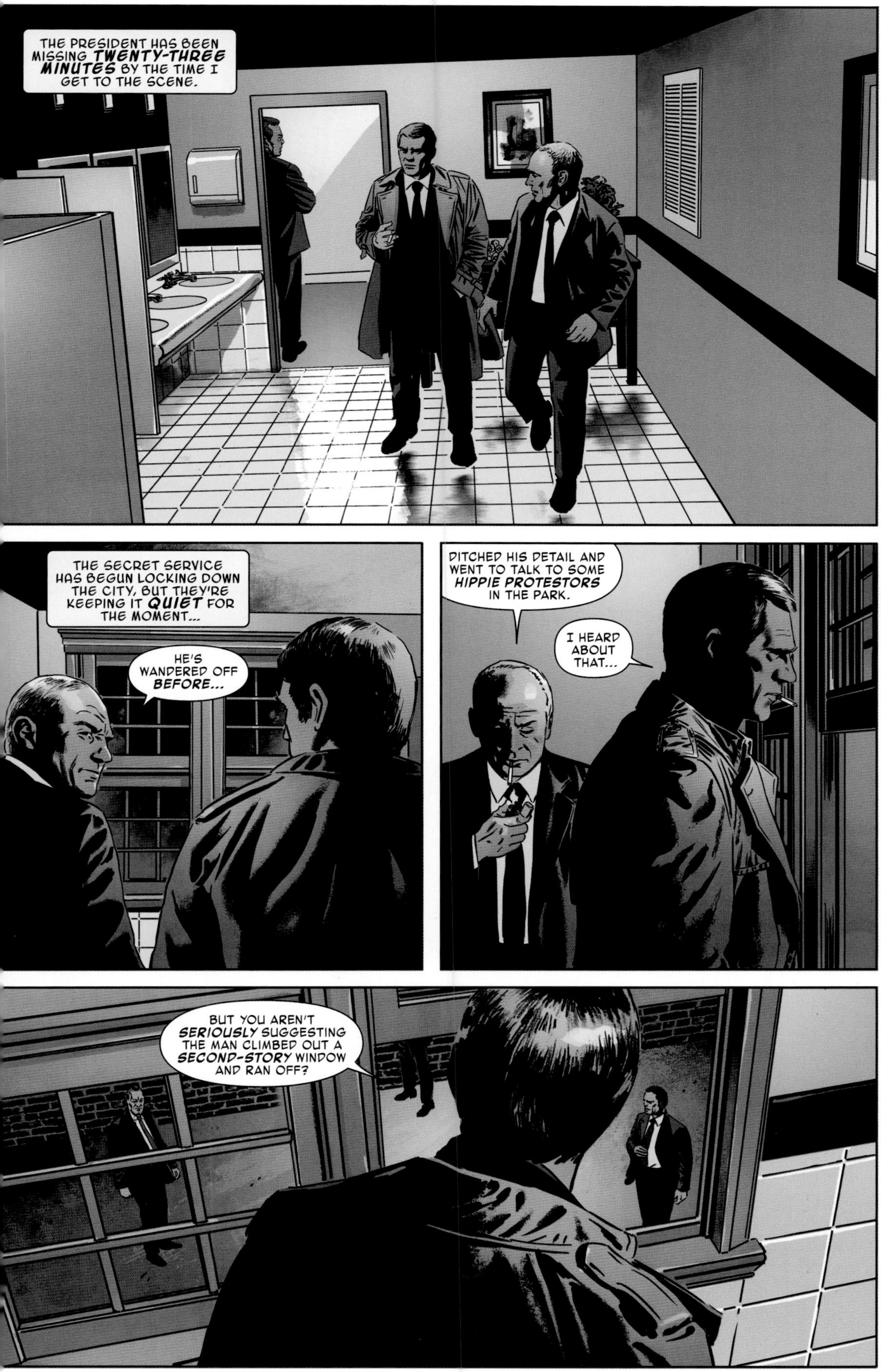

THE PRESIDENT HAS BEEN MISSING **TWENTY-THREE MINUTES** BY THE TIME I GET TO THE SCENE.
THE SECRET SERVICE HAS BEGUN LOCKING DOWN THE CITY, BUT THEY'RE KEEPING IT **QUIET** FOR THE MOMENT...
HE'S WANDERED OFF ***BEFORE...***
DITCHED HIS DETAIL AND WENT TO TALK TO SOME ***HIPPIE PROTESTORS*** IN THE PARK.
I HEARD ABOUT THAT...
BUT YOU AREN'T ***SERIOUSLY*** SUGGESTING THE MAN CLIMBED OUT A ***SECOND-STORY*** WINDOW AND RAN OFF?

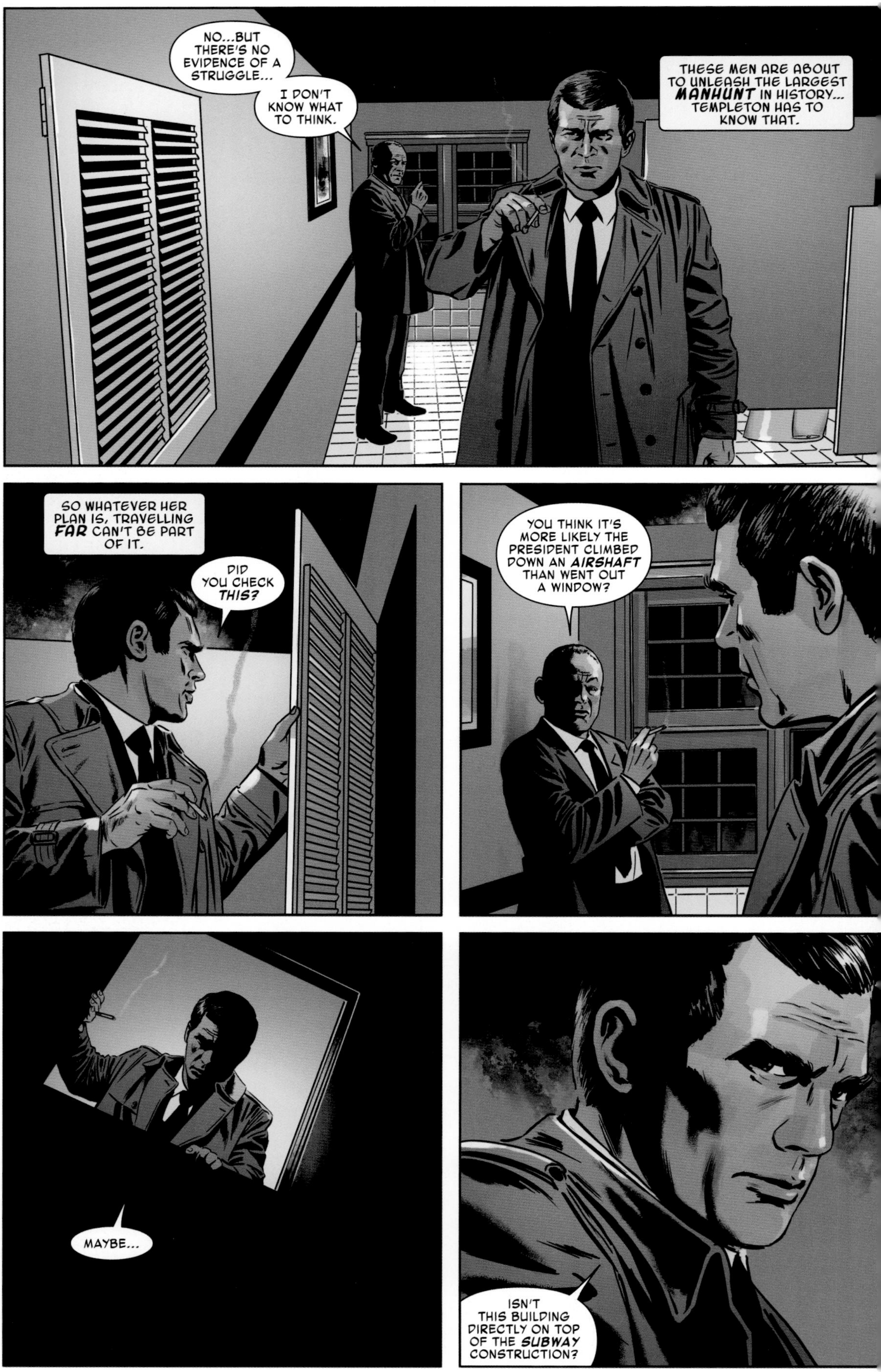
NO...BUT THERE'S NO EVIDENCE OF A STRUGGLE...
I DON'T KNOW WHAT TO THINK.
THESE MEN ARE ABOUT TO UNLEASH THE LARGEST MANHUNT IN HISTORY... TEMPLETON HAS TO KNOW THAT.
SO WHATEVER HER PLAN IS, TRAVELLING FAR CAN'T BE PART OF IT.
DID YOU CHECK THIS?
YOU THINK IT'S MORE LIKELY THE PRESIDENT CLIMBED DOWN AN AIRSHAFT THAN WENT OUT A WINDOW?
MAYBE...
ISN'T THIS BUILDING DIRECTLY ON TOP OF THE SUBWAY CONSTRUCTION?

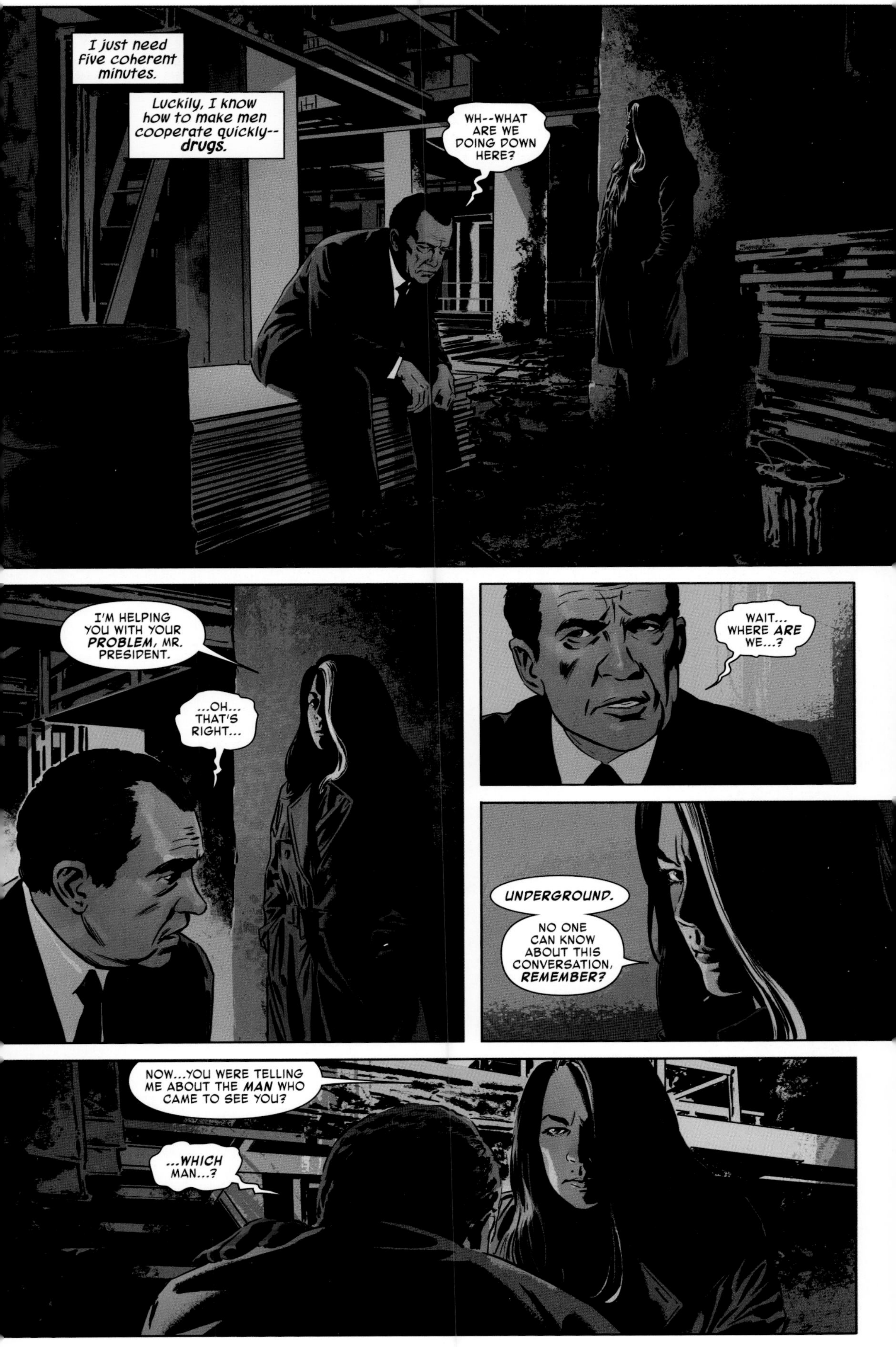
I just need five coherent minutes.
Luckily, I know how to make men cooperate quickly-- drugs.
WH--WHAT ARE WE DOING DOWN HERE?
I'M HELPING YOU WITH YOUR PROBLEM, MR. PRESIDENT.
...OH... THAT'S RIGHT...
WAIT... WHERE ARE WE...?
UNDERGROUND.
NO ONE CAN KNOW ABOUT THIS CONVERSATION, REMEMBER?
NOW...YOU WERE TELLING ME ABOUT THE MAN WHO CAME TO SEE YOU?
...WHICH MAN...?

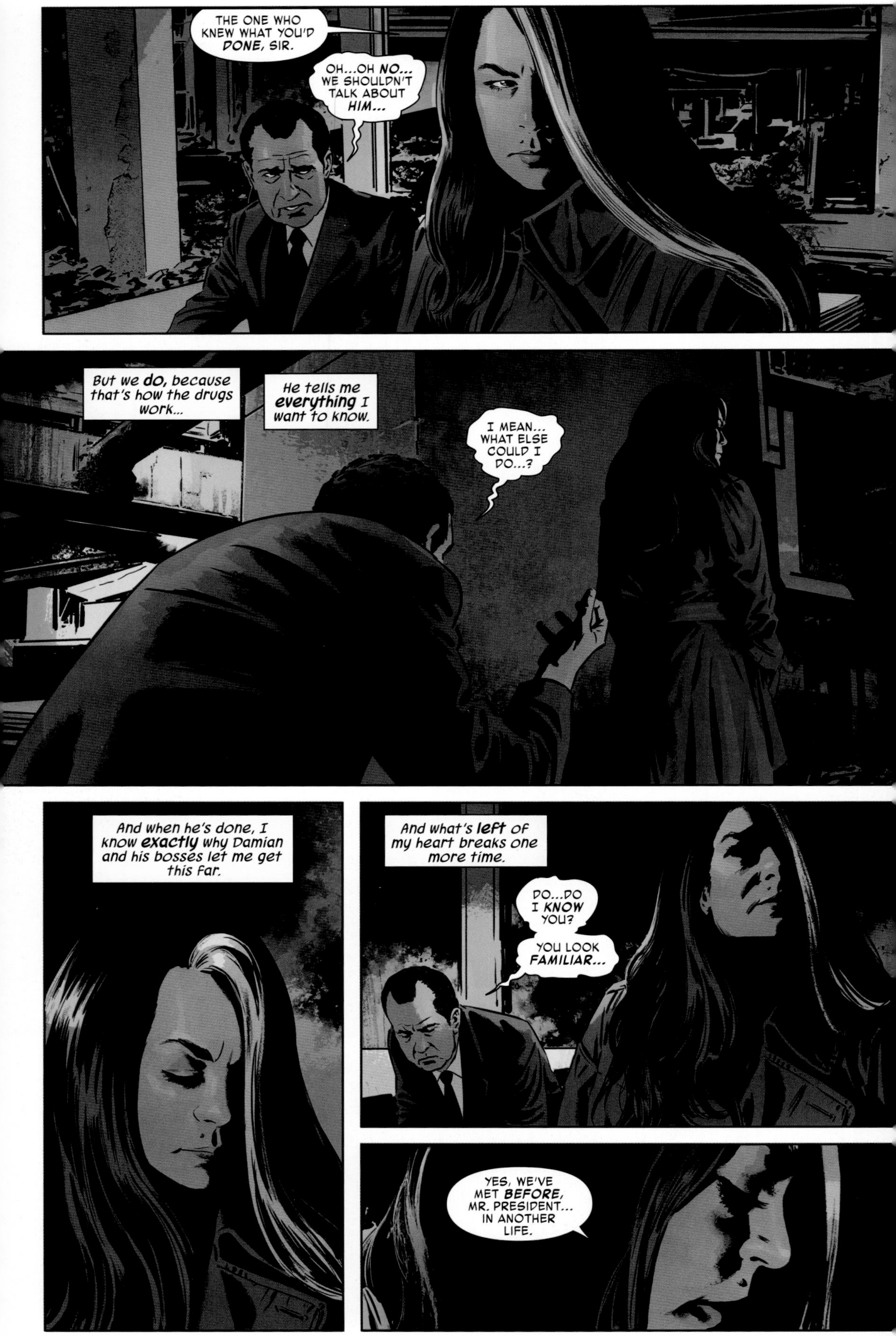
THE ONE WHO KNEW WHAT YOU'D DONE, SIR.
OH...OH NO... WE SHOULDN'T TALK ABOUT HIM...
But we do, because that's how the drugs work...
He tells me everything I want to know.
I MEAN... WHAT ELSE COULD I DO...?
And when he's done, I know exactly why Damian and his bosses let me get this far.
And what's left of my heart breaks one more time.
DO...DO I KNOW YOU?
YOU LOOK FAMILIAR...
YES, WE'VE MET BEFORE, MR. PRESIDENT... IN ANOTHER LIFE.

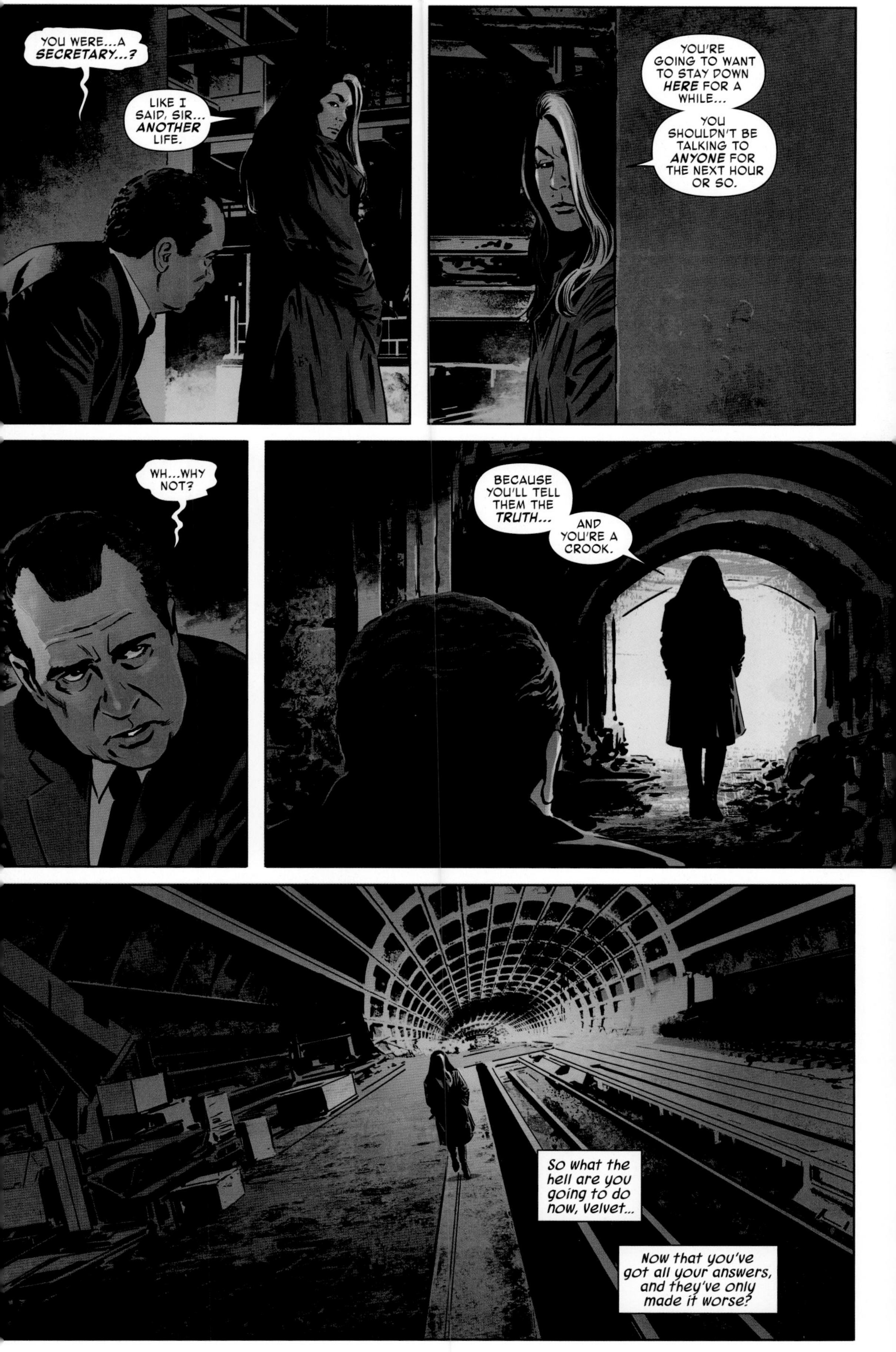
YOU WERE...A SECRETARY...?
LIKE I SAID, SIR... ANOTHER LIFE.
YOU'RE GOING TO WANT TO STAY DOWN HERE FOR A WHILE...
YOU SHOULDN'T BE TALKING TO ANYONE FOR THE NEXT HOUR OR SO.
WH...WHY NOT?
BECAUSE YOU'LL TELL THEM THE TRUTH...
AND YOU'RE A CROOK.
So what the hell are you going to do now, Velvet...
Now that you've got all your answers, and they've only made it worse?

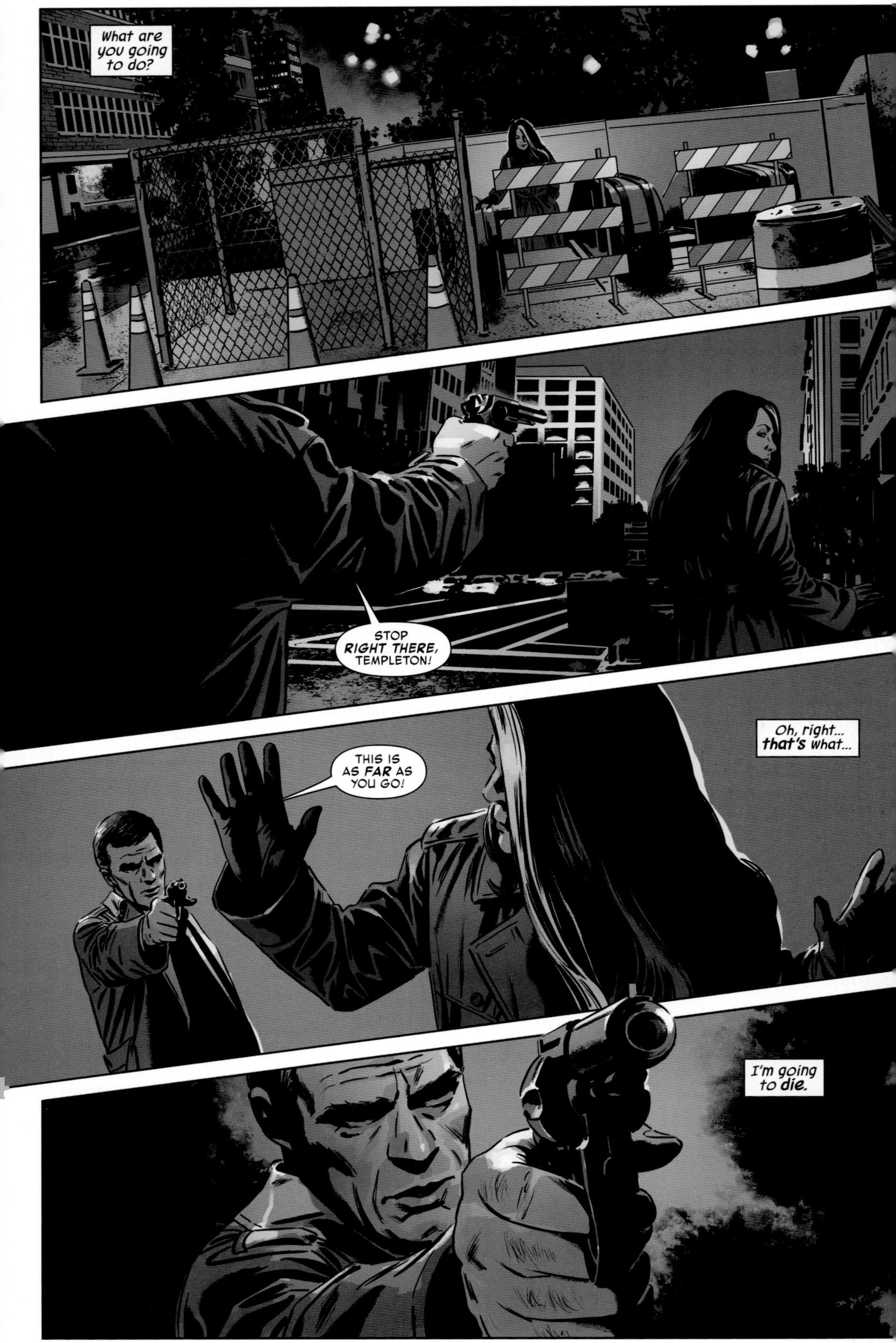
What are you going to do?
STOP RIGHT THERE, TEMPLETON!
Oh, right... that's what...
THIS IS AS FAR AS YOU GO!
I'm going to die.

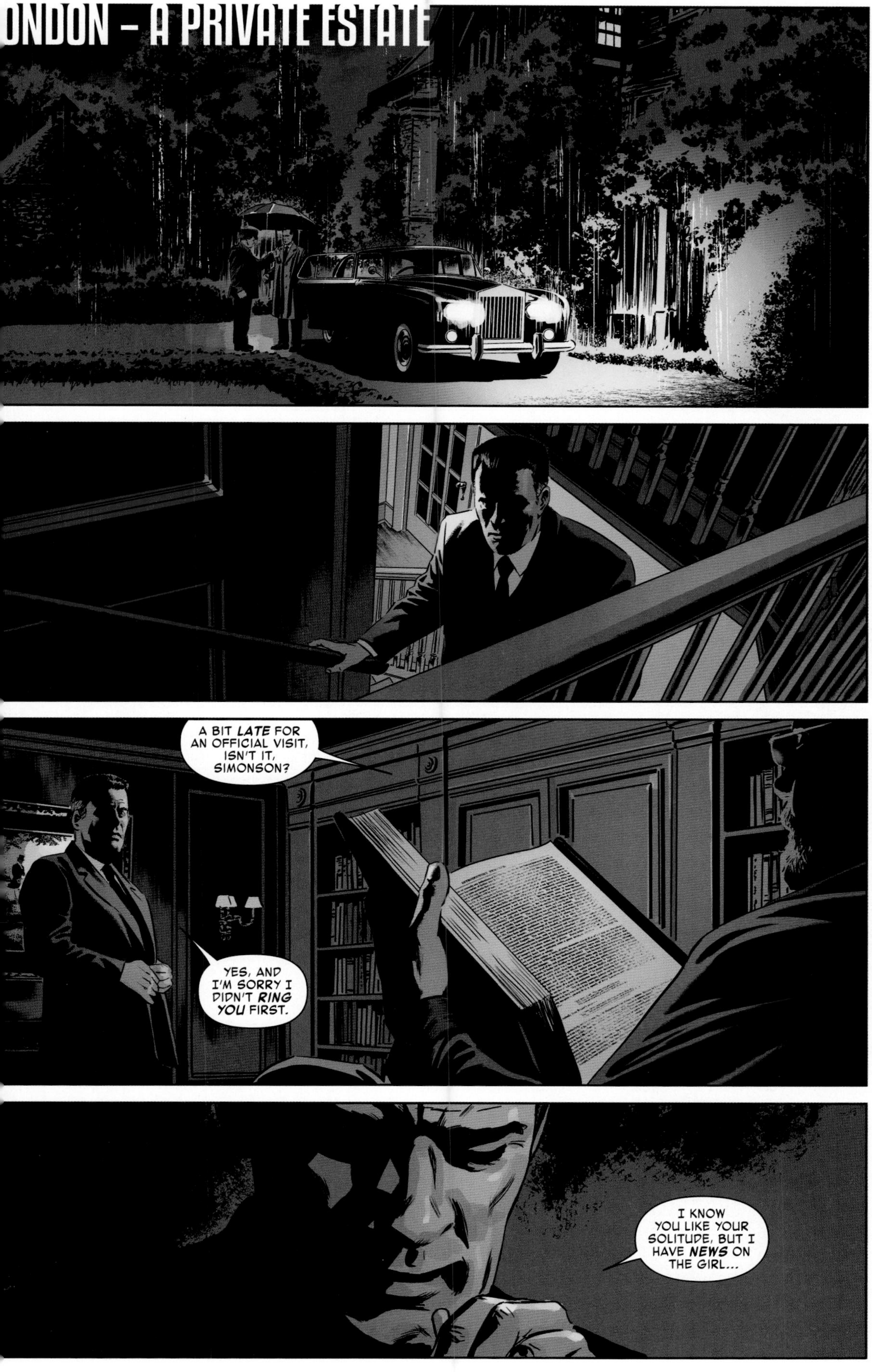
ONDON – A PRIVATE ESTATE
A BIT LATE FOR AN OFFICIAL VISIT, ISN'T IT, SIMONSON?
YES, AND I'M SORRY I DIDN'T RING YOU FIRST.
I KNOW YOU LIKE YOUR SOLITUDE, BUT I HAVE NEWS ON THE GIRL...

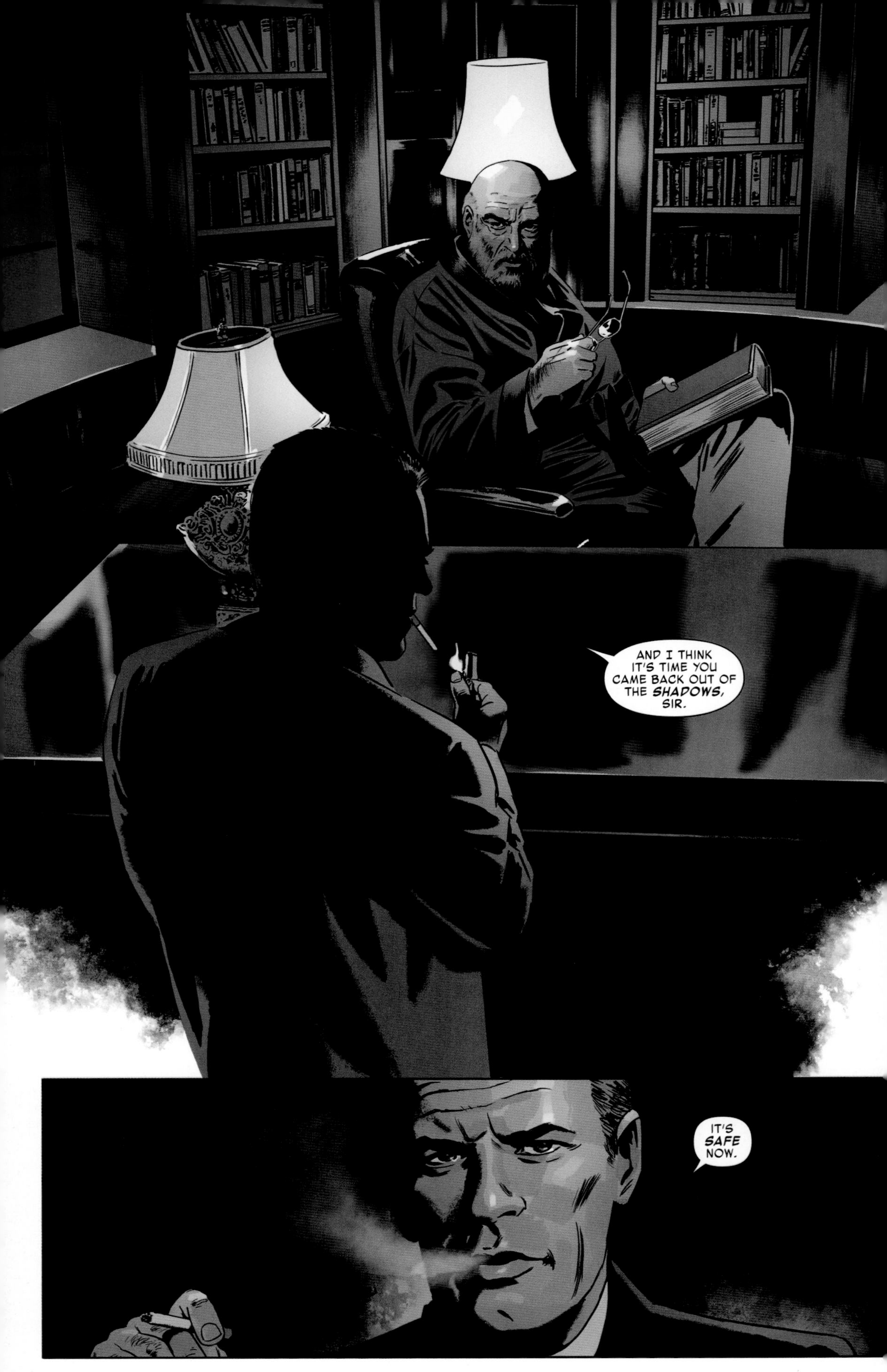
AND I THINK IT'S TIME YOU CAME BACK OUT OF THE *SHADOWS*, SIR.
IT'S *SAFE* NOW.

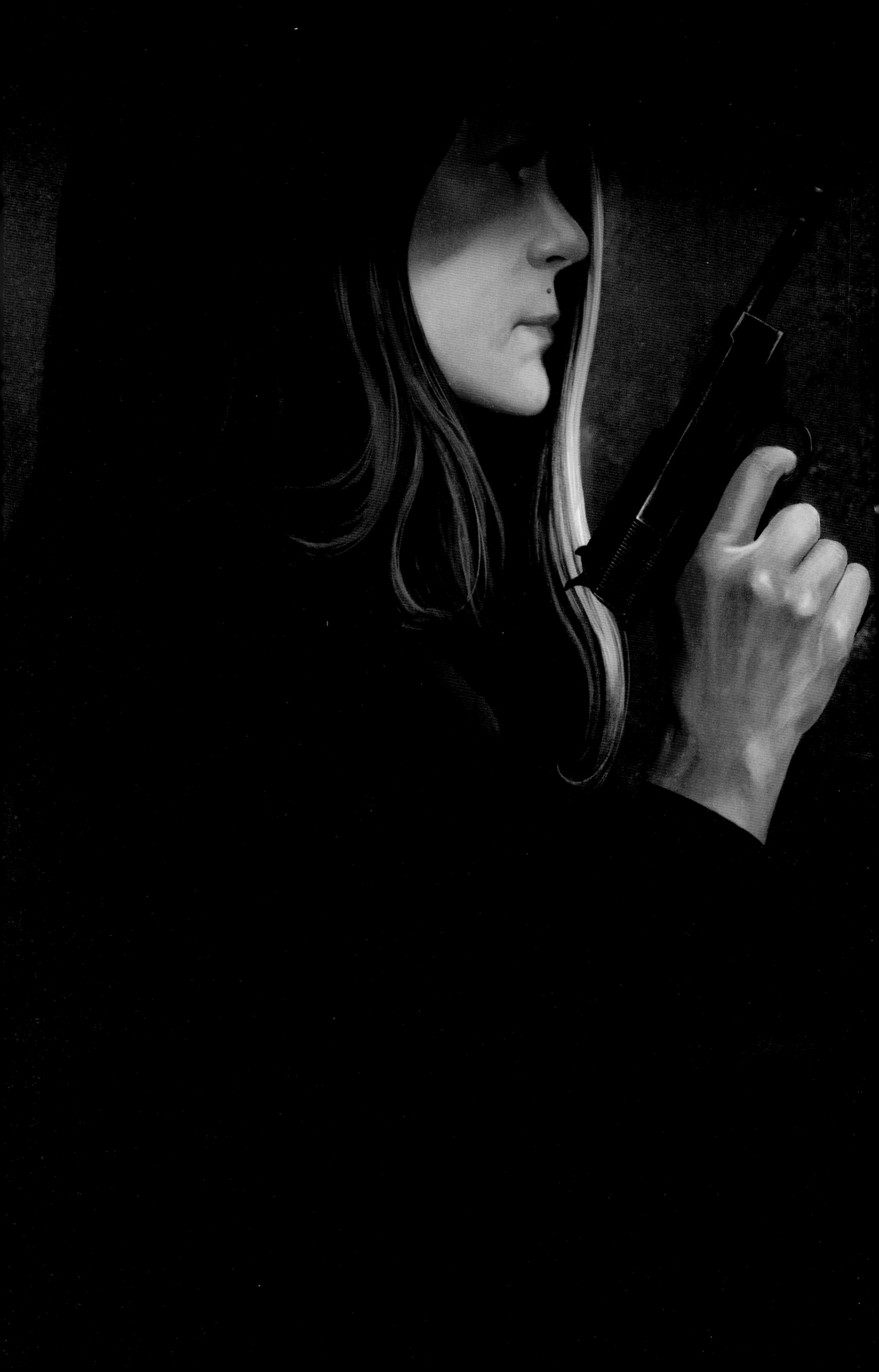

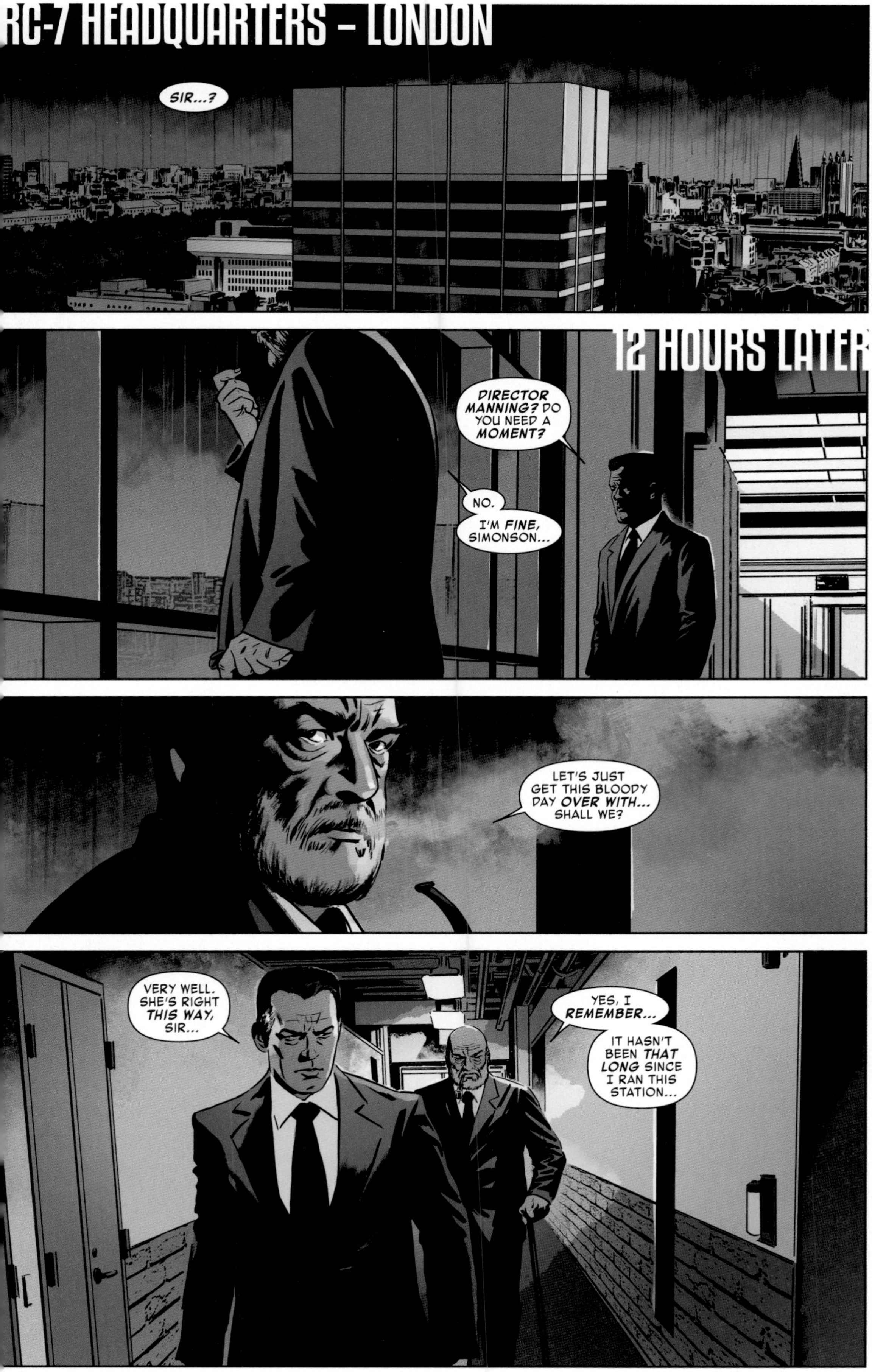
RC-7 HEADQUARTERS – LONDON
SIR...?
12 HOURS LATER
DIRECTOR MANNING? DO YOU NEED A MOMENT?
NO.
I'M FINE, SIMONSON...
LET'S JUST GET THIS BLOODY DAY OVER WITH... SHALL WE?
VERY WELL. SHE'S RIGHT THIS WAY, SIR...
YES, I REMEMBER...
IT HASN'T BEEN THAT LONG SINCE I RAN THIS STATION...

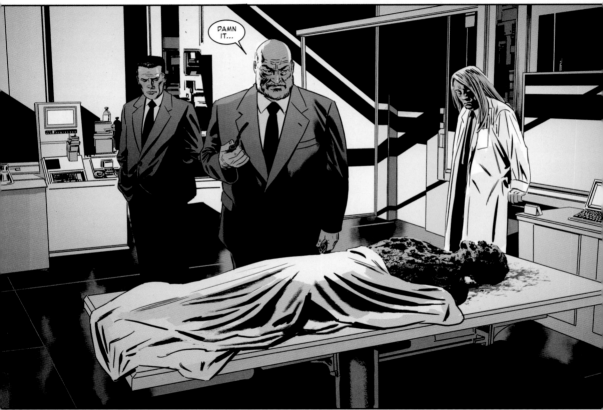

DAMN IT...

DAMN IT ALL TO HELL...

IT WASN'T MEANT TO *END* LIKE THIS...

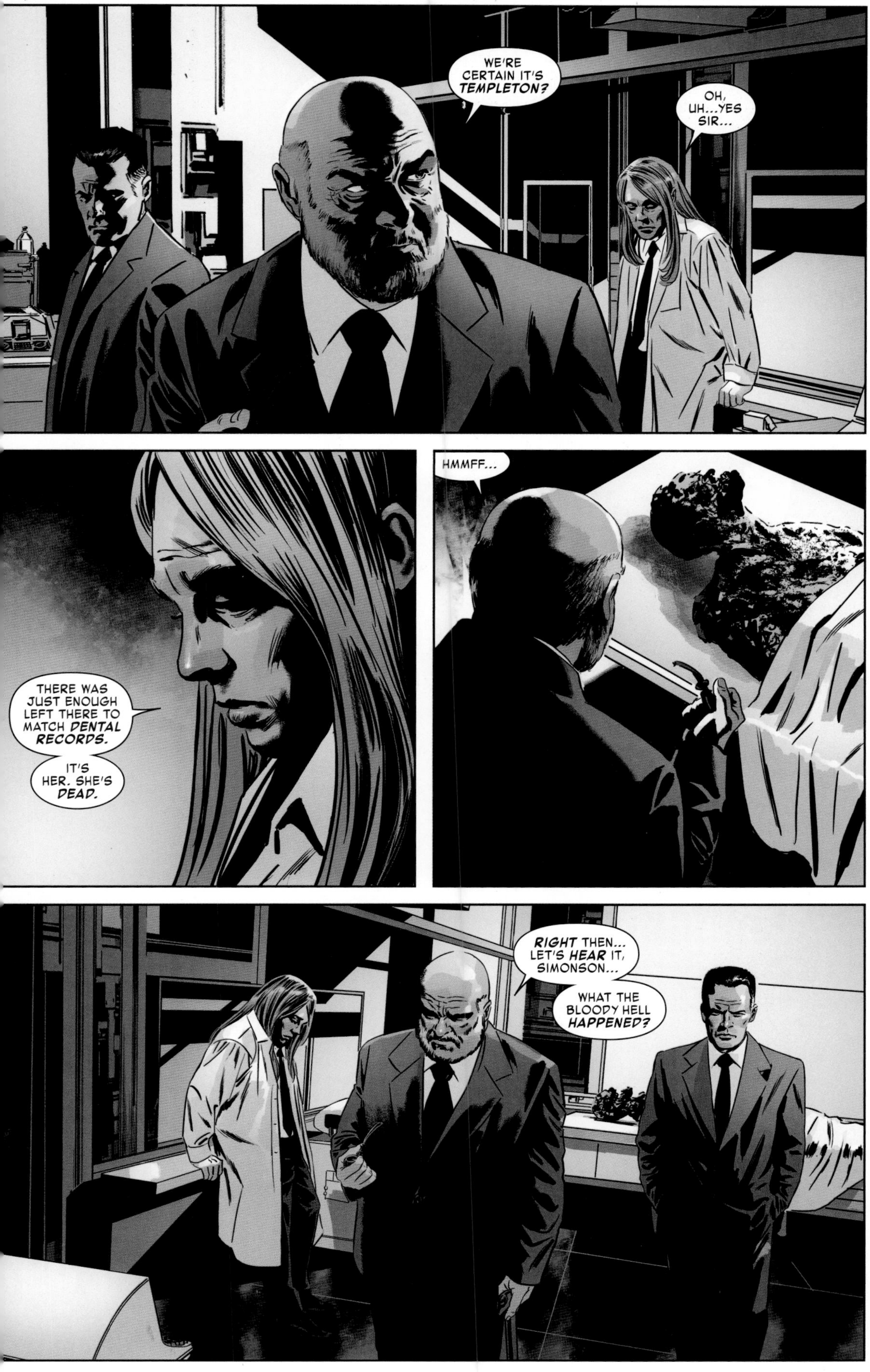
WE'RE CERTAIN IT'S TEMPLETON?
OH, UH...YES SIR...
THERE WAS JUST ENOUGH LEFT THERE TO MATCH DENTAL RECORDS.
IT'S HER. SHE'S DEAD.
HMMFF...
RIGHT THEN... LET'S HEAR IT, SIMONSON...
WHAT THE BLOODY HELL HAPPENED?

PART FIVE

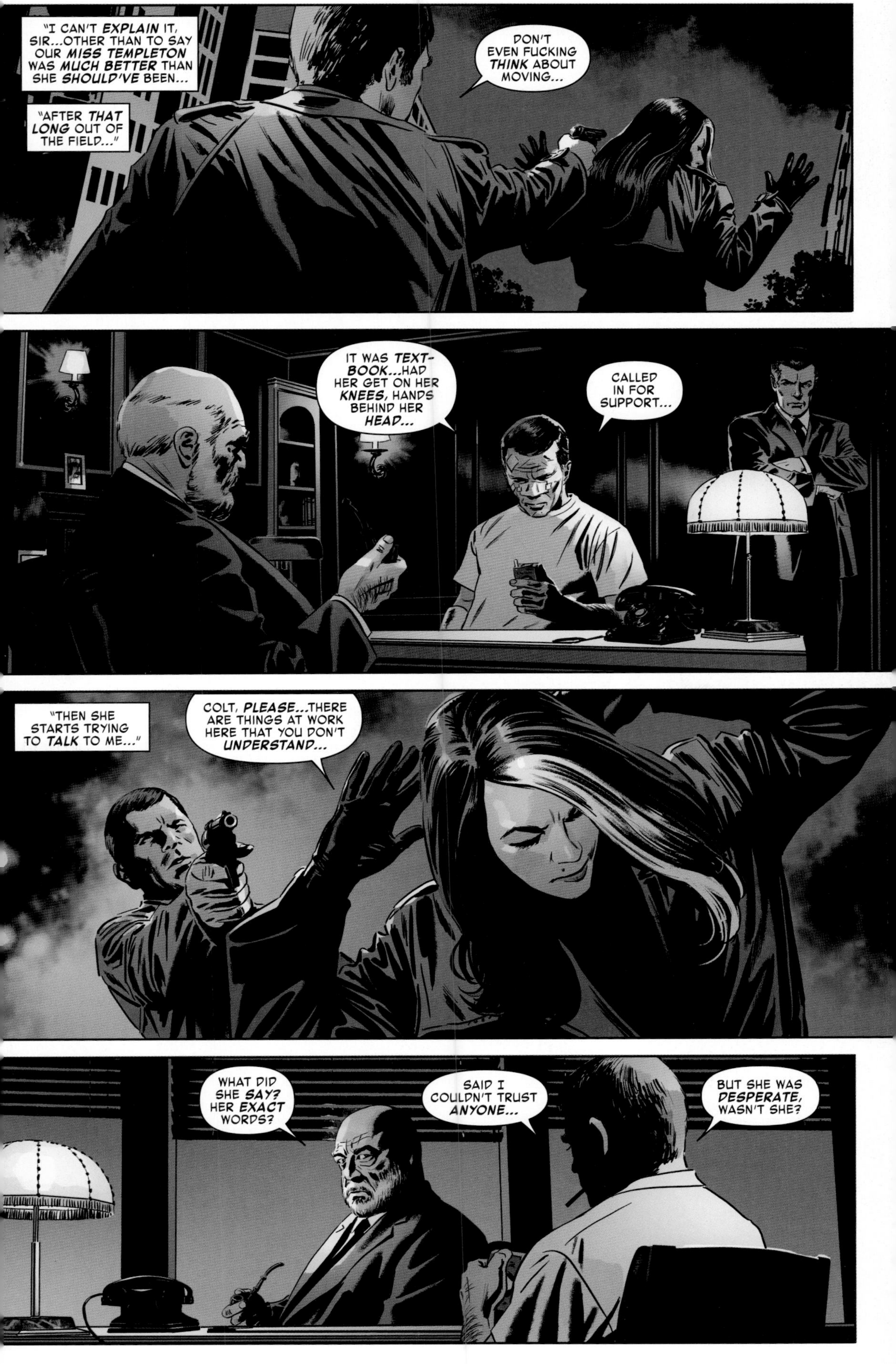
"I CAN'T EXPLAIN IT, SIR...OTHER THAN TO SAY OUR MISS TEMPLETON WAS MUCH BETTER THAN SHE SHOULD'VE BEEN...
"AFTER THAT LONG OUT OF THE FIELD..."
DON'T EVEN FUCKING THINK ABOUT MOVING...
IT WAS TEXT-BOOK...HAD HER GET ON HER KNEES, HANDS BEHIND HER HEAD...
CALLED IN FOR SUPPORT...
"THEN SHE STARTS TRYING TO TALK TO ME..."
COLT, PLEASE...THERE ARE THINGS AT WORK HERE THAT YOU DON'T UNDERSTAND...
WHAT DID SHE SAY? HER EXACT WORDS?
SAID I COULDN'T TRUST ANYONE...
BUT SHE WAS DESPERATE, WASN'T SHE?

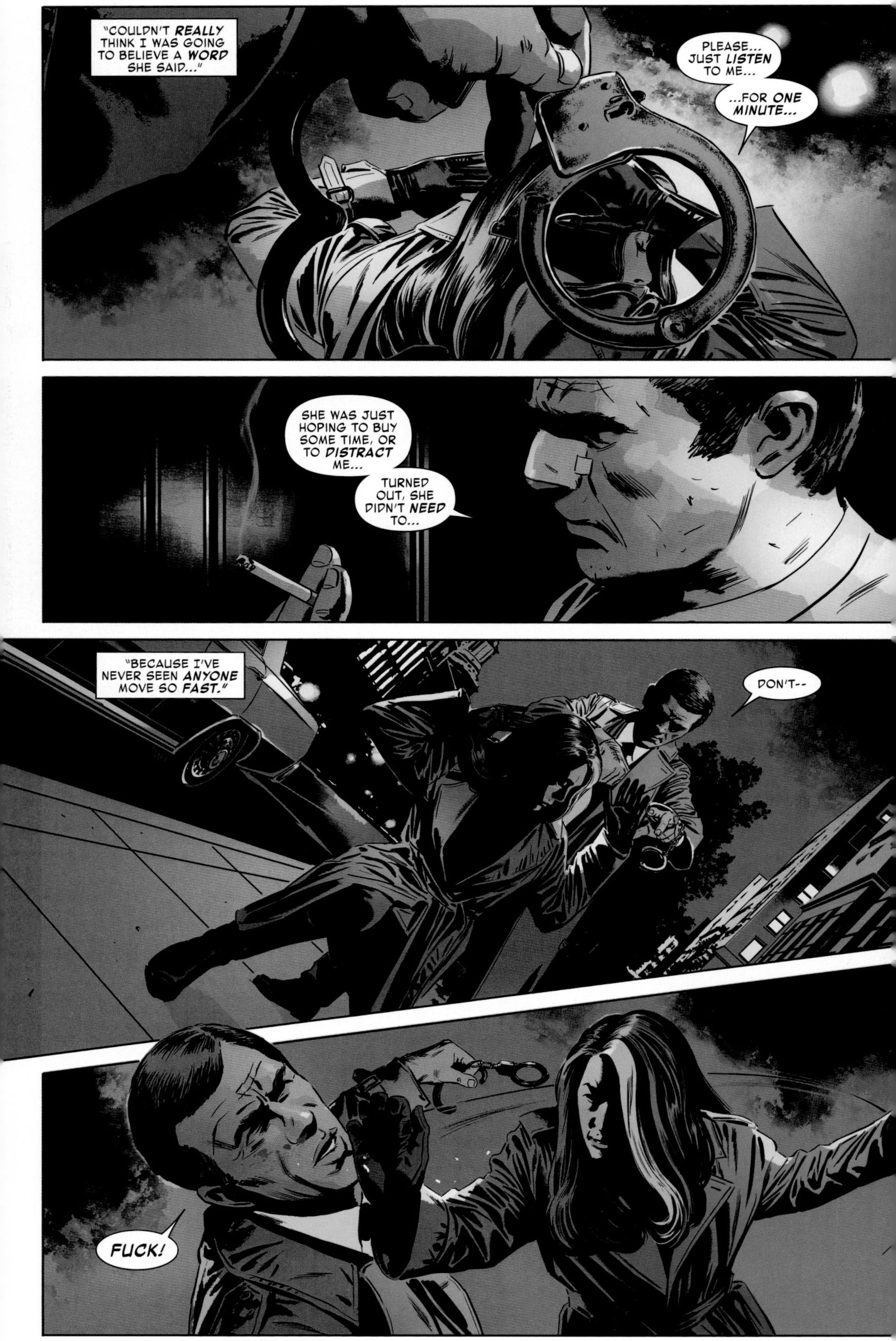
"COULDN'T REALLY THINK I WAS GOING TO BELIEVE A WORD SHE SAID..."
PLEASE... JUST LISTEN TO ME...
...FOR ONE MINUTE...
SHE WAS JUST HOPING TO BUY SOME TIME, OR TO DISTRACT ME...
TURNED OUT, SHE DIDN'T NEED TO...
"BECAUSE I'VE NEVER SEEN ANYONE MOVE SO FAST."
DON'T--
FUCK!

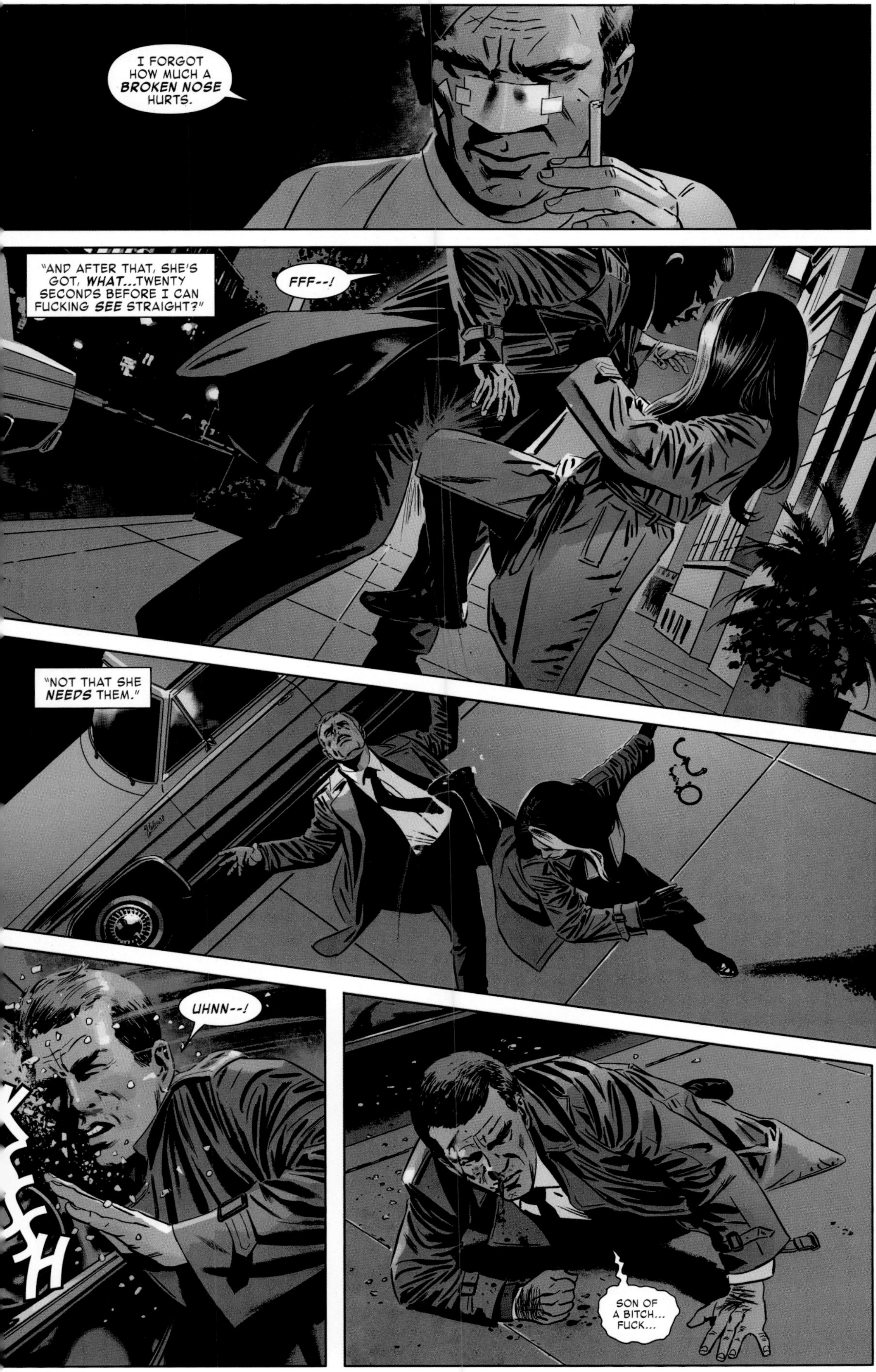
I FORGOT HOW MUCH A BROKEN NOSE HURTS.
"AND AFTER THAT, SHE'S GOT, WHAT...TWENTY SECONDS BEFORE I CAN FUCKING SEE STRAIGHT?"
FFF--!
"NOT THAT SHE NEEDS THEM."
UHNN--!
SON OF A BITCH... FUCK...

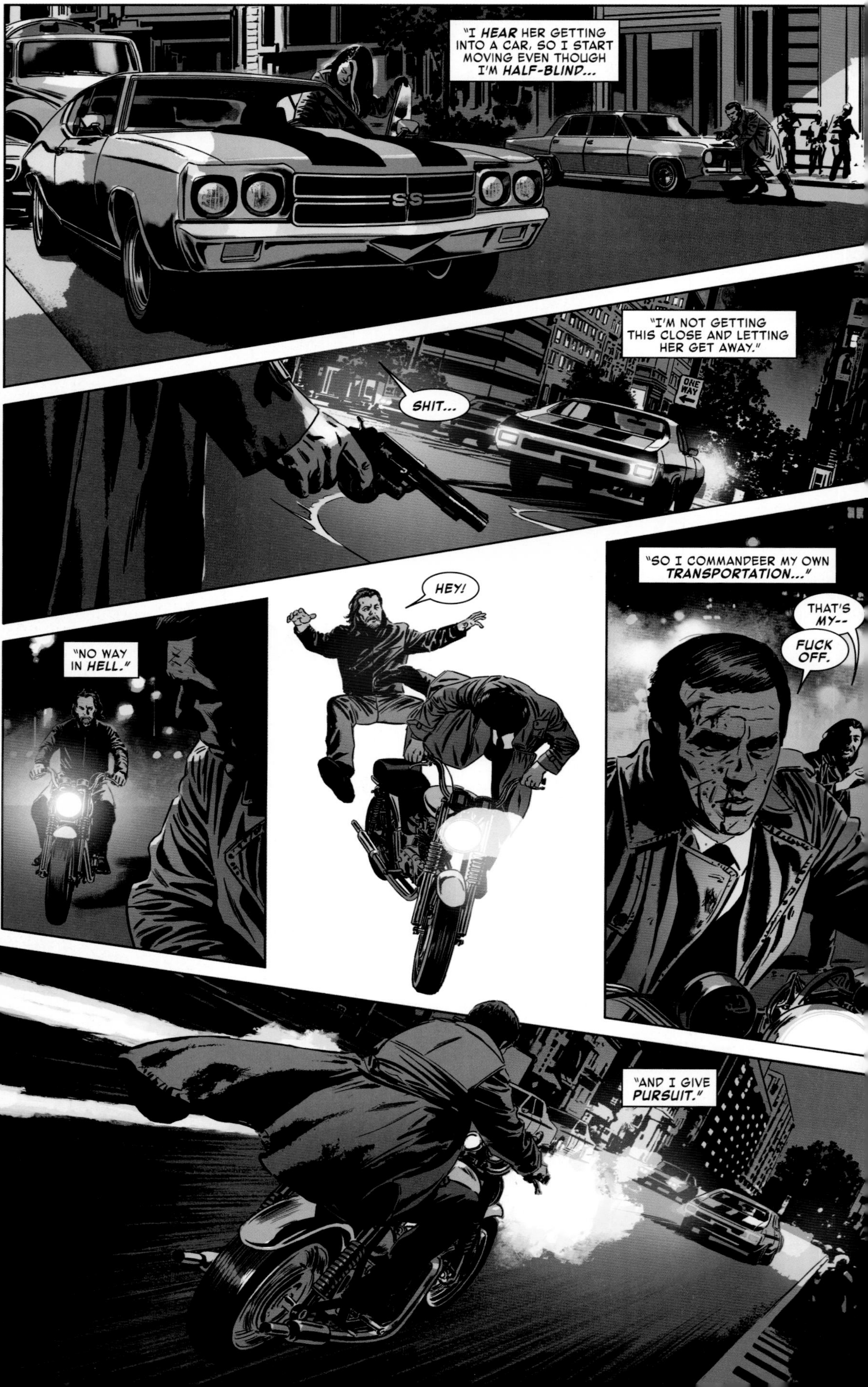
"I HEAR HER GETTING INTO A CAR, SO I START MOVING EVEN THOUGH I'M HALF-BLIND...
"I'M NOT GETTING THIS CLOSE AND LETTING HER GET AWAY."
ONE WAY
SHIT...
"NO WAY IN HELL."
HEY!
"SO I COMMANDEER MY OWN TRANSPORTATION..."
THAT'S MY--
FUCK OFF.
"AND I GIVE PURSUIT."

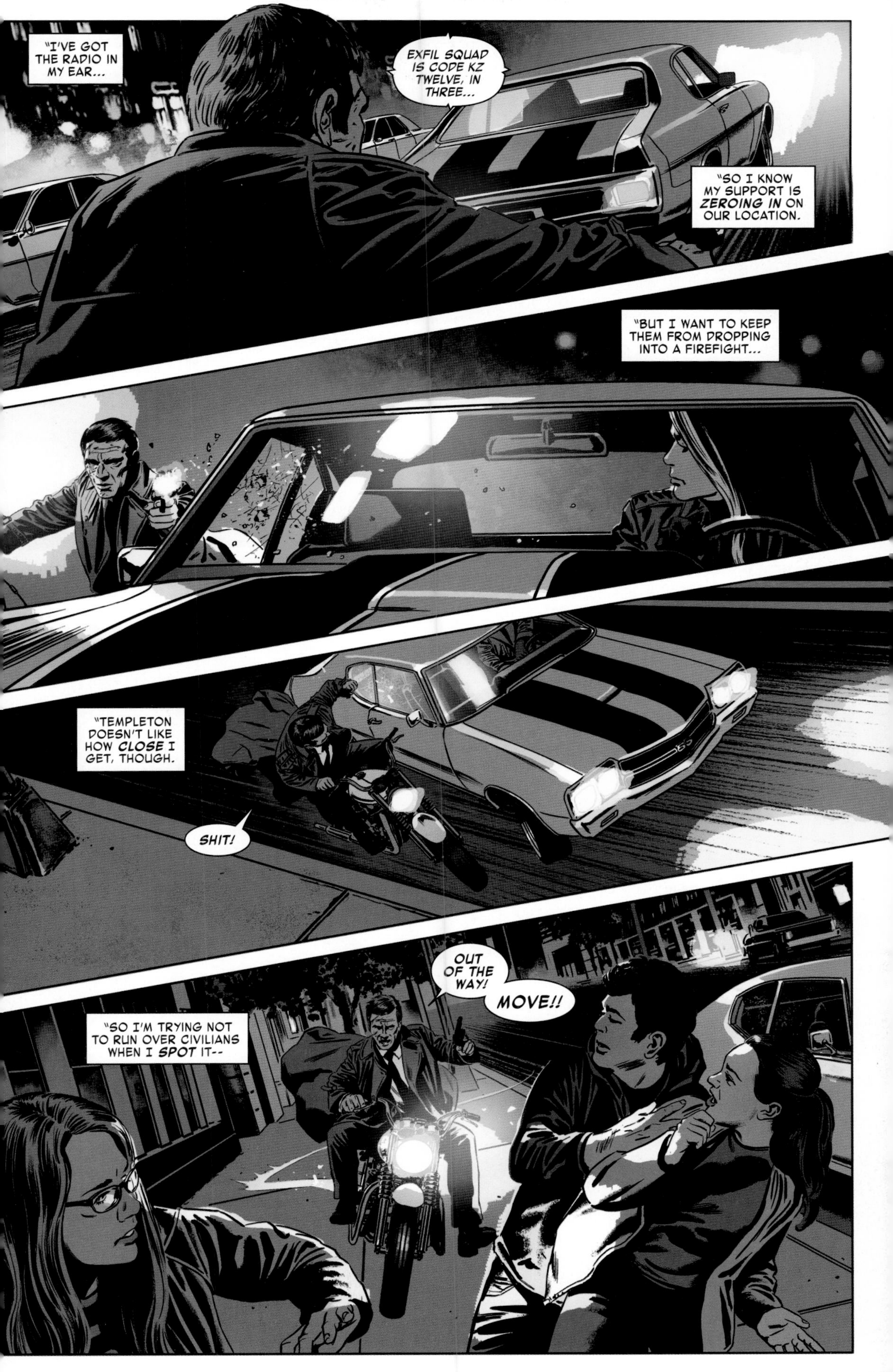
"I'VE GOT THE RADIO IN MY EAR...
EXFIL SQUAD IS CODE KZ TWELVE, IN THREE...
"SO I KNOW MY SUPPORT IS ZEROING IN ON OUR LOCATION.
"BUT I WANT TO KEEP THEM FROM DROPPING INTO A FIREFIGHT...
"TEMPLETON DOESN'T LIKE HOW CLOSE I GET, THOUGH.
SHIT!
"SO I'M TRYING NOT TO RUN OVER CIVILIANS WHEN I SPOT IT--
OUT OF THE WAY!
MOVE!!

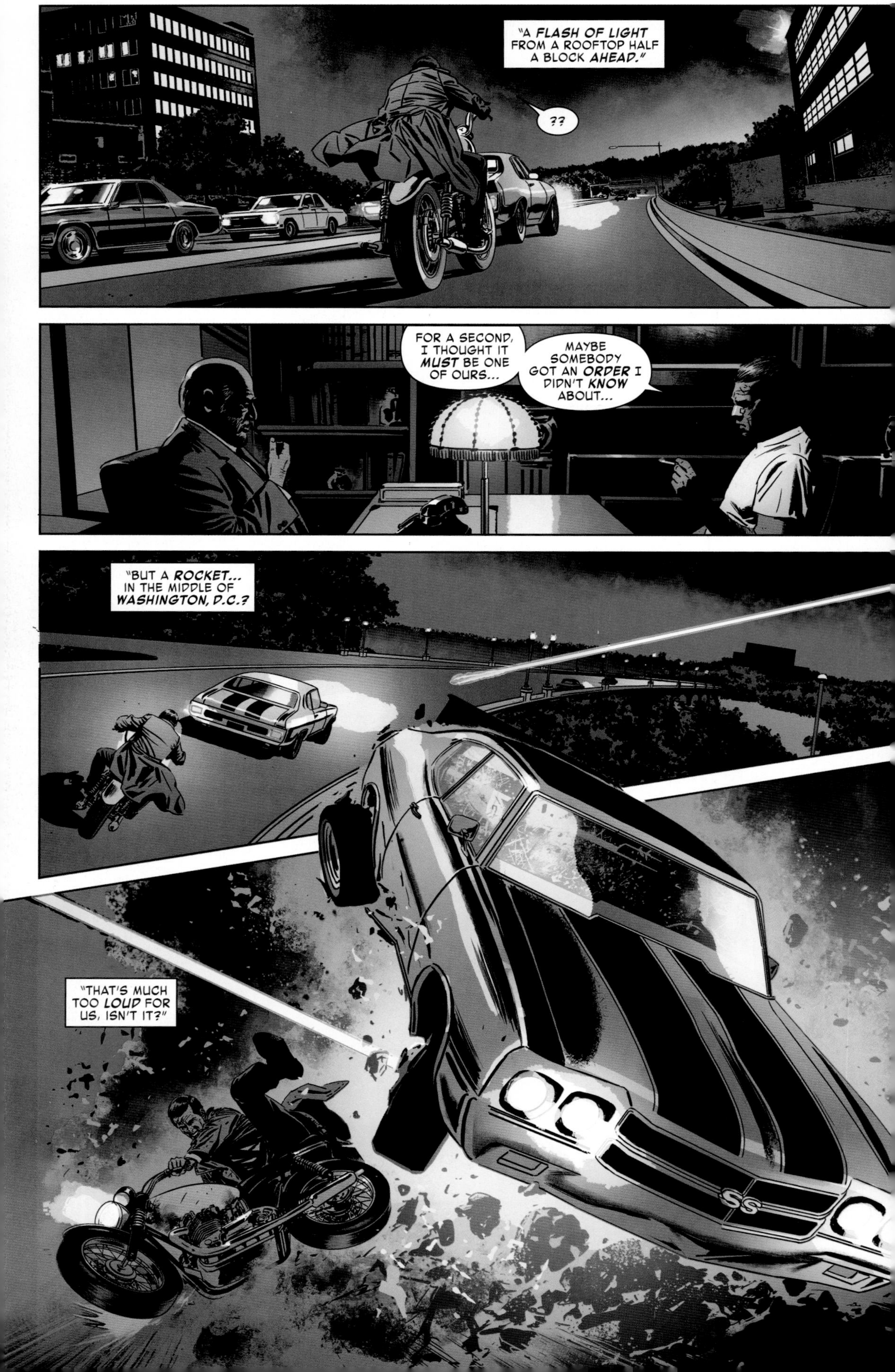
"A FLASH OF LIGHT FROM A ROOFTOP HALF A BLOCK AHEAD."
??
FOR A SECOND, I THOUGHT IT MUST BE ONE OF OURS...
MAYBE SOMEBODY GOT AN ORDER I DIDN'T KNOW ABOUT...
"BUT A ROCKET... IN THE MIDDLE OF WASHINGTON, D.C.?
"THAT'S MUCH TOO LOUD FOR US, ISN'T IT?"
SS

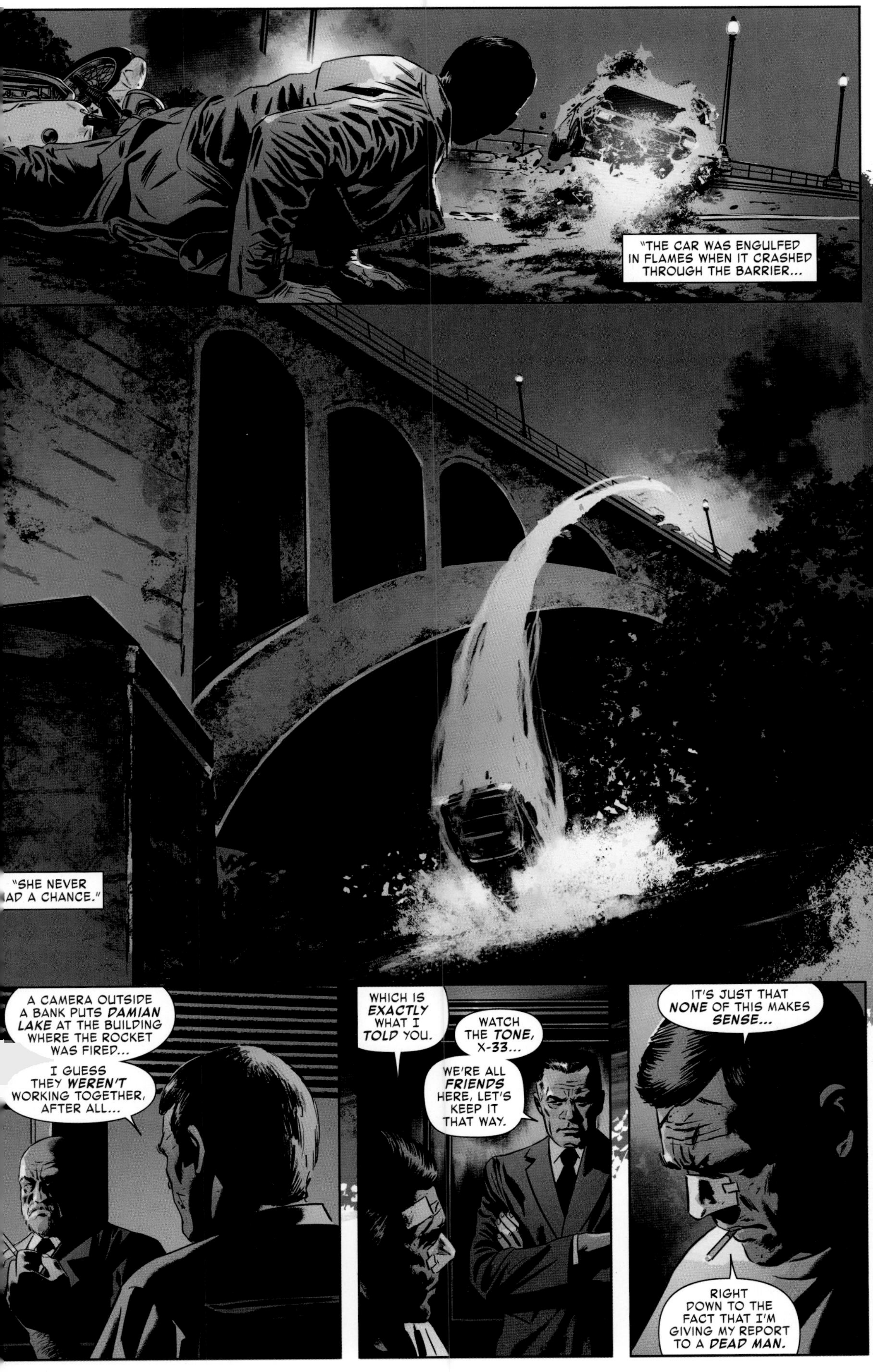
"THE CAR WAS ENGULFED IN FLAMES WHEN IT CRASHED THROUGH THE BARRIER...
"SHE NEVER
AD A CHANCE."
A CAMERA OUTSIDE A BANK PUTS DAMIAN LAKE AT THE BUILDING WHERE THE ROCKET WAS FIRED...
I GUESS THEY WEREN'T WORKING TOGETHER, AFTER ALL...
WHICH IS EXACTLY WHAT I TOLD YOU.
WATCH THE TONE, X-33...
WE'RE ALL FRIENDS HERE, LET'S KEEP IT THAT WAY.
IT'S JUST THAT NONE OF THIS MAKES SENSE...
RIGHT DOWN TO THE FACT THAT I'M GIVING MY REPORT TO A DEAD MAN.

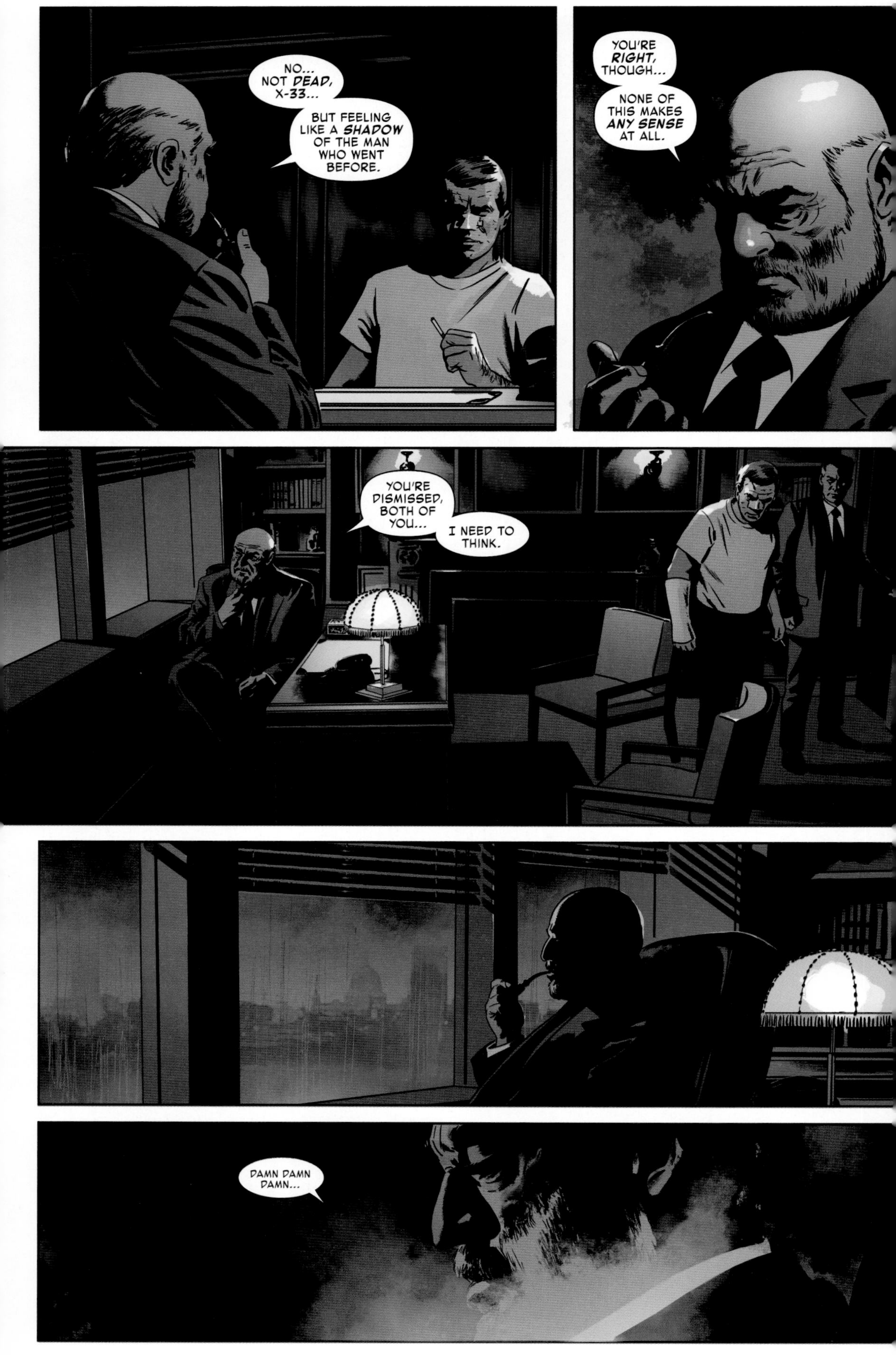
NO... NOT DEAD, X-33...
BUT FEELING LIKE A SHADOW OF THE MAN WHO WENT BEFORE.
YOU'RE RIGHT, THOUGH...
NONE OF THIS MAKES ANY SENSE AT ALL.
YOU'RE DISMISSED, BOTH OF YOU...
I NEED TO THINK.
DAMN DAMN DAMN...

THREE WEEKS LATER

WILL YOU BE NEEDING A CAR, SIR?

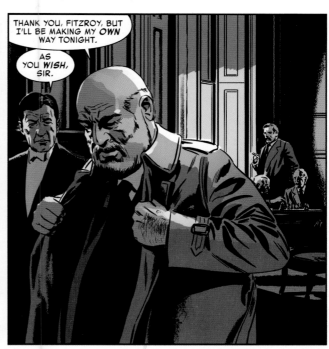

THANK YOU, FITZROY, BUT I'LL BE MAKING MY *OWN* WAY TONIGHT.

AS YOU *WISH*, SIR.

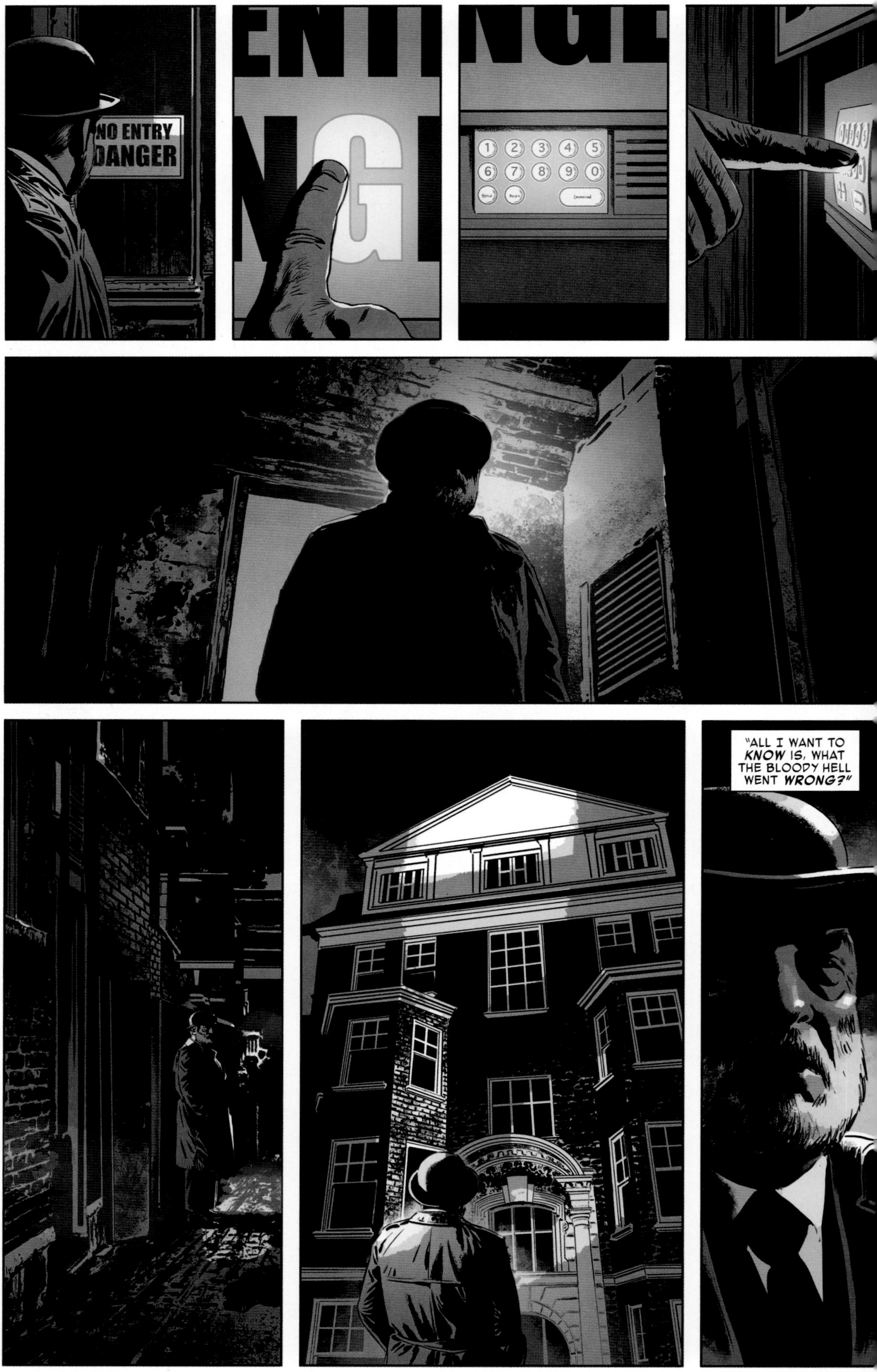
NO ENTRY
DANGER
"ALL I WANT TO KNOW IS, WHAT THE BLOODY HELL WENT WRONG?"

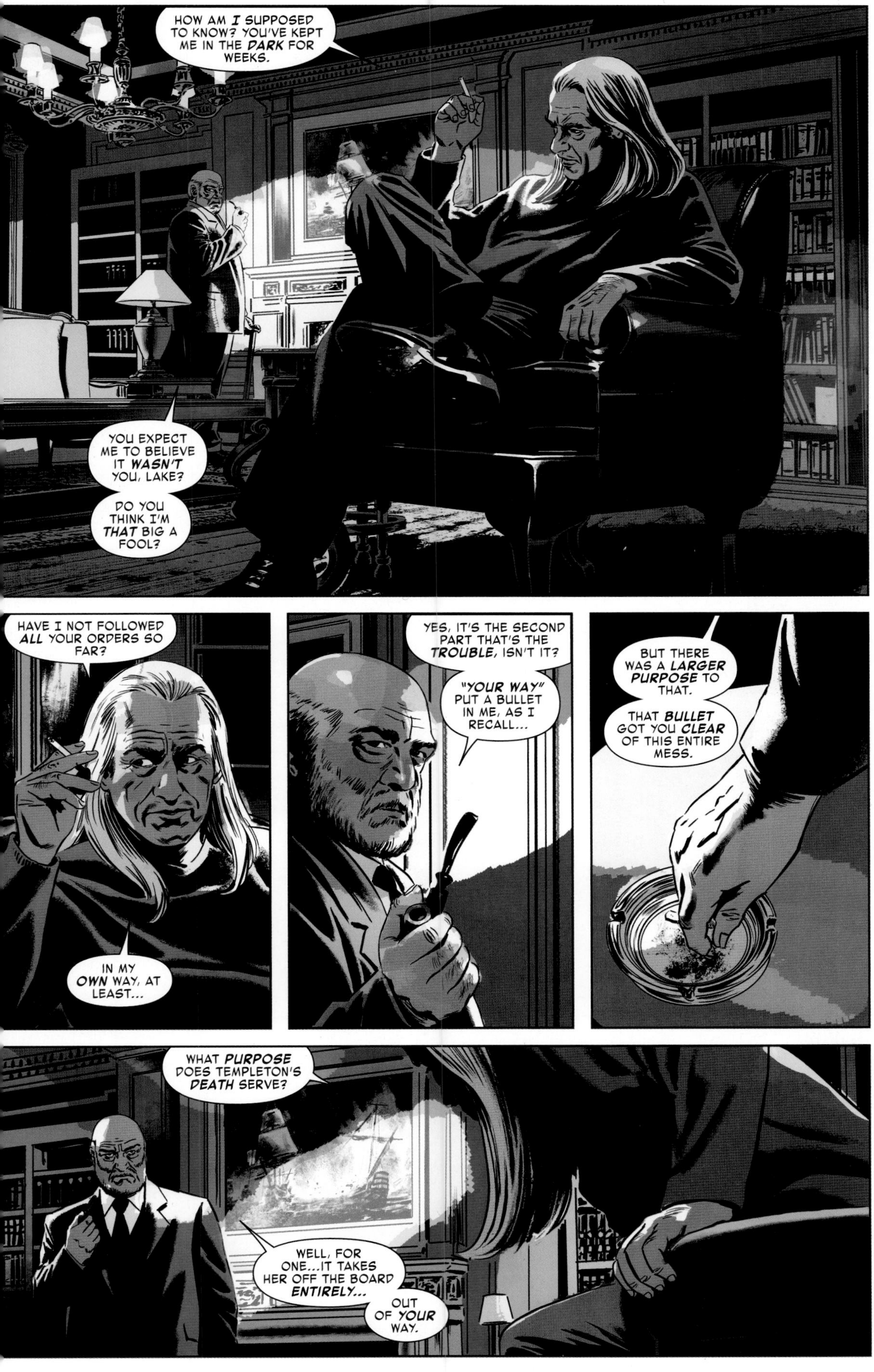

HOW AM I SUPPOSED TO KNOW? YOU'VE KEPT ME IN THE DARK FOR WEEKS.
YOU EXPECT ME TO BELIEVE IT WASN'T YOU, LAKE?
DO YOU THINK I'M THAT BIG A FOOL?
HAVE I NOT FOLLOWED ALL YOUR ORDERS SO FAR?
IN MY OWN WAY, AT LEAST...
YES, IT'S THE SECOND PART THAT'S THE TROUBLE, ISN'T IT?
"YOUR WAY" PUT A BULLET IN ME, AS I RECALL...
BUT THERE WAS A LARGER PURPOSE TO THAT.
THAT BULLET GOT YOU CLEAR OF THIS ENTIRE MESS.
WHAT PURPOSE DOES TEMPLETON'S DEATH SERVE?
WELL, FOR ONE...IT TAKES HER OFF THE BOARD ENTIRELY...
OUT OF YOUR WAY.

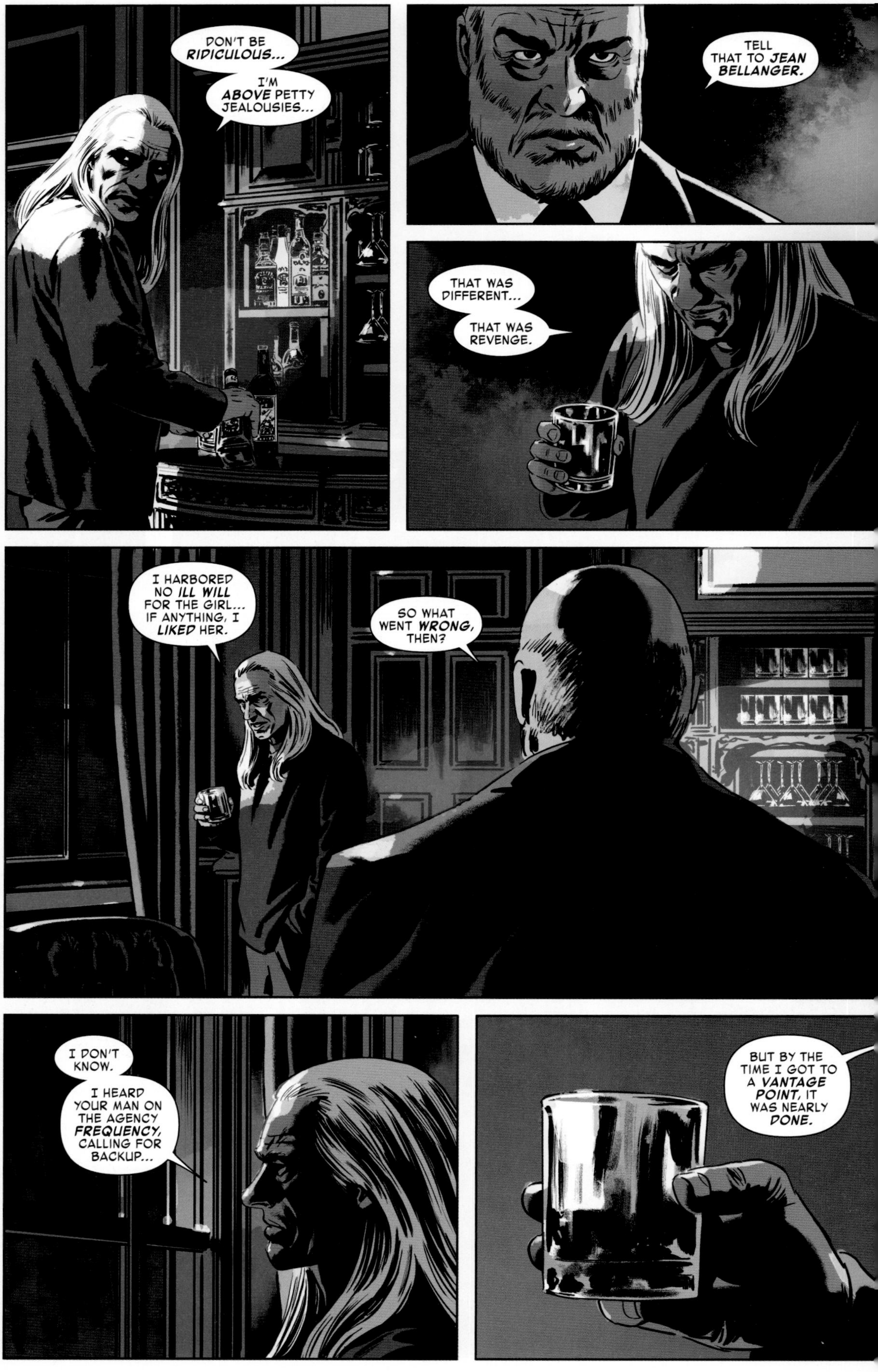

DON'T BE RIDICULOUS...
I'M ABOVE PETTY JEALOUSIES...
TELL THAT TO JEAN BELLANGER.
THAT WAS DIFFERENT...
THAT WAS REVENGE.
I HARBORED NO ILL WILL FOR THE GIRL... IF ANYTHING, I LIKED HER.
SO WHAT WENT WRONG, THEN?
I DON'T KNOW.
I HEARD YOUR MAN ON THE AGENCY FREQUENCY, CALLING FOR BACKUP...
BUT BY THE TIME I GOT TO A VANTAGE POINT, IT WAS NEARLY DONE.

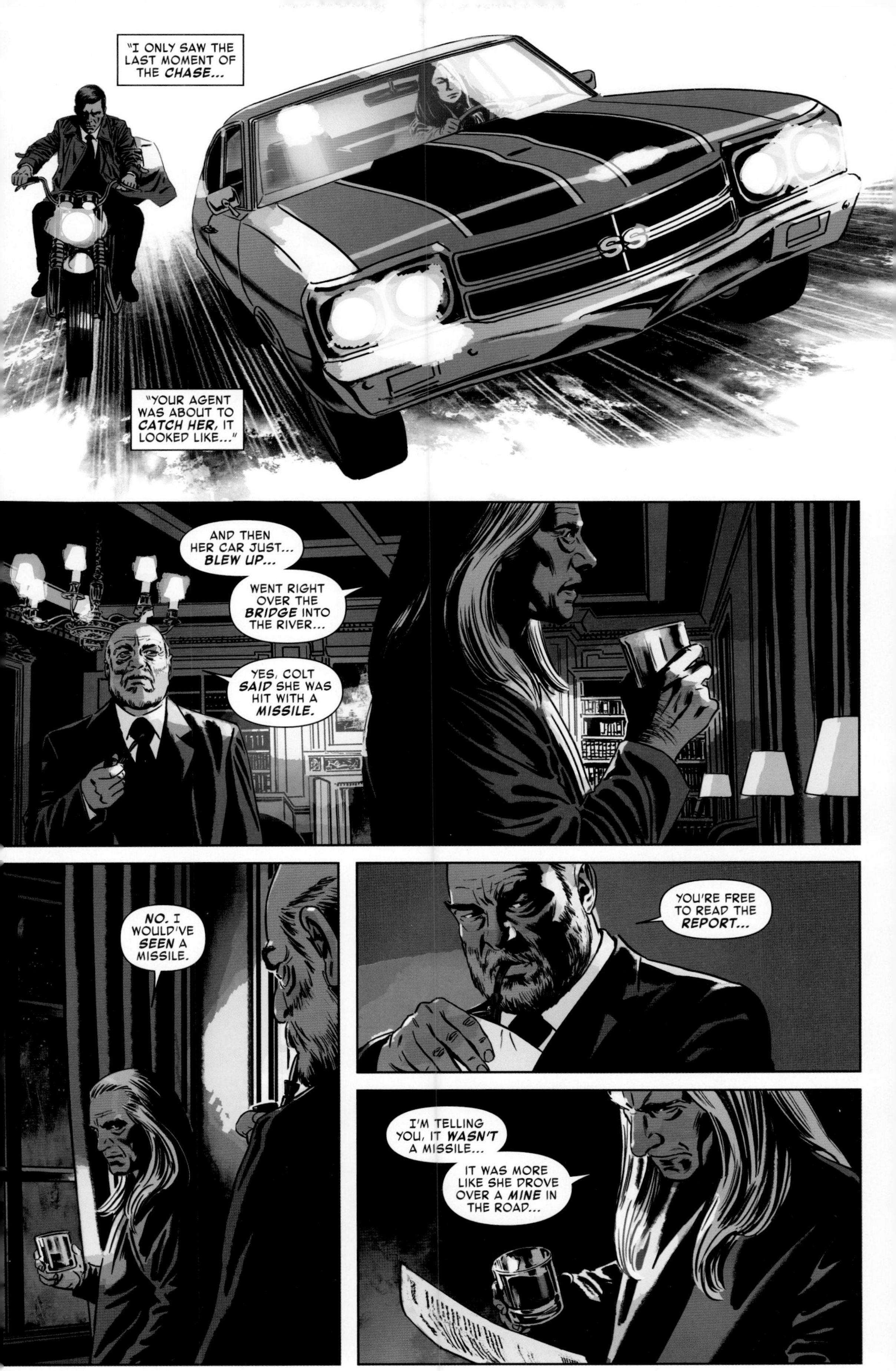

"I ONLY SAW THE LAST MOMENT OF THE CHASE...
"YOUR AGENT WAS ABOUT TO CATCH HER, IT LOOKED LIKE..."
AND THEN HER CAR JUST... BLEW UP...
WENT RIGHT OVER THE BRIDGE INTO THE RIVER...
YES, COLT SAID SHE WAS HIT WITH A MISSILE.
NO. I WOULD'VE SEEN A MISSILE.
YOU'RE FREE TO READ THE REPORT...
I'M TELLING YOU, IT WASN'T A MISSILE...
IT WAS MORE LIKE SHE DROVE OVER A MINE IN THE ROAD...

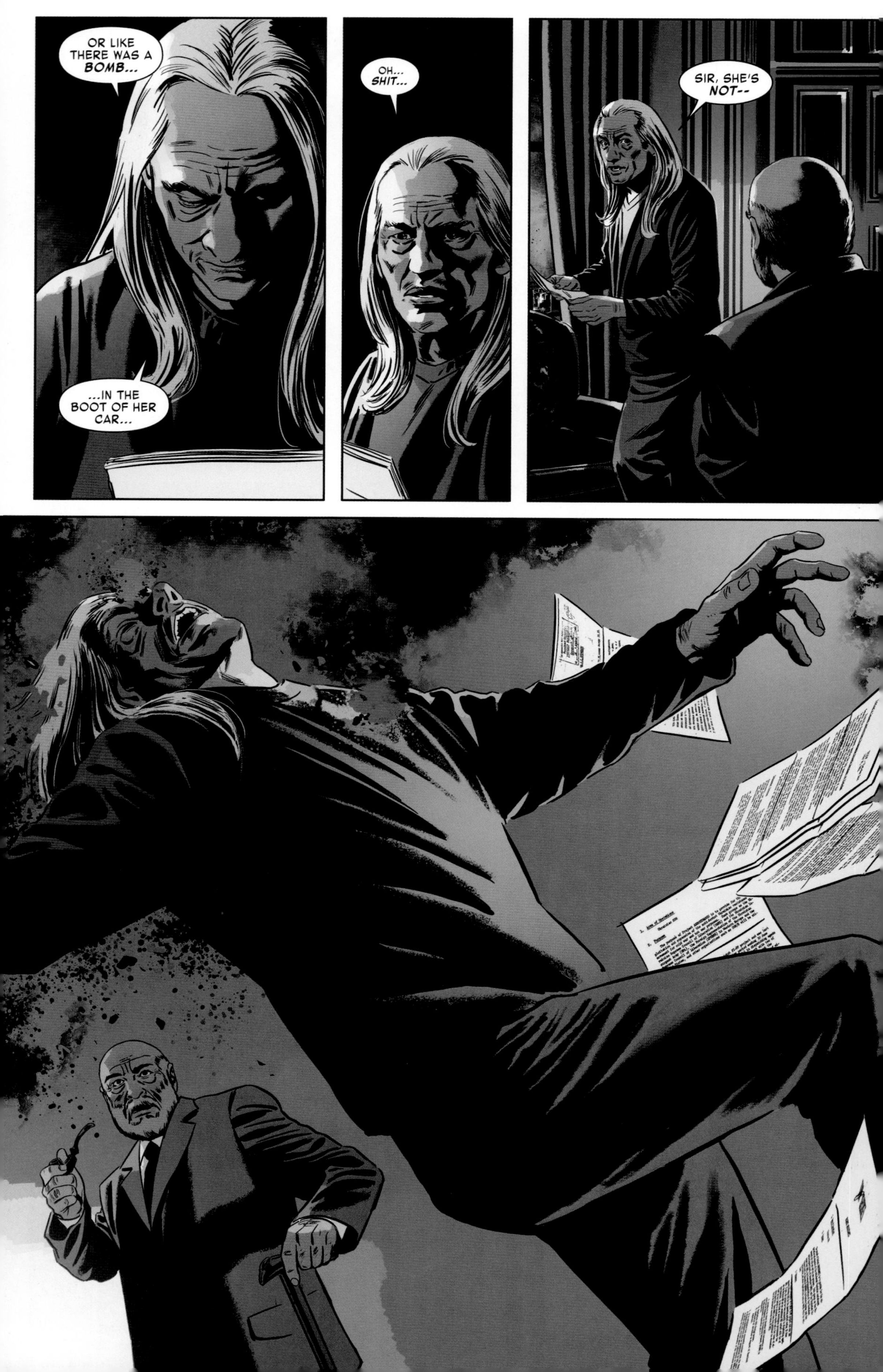
OR LIKE THERE WAS A *BOMB...*
...IN THE BOOT OF HER CAR...
OH... *SHIT...*
SIR, SHE'S *NOT--*

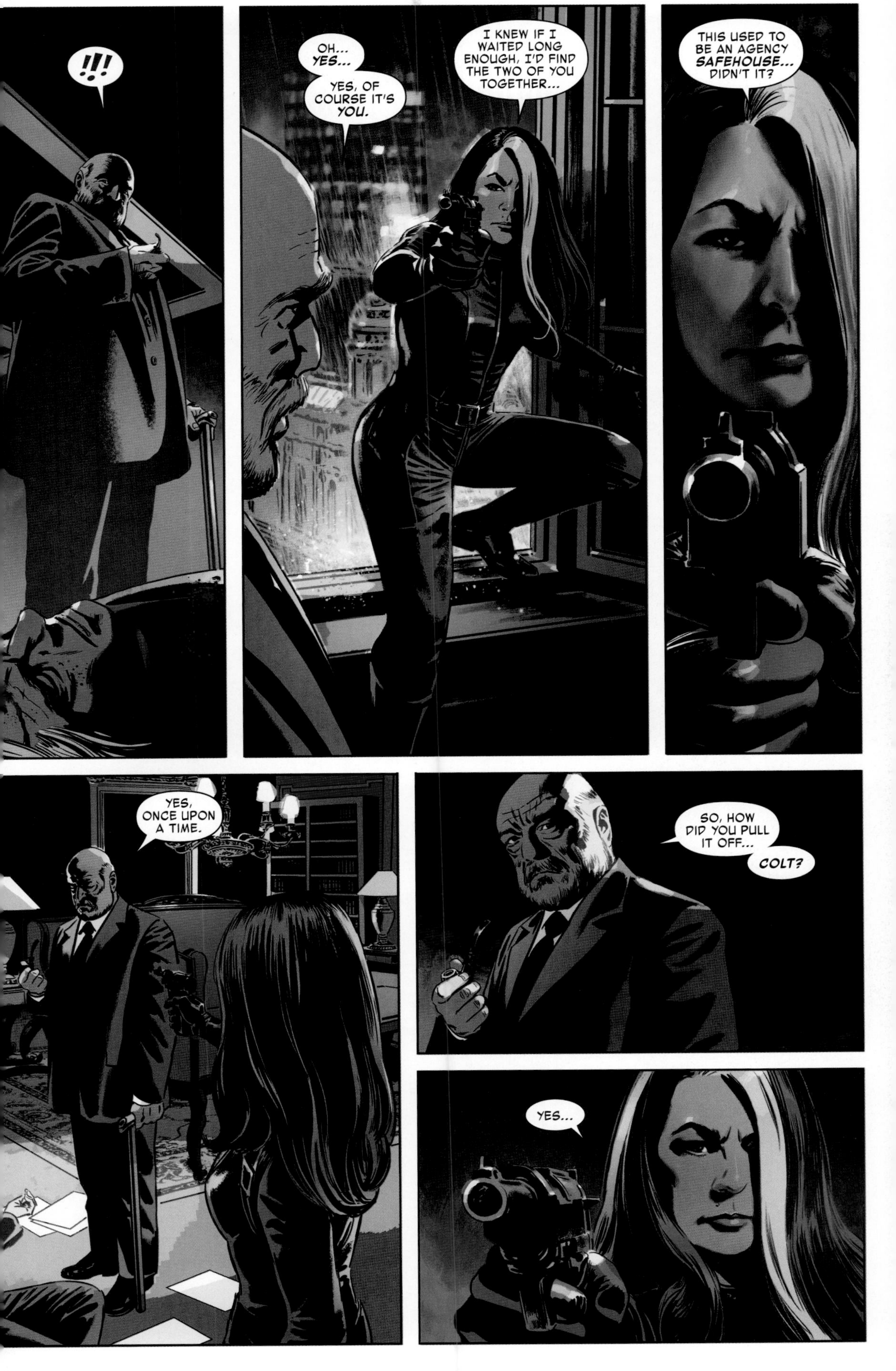
!!!
OH... YES...
YES, OF COURSE IT'S YOU.
I KNEW IF I WAITED LONG ENOUGH, I'D FIND THE TWO OF YOU TOGETHER...
THIS USED TO BE AN AGENCY SAFEHOUSE... DIDN'T IT?
YES, ONCE UPON A TIME.
SO, HOW DID YOU PULL IT OFF...
COLT?
YES...

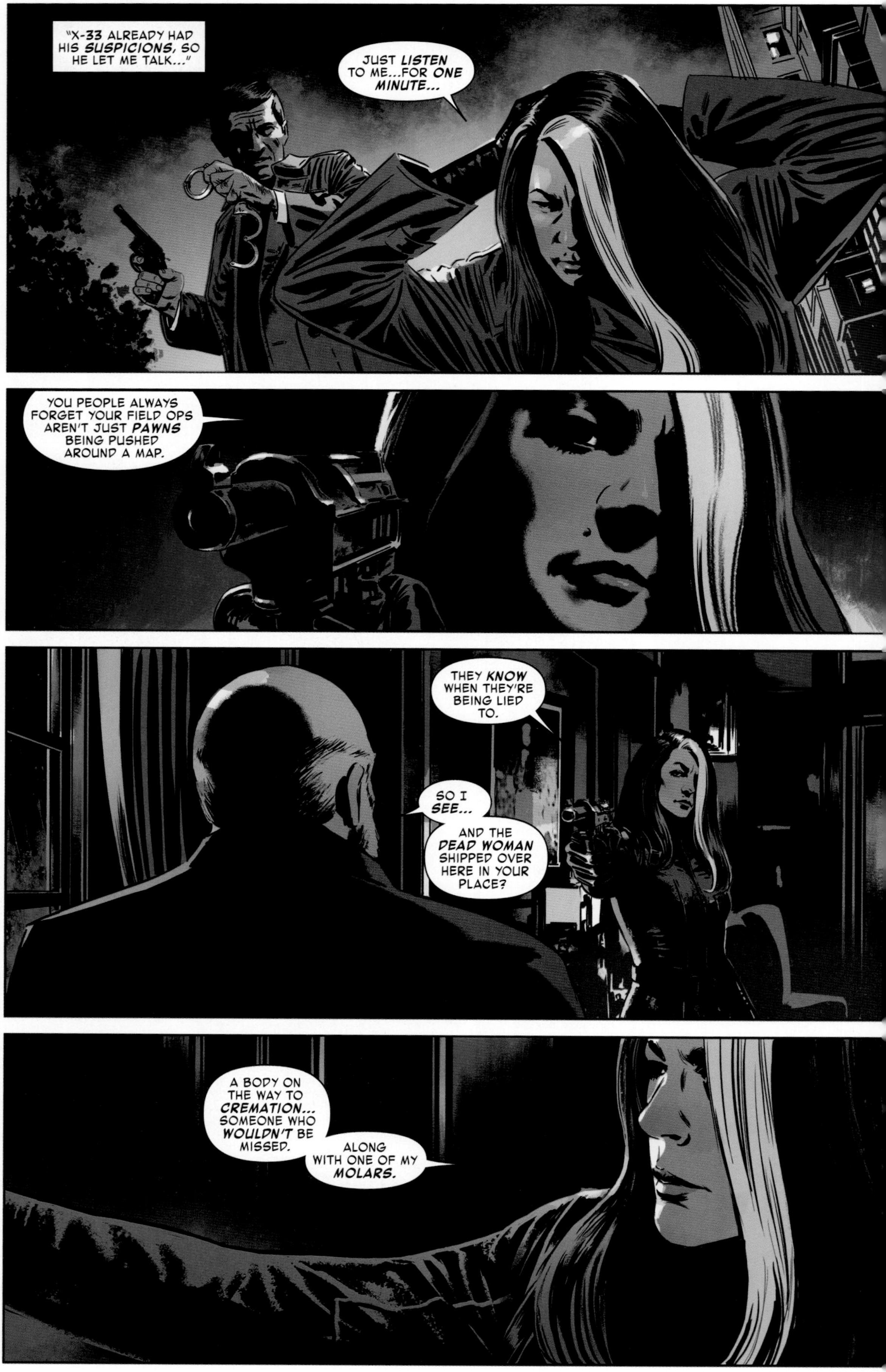
"X-33 ALREADY HAD HIS SUSPICIONS, SO HE LET ME TALK..."
JUST LISTEN TO ME...FOR ONE MINUTE...
YOU PEOPLE ALWAYS FORGET YOUR FIELD OPS AREN'T JUST PAWNS BEING PUSHED AROUND A MAP.
THEY KNOW WHEN THEY'RE BEING LIED TO.
SO I SEE...
AND THE DEAD WOMAN SHIPPED OVER HERE IN YOUR PLACE?
A BODY ON THE WAY TO CREMATION... SOMEONE WHO WOULDN'T BE MISSED.
ALONG WITH ONE OF MY MOLARS.

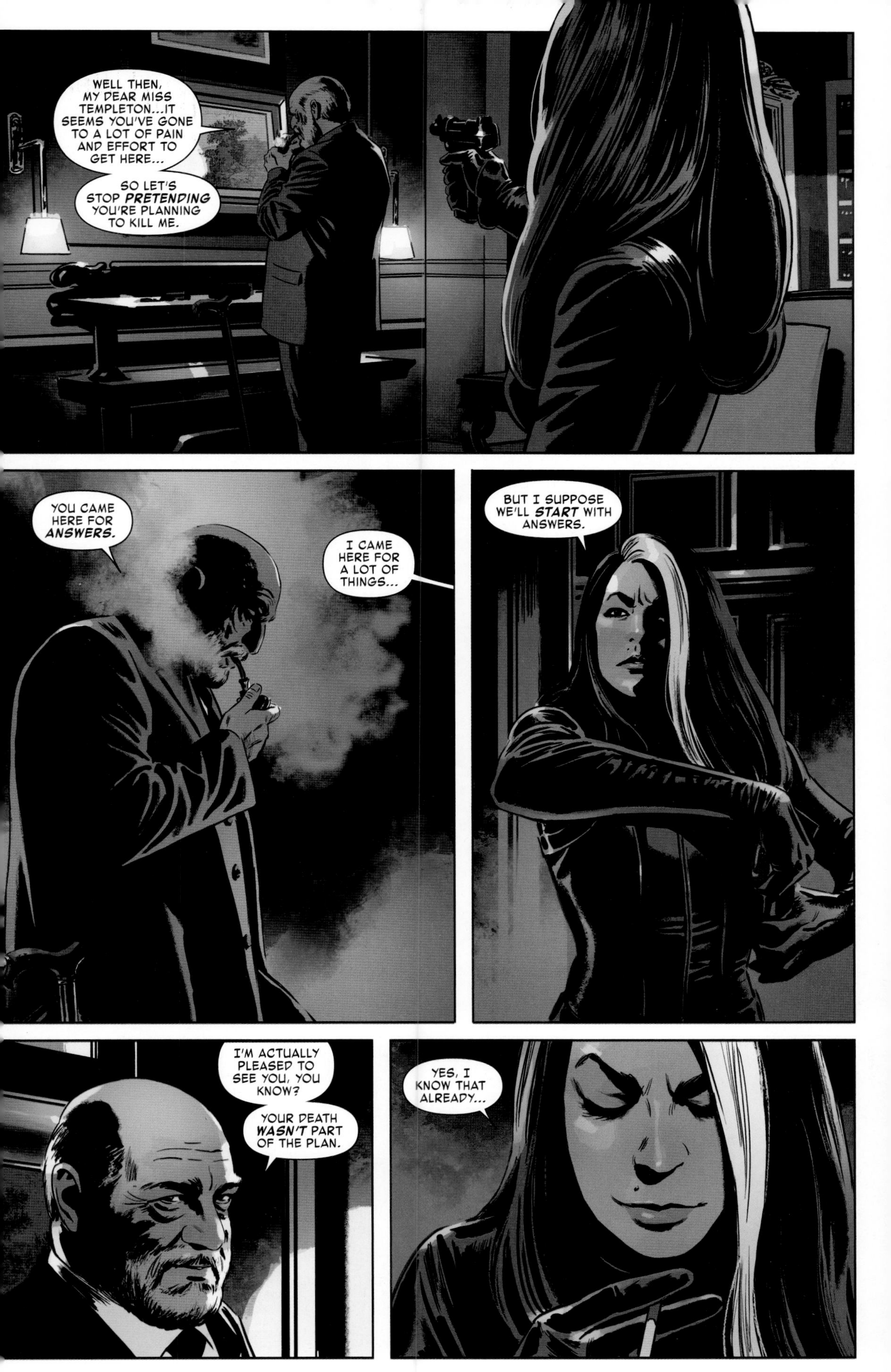
WELL THEN, MY DEAR MISS TEMPLETON...IT SEEMS YOU'VE GONE TO A LOT OF PAIN AND EFFORT TO GET HERE...
SO LET'S STOP *PRETENDING* YOU'RE PLANNING TO KILL ME.
YOU CAME HERE FOR *ANSWERS.*
I CAME HERE FOR A LOT OF THINGS...
BUT I SUPPOSE WE'LL *START* WITH ANSWERS.
I'M ACTUALLY PLEASED TO SEE YOU, YOU KNOW?
YOUR DEATH *WASN'T* PART OF THE PLAN.
YES, I KNOW THAT ALREADY...

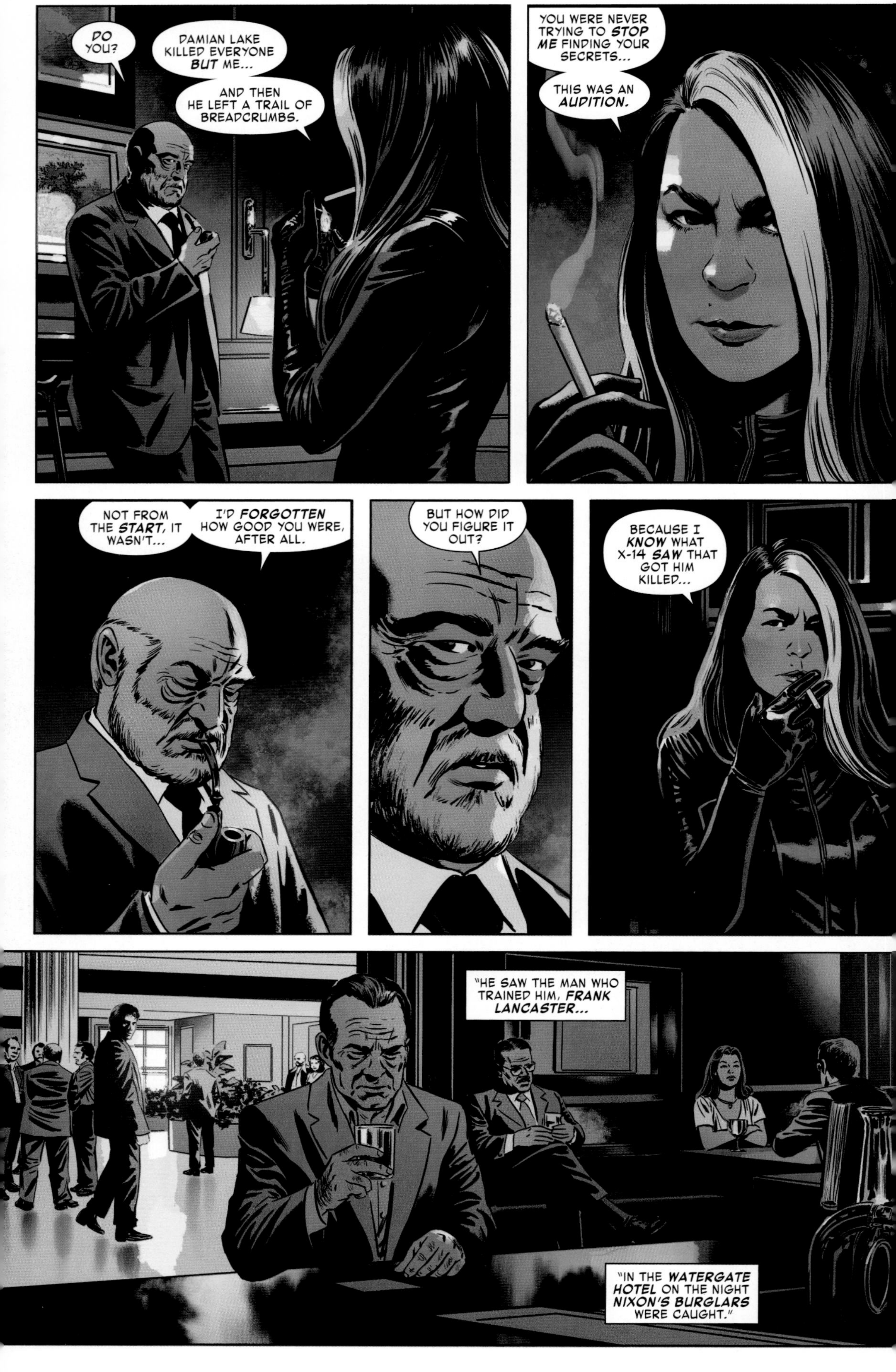
DO YOU?
DAMIAN LAKE KILLED EVERYONE BUT ME...
AND THEN HE LEFT A TRAIL OF BREADCRUMBS.
YOU WERE NEVER TRYING TO STOP ME FINDING YOUR SECRETS...
THIS WAS AN AUDITION.
NOT FROM THE START, IT WASN'T...
I'D FORGOTTEN HOW GOOD YOU WERE, AFTER ALL.
BUT HOW DID YOU FIGURE IT OUT?
BECAUSE I KNOW WHAT X-14 SAW THAT GOT HIM KILLED...
"HE SAW THE MAN WHO TRAINED HIM, FRANK LANCASTER...
"IN THE WATERGATE HOTEL ON THE NIGHT NIXON'S BURGLARS WERE CAUGHT."

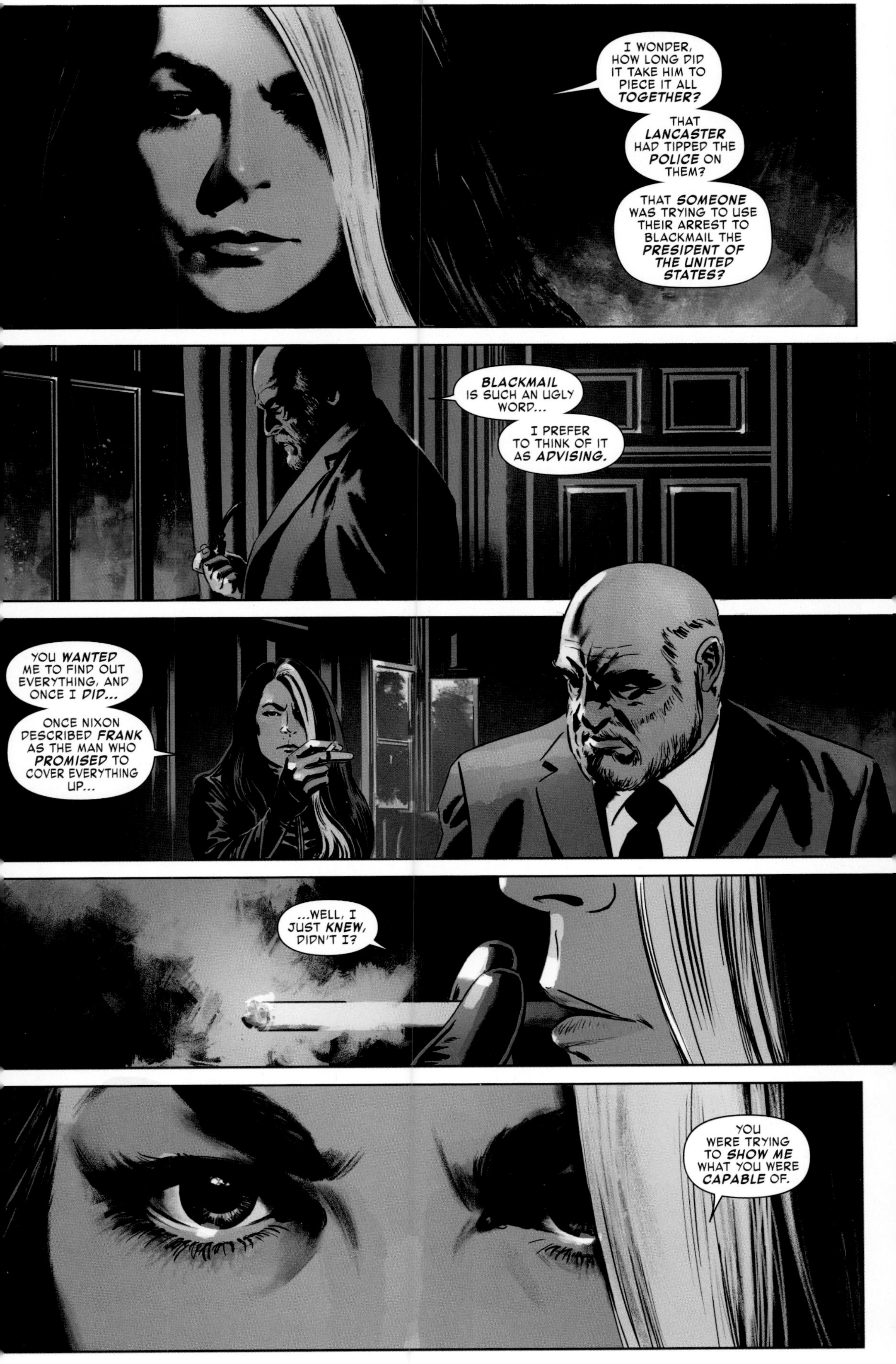
I WONDER, HOW LONG DID IT TAKE HIM TO PIECE IT ALL TOGETHER?
THAT LANCASTER HAD TIPPED THE POLICE ON THEM?
THAT SOMEONE WAS TRYING TO USE THEIR ARREST TO BLACKMAIL THE PRESIDENT OF THE UNITED STATES?
BLACKMAIL IS SUCH AN UGLY WORD...
I PREFER TO THINK OF IT AS ADVISING.
YOU WANTED ME TO FIND OUT EVERYTHING, AND ONCE I DID...
ONCE NIXON DESCRIBED FRANK AS THE MAN WHO PROMISED TO COVER EVERYTHING UP...
...WELL, I JUST KNEW, DIDN'T I?
YOU WERE TRYING TO SHOW ME WHAT YOU WERE CAPABLE OF.

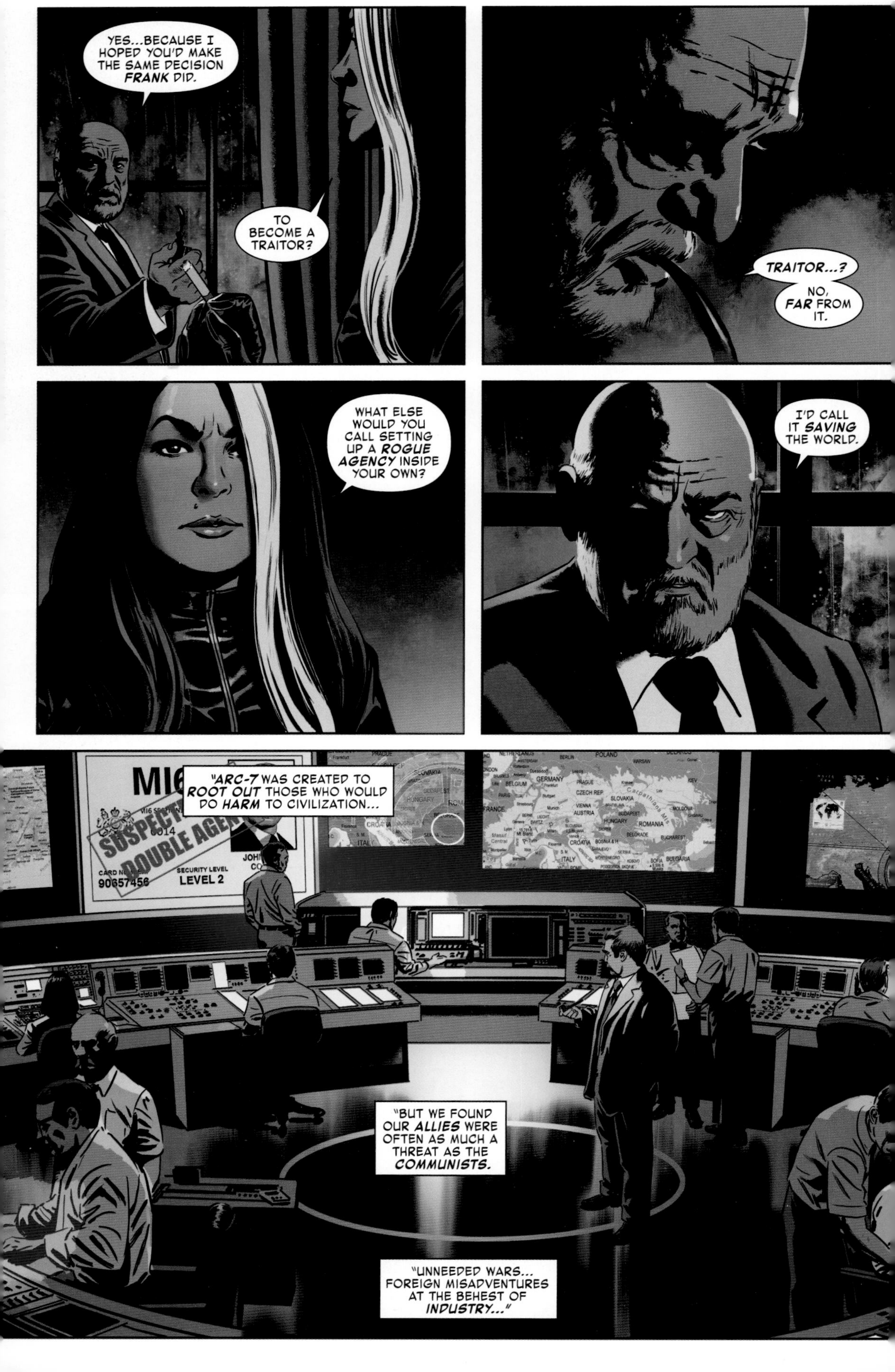
YES...BECAUSE I HOPED YOU'D MAKE THE SAME DECISION FRANK DID.
TO BECOME A TRAITOR?
TRAITOR...? NO, FAR FROM IT.
WHAT ELSE WOULD YOU CALL SETTING UP A ROGUE AGENCY INSIDE YOUR OWN?
I'D CALL IT SAVING THE WORLD.
"ARC-7 WAS CREATED TO ROOT OUT THOSE WHO WOULD DO HARM TO CIVILIZATION...
MI6
SUSPECTED DOUBLE AGENT
CARD NUMBER
90657456
SECURITY LEVEL
LEVEL 2
"BUT WE FOUND OUR ALLIES WERE OFTEN AS MUCH A THREAT AS THE COMMUNISTS.
"UNNEEDED WARS... FOREIGN MISADVENTURES AT THE BEHEST OF INDUSTRY..."

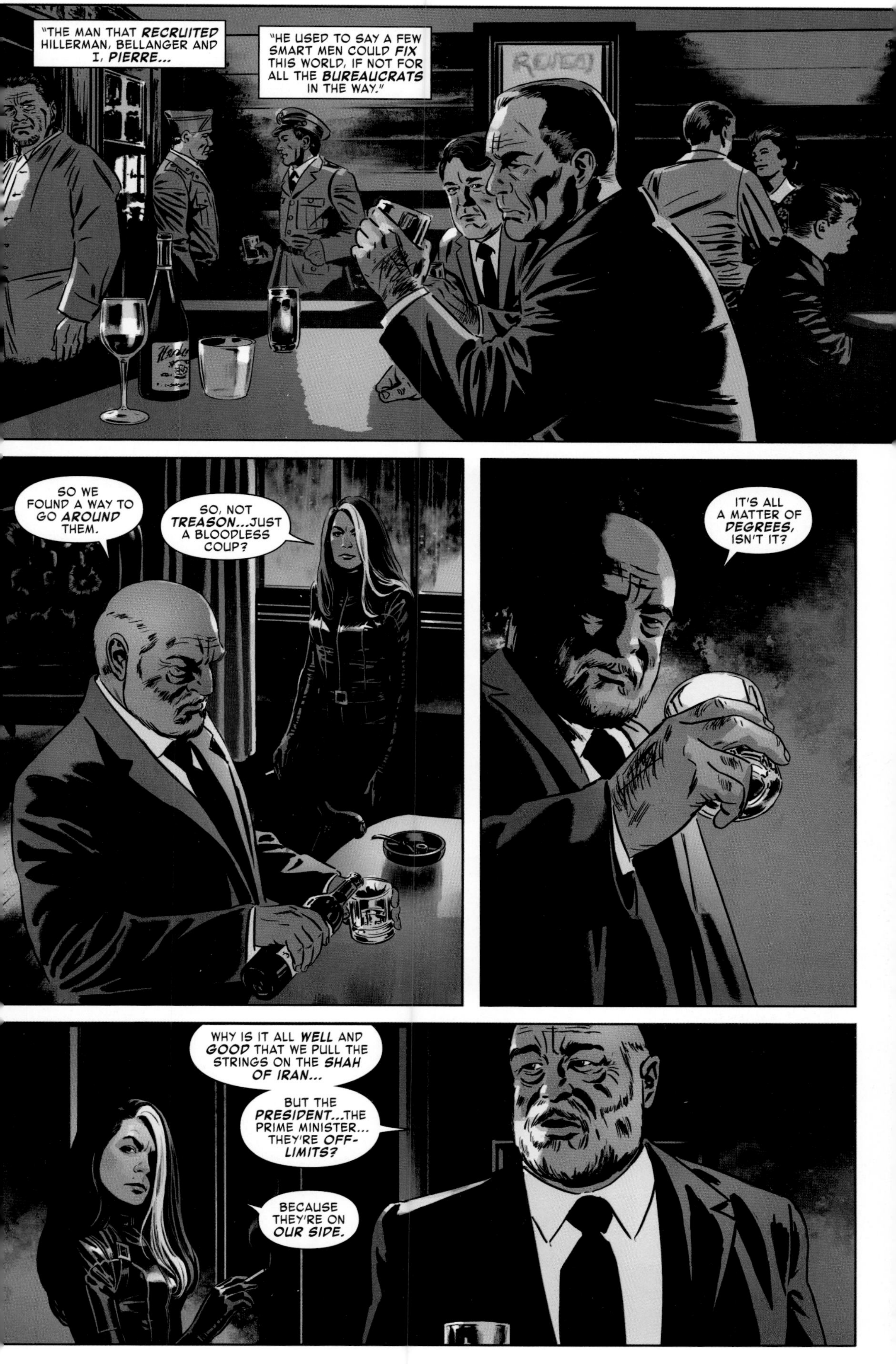
"THE MAN THAT RECRUITED HILLERMAN, BELLANGER AND I, PIERRE...
"HE USED TO SAY A FEW SMART MEN COULD FIX THIS WORLD, IF NOT FOR ALL THE BUREAUCRATS IN THE WAY."
SO WE FOUND A WAY TO GO AROUND THEM.
SO, NOT TREASON...JUST A BLOODLESS COUP?
IT'S ALL A MATTER OF DEGREES, ISN'T IT?
WHY IS IT ALL WELL AND GOOD THAT WE PULL THE STRINGS ON THE SHAH OF IRAN...
BUT THE PRESIDENT...THE PRIME MINISTER... THEY'RE OFF-LIMITS?
BECAUSE THEY'RE ON OUR SIDE.

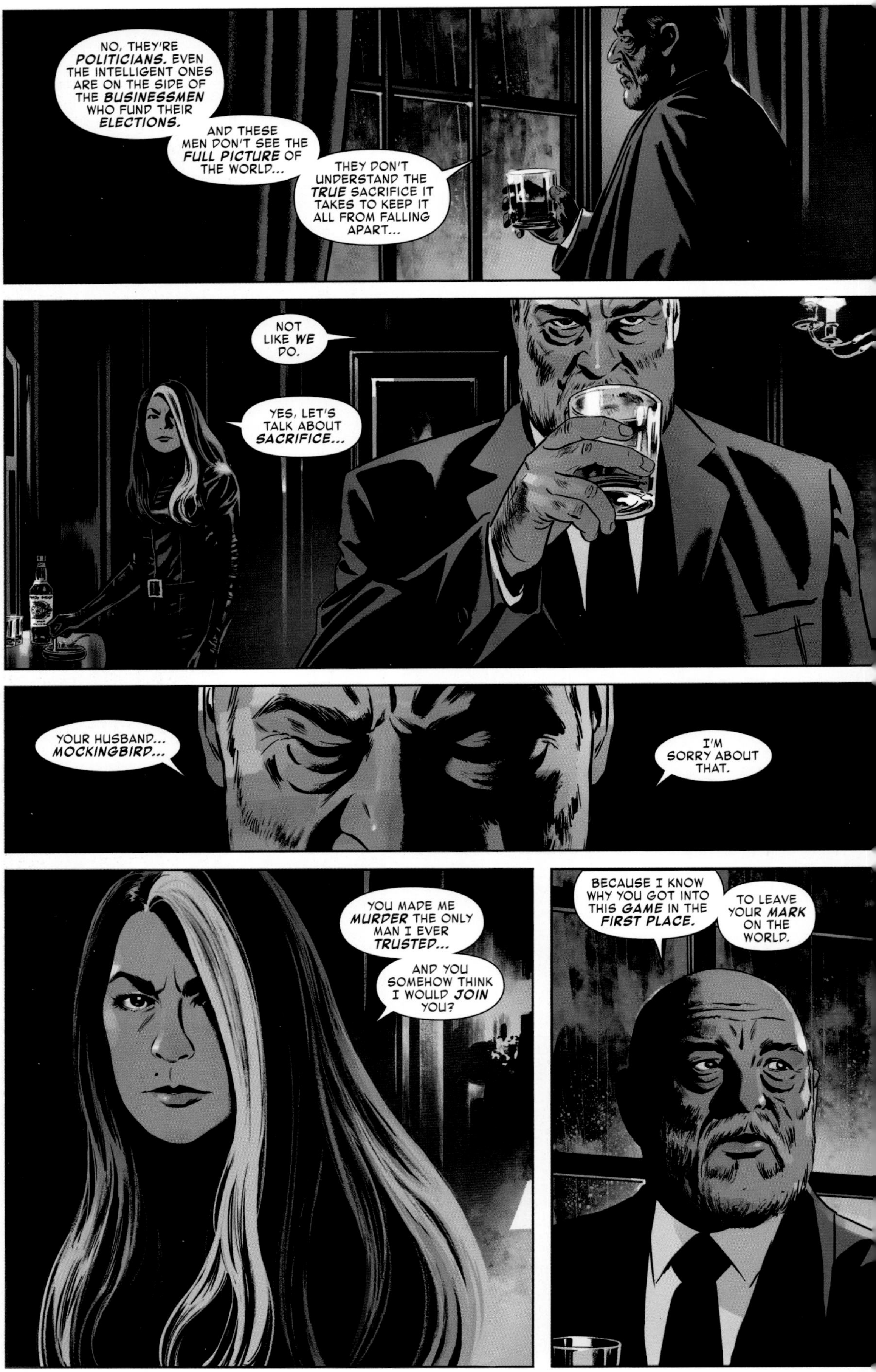

NO, THEY'RE POLITICIANS. EVEN THE INTELLIGENT ONES ARE ON THE SIDE OF THE BUSINESSMEN WHO FUND THEIR ELECTIONS.
AND THESE MEN DON'T SEE THE FULL PICTURE OF THE WORLD...
THEY DON'T UNDERSTAND THE TRUE SACRIFICE IT TAKES TO KEEP IT ALL FROM FALLING APART...
NOT LIKE WE DO.
YES, LET'S TALK ABOUT SACRIFICE...
YOUR HUSBAND... MOCKINGBIRD...
I'M SORRY ABOUT THAT.
YOU MADE ME MURDER THE ONLY MAN I EVER TRUSTED...
AND YOU SOMEHOW THINK I WOULD JOIN YOU?
BECAUSE I KNOW WHY YOU GOT INTO THIS GAME IN THE FIRST PLACE.
TO LEAVE YOUR MARK ON THE WORLD.

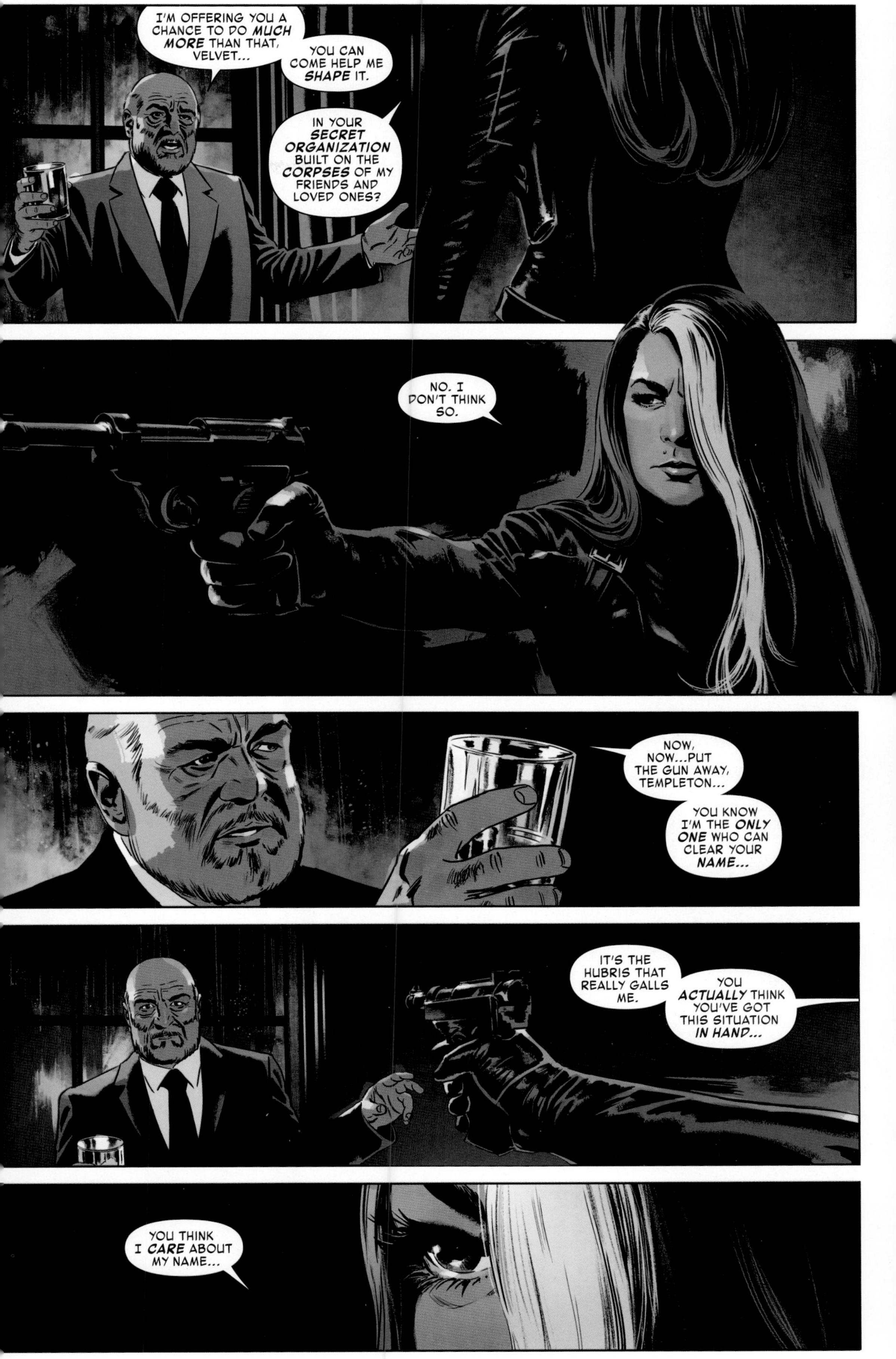
I'M OFFERING YOU A CHANCE TO DO MUCH MORE THAN THAT, VELVET...
YOU CAN COME HELP ME SHAPE IT.
IN YOUR SECRET ORGANIZATION BUILT ON THE CORPSES OF MY FRIENDS AND LOVED ONES?
NO. I DON'T THINK SO.
NOW, NOW...PUT THE GUN AWAY, TEMPLETON...
YOU KNOW I'M THE ONLY ONE WHO CAN CLEAR YOUR NAME...
IT'S THE HUBRIS THAT REALLY GALLS ME.
YOU ACTUALLY THINK YOU'VE GOT THIS SITUATION IN HAND...
YOU THINK I CARE ABOUT MY NAME...

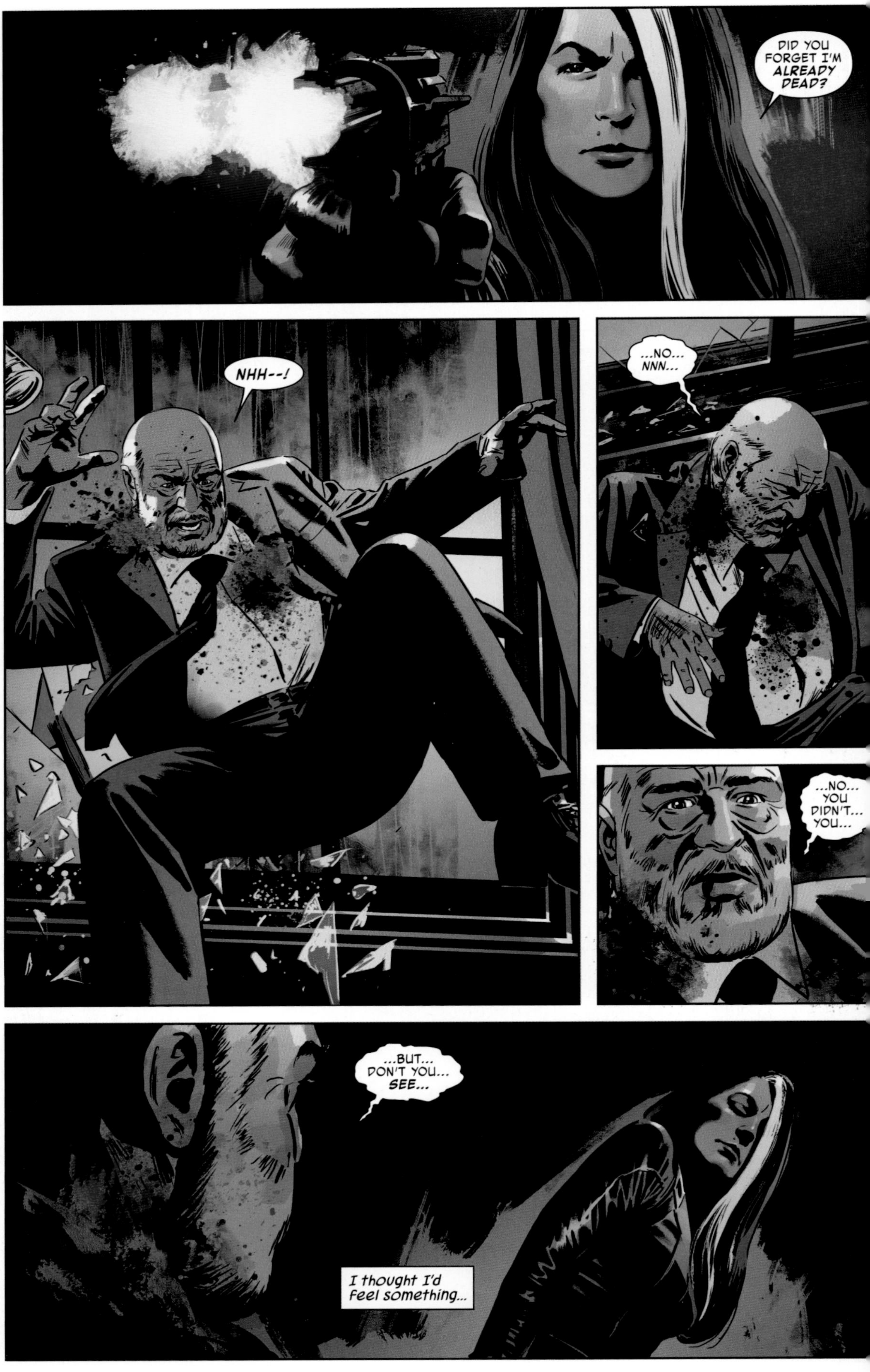
DID YOU FORGET I'M ALREADY DEAD?
NHH--!
...NO... NNN...
...NO... YOU DIDN'T... YOU...
...BUT... DON'T YOU... SEE...
I thought I'd feel something...

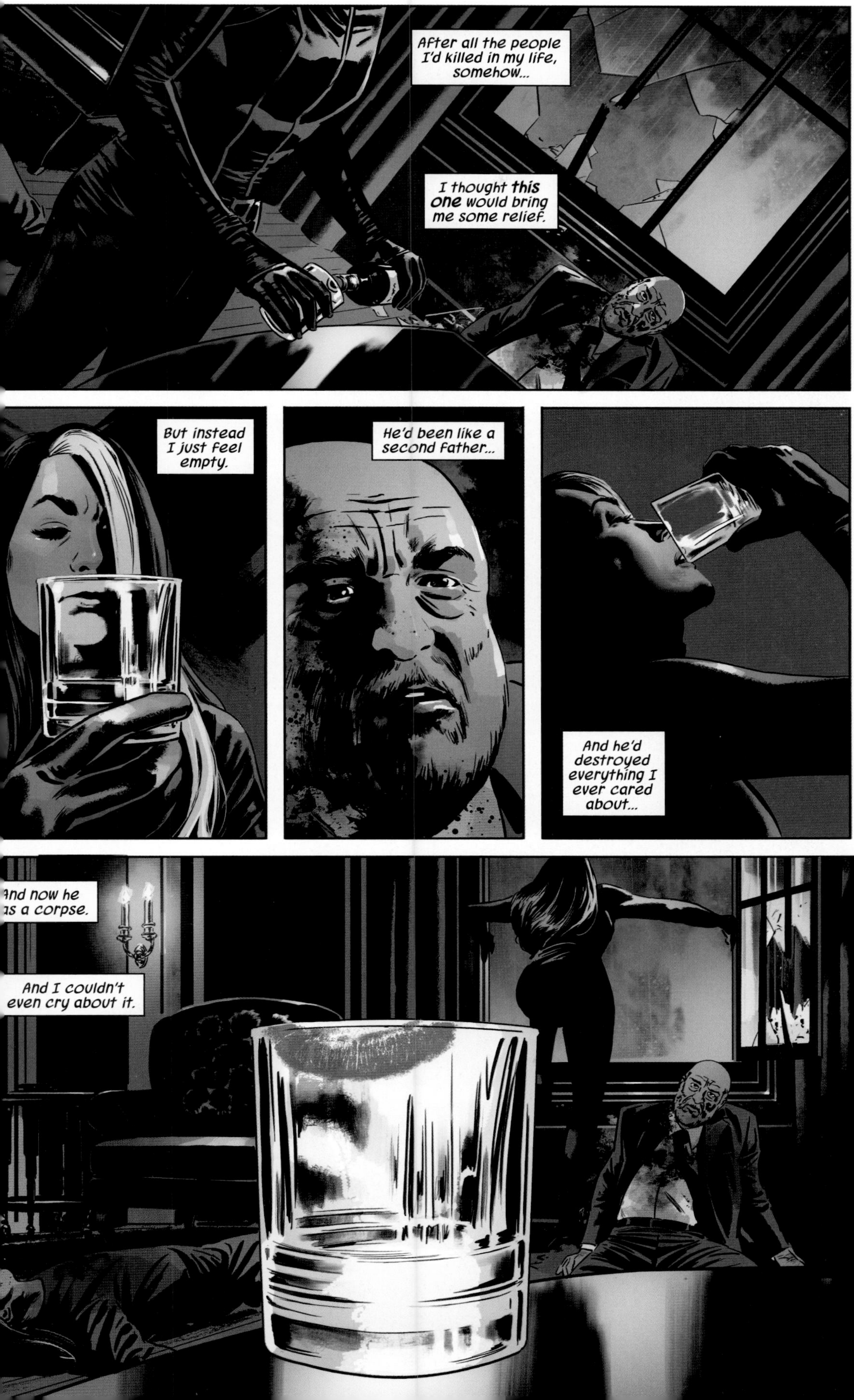
After all the people
I'd killed in my life,
somehow...
I thought this one would bring me some relief.
But instead I just feel empty.
He'd been like a second father...
And he'd destroyed everything I ever cared about...
nd now he
as a corpse.
And I couldn't even cry about it.

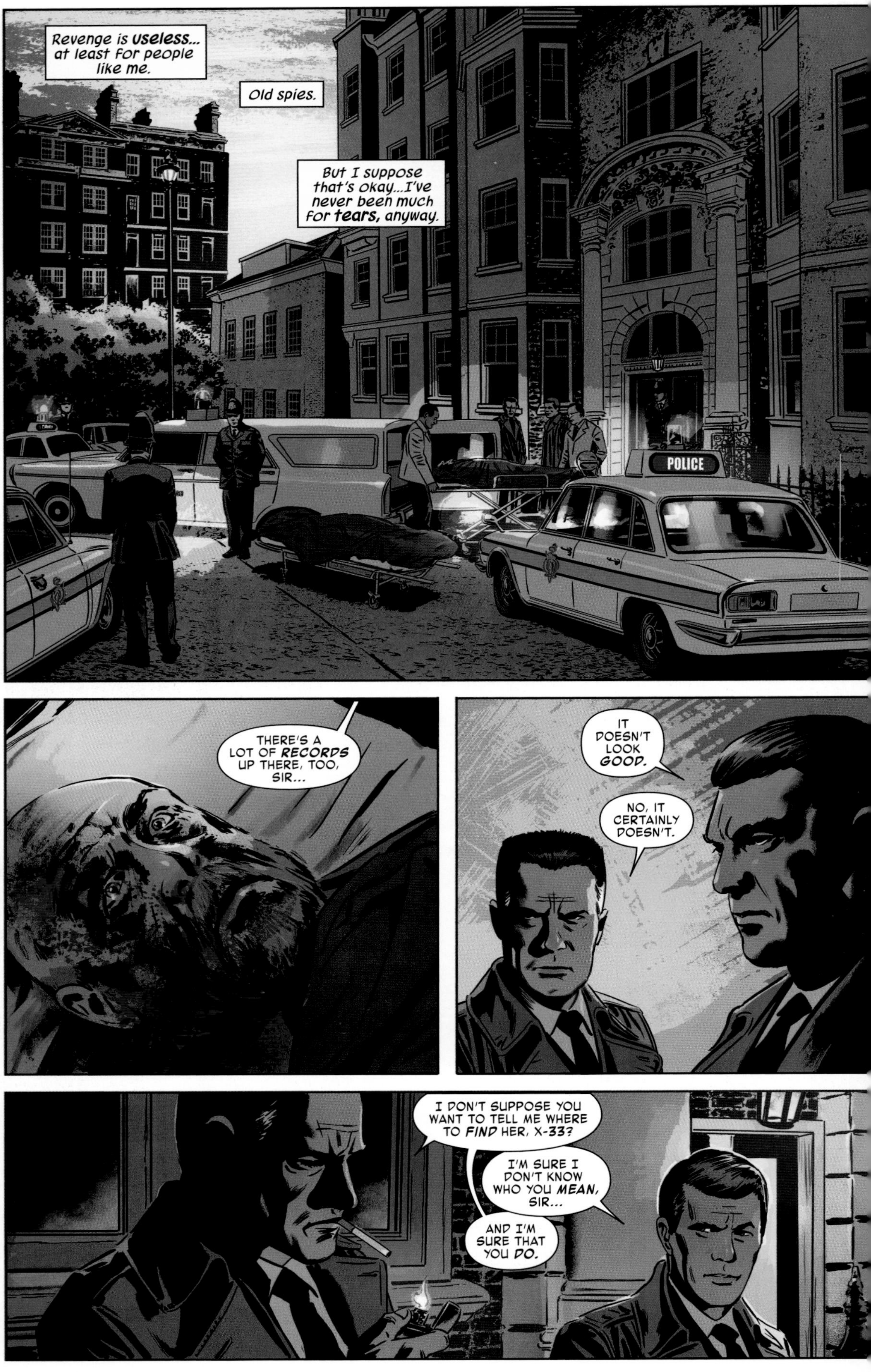

Revenge is useless... at least for people like me.
Old spies.
But I suppose that's okay...I've never been much for tears, anyway.
POLICE
THERE'S A LOT OF RECORDS UP THERE, TOO, SIR...
IT DOESN'T LOOK GOOD.
NO, IT CERTAINLY DOESN'T.
I DON'T SUPPOSE YOU WANT TO TELL ME WHERE TO FIND HER, X-33?
I'M SURE I DON'T KNOW WHO YOU MEAN, SIR...
AND I'M SURE THAT YOU DO.

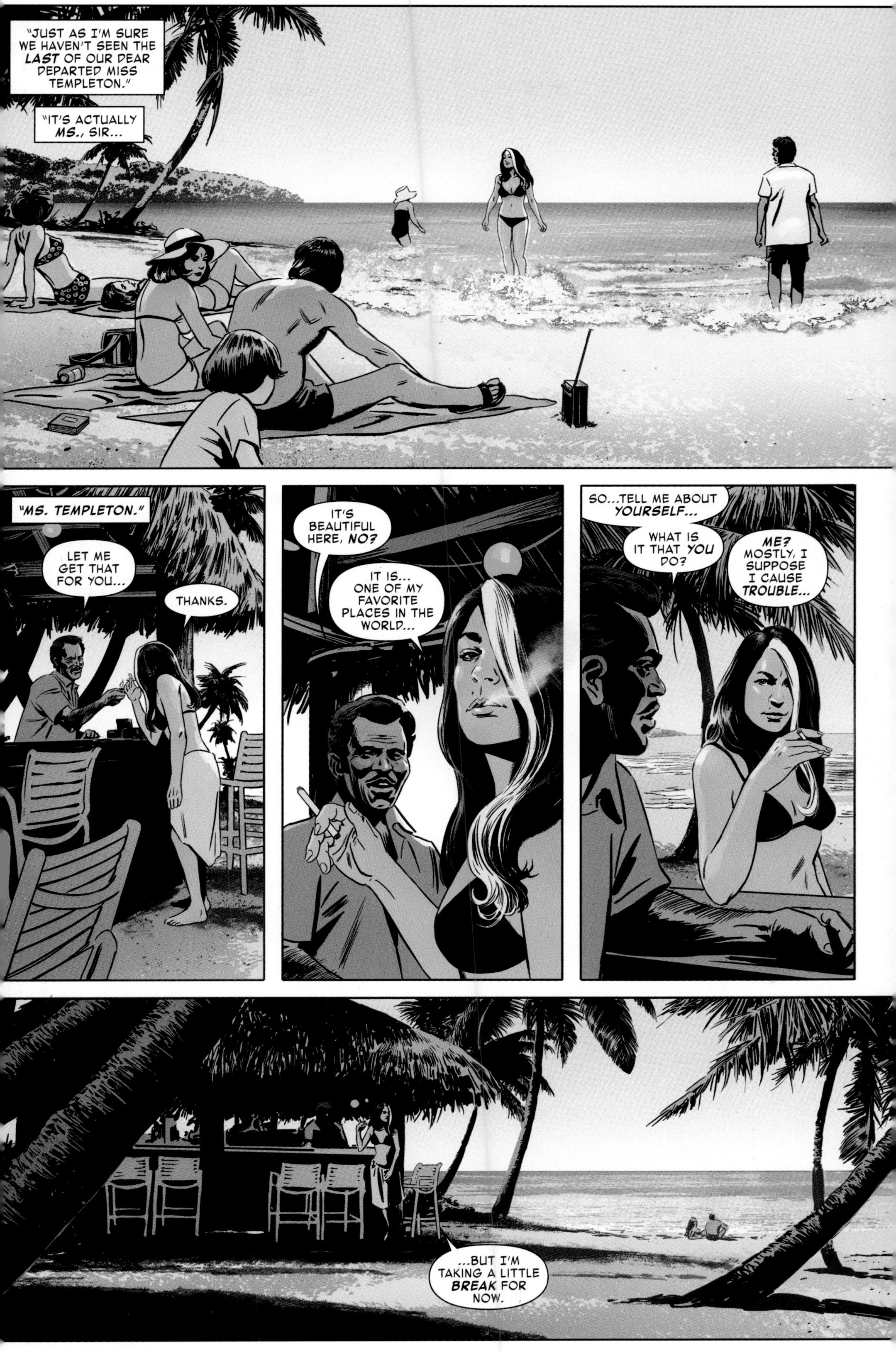
"JUST AS I'M SURE WE HAVEN'T SEEN THE LAST OF OUR DEAR DEPARTED MISS TEMPLETON."
"IT'S ACTUALLY MS., SIR...
"MS. TEMPLETON."
LET ME GET THAT FOR YOU...
THANKS.
IT'S BEAUTIFUL HERE, NO?
IT IS... ONE OF MY FAVORITE PLACES IN THE WORLD...
SO...TELL ME ABOUT YOURSELF...
WHAT IS IT THAT YOU DO?
ME? MOSTLY, I SUPPOSE I CAUSE TROUBLE...
...BUT I'M TAKING A LITTLE BREAK FOR NOW.

THE END